FLORIDA TRIANGLE

An international drugs ring, a new atomic power station and a mutant alligator help to form the multifaceted plot of this fast-moving novel. Set mainly in Citrus County, Florida, and featuring some explicit sex scenes and much violence, the story centres around an innocent man who inadvertently becomes involved with the corrupt high-ranking officials at the head of the drugs syndicate.

FLORIDA TRIANGLE

Graham Willcox

ARTHUR H. STOCKWELL LTD.
Torrs Park   Ilfracombe   Devon
Established 1898
www.ahstockwell.co.uk

British Library Cataloguing-in-Publication Data.
A catalogue record for this book is available
from the British Library.

This is a work of fiction. Names, characters, places and incidents are
the product of the author's imagination and any resemblance to actual
persons, living or dead, events or locales, is purely coincidental.

Dedication
For my wife Alison, for painting the front cover
and
for Brian Sinfield of The Burford Gallery
for his encouragement and advice with my first draft.

ISBN 978-0-7223-3779-0
Printed in Great Britain by
Arthur H. Stockwell Ltd.
Torrs Park   Ilfracombe
Devon

Contents

Chapter 1

Portsmouth, England

A stab of light reflecting off hot metal struck his eye, already wet with tears. Julian drove for the narrowing gap as the truck swung dangerously into the centre lane. It was a desperate gamble, but, half blinded by the light, he stood little chance. His left bumper clipped the truck's tail light, flinging the car into a spin with a shrill whine. Amidst flying sparks that shot across the motorway, it struck the central reservation barrier nose on with such force that it rose on end, and for a moment it seemed to pivot there horribly like a doomed vessel about to dive; and then it crashed onto its back, and seconds later exploded in a balloon of flame. Julian was killed instantly.

Gordon Richardson had taken the death of his son stoically. There were those that said he was brave to have accepted the tragedy with such composure. But this made him angry. Grieving was a personal thing, and in different people it manifested itself in different ways; his way was to stifle any outward show of emotion. It was his way of staying sane. There was nothing brave about that. His wife was different. Her grief was uncontrollable and all-empowering. She seemed to be tormented by guilt, as if she were blaming herself for the accident. It was impossible to console her, and as the days went by and turned into weeks, she drifted into clinical depression, a mental state relieved only by heavy bouts of drinking. She remained alone in her bedroom for long periods, acknowledged no one, feared everything, cried and cried.

Grief should have been a uniting force, but it had the opposite effect; it was wrenching them apart. After twenty-six years of marriage they had become strangers. The old house was oppressive. No longer did it resonate with happy times but had become a cold, inhibiting place of dark shadows to which light and laughter had become a memory.

Long before the accident they had talked of leaving to start a new life in America, but most of it had been just talk with no real commitment behind it. That had now changed. Julian's death had given the idea a tragic urgency. The other children had left, Emily to the Royal Navy, serving on HMS *Ark Royal* off the Saudi Arabian coast; Faye was a lecturer in Zoology at Sussex University and Neil had left England two years before to work in Miami as an hotel management trainee and appeared to find America, indeed, the land of opportunity. There was nothing to hold them here. Besides, according to Gordon Richardson, England was a disaster.

It was a disaster because Gordon had had enough. He was an art dealer, and a commuter of sorts. The journey to and from his gallery in Portsmouth had become a nightmare of bumper-to-bumper frustration, so that it took him one and a half hours to cover the fourteen-mile distance. The area was at pollution saturation point, at least that's how it felt. Smoke emissions from the local power station, from the petroleum refinery, from a million cars, added to his discontent; and when the cloud base was low the authorities warned people to stay indoors. It was as bad as that. Of course it was the government who were to blame; they were supposed to protect the environment, but over the past twenty years nothing much had been done. In Gordon's opinion it was now too late, tragically too late.

How different he had found the attitude in Florida, where they had bought a holiday home some years before. Local politicians and national government took conservation seriously. The protection of natural habitats alone was an important issue, the southern state was indeed a green and pleasant land.

When the Richardsons had purchased their house on the shores of Lake Henderson in Citrus County, Florida in 1998, the state was already addressing the wrongs done by previous legislature by introducing stringent controls on building and pollution. A strict speed limit had also been introduced on the roads. Now, some twelve years later, Florida had a clean and healthy environment, and the challenge to produce efficient electrical power had been put into the hands of each county. They grasped the opportunity with enthusiasm so that now, across the state of Florida, a number of small, environmentally friendly nuclear power stations had been built. Designed and pioneered by a team of nuclear scientists from Texas, they had proved so successful that Citrus County had decided to build its own unit on the shores of Lake Apopka. This would be sufficient to produce all the electricity required by the small town of Inverness. It was funded by subscriptions from local businessmen and the general public.

Now nearing completion, it was due to be commissioned within the next few weeks.

Lost in their thoughts, Gordon and Sheila Richardson stood in front of the old house. It had been their home for so long, that now the time had come to leave, feelings of regret and sadness were overwhelming. Tears fell down Sheila's smooth cheekbones, staining her neat blue dress. How pale she looked, thought Gordon. He took a clean handkerchief from his pocket and gently dried her face. She stiffened and tried to pull herself together. She was still a very attractive woman, despite of the months of anguish that had left her skin taught and darkening rings beneath her eyes. He kissed her cheek softly and she responded by tightening her grip on his hand, but that was all. A gulf still remained between them.

"Sir, if you're going to catch the plane, we'd better be moving," said the taxi driver.

At the bottom of the drive he stopped the car and Sheila turned for one last look. She said nothing but the tears were coming again. Gordon wondered what the future was to hold, but he prayed that his wife could forget. If not there was little hope for either of them.

The taxi turned right onto the A3 and two hours twenty minutes later they were checking in at the Virgin Atlantic desk at Gatwick for their flight to Orlando.

Chapter 2

Power Unit, Inverness, Florida

The 4th of July was Independence Day. It was also the day the mayor of Inverness officially opened the Community Power Unit. It was therefore a very special day for the town. The mayor had organised a big opening celebration with a fireworks display and barbecue to which everyone was invited.

Wayne Headbold, the nuclear scientist from Texas, and his assistant and live-in lover, Claire Williams, had now been in Inverness County for three months supervising the final inspections and checking the reactor and equipment so that the power supply could officially be switched on. Wayne had always worked as part of a team, but now that he had sole responsibility for the power supply to 190,000 people, he felt the burden heavy on his shoulders. His decision to leave Texas had been difficult. He was an only son with an over-protective mother, and when Claire came on the scene and the two of them fell madly in love, Wayne's mother was none too pleased. To make matters worse, Wayne was approached by the Inverness County authorities with an offer to build their new power unit.

After much soul-searching, and in spite of his mother's resistance, he decided to accept the job and to take Claire with him. His mother was incensed and put every obstacle in his way to stop him leaving. She even fabricated a stroke, something that almost shook Wayne's resolve, but Claire gave him strength, and with her support he stood, for the first time in his life, on his own two feet.

He was committed to his existing Texas contract until March. This meant that he was unable to take up his new position right away, and was therefore unable to supervise the construction of the unit and the co-ordination of the new equipment, both jobs he considered vital. The job had been entrusted to a local contractor and engineer. Unfortunately, halfway through their contract they had gone into liquidation, and it had been discovered that the supervising engineer had not been carrying out his inspection duties in accordance with his contract. This had delayed the construction programme by four months. A new contractor and supervising engineer had to be brought down from Texas to complete the job at great expense to the power company.

Although the work by the previous contractor had been suspect, Wayne had been assured by the new man and his engineer that their tests had confirmed that the eight foot deep reinforced concrete casing enclosing the reactor had been built correctly and in accordance with the specification. This Wayne had accepted. In his opinion the new contractor had carried out his contract effectively and had managed to complete the unit in accordance with the original programme and on time for the opening on July 4th. But politically things had not gone so smoothly.

When initially the mayor had suggested building a nuclear power station, albeit a small one, on the banks of Lake Apopka, there had been a public outcry, and it was only after much lobbying by the authorities, public meetings and assurances of safety, that permission was eventually granted. But there was still disquiet amongst its detractors. To make matters worse, construction costs had risen by some 20% above the original contract figure and additional shares had to be issued for the extra funding. To the dismay of many of the original shareholders, the bulk of these new shares had been bought by a Cuban, Hunaz Potra.

The new power station was situated in an isolated position on the far side of the lake, some considerable distance from the town of Inverness itself. The only other building, a local brewery, was a quarter of a mile away in the adjoining bay. The brewery produced the famous Inverness Rum and was owned by Peter Cooper.

Wayne Headbold and his assistant, Claire, had been working non-stop in the control room all day.

"I'm whacked," said Wayne. "How about we close down the tests and head for home? We could grab a bite on the way, and perhaps a bottle of wine – and you can have my body it you like."

Claire kissed his cheek, smiled and started closing down the test programme. "I love you," she said. "Now move your arse out of here."

At the time Wayne and Claire were leaving the power unit, Peter Cooper at the brewery had just slammed down the phone on 'that cock-sucker' of a manager at the First State Bank.

The manager of the bank. Jimmy Clark, had been telephoning Peter's office all day. Pam, Peter's long-suffering secretary, had made all the usual excuses, saying that her boss was either out of the office or tied up in a meeting. Being a creature of habit, Pam always left the office at about 5.30 p.m., so when the phone rang at 6.00 p.m. Peter answered it himself. It was Jimmy Clark. 'Christ,' he thought, 'why can't this guy get off my back!'

"Peter, I must speak with you about your financial position." The voice sounded agitated, but determined. "To put it bluntly, Peter, you have one month to reduce your overdraft to below $500,000. If you fail, the bank will have no alternative but to foreclose and that will be the end of the Inverness Liquor Company – Peter, are you listening?"

Peter frowned. The company had been banking with the First State since the 1920s and all the previous managers had understood, especially when cases of special Inverness Rum were delivered to their homes once a month. Jimmy Clark was different. For one thing, he combined his job as a bank manager with that of a lay preacher. He was a small, stout man, who sweated profusely and abstained from drink, claiming that alcohol was the tipple of the devil. He had small, dark beady eyes and Peter thought of him as a big hippo wallowing around in deep river mud. At their first meeting he took an instant dislike to the man. The thought of him holding the destiny of the Inverness Liquor Company in his clammy hands was enough to make the blood boil.

The company had been formed by Peter's grandfather in the 1920s, just after Prohibition. The Special Rum had been a great success, not only with the locals but also with the tourists. Business had flourished in the early 1970s, when it was decided to close the old factory and to build another larger unit on the banks of Lake Henderson. This was completed in 1975.

The formula for the brewing, distilling and the recipe for the special ingredients had been kept a secret, even from the workers. Only members of the immediate family were privileged to know.

Peter had never really wanted to be involved in the business. He'd spent most of his time over the past ten years travelling the world and generally absolving himself of any responsibility at his father's expense. When his father died from a heart attack some three years before, Peter's life had changed completely. In effect he was now head of the company, and he resented the loss of his freedom deeply.

His mother had phoned him in London the day his father died, and Peter had returned home to Florida the following morning. After the funeral, the whole family insisted that he take his new responsibilities seriously. He must stay and run the business. He protested, of course, but it was no use. For the sake of family, as well as the local community, he complied with their wishes.

But the responsibility hung heavily on his shoulders. He had always been his father's favourite son, and was known locally as the spoiled rich kid, but in spite of this, he was well liked. He was intelligent and determined, which was just as well because he was now responsible, not just for the company itself, but also for the financial security of his mother and his younger sisters. Not a problem for a successful company until, that is, Peter examined the accounts. To his horror it soon became clear that over the past few years the company had been making substantial losses. His father, never a man to confide in people, even his own family, had never discussed the financial state of the company. What Peter had been left was not a thriving business, but a company in crisis. He tried to talk to his mother and sister, Debbie, about the situation but neither would listen.

"Your father always came home with the bacon," his mother had said dismissively. "If you were half the man he was, you'd get on with the job and stop whining like a spoilt child."

His younger sister, Tracy, however, understood the dilemma. "Look, Peter," she told him, "you don't owe anybody anything. For Christ sake lead your own life. Tell Mother and Debbie to stuff the business up their butts. Let Mother sell the company and then she can live the way she wants for the rest of her life."

"You don't understand," said Peter. "We can't sell the company. It owes the bank over $500,000. It's not making any profit   it's worthless."

Peter and his sister had always been close; there was a special bond between them. In his heart he knew that the reason he had never married was because he could never hope to find anyone quite like his Tracy. For her part, Tracy had always looked up to Peter as a father figure. Her reasons for never marrying were similar to his own.

For the first eighteen months after taking over, Peter struggled to understand the business. He employed accountants to fully assess the situation. Their report made depressing reading. It recommended that the number of employees should be reduced from thirty-two to eighteen, and the sale of rum increased by at least 150%. The necessity to increase business by so much was a difficult, if not impossible, task; to make so many employees redundant was unthinkable. The factory had always employed local labour, and fathers and sons worked together. To reduce the workforce by this much would have a devastating effect on the community. He could not bring himself to do it, so he decided to continue with the existing workforce and attempt to boost sales by a nationwide advertising campaign, but this was going to cost money, more than $250,000. Since the company did not have this much, it had to raise another loan. When Peter approached the bank, the incumbent manager, Bill Cassedy, an old friend of his father's and an Inverness man, was happy to oblige. The loan, however, was secured against the factory and the family home, which left him uneasy.

Initially the advertising had brought results, but after a short time, with the exception of the Japanese market, sales slipped back again. Cash flow became a serious problem, and the arrival at the bank of Jimmy Clark and the departure of Bill Cassedy only exacerbated the situation. Peter was getting desperate; he had to do something, and fast.

He slumped back despairingly in his chair and began drumming his fingers nervously on the desk. He needed to reduce costs, but how? Cut the labour force? Out of the question. The biggest expense was the bill from the haulage and recycling company for the dumping of the sugar and rum residue left in the cooling vats, which ran to over $15,000.00 a month. However, he had been unable to reduce the cost of this necessary operation.

Through the window he could see Claire and Wayne leaving the power unit. They noticed him and both waved as they passed his office. Over the past three months he had come to know Claire and Wayne quite well, and had become fond of them both. The three of them often met after work for a drink at Murphy's Bar. As he watched them go down the road his gaze shifted to the lake, and he suddenly had an idea about the residue.

The area surrounding the power unit, to a distance of 500 feet offshore, was off limits to the public. If he could dump the residue himself, something he was perfectly capable of doing as he knew the procedure off by heart, in the lake near the power station, nobody would ever know, because no one was allowed that close. It was a perfect solution and would save the company $180,000.00 a year.

There were, of course, problems. For one thing the power plant and its surrounding area was patrolled nightly between 6.00 p.m. and 8.00 a.m. by two security guards. He would need to keep a close watch on them over the next few nights, familiarise himself with their routine, especially the time they patrolled the actual grounds and shoreline. A plan was formulating in his mind, but could it be engineered and carried out without detection?

Peter's train of thought was abruptly disturbed as the office door opened and in walked the office manager, Patrick O'Reily.

"I've closed down the plant for the night, Mr Cooper," he said. "Could you remember to lock up the warehouse when you leave, and switch on the security system? Many thanks. I'm off now."

"Okay," replied Peter. "See you Monday."

When Patrick had gone, Peter picked up the telephone and rang home. His mother answered. "Hi," he said. "It's me. I've just rung to let you know I'll be working tonight. Don't wait dinner for me."

"Oh, Peter, that's a pity." His mother sounded most disappointed. "I've invited Kaye for dinner. You know, Jimmy Clark's daughter. She seems such a nice girl. She will be disappointed."

'Fat cow,' Peter thought. He allowed himself a smile. 'Thank God I can't make it.' "Do give her my apologies, Mother, but business must come first. See you later."

He replaced the phone and positioned himself at the side window so that he could observe the security guards. He took out a little black pocketbook in which to log their movements. What surprised him was that on one occasion the two men separated, one of them leaving the complex and returning an hour or so later. With one of the guards absent for such a long period, he was certain that his plan would work. "I can do it," he said to himself. "I know I can do it."

Chapter 3

Havana, Cuba

Hunaz Potra sat in the back of the Cadillac, his attention divided by the balding head of the chauffeur in front and the goings on in the world outside beyond the tinted windows. As the car sped along the boulevard, the small Cuban flag on the front bonnet flapped in the wind. Although only seven in the morning, the temperature was already in the 80s. 'Another hot day,' he thought, and hoped that the air conditioning in his office, that had crashed the previous day, had now been fixed.

Hunaz Potra was Minister of Tourism at the Cuban Foreign Office and, as such, had a high rank in the order of things. Since Castro's death, an event still surrounded in controversy, the country had been run by his only son, Alfredo. The official government statement was that he had died of a heart attack, but Hunaz was suspicious. There were rumours. One was that Castro had been poisoned by Alfredo, but rumour was not proof. Hunaz kept his opinions to himself. One lived longer that way.

In his first public speech in Havana Square, Alfredo had vowed that he would work to reintroduce democracy within four years. The people were not convinced. It had been eleven years since the dictator's death and tyranny and poverty were as bad as ever. Most of the sugar plantations were derelict, petrol could only be obtained on the black market, unless of course you had a government car, and 70% of the population was unemployed, many of them starving. Oppression was rife. Robbery, violence and murder were commonplace, and there was a feeling of rebellion in the air. Cuba received no help from its Communist allies and was therefore solely dependent on grants and handouts from the United States.

Following the death of Castro there had been secret meetings between Alfredo and the American Foreign Office. But all negotiations had broken down, as it was soon evident that Castro's son had no intention of relinquishing his power. This effectively meant that American influence in the region would be minimal. President Bower had therefore decided that America would no longer supply financial aid to Cuba. With American aid now effectively cut off, Alfredo turned to tourism to produce urgently needed revenue. He made it top priority and appointed Hunaz Potra, a man of increasing influence and wealth in the business community, to the post of Minister of Tourism. This gave Hunaz not only unlimited opportunities to travel beyond Cuba's shores, but also, and more importantly, diplomatic immunity.

During his years in office Hunaz had been very successful at enticing rich entrepreneurs and developers to the island. Already twenty-two hotels had been built, with a further ten planned over the next few years. In addition, the airport had been extended at Havana with the most modern air-conditioned terminals. In all, tourism, mainly on account of Hunaz Potra's efforts, accounted for 50% of Cuba's wealth and, next to Alfredo, he was the most powerful man in the country.

"What the hell do I care about democracy?" he would say. He had learned a long time ago to look after number one, and that is exactly what he had done throughout his career. No one had helped him, but he'd had the ability and foresight to grab opportunities as they came along, and look how far he'd come. It is strange the way fate determines destiny.

Hunaz Potra had been brought up in poverty in a poor district on the outskirts of Havana. From the age of eight he had spent most of his life working in the cane fields, labouring from dawn until dusk for a few pesetas. His father, who never worked, took Hunaz's meagre wages and squandered them on drink and gambling. When he came home drunk, which were most days, he would beat his son. One night, when Hunaz was fourteen, his father returned home following a particularly heavy drinking session, and in a savage mood. He called for the boy, but Hunaz had hidden under the bed for protection. Frustrated and in a drunken rage at being unable to find his son, the father turned on his wife and began to beat her mercilessly. At first Hunaz covered his ears to drown his mother's screams and curled up into a ball, but his mother's cries penetrated even his hands clasped tightly to his head, so that in the end he could bear it no longer. In a state of terror, mingled with a dull controlled rage, he had crawled from beneath the bed into the kitchen. There he picked up a bread knife, returned calmly into the room, raised the knife high above his head and with all his strength embedded it in his father's back. His father's body straightened against the thrust of the knife and, still in the act of aiming a kick at his wife as she lay on the floor, he collapsed and lay groaning. There was a terrible gurgling in his throat as the blood welled up inside it. Hunaz leant over his father's body and, struggling, he managed to turn him onto his back. Only then did he realise that he was dead. For some seconds he knelt by his father's body, his mind numb.

Then his mother stirred and struggled to her feet. She was dazed and unable at first to comprehend the enormity of what had happened. And then it seemed to strike her like another blow, and she dropped on her knees beside Hunaz – and from her own bruised body came a deep anguished moan. Hunaz backed away in fear, and as he did so she turned on him, tears streaming down her face. "You've killed him!" she screamed. "You've killed him!" Her dark-rimmed eyes, stained with tears, were filled with anger. "Get out!" she cried. "Get out of my sight!"

"But – Mother . . . "

"Get out!"

Hunaz, stricken with panic, turned and fled. Confused and angry he made his way to the docks at Havana and learned to look after himself as best he could. He became mean, resolute and aggressive in order to survive. He slept wherever he could lay his head; he stole to eat and fought to stay alive. He was a rat among other rats and he eschewed normal company, which is until he met Fernando Cose, a meeting that would change his life. It had happened one hot summer evening, just before his sixteenth birthday, outside the Lobster Restaurant, just off Havana's main square. Hunaz had been hanging around as usual waiting for an opportunity to steal something, but pickings had been meagre. It was then that this man approached him. Hunaz's first reaction had been to steal his wallet and run, but the man's manner had been beguiling. He didn't threaten or raise his voice, but simply asked if he might buy Hunaz a meal. He would be delighted if the young man would accept, so Hunaz did. Who the man was, or what he did, was of no concern to a hungry dock urchin.

Fernando was the kind of man particularly attracted to young boys. All those he befriended he treated with kindness; something few of the urchins had ever experienced. With Hunaz Potra he became infatuated, and very soon man and boy were lovers. Hunaz lived with Fernando in his apartment overlooking Havana harbour, and for two years life was good. Hunaz, himself, was not homosexual, but he deferred to the older man's demands, even if at times he was forced into acts that he found distasteful – but it was better than the docks.

One evening, Fernando arrived home in an anxious state. He looked insane; there was fear in his eyes. He pushed past Hunaz, pulled back the edge of the curtain and looked out across the square. Hunaz moved towards the window, and as he did so Fernando's body jerked violently backwards and he dropped to the floor as if poleaxed. Hunaz crouched, seized with a wild animal's sense of imminent danger. He waited. Seconds passed before he felt it safe enough to crawl towards Fernando's still warm body. He was lying on his back, exactly where he had fallen, and in the centre of his forehead was a clean, neat hole – no blood, just a circular incision. Hunaz was seized by a new sensation, not fear, and not shock at the death of a friend, but a chilling feeling of despair. Once again he was totally alone. He lay there next to Fernando's body for several minutes, his eyes unable to focus properly, his breathing laboured, his pulse racing and an unreasoning feeling of anger rising in his chest. Gradually his body recovered its normal rhythm and he began to think more clearly. The anger began to subside and questions assailed him. Who had fired the shot? Why had Fernando been killed? Why had he been left alone again? Was there no God? And then he noticed something clenched in Fernando's hand. It was a white package. With difficulty he prised the fingers open one at a time until the package was freed. He held it in his hands, bemused. But any thoughts forming in his mind at that moment were shattered by a sharp rapping on the door. He turned and scrambled along the floor on his hands and knees to the safety of the settee, behind which he hid, clutching the package tightly to his chest. Beyond the door he could hear voices, and then the rapping began again, much harder this time. Hunaz didn't move. Then suddenly two gunshots exploded the silence and the door flew open. Two enormous Negroes, each grasping a revolver, burst into the room followed closely by a stocky man, dressed in a white cotton suit and a homburg, who quickly scanned the room, his eyes missing nothing. And when he spoke, it was in a quiet, restrained voice that hid a cutting edge.

"Mr Hunaz, I know you're there. Would you please stand so that we can see you."

Hunaz froze behind the settee, wishing the floor would open and swallow him up.

"Mr Hunaz, I am not a patient man. You are behind the settee, I think. If you do not show yourself in ten seconds we will shoot you."

Hunaz very slowly rose from behind the sofa, his hands raised above his head, his right hand still clutching the white package.

"That I will take," said the man in the homburg, reaching over and snatching the packet from Hunaz's hand. "It belongs to me." He had a strange half smile on his face. "Now, Hunaz," he said, "you don't know me, I'm sure. My name is Calcus Anando. I am from Puerto Rico. But this is perhaps irrelevant. Do you know what is in this package?"

Hunaz shook his head. At that moment he really didn't care. He would have liked to leave.

"This, my young friend, contains one kilo of heroin, worth a great deal of money. It belongs to me." He cast his eyes at the dead body of Fernando. "Did you know that your friend was a pimp and he dealt in drugs?"

"I didn't ask," stammered Hunaz. What Fernando did was of no concern of his. "I didn't care."

Calcus shrugged. "I can understand that," he said softly. "But what of you? How will you manage without your fine friend? After all, you're wanted for murder."

"I only wanted to protect my mother," Hunaz stammered.

"Possibly true, but do you think the police would believe you? Tut, tut, of course *I* believe you." He pointed a forefinger at Hunaz and whispered in a consoling voice, "You see, I have two problems. Number one is that you know who I am. You might even think of going to the police to tell them who killed the pimp. Bad move. And secondly, I have lost my courier."

Hunaz was mystified.

Calcus reached inside the pocket of his suit, withdrew a pistol and held it against Hunaz's head. "I could kill you now," he said. "Nobody would know – or care. On the other hand . . . "

Hunaz prepared himself to die.

"I need an assistant – I need a slave!" Calcus smiled broadly. "A slave! Do you want to become my slave, Hunaz?"

Hunaz swallowed hard. Clearly the man was mad. "What do I have to do?" he asked shakily, as if he had any choice.

"Do? You can drive my car. Be my chauffeur. Would you like that?"

Hunaz liked that.

"Okay," said Calcus briskly. "But no double-cross. Fernando – he double-crossed. You double-cross me – Zit!" He drew his finger across his throat. "You will learn quickly, my young friend."

And learn he did. Over the years he not only learned but became moderately rich. And, like his employer, whose confidence and respect he soon earned, he was ruthless. Calcus lived in Columbia and imported drugs to Cuba, mainly through the port of Havana. From Cuba the drugs were then distributed throughout the world; the main markets being America and the UK.

Hunaz rose from being a simple courier to the main distributor on the island, and became a prominent member of Cuban society. People who stood in his way, no matter how prominent, were simply removed. Removals included a number of high ranking members of the government, who met with unfortunate 'accidents'.

As a cover for his growing affluence, Hunaz purchased two hotels from the Cuban government. The deals went through just before Castro's death. These hotels were run on strictly legitimate lines – no drugs and no couriers.

By the age of forty-two, Hunaz was Minister for Tourism, a well respected member of Cuba's inner social elite, a dutiful husband to his beautiful English wife, and a proud father to a teenage daughter.

As the political situation was unstable, Hunaz's wife spent most of her time in England with their daughter, who was at a very expensive ladies' college. He had more money than he could possibly have dreamed of. He was the poor boy made good, and he felt very proud of himself.

The sound of his car turning into the drive made him look up. He waved to the two security guards at the gate. Both men, although employed by the government, received certain gratuities from Hunaz; they belonged to him.

Chuck, his American chauffeur and bodyguard, ran around the car and opened the door so that he could step out.

"Thank you, Chuck," he said breezily. "Bring the briefcases in, if you would."

He loved this feeling of power. It was like a drug. It was as if he was born to it.

The two guards ran ahead to open the huge pair of oak doors that led into the grand building that contained his office. They both saluted as he passed. He ignored them; it was his prerogative. He climbed the stairs to his office and nodded a brief good morning to his secretary.

Hunaz's office had a tall ceiling with a large fluted crystal chandelier in its centre. But for two black leather settees, in which one could have sunk without trace, and an enormous walnut desk, the office was bare. That's how he liked it – no frills.

He picked up the telephone. "Amonica, why haven't they fixed the air conditioning?" He was sweating profusely. He hated the heat, hated hot rooms. Discomfort was no longer part of his life. Why should it be? He'd left all that behind.

"They're doing it right now, Mr Hunaz," his secretary replied in a brisk tone. "Mike has assured me that he should have it working again in a few minutes."

Just as she finished speaking there was a soft thud from somewhere above, and cool air began to drift across his face. The door was still ajar and Chuck appeared carrying the three briefcases. He put them down on the settee and without a word left the room, closing the door behind him.

The telephone rang on Hunaz's private line. "Potra," he said into the receiver.

"Hunaz. It's me, Calcus. I think we have a problem."

Chapter 4

Orlando Airport

The Virgin Atlantic jumbo jet touched down at Orlando International Airport at 19.00 hours, two hours behind schedule. During the flight Sheila Richardson had looked more relaxed than at any time during the past few months, and Gordon began to congratulate himself on having made the right decision. However, while his wife appeared to be more relaxed she was still withdrawn, and her eyes had none of that lively sparkle that he used to find so beguiling. Perhaps he should take her to see a psychiatrist? he thought. It was no big deal in America – everybody had their pet shrink.

"Love you, darling," he said as he leaned over and gave her a kiss. "Seat belt on."

"Are we here?" she asked dreamily.

"About to make the descent."

It was a smooth landing, but Gordon couldn't help noticing that his wife was gripping the armrest so hard that the whites of her knuckles showed. As he reached above his head to remove his camera and travel bag, he accidentally collided with one of the passengers. He turned to apologise and was taken aback by the young woman facing him. She was anything between twenty-five and thirty, with a softly-tanned skin and the long blonde hair of a classic Sloane. She happened to be wearing a thin dress that clung to her lean frame, with nipples silhouetted against the dim light of the cabin. She clearly wore no bra.

"I'm terribly sorry," he said. "Could I help you with your luggage?"

The girl smiled, a come-on smile if ever there was one. "Thank you," she said. "Mine is the black bag with the red straps."

Gordon reached across and caught the heady fragrance of Coco Chanel. He casually touched her shoulder with his hand and felt a tingle of excitement. The girl thanked him, turned away and joined the queue to disembark.

Gordon took a deep breath and smiled nervously at Sheila. "Time to go," he said. "This is it."

Customs and Passport Control took about two hours. All their papers were in order, including the immigration documents giving details of their new business.

Before they had finally decided to emigrate to America, Gordon had approached the owner of a gallery in Inverness, Fred Hall, to buy his business. After agreeing suitable terms, he had purchased the gallery. Fred mostly dealt in prints, cheap tourist items and knick-knacks. Gordon could see the potential for an exclusive gallery selling expensive twentieth-century oils and sculpture, and possibly first edition books, to the wealthy middle class in Citrus County.

It had been two months since he had purchased the gallery; and he hoped that by now the internal alterations and decorations would be completed. All his stock of pictures from England had been packed and shipped off to America some ten days before, and as far as he was aware they would be waiting in the cargo sheds at Orlando Airport for collection and customs clearance.

As they passed through the departure lounge, Gordon began to look around for Freda Corn. Freda ran the local taxi company, which had been started by her father in the early 1970s. When her father had suddenly been taken ill, several months previously, Freda had taken over the company and was now running it single-handed. Freda was in her early forties, a rather rounded five foot six with a chubby face and a quick smile. She was married to Joe and had two kids at college.

Over the past few years she had always picked Gordon up from the airport; it was a good feeling to see a welcoming face.

They heard her voice in the crowded airport lounge before they saw her. "Mr and Mrs Richardson!"

They both turned and saw her standing on one of the plastic chairs waving her arms.

"Freda," cried Gordon. "Great to see you. How are you and how's the family?"

"So, so," Freda replied. "Welcome to your new country."

"What about your father?" asked Gordon.

Freda turned away. "Oh, he's not too bad. I went to see him at the drug rehabilitation hospital in Orlando today. They say he's making some progress."

Chapter 5

Winter Town, Orlando

Terry Craig and Bob Titcombe had been sitting in the Ford Mustang watching number 150 South Street since early morning, and were relieved when the two suspects arrived at 6.00 p.m. They had been keeping surveillance on the property for the past six days, and were beginning to think that the anonymous telephone call had been a hoax. The informant had given a detailed description of the two men who would be collecting the drugs.

Local enquiries had revealed that the property was a whore house, owned by a Puerto Rican woman called Anita Toque, and when Terry had paid a visit in the line of duty the day before, he counted five nice girls waiting for business.

Originally, in the early 1990s, all houses of disrepute had been closed down because of the AIDS scare, but a Swiss pharmaceutical company had produced a cure for the virus and prostitution was once again tolerated in the state.

The reason for his visit was to assess the layout and means of exit, to ensure that proper surveillance could be carried out. To do this he needed access to the first-floor area. Having never been to a whore house before he felt a little nervous. He was not there to sample the goods; he was on duty, but he hadn't reckoned with Nancy. Nancy was black, tall and beautiful, a seductress of infinite variety and skill, one of Madame Toque's star protégées.

She worked on the first floor, and it was Nancy who opened doors for FBI agent Terry Craig. Terry followed her upstairs to her room, Nancy closed the door behind them and, one button at a time, without saying a word, she began to undo her pink satin robe in front of his nervous gaze. His first reaction had been to ignore her, but desire was not an easy thing to thrust aside, and after all he was only human. His gaze followed the gown as it fell around her knees. He raised his eyes slowly – black legs in silk stockings, suspenders, no knickers. He could see the thick pubic hairs nesting between her thighs. Her stomach appeared perfectly flat, gently curving up to firm breasts. Nancy stood naked in front of him, an enigmatic smile playing around the corners of her mouth, legs apart. His sense of duty blown, Terry felt an overwhelming desire for this woman.

Nancy turned and locked the door, then moved towards him, closer until their mouths touched. Her tongue, probing, warm, sensuous, entered his mouth, withdrew and entered again. Terry began to press her towards him and his hands caressed her breasts and then pressed hard down into her vagina.

Slowly she unbuttoned his shirt and slid it off his firm shoulders, kissing his arm as she slipped down and quickly undid the belt of his trousers. Very slowly she pulled the zip open, and Terry's trousers fell to his feet. He swung his big arms around her, and with one sweep lifted her off her feet and straight onto the bed. He thrust deep into her and, as he did so, she kissed him harder and brought her hands tight across his back, so that he groaned and his body shuddered as the power surged out of him. The two lay entwined in the silence as their pulses slowed.

Then, casually, Nancy looked at her watch. "Hey, mister, I'm afraid you got to move. I could be missing business."

Terry was back to reality. He raised himself slowly away from the girl and sat by the side of the bed. Nancy swung herself off the bed, and as she moved towards the bathroom she stroked his face. He looked up and noticed a number of small pink marks on the side of her inner arm.

'So that's why she does this job,' he thought. 'To fuel her addiction.'

Nancy closed the bathroom door and turned on the shower.

He dressed, retrieved his clothes from where they had fallen, and then stepped into the hall to examine the layout of the upper floor. It was evident that there were only two ways out of the building; one by the front door and the other by the old timber staircase from the first-floor landing level to the side of the house. He reasoned that he could set up a surveillance of both exits from the corner of South Street and Bauldwin Street.

He quickly stepped back into the room. Nancy was still in the bathroom. He sat down on the corner of the bed to tie a loose shoelace, when from the bathroom came the sound of breaking glass, then a further sound of trash being thrown into a bucket. Craig had been in the drug squad for five years; he had heard that sound many times before. Nancy had just given herself a fix and thrown the hypodermic into the bin. When she emerged from the bathroom it was with renewed vigour. She was ready for the next customer, but Terry could not help noticing the look of despair in her eyes.

He turned and said, "See you."

She inclined her head. "Sure," she said. "Leave the two hundred with Anita. Thanks."

"Take care," said Terry as he made his way down the old staircase.

At the bottom, Anita was waiting. "Had a good time?" she asked holding out her hand.

Craig looked at her for a moment. Her eyes were rigid, without feeling, and he wondered, as he handed over the money, at the tales she could tell. He nodded to her and walked slowly through the front door, climbed into his Mustang and drove off. He could imagine Nancy preparing herself for the next customer.

At about 7.30 p.m., two men, both in their early forties, came back down the stairs at number 150 South Street, Winter Town, carrying two red holdall bags. Both men were dressed in crumpled Hawaiian shirts which hung loosely outside their blue jeans.

Jake Tale was white, six feet tall, slim and clean shaven with long blond shoulder-length hair. His face looked tired, his skin drawn tightly over high cheekbones, eyes bulging like an old catfish. As he walked down the steps he appeared to stagger slightly, and his associate, Joshua Zeal, a beefy black man, steadied him by catching hold of his shirt. "My God, man," he said, "you sure are high tonight."

Jake laughed. "That's right, Josh. Now let's get on with the job."

The two men walked briskly down the street, turned into the main boulevard of Winter Town and stopped at an old 1963 Cadillac Colorado. Jake looked around to make sure nobody was watching, took the other bag from Joshua, opened the boot and placed the two bags carefully inside. They both got into the car and Joshua fired the engine, looked both ways, pulled out into the main street and headed towards the highway.

Leaving Orlando, the Cadillac headed north on the Florida turnpike for about one hour, then turned west onto Highway 44, through Rutland and on towards Inverness.

Behind them, at a safe quarter of a mile distance, agents Craig and Titcombe kept the car continually in their sights. On two occasions the Cadillac slowed down and moved into the inside lane. Both times the agents passed in front, keeping the car focused in their rear mirror.

On the outskirts of Inverness the Cadillac turned right off the highway and made towards Murphy's Bar. They parked in the car lot, opened the boot, removed the two bags and hurriedly entered the bar, carrying the bags with them. It was 9.45 p.m. and the bar was empty except for Wayne Headbold and Peter Cooper.

As the two men entered they glanced up. "Good evening," said Wayne.

The two men nodded. Jake ordered two Budweisers and they went and sat at a table in the far corner of the bar. Murphy poured the two beers and took them over to the table. Neither of them looked up but drank their beers in silence. Wayne thought they looked nervous. It was obvious they weren't locals. He thought that perhaps they might be meeting someone; he wouldn't like to meet either of them at night in a dark alley.

Terry and Bob, meanwhile, had parked on the opposite side of the road where they had a good view of people entering or leaving the bar. Bob, who was sitting in the back seat, was just able to see the two guys' heads above the window sill at the corner table. He felt thirsty and half thought about going into the bar for a drink himself, but decided it wasn't worth the risk of blowing their cover.

After a few minutes a blue convertible Buick drew up and parked outside. A black man stepped out. What Rastos Nokes was like as a young man could only be guessed at. At seventy-five he was still a paradigm of power and strength, an enormous man with an appetite for fun equal to his size. He was the local fisherman and wildlife expert. Though mostly retired, he earned extra cash by taking tourists on fishing trips and safaris. Like his father before him, he'd always managed to earn enough to live the life he wanted, which meant doing the minimum necessary to buy food, petrol for his beloved boat, and enjoy a few beers at Murphy's every evening.

Rastos pushed the door open with a thud. "Evening all," he boomed.

Wayne and Peter raised their glasses in acknowledgement, but the two men in the corner ignored his friendly greeting.

Rastos turned to Peter. "Christ, what a day I've had," he said. "I took two New York tourists fishing today, not a single bite. I just don't know where those fucking bass are hiding, man." Then he noticed the two guys in the corner. Although he didn't say anything, Peter knew what he was thinking.

Murphy filled a glass of beer and handed it over to Rastos. "You sound as if you've had a good day," he laughed.

"Oh, wonderful," said Rastos.

He was just about to expand in more detail about the day's fishing when Kevin O'Donnel, the local sheriff, entered the bar. "Goodness, I've got a thirst," he said, but Murphy was one step ahead and had a beer ready for him.

"Unusual to see you here this time of day, Sheriff," he said questioningly.

Kevin O'Donnel was a well-built man in his mid-fifties. Slightly below average height, he always kept himself fit and was thought by some of the ladies in the town to be rather attractive. He had been Sheriff of Inverness for the past two years and was well respected by the locals. In his time as sheriff, Inverness had experienced the lowest official crime rate in Florida. When he had first come to live in the area he had been married, but after a few months his wife, Susan, had decided that the quiet life was not for her and suddenly, one Saturday night, she had packed her bags and left, leaving Kevin to bring up their only son, Paul. It had not been easy, and he had to admit that there had been problems with Paul, though nothing that could not eventually be sorted out.

The sheriff glanced at the two men in the corner without comment, drank his beer straight down, touched the brim of his hat and said, "Well, must get on. That was just what the doctor ordered."

The two agents were still waiting in their car across the street and observed the sheriff drive out onto the highway. As he passed he slowed down and glanced towards them.

Chapter 6

Mitcham Creek, Inverness

By the time the taxi reached the toll road, darkness had fallen. Freda was in full flow with local news and gossip, but the Richardsons were both too tired for conversation and, within minutes, Sheila had fallen asleep on Gordon's shoulder.

"And then Paul O'Donnel, the sheriff's son, was expelled from college," Freda went on.

Gordon became more attentive. "What happened there?" he asked.

Freda said, "As far as I know he'd been messing around with a fifteen-year-old girl from a well-known New York family. Apparently they'd been found in bed together in Paul's room in the halls of residence. The whole thing's been hushed up, but Paul had to leave."

Gordon had only met Sheriff O'Donnel briefly on two occasions. Although he hadn't much liked him, he had to acknowledge that he'd done a lot for the town. "The sheriff may know how to deal with law and order, but he sure has a problem with his own family life," he said.

Freda shook her head. "Yes, he does seem to have more than his share of bad luck – what with Susan and all."

Another bit of news that particularly interested Gordon was that Thatchum House at Alligator Island on Lake Apopka had been sold, six weeks previously, to a New York businessman called Montigue Larimer, for a reputed $4,000,000.

"Nobody appears to know much about the guy," Freda went on. "Only that he has a gorgeous wife and quite something of a daughter. They've been seen driving around town in their Ferrari, but nobody has ever seen Mr Larimer."

Gordon's interest in the Larimers was purely business. They were wealthy people, and wealthy people might buy pictures. He made a mental note to make contact once the gallery was open. "Have to pay them a visit," he told Freda.

"That won't be easy," she said. "The main gate on the bridge to the island is always guarded twenty-four hours a day, and no one gets in without clearance from Mrs Larimer."

"You're well-informed, Freda," Gordon said.

"Old Rastos told me," she replied.

"Well, if Rastos told you, it must be true."

Sheila stirred but didn't wake.

Gordon looked down at her, squeezed her hand fondly and gently kissed her on the forehead.

Eventually they arrived at Mitcham Creek. The lights leading down the drive to the house were on and he could see a light on the kitchen.

"Sheila, darling, we're here," he said, giving her a little shake. "Home at last."

She woke with a start. "Curdridge House – thank goodness," she said sleepily.

"No, darling," Gordon whispered, hoping Freda hadn't heard. "Mitcham Creek." He got the suitcases out of the car boot and placed fifty dollars in Freda's hand. "Thanks," he said.

"Not at all," replied Freda. "It's been a pleasure. Anytime you want taking anywhere, just give me a ring. Goodnight to you."

Sheila had already found her way into the kitchen where Mrs Crossley from next door had left them some sandwiches and a note.

'Very kind of her,' she thought, though she didn't feel particularly hungry, and decided to make herself a cup of tea and then to bed. Gordon said he'd follow in a minute as he wanted to check the pool and look at the lake.

He opened the patio doors, switched on the light in the pool area and strolled around the pool enclosure. The evening was still with a full moon which threw its quivering reflection upon the waters. On the far side of the lake the utility power station lights flickered through the trees, and to the east, Thatchum House on Alligator Island could be seen silhouetted against the moonlight. The air was heavy; he could feel a storm brewing.

As his eyes traversed the garden and the lake, he noticed something strange in the darkness, some way out across the water: two orange stars glowing on the surface. 'Alligator,' he thought. 'Big male by the looks of it. That's unusual around this part of the lake.' The next instant the lights went out as the alligator submerged, leaving only a gentle ripple on the still surface. Gordon yawned, returned to the house, and closed and fastened the patio doors. He checked the air conditioning, switched off the lights and made his way to the bedroom. Sheila was sitting up reading.

"You okay?" he said. "Thought you'd be asleep by now."

"Hmm, just about," she replied.

She looked lovely lying there, Gordon thought. He particularly liked her in the black lace nightie. There was something about black lace that sent the pulse racing. Must be something deep down in the subconscious. He noted the full shape of her breasts and the slim neck silhouetted against the dimly-lit table lamp next to the bed.

As he washed, he could feel that old surge of sexual energy tightening his muscles. 'This is ridiculous,' he thought. 'We've just travelled five thousand miles, spent eleven hours on an aeroplane, exhausted, washed out and I get a hard-on.' He rinsed his mouth, dried himself, threw the towel into the bath, and slipped into bed next to his wife, who was so engrossed in her book that she didn't stir.

"Shall I turn off the lights?" he said.

"No, just let me finish this chapter."

But there wasn't time. Gordon felt his penis rise and harden. He cuddled up to the black lace and traced his forefinger along the curve of her neck, but she didn't respond. He became bolder, sliding his hand gently over her firm breasts and squeezing a nipple between his finger and thumb. It was the kind of foreplay that over the past few months had evinced little response. In fact Sheila had usually recoiled from his advance with a firm, "Not now." But tonight he felt her nipple harden against the press of his finger and she began to breathe deeply. Gently he slid his left hand across her hips, stroking her stomach as he did so. As he kissed her fully on the lips, Sheila let her book drop onto the floor and pulled him towards her. Slowly he removed her negligee. She kissed his chest and her hand grasped his erect manhood, now hardened to bursting. She moaned, pulled him towards her and guided him in. As he entered she let out a gasp. "Oh, I do love you. Harder, please, harder!" He drove himself deep into her and she cried, "Now, darling, now!"

They climaxed as one but he kept moving into her body until he felt her relax, then he slowly withdrew, and they lay side by side breathing deeply. "It's good to be as one again," he whispered.

She began to sob and tears came into her eyes. "I've missed you," she whimpered. "Missed you."

Gordon held her in his arms, kissed away her salt tears, and eventually they fell asleep holding each other tight.

At Murphy's Bar the two strangers in the corner rose from their seats, paid for their drinks and left. Placing the two bags on the back seat of the car they sped off towards Lake Apopka.

Craig and Titcombe had been waiting and now followed them at a discreet distance. Jake drove the Cadillac to the south side of the lake to Carters Landing, where he parked by the water's edge. Taking a torch from under the passenger seat, he flashed it six times across the lake. Out of the darkness two lights flashed back. Suddenly a roar of engines punctuated the night, and seconds later a motor launch appeared running at full speed. As it approached the landing the engine cut back and it idled alongside the jetty. The two men left the car, ran along the landing and, as the boat passed slowly, tossed the bags onto the deck. The launch disappeared into the black emptiness of the lake as quickly as it had appeared. The whole operation had taken approximately twenty seconds.

The two FBI agents had pulled off the road and were hidden from view behind some trees. They'd witnessed the whole thing.

Both were silent for a full minute, then Bob said, "Now that's what I call a cool operation."

"Wow," said Terry, shaking his head in disbelief. "These guys are certainly organised."

Chapter 7

Mitcham Creek, Inverness

Gordon was in dreamland, but the focus of his dream was not his wife lying beside him, but the blonde he'd briefly spoken to on the plane. Suddenly the dream was shattered by the ringing of the telephone. He looked at his watch. It was 11.30 a.m. 'Christ!' he thought. Sheila still slept, and he didn't feel inclined to wake her. He rolled off the bed, still groggy with sleep, and reached the telephone in the lounge just as it was about to cut off. His naked body felt the warmth of the sun through the patio windows, and he stretched unconsciously to embrace it.

"Hello."

"It's me," said a voice. "Tim Terry. I'm at the gallery. I need to discuss the lighting and signage."

'God, is that all!' thought Gordon, but said, "How's it all going?"

"Okay, but I do need some answers quickly, the electrician's sat on his arse here waiting, so it's costing you money."

"Be with you right away," said Gordon, and slammed down the phone.

He crept back into the bedroom, quickly showered, dressed and slipped out through the side door into the garage. He glanced back at Sheila as he left. She stirred slightly, groaned in her sleep and rolled over onto her stomach. She needed him, that he knew, but his ability to keep faith with her? He meant well, he told himself. Perhaps. But these passions, they were hard to control. His weakness was for women, in particular tall blonde women with youth on their side. Well, if he meant well, he didn't work at it. Temptation was a terrible thing.

The blue convertible Pontiac he had bought two years ago was covered in a dust sheet. He dragged it off the car, eased himself into the deep leather, turned the ignition and the engine roared into life. It was like a shot of adrenaline. He pressed the remote control switch to open the garage door and, as it lifted, he eased the car into the Florida sunshine and drove off at a leisurely speed.

The storm had cleared the air, it was going to be a beautiful day. He took a long look around as he cruised along Creek Boulevard and waved to Rastos, who, as usual, was sat out on his porch in his rocking chair, keeping one eye on the lake and one eye on the people passing by. He always looked as if he were asleep, but Gordon knew differently.

As he turned on to 4th Street, he could see the sheriff's car; its blue light flashing. It was parked outside Gerry and Dorothy Makepiece's house. Coming down the road towards him at great speed with siren blaring was Deputy Sheriff Mark Wall. Beside him sat Lucy Foster, the local doctor.

Mark Wall was a tall, well-built man of forty-five with deep brown friendly eyes and cropped grey hair, which he combed forward in a vain attempt to hide his receding hairline. At one time, following the death of his boss, Sheriff Pocket, who'd been killed in a hit-and-run accident, he had thought that he might run for the job himself, but Mayor Thompson had intervened. He'd told him in no uncertain terms that a new guy from Tampa, Kevin O'Donnel, would be seeking election as sheriff, and he was not to be opposed.

Mark had thought long and hard about this. He was not the kind of man to be put off by threats, and he didn't like Mayor Thompson's high-handed attitude, but at the same time he was happy as deputy. He did his job well, and he was in no hurry to change; his time would come, so he agreed not to run.

'Looks like there's been an accident,' Gordon thought as he passed the house at about the same time as the deputy's car screeched to a halt before the drive.

The deputy clambered out, hugging the doctor's black bag, which in his haste he dropped, scattering its contents across the drive.

Lucy uttered an expletive beneath her breath and raised her hands in frustration.

Gordon was concerned that something may have happened to Gerry or Dorothy or to that daughter of theirs. The daughter's name escaped him, but he thought it was Christy or something like that.

It was Sheriff O'Donnel who opened the door to Doctor Foster. Lucy was a career doctor, in the sense that medicine was her whole life, which some held as the reason she had never married; at thirty she was running short of time. She was petite, pretty and intelligent, and had no shortage of suitors.

Sheriff O'Donnel studied her face for a moment. He had always been attracted to her, but took care to keep his feelings to himself. Now he was agitated. "Come in quick," he said with a worried look. "Though, I'm afraid you're too late. You can't help the girl, I think she's been dead for three or four hours."

"How did it happen?" asked Lucy.

"Hell, I'm no expert," said the sheriff, "but it looks to me like a drugs overdose."

Lucy threw the sheriff a withering look. His attitude to what was, after all, a tragedy, irritated her, and she pushed passed him without saying a word. The sheriff looked at his deputy, and held up his hands in a gesture of despair.

Lucy found Christy laying face down on the bed, her naked body covered by a sheet. Mrs Makepiece was sitting by the bed holding the stiff, cold white hand. She was staring into space and her eyes were full of tears; she was in deep shock.

The sheriff, who had followed Lucy into the room with his deputy, said, "I didn't move her. I wanted you to examine her first."

By the side of the bed, Lucy noticed a needle, syringe and a small plastic bag containing white powder. The sheriff was right. It was a drugs overdose. Lucy carefully closed Christy's eyelids and drew the sheet up over her face. At this point she noticed the sheriff surreptitiously pick up the needle and the plastic bag and place them in his coat pocket. She looked at him disapprovingly.

Catching her gaze, Sheriff O'Donnel beckoned her out of the room. "Doctor, do you think we can have a word?" O'Donnel weighed his words carefully. "Look," he said, "nobody must know how this girl died – at least not yet."

Lucy shot him a look of incredulity. "What!" she said angrily, her skin tightening against her cheekbones.

"Trust me, Lucy," the sheriff said quietly. "I have good reason."

The deputy sheriff, leaning against the door, was as surprised as Lucy at O'Donnel's remark and glanced across at him. From the determination in the sheriff's eyes he knew he meant what he said; he'd seen that look often.

"You go to hell!" cried Lucy. "The cause of death on the certificate will be overdose, and I'm requesting a full autopsy report." She turned her back on the sheriff. "I'll see you later, Mark," she said, and went back into the bedroom to see if she could do anything to ease the parents' pain.

Sheriff O'Donnel turned to his deputy. "I can guess what you're thinking, boy," he said, "but believe me, I have strong reasons for doing this. You don't mention to anyone how the girl died. I'll deal with Dr Foster later. When she's finished in there, I want you to arrange for an ambulance to take the body to the mortuary at Rutland. I'll speak to Dr Lane myself. Oh," he added, "and bring Dr Foster straight down to my office."

"Sure," said Mark, his eyes fixed on the old patterned tiled floor. He drew a deep breath and looked up into Kevin O'Donnel's steely eyes.

"That's an order," the sheriff said softly. "I want to see her as soon as she's free. I repeat, you don't say anything to anyone. Don't cross me on this, Mark." He turned and walked down the passage to the bedroom and knocked on the door. Without waiting for a reply, he opened it slowly. Lucy was doing her best to comfort the bereaved parents, but they were both still in a state of shock. Sheriff O'Donnel cleared his throat. "I just want to say how sorry I am about your daughter," he said haltingly.

Lucy gave him a cold stare as their eyes clashed, but she didn't speak. Gerry Makepiece nodded, but that was all. Like his wife, he was too distraught to speak.

The sheriff closed the door and left. When he reached his car the warning light was still flashing. He turned it off and drove at speed along 4th Street. Picking up his mobile phone as he drove, he dialled a number in Orlando.

Two hours later, Deputy Sheriff Mark Wall entered the sheriff's office with Lucy Foster.

O'Donnel looked up from his desk. "Well done," he said nodding to his deputy. "Now please leave us and close the door as you go."

The deputy hesitated.

"Now, Mark," said the sheriff sternly.

The deputy smiled nervously at Lucy, turned and left the room, closing the door firmly behind him.

"What's the big deal?" the sheriff's secretary asked.

"Don't ask me," Mark grunted. "I'm just the boy around here."

From his desk he could see his boss arguing with Lucy Foster through the glass panel of his office. The sheriff was stabbing his finger at Lucy to make his point, whatever that was, and was clearly angry.

Dr Foster suddenly turned to leave the room, but the sheriff blocked her way. Mark saw him take hold of Lucy's shoulders firmly and ease her into a chair. He leaned over and whispered something in her ear. Her expression at that moment changed from anger to one of shock, and she began to cry. She stood up shakily and for one moment it looked as if she was about to faint. O'Donnel steadied her in his arms for a moment, but she stiffened and pulled away.

Mark Wall, watching through the glass, wondered what was going on; none of this made any sense. He saw Lucy stand for a moment to regain her composure, and when she came out of the sheriff's office she was as white as a sheet.

"Are you okay, Lucy?" Mark asked.

"Yes, I'm fine," she said taking a deep breath. "My report on the girl's death will state that she died of a heart attack. Tell him I'll have the certificate sent round in a couple of hours." She glanced towards the sheriff's office and then back to the deputy. "Mark, we have to trust him," she said resignedly. "There's nothing else we can do." She looked tired and pale, but she was also hurt. She turned quickly, picked up her bag and slammed the door behind her as she left.

Chapter 8

Inverness Rum Brewery

Peter Cooper had now logged all the security routines for the past four nights, ever since the idea of dumping the sugar rum residue into the lake had occurred to him.

The two guards, Luke Washer and Johnny Combes, were creatures of habit. At 6.45 each evening, Luke would remain in the gatehouse while Johnny traversed the external areas, flashing his torch haphazardly around as he walked. Neither of the guards carried out their duties efficiently. Peter had noted that at about seven o'clock every night, Johnny would finish his round, then slip quietly past the gate and head off towards town, returning about an hour later. Luke would then carry out an inspection of the external perimeter of the site, after which, just like his colleague, he would disappear for an hour, between nine and ten. The two guards would then take turns every hour throughout the night, checking the perimeter fence and occasionally flashing their torches out across the lake. In four successive nights this routine had remained constant. What surprised Peter was than no one had ever checked on the guards; they seemed to do exactly as they pleased.

Peter decided that the best time to dump the residue would probably be between nine and ten o'clock each night, before the second guard returned. However, before he could finalise his plan he needed to check the exact movements of the two guards; he wanted to know where they went when each of them disappeared for an hour.

On the fifth evening he decided to follow Luke. He tracked him to the outskirts of town and was surprised to see him stop at Max Pace's old timber shack on Lake Street. Luke looked nervously around before going in.

Everyone knew Max Pace. He was a well-known troublemaker, and he'd been familiar with the local sheriff ever since he was a kid.

It had never been serious stuff, mostly petty theft and drunkenness, and, as far as Peter could remember, Max had never held down a job for more than a week. It was therefore surprising, as rumour had it, that he had money to spend; a good deal of money. He'd apparently bought a new Nissan and an old 1960s Wurlitzer jukebox. The latter had come from a very expensive shop in Miami. As he listened, Peter could hear music blasting out of the half open side window. He recognised it as 'Jailhouse Rock'. Rather appropriate for Max, he thought

The back of the shack was littered with the cadavers of old cars and general junk, and as Peter crept close in the darkness he accidentally stood on an old bicycle frame. The pedal came up hard against his shin and he bit his lip to stop himself crying out, but even then a muffled groan escaped. He crouched, fully expecting Max to come crashing through the door uttering expletives and brandishing his rusty twelve bore, which he'd never actually managed to fire. But nothing happened. He waited a few minutes and then limped around to the rear and peered though the window. In the back room he could make out Luke, Max, Tom Black and Chuck Romford. They were sitting around the kitchen table playing poker. In front of them sat a large stack of ten dollar bills. They all appeared to be well and truly drunk, and Max, as Peter watched, was so far gone that he fell off his chair, this to hoots of raucous laughter. Max was not well pleased and cursed them roundly as he clambered to his feet. But for all his faults he was not a violent man.

Peter's gaze shifted to the far side of the room which was partly in darkness, and his eyes rested on an old stone sink in which there appeared to be lying an old brown overcoat. In the dim light he could just make out more overcoats and blankets draped over the beams above. He narrowed his eyes in an effort to see better, and then suddenly he realised what they were; alligator skins. The bastards had been poaching alligators, a crime which in Florida came slightly below homicide.

Alligators had been a protected species in this part of Florida since 1995. At one time, in the early 1900s, the lakes and river around Inverness were alive with them, but by the 1980s, due to uncontrolled hunting, their numbers had dwindled to a few hundred. It was then that the conservationists persuaded the state authorities to ban the hunting of all wild alligators. Alligator skins were still big business. The consequences of this measure meant that the manufacturers of alligator products, such as handbags, shoes and other knick-knacks, were forced to import skins from overseas, and even then the trade was strictly controlled. With Florida alligator skins now virtually unobtainable, a black market emerged, and poaching became a lucrative business, with very severe sentences for those caught.

In this area, poaching of alligators was supposed to have been stamped out, so the county sheriff was in for a surprise.

Peter limped down the side of the house, avoiding the rubbish, including the bike, and made his way back to the factory. After he'd checked the burglar alarm and locked up, he climbed into the old Buick and drove to Murphy's. As he passed the power unit, he noticed Johnny Combes at the gate.

At approximately 10.15 p.m. the other guard, Luke Washer, arrived at the unit, waved to Combes and then began to carry out his inspection of the perimeter fence. As he neared the lake, he was unaware of two glowing orange eyes, some sixty feet offshore, watching his every move. As the guard swept the lake with his torch the two orange glows submerged beneath the dark waters.

Chapter 9

Bond Street, London

Gerald Fitzgibbon parked his Ferrari Testarossa in the mews garage that he rented behind his shop on the corner of Bond Street. As he climbed out of the car he lovingly stroked its sinuous curves. Beneath his hands it seemed to respond like a woman's flesh, sensual and erotic. For a moment he let his eyes rest on its perfection. He had always loved cars, and this one in particular. He pressed the remote control key and the door clicked shut as the sensors picked up the signal. "See you later," he said to the car, then turned and walked into the September sunshine, shielding his eyes from its glare. He pressed another switch and the double garage doors slowly closed. He placed the keys in the pocket of his pinstriped suit, and straightened his silk tie. Gerald always dressed well, Winchester and Oxford had seen to that. He had that air about him that spoke of privilege, and he carried his lean, six foot frame well. His face was suntanned, slightly weathered and at thirty-six he could afford a few wrinkles around the eyes when he smiled, it gave his face an extra vitality. He felt relaxed and particularly well. The fact that at that moment he happened to be between wives, might have had something to do with it.

He walked down through the mews and entered Bond Street just above Sotheby's. From this point he could see his shop on the corner with its 1930's facade and the name 'JATAME SHOES' picked out in dark gold letters over the front window. The time was 8.45 a.m. Mary Tarmore, his assistant manageress, had just arrived and was busy unlocking the front door.

'Good,' Gerald thought. 'Right on time.' He wished her good morning as he entered the shop, and heard the telephone ringing in his office. He fumbled for the key in his pocket; finally found it, unlocked the door and grabbed the phone. "Jatame Shoes."

"Gerald," said a hurried voice with an American accent, "the new

42

shipment of shoes left yesterday and they need to be picked up at Heathrow tonight."

"Have they cleared customs?" Gerald asked.

"Yes. But the clients in Kensington require the merchandise by tomorrow, midday."

There was a click and the phone went dead. Gerald held the receiver in his hand. 'Rather abrupt, today,' he thought, carefully replacing it.

"Your mail, Mr Fitzgibbon," said Mary, entering his office with a bunch of letters.

The assistant manageress had a disturbingly charming way of delivering the mail, he had always thought. He found it difficult to avert his eyes from this slim young figure in the bright-red dress with the bubbling personality. "Dinner tonight?" he heard himself saying.

"Yes," said Mary rather too eagerly, her dark-brown eyes shining. She was madly in love with her boss.

"Pick you up at your place, about 9.30? Some business to attend to this evening first." He hesitated for a moment. "Perhaps, you'd like to come down to my place for the weekend?"

"Okay," she said breezily and turned to leave, swinging her hips seductively as she did so.

Gerald looked longingly after her and sighed. He did so love these young things. He turned back to his desk and suddenly his mood changed. His hands began to tremble and he felt a cold chill. He could feel trickles of sweat on his neck and on his top lip. He pulled out a bunch of keys and knelt down in front of the safe. He tried to place a key in the lock, but his right hand was now shaking so much that he had to grasp it tightly with his left to keep it steady. He turned the key, opened the heavy door slowly and took out a small package sealed with tin foil. Placing the package on the desk, he quickly opened it, spreading the tin foil out flat. He took some of the white powder, placed it on the back of his hand, raised it to his nostrils and sniffed hard. The effect was miraculous. Within a few seconds he became calm and confident again. Slowly he took a deep breath and sniffed again. He then folded the package tightly, returned it to the safe, closed it and turned the lock, dropping the keys back into his trouser pocket and tapping his leg as he did so.

He opened the door of his office, then sat back in his chair and watched Mary arranging the shoe displays. 'Just wait until this evening, my girl,' he thought. 'It's been a long time since we've been together.' He then turned his attention to the letters on his desk and began to systematically open each envelope, putting bills to one side, cheques and requests for orders in the centre of the desk in front of him. By now the cocaine was taking over and his mind began to wander. "Sheila," he whispered aloud, "I miss you."

Mary came through from the shop. "Mr Fitzgibbon, did you call me?"

"No, sorry, Mary. I was just thinking aloud."

"Oh, you must be getting old," she joked cautiously, and went back into the shop.

Gerald's mind began to wander, recalling vividly how he and Sheila had become lovers. It had happened so innocently; he had never intended to make a play for her. They had first met at the Royal Academy Summer Exhibition, at one of its preview nights. Gerald had no detailed knowledge of art, but he'd become a collector of sorts, by way of a lusty affair with a delightful Academy employee, a girl considerably younger than himself, who'd encouraged him to invest in certain 'in vogue' pictures. He'd even become a sponsor. Unfortunately, before he'd got to grips with things, her husband found out and whisked her off to Australia, never to be seen nor heard from again.

On the evening he first met Sheila, he was admiring a large painting by Ken Howard, aptly named *Desire*, when he felt the presence of a woman standing beside him. He knew it was a woman as he could smell her perfume.

"Do you like his work?" she asked in a soft voice.

"Not particularly," he replied turning to look at her. "But his pictures have something – vitality, feeling for life, I don't know, but something."

"Yes, I know what you mean," she said. "I've always liked Ken Howard's pictures. I first bought one here at the Academy exhibition in 1990, and I've bought one every year since."

'A lady of strong convictions,' Gerald thought. 'Good looker, too. Thirty-five-ish, five foot five or thereabouts, brown eyes, long mousy hair – natural. Not bad.' "You . . ." And then he stopped.

She inclined her head. "You were about to say something?"

"No – please excuse me," Gerald said apologetically. "I was thinking . . . in fact, I was thinking how beautiful you are."

"Oh!" She coughed shyly. "Thank you, but don't you think I'm a little old to fall for that kind of patter?"

"Yes, of course," said Gerald slightly embarrassed. "I'm sorry, I didn't mean . . ."

"No problem," she said smiling and held out her hand. "I'm Sheila

Richardson. That gentleman over there talking to the young blonde goddess is my husband. He's an art dealer."

'Good for him.' Gerald thought, but said, "I'm Gerald Fitzgibbon. I sell rather expensive shoes on Bond Street."

He was just about to ask her to join him in a glass of champagne when her husband, obviously bored with the young blonde, wandered over and reached out a hand. "I'm Gordon Richardson," he said smiling and shook Gerald's hand vigorously.

"Yes, I know," said Gerald. "Your good wife has just pointed you out to me."

"Are you interested in art?" Gordon asked.

"Yes, but mainly for investment. I'm a bit of a philistine, you see, not what you'd call a connoisseur."

"Gerald says he likes this Ken Howard," Sheila interrupted.

"Gerald?"

"Oh, I'm sorry, I haven't introduced myself, my name's Gerald Fitzgibbon."

"I'm very pleased to meet you, Gerald. Now, would you care to join us in a little glass of champagne?"

"Love to," replied Gerald.

Gerald didn't remember everything that happened that evening, only that he couldn't take his eyes off Sheila Richardson, and when Gordon suggested to him that he visit the gallery at the weekend, Gerald accepted immediately, though acknowledging to himself that Gordon Richardson was not a man to whom he took an instant liking. Perhaps he was simply jealous, and this was clouding his judgement.

Over the next few months, Gerald bought a number of pictures from Gordon Richardson. The three of them often went out to dinner together whenever Sheila and Gordon were in town, but Gerald always knew what he really wanted, and it was not Gordon Richardson's company.

One Thursday afternoon at about five o'clock, Sheila came into his shop alone. He went to meet her and gave her a gentle kiss on the cheek, a formal, though affectionate, greeting between friends. Gerald desired more but was unwilling to risk her friendship by forced demands, but when he kissed her that day he detected a warmer response, a kind of wanting, something more meaningful.

She held his hand tightly for a few seconds and looked directly into his eyes. "Gerald," she said softly. "I need to be loved."

Without a reply, he took her by the hand and together they left the shop and walked down Bond Street into the mews. Gerald unlocked the garage door, backed the Ferrari out, reached over and opened the passenger door. Sheila lifted her short black skirt as she slithered into the seat beside him. As he went to move the gear stick his hand touched her leg, and he felt the black stockings against his fingers. He let his hand rest on her leg. Sheila looked down at the floor, but made no attempt to remove his hand. He revved the engine, put the car into first and gently eased the sleek red stallion into the street. Turning left, he headed off along the A3 towards the motorway.

"Gerald, where are we going?" Sheila asked after some minutes.

"I'm taking you to Arlesford Hall," replied Gerald. "We can be alone there."

For most of the journey Sheila remained silent. Gerald could feel that she was nervous, but it was an excited kind of nervousness, like an electric current that touched him too. Eventually he turned off the lane, passed between two big wrought iron gates and stopped the car. Before them ran a straight gravel drive, lined with beech and oak, whose autumn leaves were already turning to russet green, red and gold and shimmered in the late afternoon sunshine. At the end of this mile-long drive stood Arlesford Hall. Sheila stared in front of her, absorbed by the view.

"Beautiful, isn't it?" said Gerald, squeezing her hand.

"Unbelievable," replied Sheila staring. "This is all yours?"

"Yes it is, and it takes every pound I have to keep it this way. I love it. It's part of my life, my heritage and I'm very proud of it. I'll do anything to keep it." He glanced at her longingly. "Anything!" He fired the engine, let out the clutch and the car roared to life. They pulled to a halt at the main entrance where wide stone steps led up to the front door.

"It really is beautiful," said Sheila, unable to take her eyes off the house.

Gerald took her hand and led her step by step to the great oak door. He turned the brass handle and the door swung open before them to reveal a spacious oak-panelled hall. At one end a grand staircase rose in a sweeping curve to a galleried first-floor landing.

He turned and stood before her. Taking both her hands in his, he said, "I've loved you from the first moment I saw you that day at the Academy. I've never felt like this about any woman before."

"Not even your ex-wives?" said Sheila with a wry smile.

"Certainly not! Look, I tell you what, go through that door on the right. It'll lead you to the swimming pool and conservatory. Take a seat and I'll get a bottle of champagne from the fridge." And with that Gerald disappeared.

46

Now alone, Sheila opened the door and found herself in the most beautiful Victorian conservatory she had ever seen; the tropical foliage of vast palms reached for the light, and the scent of orchids pervaded the sultry air. In the centre of this virtual jungle was the pool, a sheet of clear water, shot through with reflections from the surrounding foliage. It was a small paradise. She felt relaxed, intoxicated by the luxuriant surroundings and sank down onto an old Victorian wicker settee, well supplied with ample cushions. It was like a delicious dream, and when Gerald entered carrying a silver tray with two wide-brimmed gold-edged crystal glasses, and an ice bucket from which protruded the neck of a large bottle of champagne, the dream took on reality.

He bowed to her in a gallant manner and removed the cork with a loud pop, which released a spurt of champagne over his white silk shirt. "Damn!" He contemplated the wet stain. "Never mind. Madame, your champagne." He filled the two glasses to the brim, and raised his in a toast. "To you," he said. "I adore you."

"Thank you," she said, thinking this was all too good to be true, and at the same time feeling a stab of guilt. She was, after all, a married woman.

"Are you okay?" Gerald asked anxiously. "You look a little nervous."

She nodded and took a deep breath. "Yes, I'm all right – but, well – I've never done anything like this before."

"What – never?"

"No, never," she replied, averting her eyes from his gaze. "I've been married to Gordon for twenty-five years and I've never been unfaithful."

"I won't let you down," said Gerald after a long pause. "I'm flattered that you agreed to come here with me. You're different from any woman I've ever known, or ever wanted." He took the glass from her hand and placed it on the table, then he reached out and caressed the nape of her neck, gently drawing her towards him, and their lips met.

Sheila responded a little hesitantly at first, but Gerald could feel her body relaxing as her lips pressed more forcibly against his own.

The master bedroom was situated on the first floor by way of the winding staircase. By the time they reached it, Sheila's emotions were in turmoil. It was a large bedroom, panelled throughout, and at one end stood a huge four-poster, hung with embroidered silk drapes.

"The bed's been in our family for generations," Gordon whispered. "I was born in it."

"Oh!"

47

"Come and sit by me," he said making himself comfortable at one end of the bed.

"Gerald . . ."

But her words were stifled as he took her in his arms and kissed her softly. Her resistance now gone, she drew him to her and they sunk back, locked in each other's arms. Their embrace became more attentive with each movement. Sheila felt his hands on her neck, caressing. He began to loosen her dress, one button at a time, and the passion within her rose. He kissed her exposed nipples, hard to his tongue, and gently slipped off her dress, exposing her navy slip, and then he lay back.

Sheila unbuttoned his shirt as he lay there, and slipped off his trousers and underpants, her hands gently caressing, moving down the side of his firm body until she reached between his legs.

Ferociously he stripped off the rest of her underclothes, and she rolled onto her back in complete submission. He entered her then and she began to moan as Gerald's manhood grew inside her, and cried out as her perspiring body rose against each frenzied thrust, each stab of exquisite pain – and then it was over, and they fell back exhausted.

After their first love-making they met each Thursday afternoon at Arlesford Hall. Sometimes they made love in the pool, sometimes in the summer house at the end of the garden, and once, on a perfect day, in the meadow far beyond the house.

Gerald introduced Sheila to cocaine, and at first she resisted, but one afternoon after they had made love, she consented; it was the beginning of her addiction.

As time went by, Gerald felt himself falling deeper in love, and she returned his love, but no matter how much he pleaded with her to leave her husband, she always refused. He was sure she didn't love Gordon, but she was a woman of strong loyalties, and refused to cast them aside.

Gerald became insanely jealous. He wanted her desperately, and he knew she wanted him. Whenever he brought the matter up, which was incessantly, Sheila parried his demands. Things between them began to deteriorate, until one Thursday Gerald arrived home to find that Sheila had called earlier and left a letter for him.

The handwriting was shaky: *Darling Gerald,* she wrote. *I love you more than words can say, but our relationship must end. I can't go on any longer. We can't be together any longer. I cannot face the shame of telling Gordon, or the children. I'm sorry. Forgive me. Love Sheila.*

Gerald closed his fist on the letter. He wouldn't let it end like this. He drove at full speed and arrived at Curdridge House at three in the afternoon.

Sheila saw his car coming down the drive as she sat crying by the swimming pool. He walked briskly across the lawn and threw the door open.

"You don't mean this?" he said in a tone of angry dejection. He was shaking and he held the letter in his hand. "I know you love me. We can work something out."

"How?" Sheila cried. "How? I can't tell Gordon. I'm afraid. I'm not going to leave him – I can't." She buried her face in her hands and sobbed uncontrollably.

He knelt beside her. "Please, Sheila. I accept what you say, but can't we just go on as we are, seeing each other – it's not ideal but . . ."

"That's no good either," Sheila cried through her tears. "I love you so much, but it's tearing me apart. I can't take the lies and deceit any more."

Gerald moved to console her, and for a second she drew back, but he persisted and drew her into his arms. He held her close and kissed her wet eyes. Her body relaxed, she had no strength left to resist.

They made love on the stone floor by the pool, and just as they climaxed, the door burst open and Sheila's son, Julian, burst in. "Mum, where's my green shirt . . . ?" He stopped in mid-sentence and stared at his mother. "My God!" His anguished cry died in his throat.

He turned, staggered to the door, flung it open and ran across the lawn towards his car. The wheels of the Mini Cooper spun in the gravel as he revved the engine and took off down the drive, sending stones flying.

Sheila pushed Gerald off her, grabbed her robe and stumbled after her son, struggling to cover her nakedness as she ran across the lawn calling his name. "Julian, come back! Come back!" But he was already through the gate, his foot hard down on the accelerator.

She stood, wrapping her arms around herself in an attitude of total dejection. All the strength had gone out of her. She lowered her head and wept. Gerald reached her and slid his arm across her shoulders, but she shook him off.

"Darling, I'm sorry, so sorry. I didn't mean . . ."

"Gerald, just go now," she pleaded. "I never want to see you again. Go now – please."

He knew it was over. He wanted to say something but he couldn't formulate the words, so he simply nodded and turned away; his eyes full of tears. He got into his car and started the engine. He drove past her at the gate, and when he had gone a little way he looked back. She still stood, slightly stooped, arms clutching her sides, a desperate figure silhouetted against the dark winter sky.

Gerald didn't know how he managed to get back to Arlesford Hall, but he did. He got blind drunk that evening, but it didn't ease the pain; his heart was broken.

Gerald never saw Sheila again. And Julian, he later learned, had died in a car accident that same afternoon.

He was still day-dreaming when the telephone rang. It was Kilion Rastafaf. "Hello, Gerald," he said in his thick Jamaican accent. "I understand that the goods will arrive tonight and you will deliver."

"That's right," Gerald mumbled.

"Well, I'll tell you what, man, come to my place at 9.30. I'll be waiting, man. Don't be late."

Chapter 10

Power Unit, Inverness

Wayne Headbold and Claire Williams checked all the instrumentation on the new power station three times, including all the back-up equipment. The mini nuclear power plant had been producing electric power unofficially for several days. As it would not be in full production for another three days, all the electricity produced was going back into the National Power Grid.

All the sensor checks for radiation activity, leaks and levels had been found to be working to Wayne's satisfaction; he even had the emergency outfall checked. The outfall pipe, as he had constantly assured the conservation groups and the press, would never be used. It had been installed as a last precaution in the event of a total disaster situation. The levels of coolant water surrounding the reactor, which was encased in six feet of reinforced concrete, were also monitored. The instrument checks had shown that the new power unit was working as designed.

But Wayne was not happy, and when, at eight o'clock that evening, Claire finished her final check of the instrumentation, and Wayne entered the control room she noticed that he was nervous and irritable.

He asked her to recheck the level and sensors to the water coolant, and stood by her as she did so, stroking his chin nervously.

Claire looked up at him. "Darling, why are you looking so worried?" she asked.

"Hell, I don't know," Wayne replied. "I just feel that something's not quite right."

"But we've checked and rechecked, and everything's okay. None of the sensors of level indicators shows any sign of a problem. In fact this baby seems to be running more efficiently than any of the other three we've built in Texas."

"Yes, I know," said Wayne. "We seem to be getting an energy efficiency of 90%, which is wonderful, but I still feel uneasy."

Claire placed her check card slowly on her desk. "I'm tired, Wayne," she said wearily. "Let's go home early. Think about all this in the morning."

Wayne nodded. There was no reason for his apprehension; nothing a good meal and a sound night's sleep wouldn't put to rights. He opened the control room door and shouted to the technician, "Tom, ring the main power station at Waccassa Bay, and tell them that Claire and I will be leaving in about fifteen minutes. You'll be on duty tonight."

"Okay," Tom replied breezily. "Will do."

Wayne watched him through the viewing screen, and said to Claire, "He knows Betty's on duty tonight, that's why he's so happy about his night shift. Something going on between those two?"

Claire gave a knowing smile.

Tom Crink had been headhunted from the main power station at Waccassa Bay six months previously, and had spent three months training in Texas under Wayne's supervision. He liked Tom, even though at times he found him a little vague and forgetful, but he was keen to learn, and he was enthusiastic. Besides which, he was a damn good technician, and because of this Wayne appointed him to the job of senior technician.

As for Betty Goddard, Wayne had met her several times whenever he visited Waccassa. She was a very good engineer, and from his discussions with her, he felt she had a far superior outlook and mental attitude to life than Tom. He even offered her a job, which she said she'd think about.

"Well think hard," he'd said. "Just remember that in a few years time large power stations like this one will be extinct. The future lies in the mini station."

Watching from his factory window, Peter Cooper saw Claire and Wayne leave the power plant. He checked around the brewery to ensure that everyone there had also gone, then quickly left by a side entrance, jumped into the JCB digger and turned the key. The diesel engine gave a deep roar as it sprung into life.

On Monday evening, Peter had let the tanker pick up the residue as usual. The next day he telephoned Tim Clear, the owner of the transport company, to say that he was cutting production and would need no further collection for some while. "I'll ring you at the end of the week," he told Tim abruptly, "if I need you."

Tim was dismayed. He'd been dealing with the residue from Peter's company for the past ten years. "But no one else in the area has a licence for residue storage," he pointed out. "Even on a reduced production, you've still got to get rid of the stuff."

"Look, I'm trying a new system of production," Peter replied haltingly. "I'll ring you," and with that he replaced the phone. He felt nervous and he noticed his hand was shaking. Tim had been a good friend to the company over the years, and Peter knew that the loss of this contact would be a blow to him, but there was simply no alternative.

He drove the JCB down to the cooling residue vats and opened the holds. The sweet, sickly smell of sugar and rum met his nostrils. He dug the bucket into the crystals and slowly began loading the small barge that he'd moored to the jetty. As this was to be the first trip he decided to limit the load, and after about half an hour, when the barge looked half full, he closed the doors to the residue storage pit, returned the JCB, and then covered the hold with tarpaulins. He looked at his watch. It was 8.30.

"Another hour yet," he said to himself.

Back at his office, he opened the walnut art deco veneered cabinet and poured himself a stiff glass of Inverness Rum. He looked out of the window across the lake towards the power unit, and coughed as the strong liquid slid down his throat. Suddenly the door to his office was flung open with such force that Peter dropped his glass, which shattered into a million fragments on the floor.

It was Johnny Combes, the security guard. "Sorry, I didn't mean to startle you," he said, "but I heard someone using the JCB down by the lake. I thought you'd better know quick."

Peter drew his breath. "Oh! That was me," he said shakily. "I've been wanting to drive that damn machine for years, so I thought I'd have a go while no one was around." It didn't sound plausible but it was the best he could do. He noticed just then that Combes was swaying slightly. Could he have been drinking?

Combes said, "I heard business was not good."

"It's okay," said Peter, thinking it was none of his business.

"You're not thinking of getting rid of the digger driver are you, Mr Cooper?" Combes said unsteadily. "Makepiece is on a downer at the moment. You've heard about his daughter?"

"Not at all," said Peter sharply, ignoring the reference to Makepiece's daughter. "I just wanted to have a go in the thing, that's all. Makepiece is not going to lose his job."

Combes looked unsure but said, "Okay, Mr Cooper. Don't lose your temper. I'm leaving." He turned and walked unsteadily through the door, leaving Peter drained.

He picked up the pieces of shattered glass and threw them into the waste bin. He was angry with himself. He'd handled the situation badly, but perhaps Combes hadn't noticed. He had, after all, been drinking. In future he'd have to make sure that he only used the digger between 8.30 and 9.

He moved to the window and saw Combes leaving the building. Luke waved to him as he passed through the gate en route to Max Pace's place.

As soon as he was gone, Peter made his way down to the barge. It was a dark night with low cloud cover, but there was just enough light to see by. Once aboard he pressed the switch to start the silent electric motor and gently eased the barge away from the shore, heading south towards the power unit. But his actions had not gone unnoticed. Luke, at the security gate, had seen the barge leave and had followed its route with his binoculars.

As the barge rounded the cove, the old male alligator, lying in his den, felt the engine's vibration through the soft sand. He was a huge creature, a good twelve feet in length, and about forty years old. Considering the amount of hunting that went on in the area in the 1970s and early 80s, it was a miracle that he'd survived to such an age. His den was just around the point of the lake between the rum factory and the new power unit, and when the latter was under construction the alligator kept well away from human contact. He slipped gently into the water and watched the barge as it approached. Only his two bright orange eyes were visible above the waterline, and then they, too, were extinguished as the alligator submerged out of sight. Peter saw nothing as he passed close by.

As he reached the drop point he turned the single bow light off and drifted silently into the bulrushes. Slowly he opened the side loading panel, pressed the switch to operate the jacks that lifted the false base of the barge up at an angle, and watched nervously as the crystal residue slid over the side and vanished beneath the dark surface. The noise of the crystals hitting the water broke the silence and made Peter wince. The depth of the water at this point was about twenty feet, and as the crystals floated gently to the bed of the lake they flashed and glistened like a shoal of small fish. And as he watched he was suddenly aware of turmoil beneath the surface. A shoal of bass swept in and began to gorge themselves on the crystals. Their appetite was ferocious, and they sucked in great gaping mouthfuls of the crystals. The alligator sensed the vibrations of the feeding shoal through the water. He had not eaten for some time and he was hungry. He was also nervous of the boat.

When the last of the residue had been emptied from the barge, Peter raised the side and lowered the tilting bar. Slowly he turned the barge around and headed back to the factory, passing within a few feet of the submerged alligator.

As soon as the boat had gone, the alligator made for the shoal of bass. He swept straight in and gorged himself on the easy prey, then turning on his belly, he returned to his den. At the first attack the shoal had dispersed, but within a few minutes it had regrouped and was back feeding on the crystals. The alligator made two more sorties on the bass shoal, but when he returned a fourth time the fish had moved on. His belly full, he remained still, lying just below the surface, the only movement the gentle swish of his tail against the motion of the current. He would not need to feed again for another week.

Chapter 11

Customs Building, Orlando

It had now been ten days since the Richardsons had moved to Florida. Sheila had at first appeared relaxed, even attentive towards her husband, though this did not extend to love-making. Very soon, however, she began to slip back into depression, and once again became withdrawn and hopelessly vague. There were mood swings, times when she would laugh and become almost like her old self, only to plunge once more into the depths of despair.

He had tried to interest her in the gallery but with little response. She would sit by the pool in the evenings, drinking heavily and staring into space. Sooner or later, if she got no better, he would have to persuade her to seek professional help, but he felt that time had not yet come, and he still hoped and prayed that she would eventually emerge from the shock of Julian's death.

At that moment, however, Gordon was facing another problem. The fitting out of the new gallery was due to be completed by the weekend, after which he had planned to hang the pictures. The trouble was that the shipment of paintings coming from England had been held up by customs. Gordon had made numerous telephone calls to ascertain the problem, only to be met with evasive answers and demands for the filling in of more forms. Gordon was baffled. As far as he was aware the import documents were in order, and he had completed all the necessary forms, but customs still refused to release the shipment.

Eventually, in a state of total frustration, he had managed to track down the customs and excise chief in Orlando, a Mr Macceffy, who had agreed to meet him at the customs office that Wednesday afternoon at three o'clock.

As Gordon pulled into the parking lot at the Customs House he was stopped at the gate and his car searched. A completely unnecessary precaution, he thought, since he was coming to see their boss. The older guard made a telephone call and then waved him through. Gordon parked his car, locked the doors, and turned towards the main entrance.

As he glanced upwards he was surprised to see Sheriff O'Donnel walking towards the automatic glass doors, accompanied by a small thin man with a rat-like face. Both men were dressed in lounge suits. Outside, at the top of the steps, the sheriff turned to the little man and they shook hands. Rat face then went back into the building, whilst the sheriff walked at a brisk pace towards his car. He stopped at a light-blue Rolls-Royce Corniche convertible. Pressing the automatic key he opened the door, climbed in and started the engine. The power hood automatically lowered. He drove off through the main gate, where he was waved straight through by the security guard.

Gordon pondered on what he had just seen. The sheriff in a Rolls-Royce? Perhaps he had family money? Perhaps he'd just won the lottery? What the hell! It was none of his business after all. At that moment he had enough to think about. Gordon withdrew a white envelope from his inside pocket, checked that he had all the documents he needed, straightened his tie nervously, and walked to the main entrance, then through into the foyer.

The blonde behind the reception desk had her back to him, so he pressed the bell on the desk. The girl turned round. To his astonishment it was the girl he'd bumped into on the plane. Recognition was mutual.

"Well," she said smiling, "we meet again."

"Small world," he said, returning the smile.

"And what can I do for you Mr . . . ?"

"Richardson. Gordon Richardson. I have an appointment with Mr Macceffy – at three o'clock."

"Right. I'll let Mr Macceffy know that you've arrived." She picked up the telephone and punched in the number for the excise officer. Gordon couldn't quite believe that he'd met this girl again. He was already captivated and could hardly take his eyes off her.

Replacing the telephone, she turned to him and said, "If you'll go up to the eighth floor, Mr Macceffy's secretary will meet you at the lift."

Gordon nodded. "Perhaps I'll see you on my way down?" he said hopefully.

"Perhaps," she said coquettishly reclining her head.

As he walked towards the lift he could feel the bristles on the back of his neck stiffen. He was sure she was watching him; sure the attraction was mutual. He pressed the call button and stepped into the lift without looking back.

A slim young man, wearing a blue pinstripe suit and pink shirt, met him as he stepped out of the lift on level eight. "Mr Richardson?" he said in a light, fluffy voice. Without waiting for confirmation he continued, "I'm Geoffrey, Mr Macceffy's personal secretary. Would you follow me, please, and I will show you to Mr Macceffy's office."

Gordon followed him along the carpeted corridor, at the end of which they turned left and entered into what he could only describe as an office of palatial magnitude. It was furnished with exquisite furniture from the art deco period. There were some magnificent pictures and a number of Grecian statues.

'Very, very nice,' he thought. 'I could sell most of this stuff with one phone call.'

Sitting at a large veneered walnut desk was Macceffy. To Gordon's surprise it was the very same little rat-faced man he had seen talking to the sheriff at the main entrance.

Macceffy rose from his chair and shook Gordon's hand limply. "Do sit down," he said. "Can I order you a coffee, tea – or something stronger?"

Gordon declined the offer. "No thanks, I'm fine," he said.

"Well, Mr Richardson," said Macceffy, settling back into his chair with a confident smirk on his face, "we appear to have a problem clearing your pictures."

"That's right," said Gordon, "and I don't quite see why. All my papers are in order?"

"Yes, they are," said Macceffy. "However, there is one little problem. We are of the opinion, and by 'we' I mean the department, that the valuation you have put on this shipment of $3,000,000 is not accurate."

Gordon's eyes widened. "That valuation was agreed in England with customs and excise, and they found it acceptable."

Macceffy pursed his lips. "Well, I'm afraid, Mr Richardson, that I don't." He hesitated. "We don't."

Gordon shifted irritably in his seat. "What are you trying to say?" he asked. "That you want the paintings totally revalued? But that will take days! I'm due to open my gallery next week. I can't wait that long."

"It appears to me," said Macceffy, rubbing his eyes as if the whole thing was a huge bore, "that you have a real problem."

Gordon stared at the carpet in an attempt to keep his temper under control. "Have you any alternative suggestions?" he asked coldly.

Macceffy shuffled papers on his desk. "There's one possible way," he said after a long pause.

"And what might that be?" Gordon asked.

"Well, there is a local haulage and delivery service that we use. If you were to ask them to handle the delivery, I'm sure they would oblige."

"Where's the catch?"

"No catch," said Macceffy as if hurt by such an accusation. "Their charges are somewhat high, but . . ."

"High? How high is high?"

"Eighty thousand dollars should cover the charges."

"But that's extortionate!"

Macceffy shrugged and made to push back his chair to indicate that the meeting was over.

Gordon's jaw stiffened and he stared menacingly at Macceffy. "I know, I've no alternative," he said resignedly.

"Yes you do," said Macceffy. "We can have the pictures revalued and follow the normal channels. The paperwork shouldn't take more than six weeks." Macceffy spoke as if he were enjoying the charade.

Gordon considered for a moment and then said, "Okay, this haulage company can pick up the pictures and deliver them to my gallery, but it must be this week."

"Good," replied Macceffy, clearly feeling pleased with himself. He then added, "Oh, and by the way, payment will be cash on delivery."

"I thought it might be," said Gordon.

Macceffy wrote a telephone number and a contact name on a piece of paper and handed it across the desk. "Ring this number," he instructed. "Tell them you have arranged with me for them to pick up your pictures from the customs compound. Give them full details of the delivery address. Put the money in a plain white envelope and hand it to the driver."

"What about the customs clearance papers?" Gordon asked.

"They're already made out and signed," Macceffy said opening a drawer, taking out a sheaf of papers and handing them over. Gordon examined them carefully. They were all in order, all signed and gave clearance for the pictures to be released from the compound. They also gave permission for the Florida Haulage Company to collect them from the customs shed.

"Thanks," Gordon said, "for nothing."

A thin smile crossed Macceffy's narrow face, showing sharp white teeth. He stroked his moustache as he rose from his chair.

"Mr Richardson," he said patronisingly, "you're in Florida. Relax. Take life as it comes. If you don't you'll not survive, believe me, I know." He pressed a switch below his desk and a few seconds later his secretary entered. "Show Mr Richardson out, Geoffrey. Oh and by the way," he said turning to Gordon. "Have a good day."

Gordon was furious at the way he'd been treated, but by the time he reached the ground floor he'd got a grip on himself. He was disappointed to see that the girl was no longer at the reception desk. It was now manned by a middle-aged woman with greasy hair and horn-rimmed glasses. He asked where the girl had gone.

"Oh, you mean Jean," drawled the woman. "It's her half day. She won't be back until the morning."

"Do you know where she lives?"

"I'm sorry," the woman said. "I'm only temporary. I don't even know her second name. Anyway, if I did I couldn't let you have it – rules you know."

Outside the glare of the sun made him cover his eyes with his hand. As he walked towards his car he loosened his tie and unbuttoned his shirt at the neck, more out of frustration and annoyance than because of the heat. He climbed into his car and in frustration gripped the steering wheel so hard that his knuckles showed white. Just as he was about to put the key into the ignition he realised he was not alone. Sitting next to him in the passenger seat was the girl from reception. Surprise was combined with a quickening of his pulse.

She held out an elegant hand with long fingers tipped with manicured nails. "Jean Manley," she said. "I've never yet thanked you for helping me when we met on the plane."

Still gripping her hand and wondering why God had just smiled upon him, Gordon said, "Is this an official thank you?"

"If you like."

"Calls for a drink?"

"That would be nice, but please could you let go of my hand."

Chapter 12

Power Unit, Inverness

It was the official opening of the new mini power station. The car park had been decorated with American flags, balloons and bunting, and the grounds were decked out with brightly coloured flowers and shrubs especially for the occasion.

A marquee had been erected on the lawn in front of the lake, and the catering company had started delivering the food in large ice-cooled plastic containers. Two mechanics were fixing the portable air-conditioning system and the band were busy practising on the makeshift stage.

Inside the power station, Claire Williams and Wayne Headbold were making final preparations, checking equipment and carrying out all the necessary safety checks. A security guard was sticking a 'No Admittance' sign on the door of the control room.

Claire glanced at Wayne. 'How tired he looked,' she thought. Was all this really worth the effort? Well, by this afternoon they would know.

The door to the central control room opened and Mayor Thompson entered. The mayor was forty-eight years old, portly, with a bold chin and dark-brown eyes, around which the skin crinkled when he smiled. Being a special day, he was wearing a light-blue lounge suit.

"Just called in to make sure that everything's okay for this afternoon," he said, enthusiastically looking around. "It all looks great. I want you to know how much we appreciate the work you two people are doing for our community. Good luck, and I'll see you at 2.30."

After he had left, Wayne looked at Claire. "It must be tough being the mayor *and* a director of a power company," he said.

They both laughed.

'That's better,' thought Claire. 'I love him more when he smiles.'

As the mayor passed the security gate, Peter Cooper was entering the car park, the boot of his car stacked with three cases of Inverness Rum for the party. He had been dumping the residue in the lake for over a week now, and as far as he was aware he had not been detected. Last evening, however, he had decided that it would be imprudent to take the barge out as he knew people would be working late, erecting the marquee and generally getting ready for the party. He waved to the mayor, but as he did so he felt a little guilty.

He pulled up in front of the marquee and began unloading the car, placing each case of rum on the long table near to the bar. As he left the marquee he saw Johnny Combes coming towards him.

"Morning, Mr Cooper," Combes said. "I couldn't help noticing that you were out with the excavator a couple of nights ago. You are sure that Gerry's job is not on the line?"

"His job's safe," replied Peter sharply. "I told you before. Anyway, it's none of your bloody business!"

Combes shrugged his shoulders. Peter brushed him aside to get back to his car, but there were beads of sweat on his face. As he drove off he glanced in his wing mirror and saw Johnny Combes watching him. 'What the hell is he up to?' he thought. 'He's fishing around, the creep.'

Earlier that morning, Gordon had finally taken delivery of his pictures at the gallery and had paid the driver the 'haulage fee'. He still felt a bitter resentment towards the customs chief. The whole system was rotten, but he knew it was pointless pursuing the matter. At least he had the paintings in time for next Saturday's opening.

Sheila, surprisingly, had agreed to help him unpack and hang the pictures, and the printers had promised faithfully to have the brochures ready by Tuesday morning.

"Talking to yourself now?" Sheila said.

"Just thinking aloud," Gordon said smiling. "Do you think this Clausen is hung at the right height?"

Sheila stood back and studied the picture. She appeared unsteady on her feet. "Looks about right – perhaps a little more light."

Gordon adjusted the spotlight. "Okay, will that do?"

"Yes, that's perfect." She reached out tentatively and touched his hand, and he responded by reaching out to her, but she pulled away as if repelled by contact with him, and disappeared into the office.

He heard her pour a drink, and he glanced at his watch, it was ten past eleven. "Drink time," he whispered to himself, and felt a deep sadness creep over him.

Jean wouldn't recoil from his touch like Sheila had. His thoughts drifted back to that afternoon at Orlando when he'd found her sitting in the car. They'd driven out along the Florida turnpike and finished up at a restaurant beside Lake Touissa. They'd had a light prawn salad and a bottle of Chablis, and had talked; relaxed talk about everything under the sun. He felt rejuvenated by this girl, even if she was young enough to be his daughter. She'd asked him questions about his business and his move from England, and Gordon had answered readily, but she didn't ask the obvious one – was he married? She was also strangely inquisitive about his meeting with Macceffy. He told her that he'd had some trouble getting a shipment of paintings released from customs, but that the issue had now been resolved.

"So that's okay, then," she said smiling.

The afternoon had passed all too quickly, and at six o'clock Jean said she had to leave. She had to be home by seven and she lived half an hour away on a condominium on the edge of Lake Tecko, near Orlando.

They arrived at 6.30 and Gordon was half expecting to be invited in for a drink, but instead she leaned across and gave him a kiss on the cheek. Gordon put a hand on her neck and pulled her towards him, but she pushed him gently, but firmly, away. "I really do have a meeting at seven," she said almost regretfully. She put her hand into her jacket pocket. "Here's my card," she said. "Give me a ring tomorrow." And with that she was gone.

Ever since that evening he hadn't been able to forget about Jean Manley, and every day he'd wanted to phone her. What had stopped him was the thought of his wife. She needed him more than ever. He felt a strong responsibility towards her, even if they no longer loved one another as they once used to. His train of thought was suddenly broken when he felt a touch on the shoulder.

"Shucks, I didn't mean to frighten you," said Mayor Thompson, taking a step backwards and at the same time thrusting forward his hand.

Gordon shook it. "What can I do for you, Mayor?" he asked.

The mayor cleared his throat. "Well," he said, "as you are now a permanent member of this community, I have come to invite you and your wife to the official opening party for the new mini power station this afternoon. I do hope you will agree to come."

Gordon said he would be delighted, and asked what time it started.

"Oh, be there around 2.45. I'm sure you'll meet some interesting people, especially in your line of business. Me, I know nothing about art, wish I did." He took a perfunctory glance around the gallery, then reached inside his coat and took out a gold-edged invitation card made out to Sheila and Gordon. "There's your invite," he said. Then, glancing down at his gold Rolex, he exclaimed, "Look, I must go. It's a busy day. See you both later, then."

As the mayor left he almost collided with Sheila, who was making her way unsteadily from the office to the gallery. "Who was that?" she said with an obvious slur to her voice.

"The mayor," replied Gordon. "You must have recognised him."

"Didn't," Sheila said. "What did he want, anyway? Is he going to buy a picture?"

"I don't think so," said Gordon. "He called to invite us to the official opening of the power station this afternoon. I said we'd love to accept."

Sheila's face dropped. "I can't," she said, her voice unsteady. "I can't face all those people – not yet. I'm not ready."

"But, darling, that's ridiculous. Of course you can. I need you by my side. Please, please make the effort."

Sheila bit her lip and turned away from him. She was fighting her demons. Gordon knew that, but he felt he had to get her to come; try to draw her out of herself.

At length she said, "If – if I come, you won't leave me alone will you? I couldn't bear to be alone."

"I promise," Gordon said nervously. "I'll be as attentive as a young puppy. I promise."

Sheila looked unconvinced, but she nodded to herself and went back into the office.

At three o'clock, Gordon arrived with his wife at the opening. Johnny Combes showed him where to park his Pontiac, amongst one of the gleaming rows of automobiles cooking in the sun. He noticed a red Ferrari 250 GT Spider parked adjacent to the sheriff's car. He'd always been fascinated by Ferraris. They were works of art. In England he'd owned a 348TS in the 1990s. He'd sold it four years before to a West German multimillionaire for £200,000. He yearned to sit behind the wheel of a black horse again and feel the power of the V12 engine and the excitement of the breathtaking acceleration.

At the hospitality tent the college band was playing an old Beatles song, 'Let it Be'. It reminded him of home. The marquee was full of VIPs eating, drinking and generally making polite conversation. The whole thing reminded him of an English country fair on a warm summer's day.

Although, even before they had moved to America, they had been visiting Inverness for some twelve years, they hadn't made any real friends, though they recognised a lot of faces. Gordon made it his business to get to know most people of importance – or notoriety – in the area, but even then he was only on nodding terms. He cast his eyes over the crowd. In the far corner he saw the sheriff and the mayor in conversation with a tall beautiful woman in her late thirties. She was dressed in expensive designer clothes, and the necklace sparkling on her slim neck was no dress jewellery.

"That must be Mrs Larimer," he whispered to Sheila, nodding in the direction of the group.

"Who's that next to the sheriff?" she asked.

"That young tall guy? That's the sheriff's son, Paul. He's the one who's just been expelled from college."

"Oh, him."

As the waiter went past, Gordon grabbed two glasses of champagne and handed one to his wife, but she had moved away and appeared to be mesmerised by the mayor's party, particularly by the sheriff's son.

"Are you okay, darling?" he said touching her hand with the glass.

"Oh! Yes, sure," she replied hesitantly taking the glass. She raised the champagne to her lips but didn't take her eyes off Paul.

At that moment the mayor noticed the Richardsons, and beckoned them over. Gordon gave a wave in recognition, and, taking hold of his wife's arm, guided her through the throng of people to the mayor's party.

Mayor Thompson shook Gordon's hand heartily, as if he were an old friend, and welcomed him to their grand occasion.

"This is Sheila and Gordon Richardson," he announced. "They have just joined the community, and Gordon has recently opened a very exclusive art gallery on the boulevard. Now, let me introduce you: the sheriff and his son, Paul, I'm sure you know. And this is Mrs Larimer, who has also just moved into the area. Her husband has bought Thatchum House on Alligator Island."

"Yes, so I heard," said Gordon. "Pleased to meet you."

Mrs Larimer smiled enigmatically and raised her glass in acknowledgement.

"I understand you have a beautiful daughter," he said.

"I'm pleased you think so," she replied in a perfect English accent. "She's over there, talking to Peter Cooper."

Gordon followed her gaze, his eyes coming to rest on a tall, sophisticated young woman with the most exquisite features. Peter Cooper appeared to be quite spellbound. 'Lucky him,' Gordon thought and turned to his wife to see if she wanted another drink, but Sheila wasn't there.

"Your wife's gone with Paul to get some food," said Mrs Larimer.

"Let her enjoy herself. Come here and tell me about this new gallery of yours." She linked her arm through his. "Perhaps I might become one of your clients."

As she led him away from the others, he couldn't help noticing that Sheriff O'Donnel was watching them intently. He couldn't think why. Why should either of them be of interest to the sheriff?

Waiters in black tuxedos were serving food at the far end of the marquee. Gordon noticed that his wife and the sheriff's son were in deep conversation at a corner table. She was smiling and appeared to be enjoying herself. She was also drinking heavily, judging by the number of champagne glasses on the table.

While Mrs Larimer was deciding between lobster, bass or salmon, Gordon stood back for a better appraisal. From her poise and sense of dress it was perfectly obvious that, like all sophisticated moneyed people, she was at ease with her wealth. She would certainly know how to spend it, yet there was something in her manner and speech that suggested a certain ambiguity – she was not quite what she seemed. Gordon couldn't quite put his finger on it. She was a most beautiful woman. Her bearing and the way she spoke suggested a strong mind and a sharp intelligence. She was the type of woman that made most men feel ill at ease, particularly weaker men. Gordon himself felt apprehensive, yet he was very much drawn to this woman, as he was drawn to all women of beauty.

"Where do you come from in England?" he asked.

"Please call me Jessica," she replied. "I come from Gloucester originally, but I worked in London as a model before emigrating to the States. That was nearly three years ago."

"Is that were you met your husband, in London?" Gordon asked.

Jessica hesitated for a second. Then she said warily, "Yes, as a matter of fact it was. We met at a party at the Houses of Parliament, and one thing led to another, and here I am."

Gordon was just about to ask about her daughter when he felt a light touch on the palm of his right hand. He expected it to be Sheila, but when he turned he was confronted by Jean Manley. "Hello," she said charmingly. She then whispered, "You didn't ring me."

For a few seconds surprise took away his ability to think clearly, and his brain searched for words.

Taking her aside he said in a low voice, "What on earth are you doing here?"

She replied that she'd been invited to come with Mr Macceffy, who had an invitation, so she'd said yes.

Gordon suddenly remembered his manners and turned back to Jessica. "Do forgive me," he said. "This is a friend of mine, Jean

Manley. She works at customs and excise in Orlando."

"Pleased to meet you," said Mrs Larimer with a knowing look, and held out a slim, manicured hand. "Mr Richardson, you are a dark horse, you know. How long did you say you'd been a permanent resident of Florida – three weeks? Well, I must say I like your taste in American women."

Gordon felt a rush of blood to his head. He was just about to say something when Senator Page entered the tent, surrounded by a number of hangers-on. The senator was a tall, slim man with clean-cut features. There was the touch of the Latin about him in the way he swept his dark hair back from his forehead, and in the high cheekbones. He waved to the mayor's party and strode across the room with the confidence of a man used to having his own way, shaking a hand here and there whenever one was proffered. Hand-shaking had become part of the ritual, it had no meaning apart from that of an emperor acknowledging his subjects.

Mrs Larimer had noticed him and began to wave at him vigorously, and then without a word barged through the crowd towards him, pushing anyone aside who got in her way.

Gordon turned his attention to Jean, and those liquid blue eyes met his – and there was hurt in them.

"I asked you before," she said softly, "why didn't you telephone me? I was waiting for you to telephone."

Gordon stroked his forehead nervously. "Because," he said searching for words, "because I felt I owed it to my wife not to ring you. She's ill. She needs my help."

At this Jean looked away, as if physically stung. For some time neither of them spoke. Then she said accusingly, "You didn't tell me you were married."

"You didn't ask," Gordon replied sharply.

"It's no good avoiding me," she said, suddenly changing her tone. "I know the way you feel about me. We must meet. Let's meet later. Ten o'clock, by the lake, at the same restaurant." She was almost eager, as if she felt threatened by this turn of events and needed to consolidate her position.

Gordon said nothing but nodded in agreement and their hands touched briefly. Jean stepped back, smiled sweetly, lifted her glass and turned away to join Macceffy who was in conversation with the mayor. Gordon watched her as she moved through the crowd of guests and noted that every male eye turned towards her. But what was she doing with Macceffy, that rat-faced jerk? Why was he here anyway? He wanted answers.

He was about to leave the tent when Rastos Nokes approached

him. He'd only had a passing acquaintance with Nokes. In fact he didn't think he'd ever actually spoken to him. Today he looked different. Instead of his usual lumberjack shirt and patched jeans, he was wearing a suit; a light grey summer one. He should have looked smart but he didn't; the blue denim shirt was tight around his midriff and about to burst asunder at any minute. He was sweating profusely and looked uncomfortable in surroundings that were clearly alien to him.

He introduced himself. "Rastos Nokes," he said in a deep drawl.

"Yes, I know," Gordon said shaking his hand. "Pleased to meet you."

"Ever go fishing, Mr Richardson?" asked Nokes.

"Sure," said Gordon, "at least I've tried once or twice, but not a lot of success. Bad fisherman, I guess."

Rastos beamed. "Tell you what," he said. "I'll take you out on Sunday if you like. The lake's providing some big fish at the moment. I don't know where they've been hiding all these years, but they're definitely there, and I ain't complaining." He chuckled to himself, but his hand shook so much that he spilt beer onto his expanded gut.

"Okay," Gordon said smiling, "you've got a deal. Next Sunday." He looked at his watch and realised that it was already seven o'clock. Sheila had still not turned up. 'If she's out in the grounds,' he thought, 'I'd better find her. It's getting dark.' "Excuse me," he said. "I must find my wife. See you on Sunday."

"Six o'clock on the jetty," Rastos reminded him.

Gordon was just about to make his way into the garden, hoping Sheila might be in there, when the college band, which up until now had been playing chamber music, suddenly stopped and collectively rose to its feet. The whole congregation ceased talking. It was almost as if someone had waved a magic wand and suspended them in time. The band then struck up the National Anthem and everyone stood to attention.

Whilst all of this was going on, Senator Wesley Page, accompanied by the mayor, was making his way to the rostrum, positioned just to the edge of the stage. Both men waited for the band to finish before making their entrance. When it stopped the band sat down and a spontaneous cheer from the crowd erupted. People clapped and hooted and banged their feet, so that the mayor had to raise his hands for silence. Gradually the noise subsided until the only sound was a soft murmur accompanied by the occasional clink of glasses.

"Ladies, gentlemen, friends," the mayor began. "As you are all aware this is a very special day for the whole community. Today we produce our own cheap power."

The crowd roared its approval.

"Now, friends, residents of Inverness and honoured guests," the mayor continued, "let me hand you over to Senator Page, a good friend, a director of the power company and a servant of this community for many years. He has graciously agreed to carry out the opening ceremony and turn on the switch."

The mayor sat down to another clamour of applause, and Senator Page rose and took his place at the rostrum. He raised his hands for silence. "Friends!" he said as the murmur died down. "Welcome to this special occasion. Today in Florida we are making history. It is not just a question of cheap power for the community, it is also about protecting our environment – reducing pollution, leaving the world a fit place for our children and their grandchildren. We, the board, thank you for your financial help and the foresight in helping to bring this project to fruition. As you are all aware, there have been teething problems, more particularly with the choice of contractor, but this was quickly resolved and the project is now complete and ready to roll."

Everyone cheered.

"Just before I flick the switch," the senator continued, "I would like all of us here to pay tribute to Wayne Headbold and Claire Williams who conceived the idea and designed the unit."

Wayne and Claire, who were standing together at the entrance to the tent, smiled embarrassingly as they received a round of applause.

The senator raised his glass of champagne in their direction. "Thank you both," he said warmly. "We, the community, appreciate what you have done for us." The senator now moved towards a big red switch, especially decorated with an American flag for the occasion. Suddenly all the lights went out in the tent, leaving the crowd, for a brief moment, in complete darkness. "Ladies, gentlemen, friends!" he cried. "Let there be light!" and with this he activated the switch that turned on the power unit.

All the lights came back on and the band struck up with the 'Stars and Stripes'. At the same time a fireworks display started on the edge of the lake. People moved outside to witness the spectacle, and there was much laughing and cheering and slapping of backs.

Just before the senator pulled the switch, Wayne had returned to the control room, and on being given a signal by Claire had dipped the lights, then flipped the control panel knob to independent mode. At that moment he also extinguished the link with the main power station at Waccassa Bay. The nuclear reactor then swung to full power output.

"We did it!" shouted Wayne. "We did it, Claire. The mini power station is now fully independent."

The radioactive water within the tubes and casings began to pump around the two reactors to maintain temperature; but what nobody knew or could possibly have suspected, was that a minor hairline stress crack had developed in the concrete. It was so small that it could not be identified by the human eye. Even the sensors located around the concrete casing were unable to monitor the fracture, but, as the unit went into full power, minute globules of radioactive water seeped down through the crack in the concrete like a dripping tap, and into the subsoil below.

The party was now in full swing; the guests blissfully unaware of the possible catastrophe that could threaten their whole community. The fireworks splashed a heaven of colour and light over the lake, turning the water into a kaleidoscope.

On the shore, the alligator slipped from its den quietly, as it had done every evening for the past few weeks, and headed for the area where Peter Cooper had been dumping the residue. It was aware of the presence of humans on the bank, but the need for sustenance overcame caution. As it stealthily snaked across the lake, just below the surface, it sensed no vibrations from fish or boat. It made three sweeps in all, and each time it found no fish in the deep pool. Tonight the old alligator would have to hunt elsewhere for its prey.

By ten o'clock the party was drawing to a close, and most of the guests had departed, or were getting ready to depart. Gordon had said his goodbyes and was looking around for Sheila. Earlier he had found her at the lakeside with Paul O'Donnel, and the two of them had returned to the party together.

During the festivities they had both been introduced to Dr Foster, and Gordon had thought it an opportune time to ask her about the death of Christy Makepiece. "You see," he said, "we lost our own son six months ago, and we know how the parents must be feeling. It's not an easy thing to deal with." Instantly he regretted what he'd said and turned towards his wife, but once again she had gone. Turning back to Lucy he apologised. "I'm sorry," he said. "She keeps doing that, wandering off. The business with Julian still upsets her terribly."

Lucy appeared to be on edge. She said nervously, "Christy's death was unusual, Mr Richardson, a tragedy. She was so young. And, I'd rather not discuss it any further, if you don't mind."

"Well, of course, of course," said Gordon. "I'm sorry."

She didn't want to talk about it. He could see she was on edge, and as soon as she noticed the sheriff, she hastily excused herself

70

and rushed over to speak to him. It was all rather odd.

Odder still was the obvious fact that the sheriff would have preferred not to be talking to Lucy Foster, and after a few exchanges he appeared to end the conversation by waving her angrily away. He then walked over to join the senator's group, which included the mayor, Macceffy and a Spanish-looking gentleman, at the far side of the tent. Gordon couldn't help noticing what a strange fivesome they made. They all appeared to have something in common, something that seemed to bond them together, but what it could be he had no idea. When they left a few minutes later, they left together in a group.

Gordon was suddenly shaken from his musings by the sound of breaking glass coming from the area of the bar. To his horror, he saw that the cause of the commotion was his wife, who had collapsed across a table full of empty glasses and wine bottles. Luckily she had ended up on the floor beyond the table and thereby beyond the broken glass. She staggered to her feet holding a hand to her head.

'Oh, God, she's flipped,' thought Gordon. 'I've never seen her like this before.' He ran over to her and put his arm around her waist. "Time to go home, darling." he said quietly.

Turning to the waiter he apologised for the mess his wife had caused, but the waiter simply raised his hands philosophically, as if this kind of thing was a regrettable but normal occurrence, and said, "Senor, it is not problem. I will see to it."

Sheila began to cry. "Oh, God, Paul – he's like Julian, so much like him." She said this out loud, oblivious to all the people in the bar silently staring at her.

Gordon was anxious to get her out before she made a complete fool of herself – and him – and managed to get her to the door, apologising to people as he pushed his way through.

Lucy Foster then appeared and asked if there was anything she could do, but Gordon told her that there wasn't, but thanked her anyway, adding that only his wife could help herself. Lucy nodded. "You know where I am if you need me," she said.

Once at the car, Gordon helped his wife into the passenger seat and closed the door. She lay back and began to sob. "Gordon, I'm sorry, but Paul reminds me so much of Julian. It was just too much to take. I miss him so much. I killed him."

Gordon took a deep breath, trying very hard to control his own emotions. "Try to understand, darling," he said calmly, "you did not kill him. It was an accident. You must understand that. Nobody was to blame." Gordon could not understand why his wife kept blaming herself. Accidents happen, everyone knew that. But why did she keep persecuting herself with guilt? Julian was dead, but life goes on. He missed his youngest terribly, but his grief had now ebbed. Getting depressed and drinking wasn't going to bring him back. Nothing could do that. He started the engine, dropped the car into gear and drove off through the main gate, watched by the remaining partygoers.

By the time they reached Mitcham Creek, Sheila was already asleep, her eyes still red with tears. He picked her up in his arms and carried her into the house, pushing the door open with his foot. As he laid her on the bed she murmured something about Julian. "Julian hadn't seen me," he thought she said. Then she sighed, rolled over and fell asleep.

Gordon was mystified. What did she mean, 'Julian hadn't seen me? What had she done that Julian should not have seen? Perhaps in her ravings she still has some weird idea that he's still alive?' he thought.

Glancing at his watch he realised it was 9.45 p.m. "Damn! Jean." He said it aloud and winced. Had Sheila heard? But no, she was well asleep and wouldn't wake until the morning. Yet he still hesitated. He had promised to meet Jean. It was a promise. If he felt guilty about this, leaving his wife to meet another woman, it was overridden by alternative desire. He excused himself that there was no harm in it, and a promise was a promise. If he got a move on he might just get there in time. Picking up his car keys, he scribbled a note, just in case his wife woke up. Then he left and drove through the balmy Florida night to his rendezvous.

By the time he reached the restaurant on the shores of the lake it was nearly eleven o'clock. He parked the car and hurried to the restaurant, half expecting Jean to be waiting for him. Both the bar and the restaurant were packed, but Jean was nowhere to be seen. He reprimanded himself for being late and, disappointed, made his way back to the car.

He had just started the engine and was about to reverse out of the parking space when he heard a screech and smelled the burning of tyres as a white convertible pulled to an abrupt stop right in front of him.

"You're late, you bastard," Jean cried, jumping up from the driving seat.

"Guilty," Gordon responded smiling, and held out his arms in an appeal for forgiveness, at the same time hoping beyond hope that her greeting was meant as a term of endearment.

"Follow me," she yelled, ramming the car into gear. The engine roared and, with the back wheels spinning, she took off down the highway, blonde hair flowing behind in the slipstream. Gordon complied. He was captured, hooked, and he knew it, but how would she play him?

He had no idea where she was leading, and he didn't care. He was captivated by this woman and just wanted to be close to her. All thoughts of Sheila had, for that moment, fled. So he followed her, beeping his horn with delight like a boy on the dodgems, and waving to her as they roared along the highway.

After about forty minutes she took a right turn along an old dirt track, throwing up dust like a fog into the car following, so that Gordon, not being able to see, almost lost control and was in danger of embedding himself in a tree. After several miles Jean pulled to a stop near the shore of a lake. She jumped out of the car, perched herself on the bonnet and stared out across the water. Gordon screeched to a halt behind, sending even more dust into the atmosphere, turned off the engine and sat for a few moments to compose himself. His heart was working overtime and he needed a period of rest, no matter how brief, to get himself under control.

When, after a minute or so, he thought he'd achieved this, he opened the car door and walked as calmly as he could to the front of the convertible. She was still sitting there, though now she was astride it, her legs apart. Neither of them spoke, there was no need, the need was in the loins. He could feel her longing, too, in her short rapid breathing as he moved closer towards her. When they were face-to-face he cupped his hands around the back of her waist and pulled her savagely towards him.

As she slid off the smooth bonnet she said, "Ouch, that's hot."

But Gordon was in no mood for witticisms. Gently he lifted her blouse up and over her head. She was wearing no bra. He threw the garment into the air. Her lips felt moist to his kiss; he could feel the inner softness of her mouth as their tongues entwined. She threaded her arms around his neck, drew him even closer with each sharp breath. He felt her breasts pushing against him. With both hands he stroked her slim thighs as he moved towards her bulging vagina, stroking, stroking all the time until he could feel the moist juices seeping through her silk panties, and still he stroked her. And then she reached down and slowly pulled the zip of his trousers down and he could feel her slim hands reaching inside for him, and then it was she who stroked, up and down until she found the gap in his underpants, then grasped him so that for an instant he felt a stab of pain. Jean, realising that she was being over zealous, softened the motion of her strokes, feeling the end of his penis with her fingernails and spreading the moisture onto his taught stomach muscles. He

73

pulled away from her, lowered his head and kissed her stomach, pressing his tongue into her belly button. With his left hand he stripped off her skirt, with his right removed her panties and then moved his hand once again up her thighs. She opened her legs wide as his fingers moved inside her, probing deeper as she pushed against them.

Together they slipped to the ground. She struggled to remove his trousers and underpants, then held his erect penis, gently at first, then harder as the strokes became faster. Gordon could feel her vagina getting bigger and bigger as his hand pressed deeper, and suddenly the movements began to quicken. He could feel her body harden and tighten and, as she rose to her climax, she held onto him. As they both moved in a frenzy, she began to groan. Suddenly she placed both hands around his penis and began pumping – harder and harder with each stroke. Gordon could feel his penis extending and rising and, as Jean's fingernails dug into him, he exploded.

As their passion receded they lay together on the dry earth. He kissed her gently and she responded by feeling for his penis and stroking it softly. And so they remained until the passion began to build again and she rolled into him and kissed him hard and felt him rise once more. Her breathing became heavy, and he picked her up and laid her on the bonnet of the Corvette. Their lips met again and Gordon fell on top of her, and with her hand she guided his penis into her. Her vagina was large and moist and they pressed their bodies together, driving into each other with strong rhythmic movements, faster and faster until Jean brought her legs up around his shoulders. Gordon pushed deeper and deeper into her, his manhood growing to bursting with every thrust.

"Now, darling, now!" she cried. "Now, please!"

And Gordon, at the pinnacle of his exquisite pain, shot into her. She still moved against him, gripped him harder and harder until he was completely sucked dry of juice and energy.

After it was over they lay on the bare earth, gazing up at the clear, starry sky, their bodies barely touching.

"That was wonderful," she murmured.

He pulled her towards him then wrapped his arms around her, and together they drifted off to sleep.

By the time Gordon got home it was 7.30 a.m. He crept in through the lounge and eased open the bedroom door. Sheila was still asleep. He slipped under the sheets next to her and within a few minutes he was fast asleep.

Chapter 13

Havana, Cuba

Sitting in his office, Hunaz was ill at ease. He picked up the telephone, punched out a number and waited. Within seconds he was on line.

"Calcus? It's me, Hunaz," he said without waiting for confirmation. "I've checked my end of operations throughout the whole of Cuba. Ten kilograms have left here each month for the States. I'm sure that none of my team's double-crossing me. If anyone would know, I would."

There was a moment's silence at the other end, then Calcius snapped, "You know what this means?"

"Don't worry," said Hunaz, adopting a casual tone and ignoring the unspoken threat. "I'll sort it out myself. If we're losing any it will be through London or Florida. Rest assured, I'll find those responsible."

"Of course you will," Calcus said, "but be careful. Nothing must go wrong." Then the phone went dead.

Hunaz slowly replaced the receiver. His mind was racing, calculating his next move. The next shipment was due the following week. He would first have to establish that none of the merchandise was being lost between Cuba and Orlando. That was the first step. He looked at his watch and realised that it was twelve o'clock. It was just possible to catch the senator before lunch. He picked up the phone again, dialled a number and listened to the ringing tone.

After some time a female voice answered in a soft assured Florida accent, "Senator Page's office. How can I help you?"

"I'd like to speak to the senator," Hunaz said.

"May I ask who's calling?" enquired the voice politely.

Hunaz said forcibly, "Just tell him Mr Hunaz wants to speak to him. It's urgent."

"I see." The voice this time stiffened. "Hold the line, please."

He heard a click and then silence.

"Just putting you through," the woman suddenly said.

"Hello, Hunaz," said the senator as the phone came to life. "This is a pleasure."

"This is not a pleasure, Wesley," said Hunaz coldly. "We have a problem."

The senator's voice lost some of its ebullience. "What problem?" he retorted. "The operation is working as smooth as clockwork."

"Not so," said Hunaz. "By the time the merchandise reaches the final customer in London, two kilograms are missing, that's *$100,000* every month." He emphasised the figure to make sure his point reached home.

It had. The senator began to stammer. "That can't be right," he said.

Hunaz sighed. "My friend," he said in a slow authoritative voice, "this has been going on for two years. At first it was every three months and only a few grams, now it's every month, and last time it was two kilograms." Hunaz waited for a reaction, but the telephone was silent. "Wesley, are you still there?" he snapped.

"Yes, I'm still here," replied the senator. "I'm sure the problem is not in my section."

"Well, I'm sure too," Hunaz said, "but we have to check."

"How do we do that?" the senator asked.

Hunaz said, "There's only one way. You will have to meet the boat in St Petersburg harbour, weigh the merchandise and transport it to Orlando yourself."

"I can't do that!" responded the senator angrily. "I may be recognised."

"Wesley," said Hunaz, "you have no choice. Wear a disguise, anything, but it has to be done by you and you alone, understand?"

Again there was a drawn-out silence.

"Okay," Wesley replied wearily, "but I don't like it. What if I'm recognised? I'll be ruined."

"You'd better make sure you're not recognised," Hunaz retorted. "And you must tell no one."

"When is the shipment due?"

"Friday, on board the yacht, *Simica*. It will dock in St Petersburg at around 5 p.m. The captain's name is Meriton Duff, and he'll be expecting you. I'll handle it personally at the Havana end."

"And I thought we had a smooth operation here," said the senator. "Hell, why do people get so greedy."

"Human nature," said Hunaz. "By the way, who's your secretary? She's new isn't she?"

"That's Jean," replied the senator. "She hasn't been with me long. I met her at a function in Inverness. She was working in customs and excise in Orlando. Said she was bored. Alice was leaving to have a baby, so I offered her a job. Accepted immediately."

"Sounds competent," said Hunaz. "And sexy."

"You're right there," agreed the senator. "And she's mine, or I hope she'll be mine," and he laughed out loud.

Hunaz simply smiled to himself. "Must go," he said. "Ring me when you've delivered – and be careful."

The senator replaced the receiver, leaned back in his chair, and focused his attention on the blank wall in front of him. He found it helped him think more clearly, but this time his thoughts were interrupted.

Jean was buzzing him. "Oh, Senator, I don't seem to have Mr Hunaz's number in my telephone listings," she said.

"Don't worry about that," said the senator. "He's just a personal friend. You don't need to have it. I always ring him myself – and usually from home."

"But what if you forget his number? Don't you think we should . . ."

"I won't forget," said the senator brusquely, and hung up.

Chapter 14

Power Unit, Inverness

"That's great, Betty," said Wayne. "You won't regret it. When can you start?"

Betty leaned over the control panel and said, "I'm only on a weekly contract. I could start a week on Monday."

"Fine," said Wayne, and he shook Betty's hand. "I think you had better let Tom know. He's in the power room."

"Okay," she said. And then added breezily as she left the control room, "See you next week."

It was Sunday morning and Wayne had left Claire at home in bed. He looked at his watch. It was eleven o'clock. 'Safe to ring her now,' he thought. But from the sound of the sleepy voice on the other end of the line, he knew he'd woken her. "Hope I didn't wake you," he chuckled.

"You swine. You know you did."

"Betty's said yes. Had to tell you."

"Oh, that's fantastic," said Claire. "Perhaps now we'll get more free time. You've been working too hard these past few weeks. You need to ease off."

Wayne laughed. "Okay, okay. Now, if you get dressed and come down to the plant we could go for lunch at the Harbour Lights."

"Lovely," said Claire. "I'll get a shower and be down in an hour."

Wayne replaced the phone and wandered over to the main control panel. Claire was right, he had been working too hard. Perhaps that was why he worried. He looked at the dials, they were all functioning correctly, but the dial that measured the volume of water in the coolant reactor and gave a 'full' reading, was flickering. Had the manufacturer not given him a full and unequivocal guarantee that the instrumentation was all sound, with no faults whatsoever, he would have felt concerned. He tapped the dial three times; there was no change, the needle was still flickering.

What Wayne did not know was, that due to the constant vibration and continuing water seepage, the hair crack in the concrete casing was now beginning to open up and extend. The constant flow of contaminated water was seeping down through the porous subsoil and entering the underground spring some twenty feet below the plant. This spring fed into Lake Apopka at exactly the point where Peter Cooper was dumping his rum residue.

Peter had now been carrying out the dumping operation for four weeks, and to his surprise he was finding the routine easy to handle. His mother thought he was working late at the office, and to give himself a further alibi, he always called in at Murphy's Bar for a drink on his way home.

Each evening the alligator also followed its same routine, moving ponderously to the water's edge as it sensed the vibrations from the barge. Gliding just below the surface, its orange eyes were fixed on the boat as it slid silently past on its way back to the factory. The bass, however, lacked the patience of the alligator. Each evening they congregated by the spring outlet at the bed of the lake and waited for the silver-brown crystals to descend through the water towards them. Then they would feed with such a frenzy that within ten minutes almost all the residue had been devoured. It was at this time that the alligator attacked, taking out ten big bass or more in a single sweep. The fish were beginning to grow alarmingly fast, and some of the older specimens were doubling their body weight in weeks. The sugar residue appeared to have the effect of stimulating their desire for food, and they were now feeding all day on worms and silverfish.

During the past two weeks, Rastos had become an angling legend Three times alone in the space of seven days he had broken the record for the heaviest bass taken locally, the last one weighing in at nineteen and a half pounds.

Lake Apopka was linked to the larger lake by a canal. A steel grid sluice gate had been placed across each of the locks some years previously to reduce the risk of any disease or contamination passing from one lake to the other.

News of the record bass spread, attracting anglers from the far corners of the county, so that very soon there was a fishing boat in every bay and inlet, with the exception of the area around the power station marked 'Off Limits'.

The old alligator was well aware of the increased activity on the lake, and stayed in its den during the day. Like the bass it was growing at a far greater rate than normal. It was becoming bolder, venturing out as the barge was still on its way back to the factory. And instead of heading straight back to shore, it would loiter around the spring outlet and snap up the few crystal leftover by the feeding bass.

But the radioactive water from the spring was now beginning to contaminate everything in the immediate vicinity, including the crystals, which in turn passed into the stomachs of the fish and the alligator. The more of both the alligator consumed, the more dependent it became on them. Constant forays to its feeding ground eventually reduced the number of fish waiting in the waters for the crystals, so that it began to consume more crystals and less fish. If its feeding habits had changed, so had its physical and mental characteristics. Apart from its increasing body size, its snub-nosed features were taking on a more elongated look, and its rows of razor sharp teeth were growing unevenly. Normally a retiring creature, avoiding man wherever possible, it was becoming psychotic. Its mind functioning incongruously. Its increasing boldness was accompanied by increasing aggressiveness, and it was quickly losing its traditional fear of man.

Chapter 15

Mitcham Creek, Inverness

Gordon rose early, taking care not to wake his wife who was still sleeping. He closed the bedroom door behind him, went into the bathroom and took a quick shower.

It had now been six weeks since the incident at the power station when Sheila had got drunk, and two weeks since the opening of the art gallery, though the official opening was yet to take place.

Sheila was drinking more and more. It was not unusual to find her at the poolside before lunch in an alcoholic haze. He had tried to talk to her about her problem on numerous occasions, but each time she accused him of being selfish and cold towards her. She was, of course, right; he wasn't exactly the adoring husband and he was involved in an extramarital relationship that might not have escaped her notice had she been her normal self. But she was not her normal self, she was an alcoholic, so who could blame his infidelity?

"You don't understand," she would cry time and time again. "You don't understand. I've lost my son. Lost him for ever, and it's my fault." And then she would sob uncontrollably. There was no placating her. Her grief was such that no amount of reasoning had any effect.

For his part, Gordon was dutiful towards her, tried in many ways to help her, but he realised she was probably beyond help, and increasingly his attention focused elsewhere; Jean Manley was never out of his thoughts.

After the party at the power station, he had made an appointment for Sheila to see Dr Foster, but unbeknown to him she had not kept it. She had left the house, but instead of going to the clinic, had headed for Murphy's Bar, and had been brought home that evening, severely drunk, by a very apologetic and embarrassed Peter Cooper.

Gordon had opened his gallery unofficially about a week later, deciding, after what had happened, to delay the grand opening for a few weeks. Trade, anyway, had not been particularly buoyant, but he didn't mind too much as the lull gave him more time to see Jean. They usually met three times a week. Gordon knew that he loved her, needed her passionately, and hated to be apart from her. But where he quite stood in her eyes he wasn't sure. She had never once said how much he meant to her, and when one day she told him that she was leaving her job with customs and excise to work as a personal assistant to Senator Page in St Petersburg, he was devastated.

"Are you sure that's what you want?" he asked her, hoping she would change her mind.

"Yes, I'm sure," she replied firmly.

"But, we won't be able to meet. I've heard the senator works long hours, and some weeks you'll probably be in Washington. I won't be able to see you at all." Gordon was distraught at the prospect, but Jean clearly didn't feel as strongly as he did about parting.

All she said was, "We'll work it out. You must understand that I run my own life. This is what I want. I need my own space for a bit."

Gordon shrugged despairingly. "Okay, if that's what you really want. We'll just have to fit things round it, that's all."

That evening they made love at her apartment, but there was a tension between them. Jean was restless and she appeared to be preoccupied with other thoughts.

After her move to St Petersburg their liaisons became less regular, though they still managed to meet in the evenings once a week. One evening they made love in her new apartment off Clearwater Beach. As they lay in each other's arms the telephone rang. Jean grabbed it. It was Senator Page. Gordon could not hear what was being said, but Jean quickly began to organise herself.

"I must go to Washington," she said, kissing him on the nose. "The senator needs my help." Quickly she showered and dressed. "Ring me tomorrow," she called back as she closed the door behind her.

He felt a sense of anger, rejection. Unjustified, of course. She had to go. It was her job. He realised he was jealous, and jealousy could eat away at the soul. It was bad for one's health.

Some days later he was sitting at his desk, his mind still on Jean Manley, when the phone rang. It was the local printer, Jake Hughes, telling him that the brochures for the grand gallery opening were ready. Gordon told him to deliver them at the gallery at twelve noon. He had a lot of things to do, and he still hadn't completed his list of potential customers. He thought he might contact Mayor Thompson. He was bound to know all the people with money in the area. He picked up the local telephone directory and scanned through the pages until he found the listing for the mayor's company, Inverness Leisure Industries.

He dialled the number and was surprised that Abe Thompson himself answered the phone. "Leisure Industries," announced the mayor in his deep southern drawl.

"Mayor Thompson?" enquired Gordon.

"Yes, speaking."

"It's Gordon Richardson from the Inverness Gallery. Do you remember me?"

"Sure I do. How's that wife of yours?"

"Oh, she's much better, I guess," said Gordon, hoping to make light of the incident. "I do apologise for what happened." He hesitated for a second before continuing. "Look, I wonder if you could do me a favour? I'm planning to hold a grand opening for the gallery in a couple of weeks – you know, the full works, champagne, food, all that, but what I really need is a list of people who may be interested in art and investment. I thought that maybe you could help me."

There was a moment's pause on the other end of the phone, and Gordon thought he'd blown it. Then the mayor said, "Sure thing, Gordon, be delighted to help. I'll get my secretary to run off a list from the computer, but it's for your eyes only. No one else's."

"Yes, of course," said Gordon delighted. "I'm most obliged to you. I hope you'll be able to come yourself to the party."

"Yea, and I might even buy one of those paintings; you never know." He hesitated. "Look, Gordon, you must excuse me, I'm waiting for an important phone call. I'll have to ring off. Hope you don't mind." There was a click, then a long buzz.

Gordon spent the rest of the morning checking over the proofs for the catalogue. He had decided to consult Sheila regarding the menu for the food and drink. It would give her something to do; take her mind off things.

At two o'clock he was still working at his desk when the telephone rang. "Hi, it's me. You okay?" The voice was hesitant but instantly recognisable.

"Jean! Where the hell have you been for the past four days?"

"Oh, I've been so busy in Washington with the senator," she said apologetically. "I did ring you but you weren't in the gallery."

"I've been down to Miami for two days at an auction. I rang the senator's office, but all they would say was that you were away on business, and they didn't know when you'd be back."

"Well," she said breezily, "I'm at home. Why don't you close the gallery and come over now? I'll be waiting for you." There was a sense of delicious urgency in her voice.

"I'm on my way," he said. Before he left he tried to phone Sheila, to say that he was leaving the gallery for a while to view a picture at someone's house, but there was no reply. She was probably at the pool, he thought, or lying in bed drunk. He slipped his jacket on, set the security alarm, and locked the door.

As he headed out of town he noticed Sheila's car leaving the drive to Max Pace's place. 'What on earth is she doing there?' he thought. He put his foot hard on the accelerator and came up close behind her car, flashing his lights. She saw him coming and pulled over to the side of the road. Gordon pulled up behind her.

Sheila wound her window down. "Hello, darling. I thought you were at the gallery." Her voice was unusually composed. For once she was in control of herself.

"Hi," he said. "I've just tried to telephone you at home. I'm off to St Petersburg to look at some paintings. I'll be back late. I was going to tell you not to wait up."

"That's okay," she said in a steady voice. "Perhaps I'll have an early night."

Gordon took hold of her hand. For all her outward composure, her skin felt moist with perspiration and her eyes were inattentive. "Darling, are you all right?"

"Of course."

"What were you doing at Max Pace's?"

"Oh!" she hesitated. "I found some of my old clothes in one of the suitcases when I was unpacking. I didn't really want them so I thought his poor wife might like them."

"That's a very kind thing to do," he said, surprised that her condition allowed her to take such positive action. Of late it was quite unlike her. "You'll be all right, then?" he said.

She gave a nervous laugh. "Yes, of course. You go and see your pictures."

He gave her a kiss, but there was no real response. "Okay, but see you soon," he said. He was eager to get to St Petersburg as quickly as possible.

After Gordon had left, Sheila stayed by the road for a few minutes.

Her hands were shaking and globules of perspiration were trickling down her face. She opened the glove compartment and took out a plastic envelope containing some white powder and a tube. She laid the cocaine on a small sheet of paper, and, with the tube, sniffed the powder up into her nostrils. Almost instantly she stopped perspiring and a feeling of confidence and well-being swept over her. She placed the remaining powder and the tube into the bag and slid it under her seat. Then she turned the ignition, looked both ways and moved off in the direction of Murphy's Bar.

Chapter 16

White Sands Apartments, St Petersburg

Gordon arrived at the White Sands Apartments one hour and twenty minutes after leaving Inverness. He had not seen Jean Manley for nearly a week, and his desire for her was taking over his whole mind and body. He had been thinking of nothing else ever since she'd phoned. Now, as he drove into the car park, she was there, waving to him from the apartment balcony.

There were no stairs. If there had been he'd have taken them three at a time. He pressed the lift button and waited impatiently. "Come on! Come on!" That was the trouble with lifts, they took their time. They were not people friendly, they would hurry for no one.

When eventually the lift did arrive and the door opened, she was standing there, beneath the dim light at the back of the lift. She had on a white silk robe tied at the waist which pulled the material tight against her body, forcing the nipples of her breasts hard up against it.

"I had to see you," she said. "I couldn't wait any longer."

He said nothing, but moved towards her, took her in his arms and pressed her body close to his, kissing her neck, her forehead, her lips and moving down towards her breasts, hard to the touch. Her hand slipped between his thighs. Gordon pressed the button for the third floor and the doors closed behind them. As the lift began to move upwards she reached out and punched the stop button, which caused the lift to stop with a sudden thump. And then she had her hand in his fly, pulling the zip down with a frantic urgency. Then the hand reached into his underpants, freeing his erect penis from its cloaked prison. She reached over, above his head, taking hold of a bar which crossed above, and, stretching her body, opened her legs to him. He entered her then with urgent thrusting, driving himself hard into her, losing all sense but that of animal passion. Harder,

harder, and with each stroke she moaned and moved against him, forcing his swollen penis deeper until he could hold himself no longer, and ejaculated, exploding inside her, and still he thrust as if nothing could satisfy him, until he was spent.

"Don't you go away again," he whispered in her ear.

If she replied he didn't hear as a sound of hammering was driving wedges into his soporific brain. Someone was banging on the lift door. "Are you okay in there?" came a man's worried voice from the other side of the thin sheet of metal that separated them from reality.

Jean slipped away from his embrace and giggled as she rearranged herself. "Yes, Burt," she called. "The button's stuck, but I think it seems to be okay now." She pushed the third-floor button and the lift lurched into life.

When it stopped they glanced each way to check that the corridor was clear, and, giggling like children on a clandestine errand, they ran down the corridor, crashed into the apartment, fell over each other and collapsed together onto a leather settee, where they lay in one another's arms, breathless.

"I love you, Miss Jean," he said, stroking the long blonde hair away from her face.

"I know," she whispered back, and kissed him gently on the lips.

Chapter 17

Florida Towers, St Petersburg

Senator Page entered his dressing room and studied himself carefully in the mirror. He was stripped down to his boxer shorts and he examined his face and body closely. 'I hope this works,' he thought. 'If I'm recognised I'm dead meat.'

He ran some warm water into the sink and placed two hand towels by the basin. Then he reached into the vanity unit, took out a dark-brown plastic bottle and carefully read the instructions. Gently he unscrewed the top and emptied the contents onto his hair, massaging the red liquid into his scalp, and as he did so a change took place, his light-grey hair turned ginger.

He wiped his face and hands with the nearest towel and checked himself in the mirror. Satisfied, he entered the shower, turned on the mixer taps, and gave his new ginger hair a good rinse. When he was certain the dye was there to stay, he dried and once again looked at himself in the mirror. One more touch was needed. He combed his hair back and added Brylcream to keep it flat. The image in the mirror that returned his gaze was not that of Senator Page, but someone quite different. He nodded approvingly. 'That should do the trick,' he thought

He put his clothes in the closet, grabbed a white casual shirt, a pair of blue jeans and white canvas shoes, and returned to the bedroom. All the clothes were new. He had bought them earlier in the day at the local supermarket, and when he got home he had creased them up and tossed them in a heap at the bottom of the closet to make it look as if they were well worn. When he had finished dressing he put on a pair of dark sunglasses. He glanced at his Rolex. It was 5.45 p.m. 'Just about now they should be entering St Petersburg harbour,' he thought.

The telephone rang, which startled him, an indication of how nervous he was feeling. He sat down on the edge of the bed and took several deep breaths to calm himself before picking up the phone. "Senator Page," he said with all the confidence he could muster.

"It's me," a voice replied. "The boat's just docked. The goods were intact when they left here. The password is 'Sugar Importer'."

"Understood," said the senator, and replaced the receiver.

Once again he checked his appearance in the mirror, picked up a roll of dollar bills from the table and stuffed them into his shirt pocket. "No credit cards, no wallet," he said to himself. Finally, from under the settee he pulled out a revolver and slipped it into his trouser pocket. Checking that the housekeeper and his secretary were not around, he quietly crept along the landing, down the stairs. across the hall, and slipped unnoticed through the front door and into Clearwater Avenue. He reached the hired Datsun and felt for the keys which he had previously hidden under the seat. Once he had made sure no one was watching, he drove off at a leisurely speed towards the docks, passing the house as he did so.

But he had not gone entirely unnoticed. From behind the drawn-back curtains in her office, Jean Manley had observed someone with bright ginger hair leave the building. She had watched him get into the Datsun and drive off. Immediately she picked up the telephone and hurriedly dialled a number. When it was answered she said, "Someone has just left. He has bright ginger hair and is wearing jeans and a white shirt. He's driving a white Datsun – don't lose him."

When Senator Page reached the harbour, he parked his car in the old part of town and walked the 400 or so yards to the wharf. The *Simica* had just docked, and the captain was in the process of securing the boat to the catwalk.

"Are you Meriton Duff?" the senator called out.

The captain nodded.

"Mr Hunaz asked me to call."

The captain looked about him. "What happened to the usual guys?" he asked.

"They've been given a few days off," replied the senator. He thought it was a weak explanation, and was sure that Duff wouldn't buy it, but he apparently did. He nodded and beckoned the senator to follow him onto the boat and down into the lower deck.

"Like a drink?"

"No thanks," said the senator. "I'll just take the merchandise and be off."

The captain said, "Password."

"Sugar importer," replied the senator.

"Wait here, I won't be a moment," the captain said, and he disappeared through a door at the far end of the cabin. Beyond it there was the sound of a key turning in a lock, and then the creak of a door opening. After some minutes the captain returned carrying a red sports bag. "This what you came for?" he said dropping the bag onto the table.

Wesley opened it up and checked the contents. Two rectangular packages about four inches deep lay in the bottom, both sealed with black plastic and taped over in the form of a cross. "Looks okay," he said, zipping the bag up again. "I'd better be off."

"Sure you won't have a drink?" said the captain. "Plenty here."

"No thanks, too early for me." He shook the captain's hand and left.

Back in the old town, he made his way to the corner where he'd parked the car. Once inside, he placed the red bag between his knees. From another bag he pulled out a pair of small electric scales, which he fixed to the dashboard. He set the pointer to zero and without lifting the bag from between his legs, picked up the two packages and placed them on the scales. He examined the reading closely. It read 10 kilograms. "Well that's okay," he said to himself. "So far so good." He replaced the two packages, zipped up the bag, started the engine and drove off towards Route A91.

As the senator pulled away, and unbeknown to him, a blue Ford Mustang slid away from the kerb some fifty feet further down the road.

The drive from Clearwater to Orlando was uneventful, and he arrived at 150 South Street at around eight o'clock in the evening. Parking his car at an appropriate distance away from the brothel, he casually walked to the front door and rang the bell.

The door was opened by Anita Togue. "Yes?" she asked in her sharp Brazilian accent, at the same time looking Wesley up and down with cold grey eyes.

"I came to deliver the sugar," the senator said in a half whisper, and handed over the red bag.

The woman took it and told him to wait. She disappeared into the room behind and came back a few seconds later minus the bag.

"You're new," she said opening the door wider so that Wesley could see inside. A number of girls were seated around a parlour. "You want to sample the goods? They're nice girls. I only have the best."

"No thanks," he said. "I must be going."

She nodded knowingly. "Well, some men have it, some don't," she said caustically.

The senator smiled. "I don't have the time," he said, stifling a strong desire to do her harm.

As he made his way back to his car, he passed Terry Craig and Bob Titcombe sitting in their Ford Mustang. They were pretending to be reading newspapers, but as Wesley went by they both took a careful look at him, and Titcombe took a photograph with the hidden camera which was fixed to the inside of the left wing mirror.

"The guy looks vaguely familiar," Craig remarked.

"Well, I've never seen him before," said Titcombe. "And he certainly hasn't driven all the way from St Petersburg for a quick fuck. He arrived with a red bag. He's left without it."

When Wesley Page reached his car, he did not drive off immediately, but sat in the driver's seat watching the house. After about half an hour he saw two men arrive. They fitted exactly the descriptions given by Hunaz. The men quickly entered the house, and a few minutes later emerged from the back stairs carrying the red bag.

Craig and Titcombe also watched the operation. "Same procedure as the last three times," Craig observed.

"You'd think they'd vary it a bit," said Titcombe. "Not a very smart bunch."

The two men put the bag in the boot of their Cadillac and drove off towards Highway 44 and Inverness.

Craig started the engine and was about to follow, when the Datsun passed them on the tail of the Cadillac.

"Looks like Big Daddy's making sure his sweets get to the children," said Craig.

"Okay," instructed Titcombe, "let's back off and take the short cut to Inverness. We can wait for both cars at the Highway 19 junction."

Craig rammed the car into gear, spun round in a U-turn and shot down the road in the opposite direction.

Wesley followed the Cadillac at a discreet distance all the way up to Inverness, and by the time both cars passed the junction with Highway 19 the two officers were in position watching the road.

"There go our babies," said Titcombe nudging his companion.

"Right on time. We go now?"

"Right, but let's keep our distance. We don't want to blow our cover."

The Cadillac sped through the town heading for Carters' Landing, the usual dropping-off point. Wesley wasn't far behind, and as the Cadillac pulled to a halt. the senator accelerated and screamed to a stop alongside. The car had barely stopped before he was out and beside the Cadillac, a gun in his hand.

"Out!" he ordered, holding the gun at the driver's head.

The driver was Jake Tale, and his face had gone white. His companion, Joshua Zeal, who was holding the red bag on his lap, tried to say something, but the senator cut him short.

"Now! but slowly, hand me the bag." The black man jerked his shoulders, as if didn't understand, but the senator was in no mood for delaying tactics. "Now, goddam it, now!"

Tale began to open the door. Wesley quickly stepped back clear of the door to avoid being hit as it was swung open. When they were both clear of the car, he told Zeal to place the bag on the bonnet. When this was done he motioned them to the rear of the car and instructed Tale to open the boot.

When the man hesitated, Wesley placed the barrel of the gun against his temple. "Open it." he said menacingly.

The boot sprung open.

"Now, get inside," Wesley ordered.

The man began to protest. "You don't know who we are," he said. "You're making a mistake."

Wesley cocked the trigger. Tale climbed in. "You too," said the senator waving his gun at Zeal.

"Mister, you're going to regret this . . ." Zeal began, but Wesley levelled the gun at the man's head which had the intended effect. Zeal climbed in, and Wesley slammed the boot shut.

He then ran over to his car, took a torch from the dashboard, unzipped the bag and examined the contents. The two packs were both there, intact; they had not been tampered with. As he zipped up the bag he heard the sound of a motor launch somewhere out across the lake. It was approaching fast. Grabbing the bag he ran across to the landing and flashed his torch into the darkness six times. The boat came at high speed and as it passed Wesley threw the bag onto the deck. It then disappeared back into the night as swiftly as it had come, the sound of engines receding into the night to leave behind it a trail of silence.

"From Cuba to here, the goods are intact," he said to himself.

But the silence was now broken by another sound, a hammering from inside the boot of the Cadillac. Wesley walked swiftly towards it, climbed in and started the engine. He rammed the car into gear

92

and accelerated along the landing towards the lake, aiming for the end of the jetty and the blackness beyond. Muffled cries were coming from the boot and the hammering intensified, but even this was drowned by the clatter of wheels against the wooden decking of the jetty. At the very last minute, Wesley dived, hitting the ground in a roll as the car leapt into space. For a second or two it was suspended in air, and then it struck the water nose on and began to sink. There was a sound like a can of Coke bursting, and then it was gone.

The two officers, sitting in their car some distance away, had watched the whole scenario unfold. The climax to it was as unexpected as it was horrible. The first reaction of both of them was to run towards the car, but their professionalism told them there was nothing they could do. Besides which, such a move would have ruined their operation.

It was Bob Titcombe who reacted first. "Get on to the local police," he said. "Tell them there's a car in the lake – with two bodies in it." And then he added. "Whoever that bastard is, we'll get him."

Chapter 18

Lake Apopka, Inverness

Out on the lake, Peter Cooper quietly steered the barge offshore. Suddenly he heard the dull thud of a pounding engine coming across the lake in the darkness. He quickly pushed the lever on the old electric motor to 'Stop', switched off the small navigation light on the bow and drifted silently into the long reeds for cover.

It was a very dark night with no moon, and the boat was nearly onto him before he was aware of it. He was scared. He thought someone must have found out, but the boat sped on past unaware. Seconds later the engine was cut and the launch began to drift, eventually stopping near to where Peter had been dumping the residue.

He saw two men silhouetted against the light from the engine room. Both seemed to be intent on examining some packages, one of which they were in the process of opening. One of the men poured something from a large polythene bag into a smaller one, hurriedly wrapping the smaller package in silver foil. As they were turned away from him, Peter was unable to recognise either of them. As he watched, one of them came to the edge of the bow and dropped the silver package, with a weight tied to it, into the lake. Then the motor gave a roar and the boat disappeared into the darkness as quickly as it had appeared, heading in the direction of Inverness Leisure Industries on the far shore.

Peter was frightened. What were those men doing there near his dumping ground? They may have been fishermen baiting a swim for later, but he felt this unlikely. Whatever the reason for their presence, he had to jettison the residue and he didn't have much time left. As soon as the coast was clear he started the motor, moved over to the drop area and released the contents as quickly as he could. Then, turning the lever onto full power, he headed back to the factory hugging the shore. He did not switch on his navigation lights.

The old alligator had watched the barge and launch enter the dumping area, and it felt no fear as it drifted on the surface of the still, mirrored water just twenty feet away. Its body contaminated with radioactive waste, it had become a ferocious feeder. When the package had been thrown into the water, the alligator instantly submerged, diving below the boat, scattering the fish as it went amongst them feeding, its great jaws hoovering up fish as well as the silver foil package, which instantly burst on impact with sharp teeth; the white powder mixing with the chewed flesh of writhing bass. And now, as more crystals filtered down through the water, its feeding took on a new and frenzied urgency. It was a creature in torment and it was growing into a giant.

Chapter 19

FBI Headquarters, Tampa Bay

Bob Titcombe and Terry Craig arrived at FBI headquarters in Tampa Bay at 9.30 the next morning. Up until now they had kept their chief only partly in the picture regarding their activities. At the weekly briefing they had confirmed their identification of the couriers taking the cocaine from Orlando to Inverness. They both felt, until the previous evening, that they had the surveillance under control. It wasn't until after they had witnessed the drowning of the two men in the boot of the Cadillac that they had decided to tell their chief everything.

As they entered the main office there was a buzz of activity with telephones ringing and groups of officers discussing their activities from the previous evening's surveillances. Through the glass-panelled door, Craig could see Chief Jacobs sitting at his desk, a telephone clamped to his ear. Craig knocked. Jacobs looked up and beckoned both men into his office, pointing at two leather chairs in front of the desk. He didn't look too pleased.

The chief finished his telephone call, and with slow deliberation replaced the receiver. He pushed his chair back and stretched. "Well, this is a pleasure," he said in a tone indicating that it wasn't. "Suppose you two fucking wise guys tell me the whole story."

"Look," began Craig rising from his chair, "we've kept things a little tight on this one, and we wanted to make sure we didn't blow our cover."

"And a right fucking mess you both made of things!" shouted the chief with a flash of anger. "Sit down, Craig."

"What do you mean a mess?" Titcombe said.

The chief leaned forward in his seat and looked at them both coldly. "That was the Deputy Commissioner of the Narcotics Squad," he said. "Two guys died last night in Inverness, drowned in the boot of a car." He paused for a second, drawing in breath. "Those two guys were undercover agents, and you two arseholes just sat there and watched it happen!"

"Christ!" Craig stammered feeling his collar tightening. "We didn't know. We checked their background; they appeared to be kosher. We thought they were both bums, no good couriers, not bloody agents. Why didn't somebody let us know?"

"I'll tell you why," the chief snapped. "Because you didn't tell me the full story, that's bloody well why, and anyway, Narcotics didn't say. Anyway, it's all beside the point. You're both off the case, and think yourselves lucky that you've not been suspended from duty!" The chief was breathing heavily. He was a big man, and of late the shenanigans of some of his officers had begun to give him palpitations. These two were hardly an exception. "Now get your arses out of my office," he growled. "See Dave about your next assignment, and in future you share your information – you hear?"

The two officers nodded but didn't reply. They weren't going to argue with the boss in this mood. They knew what he was saying was true. They'd fucked it up.

The main office was silent, its inmates having been riveted by the goings on in the chief's office. They had probably heard every word.

"Damn the Narcotics," said Craig, ignoring the stares. "They think they're bloody God."

"So what's new!" rejoined his companion.

Back in his office, Chief Jacobs sat quietly in his chair, drumming his fingers on his desk and trying to regain control of himself. After some minutes he made a decision and picked up the telephone. "May, get me Deputy Commissioner Lyons at Narcotics, and make sure the call is scrambled."

A few minutes later the telephone rang. "I have the deputy commissioner," May said as she put the chief through.

"Hi, Jack. It's John Jacobs again. Look. I dealt with that matter of last night. They're now both off the case. I'm sure sorry about your two guys, but if you don't let me know what's going on, it's difficult to control the situation."

"John, it was just not possible. This thing goes right up to the highest level. I've told you too much already. All your men involved in the matter must be ordered to stop their investigations immediately. And, John, when I say immediately, I mean *now*, this second."

The chief began to object. "But we've put a lot of work into this case, Jack. Why don't we work together as a team?"

"Can't be done, John. I can't oblige you this time. I've told you all I can." There was a pause as the commissioner let this sink in. "Look, all I will say to you is this: we're dealing with a tough bunch who'll stop at nothing to achieve what they want. The death of my agents is proof of that. I'll tell you again, John, you must stop all surveillance, all investigation. Do I have your word?" The commissioner hesitated for a few seconds, waiting for a reply. "John," he said at length, "are you still there?"

"Yes, I'm here," replied the chief in a tone that reflected his displeasure. "You have my word, we stop immediately, but I want a promise. When this is all over you tell me everything."

"John, I promise. I owe you that." Then the line went dead.

The chief pressed a red button on his phone. "Ken, would you come into the office for a moment."

Captain Ken Barclay was fifty-eight years old, a highly respected officer who had worked for the FBI for thirty years, and was looking forward to retirement in two years' time. Now, as he stood in the chief's office, he wondered why his boss looked so dispirited. He was soon to find out.

"Ken, I've got some bad news," he said rubbing tired eyes. "The Cuba/Orlando surveillance has to be cancelled with immediate effect."

Barclay frowned. "You can't mean that?"

"I can and I do. Directive from above, I'm afraid. I know how you must feel but – that's it."

"Shit! Is this because of last night?"

"Partly," said the chief, "but I think we were close to being called off anyway. The death of those two guys simply brought it forward a few weeks."

Barclay raised his eyes towards the nicotine-stained ceiling. "Okay," he said dejectedly, "I'll tell the boys. But wait till I get my hands on Craig and Titcombe."

"Hey! Cool it," said the chief. "They're both young. You and I would have done exactly the same thing. Remember that surveillance we did together in New York in 92, when our chief suspect was shot by one of our own men?"

Barclay nodded. "But all that bloody work."

"Aye, but that's the way it is. By the way, that reminds me, I need a full report on all of our surveillance information. We might not be on this any more but we might as well help Narcotics; they're going to need all the help they can get."

"You want to lick their arses, too?" Barclay quipped as he left the office, slamming the door behind him.

The chief smiled. "Still the same old Ken. If he'd kept his mouth shut over the years he could have gone to the top of the tree."

Chapter 20

London, England

Slowly the red Ford Transit moved along with the traffic on the M4 motorway. Gerald Fitzgibbon had been making this journey to the airport every four weeks for the last five years. It had become routine and tedious, and he was now anxious to load up the stuff and get over to Mary's place. He'd been taking out his assistant manageress, Mary Tarmore, every Saturday night for several weeks and they usually spent their Sunday nights at Arlesford Hall. It was a pleasant arrangement and Gerald knew her feelings towards him. For his part, he reciprocated when it suited him.

He took a left turn off the motorway and at the next roundabout followed the sign towards Cargo and Customs. He came to a stop at a steel-meshed gate beside the guard house and pressed the button to unwind his window.

"Good evening, Mr Fitzgibbon," the guard said. "It's never four weeks since you were last here?"

"Afraid so," replied Gerald. "A shipment came in yesterday."

The guard nodded. "I'd better see your papers, sir, if you don't mind. Have to keep the bureaucrats happy."

Gerald smiled and handed them over.

"That all looks okay, sir," he said and opened the electronic gates.

Gerald drove through and pulled up at the main offices where the customs inspector was waiting for him.

"Everything's been cleared and stacked ready for collection," he said. "The goods are in Shed A."

Gerald thanked him and asked about the clearance papers.

"All in order," replied the inspector, pulling a white envelope from his inside pocket. "Just give this to the security officer as usual."

Gerald nodded and drove over to Cargo Shed A, where he showed his papers and loaded up the five tea chests full of alligator shoes, handbags and belts. All the chests were marked with the manufacturer's name, Leisure Industries, Inverness, Florida.

Once the loading had been completed he quickly left, clearing the customs check at the exit gate without any trouble, and was soon driving back along the M4.

He reached his shop in Bond Street at around seven in the evening and parked on the pavement outside. He unloaded the chests and carried them, one by one, into the rear office. By the time he was finished he was perspiring heavily; he was not used to heavy work.

He locked the door to the shop, returned to his office and closed and locked the door behind him. He switched off the main light and flicked on a table lamp by the desk, which gave him just enough light to see by. Then, with a paperknife, he broke the seal on the first chest and began to remove the contents, unwrapping each item carefully. Handbags, belts and wallets he placed on the floor next to the wall, but pairs of shoes and boots he laid on his desk. He repeated this procedure until all the chests had been unpacked.

His desk was now covered with a colourful array of footwear; twenty-four pairs in all. He wondered which contained the substance he was searching for. Even after five years he still couldn't tell. Picking up a grey alligator-skin boot he carefully examined it, concentrating his attention on the heel. With the paperknife he attempted to prise the heel away but found it to be solid. 'Obviously for the shop,' he thought and deposited the pair amongst the handbags and wallets. He knew that of the twenty-four pairs of shoes and boots only eight would contain what he was looking for; the rest were for legitimate sale. He picked up another shoe, this time a light brogue, and slid the knife between the sole and the heel. There was the sound of sticky tape tearing and the heel loosened. Holding the shoe tightly in his left hand, he forced the heel sideways until it came off in his hand. He tapped the shoe on the edge of his desk and a small black plastic package fell onto the carpet. He quickly picked it up and placed it in the open briefcase lying on a chair nearby.

Systematically he went through every pair of shoes until he had uncovered sixteen of the packages, which he placed side by side in the briefcase, until there were two shiny black rows of small fat packages staring back at him. It represented a great deal of money, more than he was likely to see again in his lifetime. He allowed himself a few seconds of reflection, then he went to the safe in the corner of the room, punched in the code, opened the heavy door and placed a single package inside, covering it with some papers. He closed the door, spun the dial, and locked the safe.

Back at his desk he snapped the briefcase shut and glanced at his watch. The whole procedure had taken him almost exactly one hour.

He gathered up the broken shoes, threw them into one of the open chests, then, when it was full, struggled with it to the van.

Some fifty yards from the shop, Hunaz Potra sat quietly in the rear passenger seat of his Rolls, puffing on a huge Havana cigar, watching Gerald's every move. He paid particular attention as Gerald went back into the shop and returned carrying a black briefcase. He was in a hurry as if late for an appointment, and as soon as he had driven off the Rolls cruised silently to the front of the shop.

It was the driver who got out first, a small wiry Puerto Rican, a veteran burglar to whom every security system or complex lock was a challenge. It took him only ten seconds to disarm the shop alarm, and even less, with the help of a set of special keys, to open the lock.

Even Hunaz had to acknowledge that his man was good, though he would never tell him that. He pushed past him into the shop without so much as a word and made for the shoes on the floor by the wall in Gerald's office, where he counted the pairs. He seemed satisfied and, turning to his driver, ordered the safe to be opened.

But Plateno was one step ahead. He already had his ear pressed to the safe as his fingers caressed the dial and moved it one click at a time. It was an irritatingly slow process and Hunaz was impatient.

"Come on, get a move on," he snapped, but Plateno was in no mood to be hurried. He was savouring the rare feeling of being in control, so he continued without hurry until he heard the sound he wanted, an almost imperceptible 'clunk'. Next, taking a bunch of skeleton keys from his trouser pocket, he tried them one at a time. On the fourth attempt the lock turned. He eased the door open and stood back.

Hunaz reached inside, rifled through a mass of old envelopes and legal documents tied into bundles with rubber bands until, from under a pile of letters, he withdrew the small black package he was looking for. He held it reverently in his hand for a few brief seconds before placing it gently in his pocket. From another pocket he took an identical package which he returned to the safe, stuffing it back beneath the pile of letters. This done, he retraced his steps, leaving Plateno to close the safe and reset the door alarm.

Back in the safety of the car, Hunaz paid the Puerto Rican a rare compliment. "You did a good job tonight," he said. And then he added, "I'll see your son is released from Havana Prison as soon as I return home."

Plateno responded with a wide smile. "Thank you, Senor Hunaz," he said. "You are truly a man of your word."

Hunaz relaxed into the soft leather of the seat and reflected on the magnanimity of his action. It was a gratifying thing to hold someone's future in one's hands.

Chapter 21

London, England

As Gerald drove through the darkening streets of London heading towards Kilion Rastafaf's residence in Chelsea, he thought about the past five and a half years, and how he had become involved in the drug racket.

At Oxford he had experimented with various drugs, from marijuana to LSD, and in his final year he began taking cocaine on a regular basis. In those days, in the late 1990s, drug taking was common, even well-known politicians occasionally took 'the powder' as it was colloquially known. With Gerald it became a habit that he never imagined would eventually control his life.

After graduating, he joined his father in the family business in their Bond Street shop. He liked the work and the rich young women who came into the store, and for some time he felt settled. Then things changed.

One evening he made a visit to his regular bar in Kensington. He'd agreed to meet a girl there, a very attractive brunette he'd met at the store that morning. He also needed more cocaine; Jack the barman was the supplier. But the girl hadn't shown. Gerald had waited long enough to down two large gin and tonics, by which time he'd decided to give the thing up as a bad job and head for Kenny's nightclub.

He drained his glass and was just about leave when the guy at the bar next to him turned and said, "I see you like a sniff of the white powder."

Gerald didn't answer.

"Hey, come on now. I'm not trying to embarrass you. Oh, and I'm not the law, either, I'm here on business." He was holding Gerald's arm gently but firmly to stop him leaving.

"You've been watching me," Gerald said accusingly.

"Nooo. Just interested," said the American, holding out his hand.

"My name's Abe Thompson. As I said, I'm here on business. Manufacture leather goods, from alligators. I'm trying to sell the stuff to Harrods, but the po-faced bitch of a buyer gave me the cold shoulder." He chuckled as if it were a private joke and shook his head in despair.

"You'll have to try harder," Gerald said.

The American shrugged.

"You take the stuff?"

"Cocaine? Me? Hell, no – at least, not on a regular basis. Maybe once or twice a month," said Abe.

"Then why were you watching me collect?"

The American shrugged again. "Just noticed," he said. "You ought to be more careful, no telling who's watching. Look – can I get you a drink?"

Gerald wasn't sure what the American was after, but he was curious. He also acknowledged to himself that he had been careless. If one person had noticed the transaction. there may have been others. Notwithstanding that, there was no harm in a free drink.

"Okay," he said. "Mine's a gin and tonic."

"Very English," remarked Abe hailing the barman. "Mine's a bourbon – on the rocks."

By twelve o'clock the barman was beginning to wonder how Gerald and his new-found friend, Abe the American, were holding themselves erect, when by the law of gravity they should have been flat on their backs. They had both consumed a prodigious quantity of alcohol and were bosom buddies. They had left together having, in effect, drunk themselves sober.

Next morning, however, Gerald had no recollection of leaving the bar or how he had got home. His head was bursting, and his mouth tasted foul. Lying on his bed fully clothed with his head on the pillow, which felt as if it had lumps of rock embedded in it, he did not at first know where he was. It was only after some minutes of staring at the ceiling, watching a spider negotiate the light bulb, that he realised that he was indeed in his own mews flat. He managed to raise himself from the bed, but slowly so that the blood did not rush too quickly to his brain and flood it, and staggered into the bathroom where he thrust his head under the bathroom tap and turned on the cold water.

Just as he was beginning to drown, the telephone rang. It sounded like an alarm bell at full pitch. He fumbled for a towel, patted his face with it tenderly, reached the kitchen and lunged for the telephone.

The voice on the end of the line screamed into his ear, at least it felt like a scream: "Gerald, is that you?" It was a woman's voice and it was nervous.

"Yes, who's that?"

"It's me, Ellinor. I've been trying to get hold of you all night." The voice trailed off into sobs.

"What's happened?" Gerald asked calmly, the grunge in his brain dispersing like morning mist before the sun.

Amidst more sobs his sister said, "It's Daddy. He's disappeared."

Gerald felt a sudden sense of panic which made the headache worse. "What do you mean, he's disappeared?"

There was a whimper on the end of the line.

"Ellinor, I'm sorry, I didn't mean to shout. Now tell me what happened." He was trying to sound composed, but his pulse was racing.

"Well," she sniffed, "he went fishing on the lake last night after dinner. I went to bed at eleven, but this morning he didn't come down for breakfast and his bed hadn't been slept in."

"Have you checked the lake?"

"Of course I've checked the lake. The boat's moored in the middle of it with all his fishing tackle aboard – but there's no sign of Daddy."

Gerald tried to rationalise this thoughts. It wasn't easy as the drugs and drink still swilling around his system were slowing down his thinking process. "Ellinor, phone the police. I'll be home within the next hour. I'm leaving now."

By the time he had washed, dressed and driven like a maniac to Arlesford Hall, an hour had passed. The grounds were full of police cars and an ambulance was parked by the lake. He turned off the drive, and headed directly towards the lakeside, leaving deep ruts in the wet grass.

Ellinor was there being comforted by Jim Leggatt, the butler. He stopped the car and ran over to them. Ellinor met him halfway. She was clearly in a state of distress.

"Gerald, oh, Gerald, they've found him." There were tears in her eyes, and she was fighting to constrain herself. "He was floating face down in the water near the weir. Oh, Gerald – he's dead."

As she said this she seemed to lose all strength and fell into his arms. They had never been close, but their mutual sense of loss at that moment was overwhelming. He kissed her on the cheek, and they held on to one another tightly, gathering mutual strength and comfort.

The autopsy later that week indicated that his father had not died from drowning, no water had been found in his lungs. What the autopsy had revealed was the presence of a large quantity of arsenic. Gerald's father had died from arsenic poisoning. Sir John had taken his own life.

Gerald experience feelings of shock and anger. He was aware that his father had been depressed since the death of his mother, who had died suddenly eighteen months before. The old man had missed her terribly, but he thought his father was getting back to normal. They'd even talked about the three of them taking a holiday at the villa in Portugal this coming summer, something they had not done for years.

The funeral was a quiet affair, held at the small Norman church at Arlesford. His father was buried next to his mother in the grounds of the hall.

When the funeral was over, Gerald and his sister walked down to the lakeside. Ellinor had always been particularly close to her father, much closer than Gerald had been, so his death, and particularly the manner of his death, was something that she found difficult to come to terms with. Sadness surrounded her like a dark cloak. They had hardly spoken since they had left the church. With both parents gone there was now only the two of them.

There were other matters, however, that were preying upon his mind. His father's solicitor had phoned soon after he had learned of the tragedy. The news was not good; his father had left the business in difficult financial straits. After inheritance tax and all the other debts had been paid there was precious little left, certainly nothing for his offspring. Put bluntly the business and Gerald were broke. He had intended to break the news to Ellinor that very afternoon, but in her state of vulnerability he decided to wait for a more opportune time.

It was she, however, who broke the silence. "Gerald," she said, turning to face him, "I have something to tell you. I have decided to go away. I can't stay here – not with all these memories."

"But, Ellinor, this house is your home, yours and mine. You can't go. Don't think about it."

As well as surprise he felt a sudden hurt. It was unfair of her to leave everything and run. But then he realised *he* was being selfish. It was her life. It was up to her. But he didn't want her to go; he would try to persuade her not to.

"Give it time," he said to her. "Let things settle and you might feel differently."

"No, Gerald," she said firmly. "I've decided. I'm joining Peter Nutty in Australia."

"Peter Nutty? But you don't love him! You're making a dreadful mistake. And you can't hide away, that won't help. Ellinor, you must listen . . ."

She stopped him with an outstretched palm. "I've made up my mind," she said. "I'm leaving this evening. I've spoken to Dean Rutledge. I've signed an affidavit giving you the house and business. I want none of it." She grasped Gerald's hand and, rising on her toes, she kissed him on the cheek. "Goodbye, Gerald," she said. "I will write." And then she was gone.

He watched her receding figure for some minutes as a feeling of despair crept over him. The dying sun, an orange ball of fire low in the west, seemed to mirror his mood. It was slipping away, leaving a trail of shimmering light across the still surface of the lake. Gerald could feel its warmth across his face, but it would soon cool to be replaced by long shadows and finally darkness. He looked up into the sky where faint pinpricks of stars were beginning to puncture the darkening sky. He was alone for the first time in his life, and the great arc of the world around him was empty. He was a lonely, frightened figure as he stood by that lakeshore, and when he looked down into the water he saw his reflection staring back at him. It was that of a haunted man.

Chapter 22

Arlesford Hall, England

One evening, a few weeks after his father's death, Gerald was sitting in the library of Arlesford Hall cataloguing his father's antiques and pictures when the telephone rang.

"Gerald, is that you?" said an American voice which was faintly familiar.

"Speaking, but who is this?"

"Abraham Thompson. You remember? You asked me to contact you when the shoes were ready."

Gerald was trying to search his brain, and then it clicked. "Oh, yes. Phantom's Bar. Christ that seems a lifetime ago."

"I've been trying to get hold of you for the past two weeks. You're a hard man to pin down."

"I've had things on my mind," Gerald said. "What shoes?"

"Gerald, we did a deal, remember? Forty-eight pairs of alligator shoes."

Gerald tried to think back. The memory of that night was largely a blur. He could vaguely remember shaking hands, and there may have been a back slap, but he couldn't remember any deal. "I do remember something," he said, "but . . ."

"Good," broke in Abe. "Now you remember. The goods will be at Heathrow tomorrow. I'll have my agent deliver them to the shop as soon as they've cleared customs."

Gerald's befuddled mind was still unable to grasp the situation. He stumbled with his speech. "Excuse me – but – how much are these shoes going to cost me?"

"Nothing, old man, nothing. Just remember the deal."

"What deal?" Gerald was becoming agitated. He couldn't remember a deal, but before he could ask the question again the phone went dead.

On the following Thursday morning four packing cases arrived at the Bond Street shop, just as Abe had said they would. At first he wasn't going to touch them, but curiosity got the better of him and he opened the first package. He examined the shoes carefully; they were certainly of good quality and he knew he would have no problem selling them, but he felt nervous. The telephone interrupted his thoughts.

"Gerald, Abe here. You've got the goods yet?"

"Yes I have, and fine shoes they are."

"Get a knife and see if you can prise off the heels," said Abe.

"What on earth for?"

"Just do it. It'll be worth your while."

Gerald's first reaction was to ignore such a silly request. Why on earth should he damage what were in fact very good shoes, but for some reason he didn't argue but went and fetched a knife, and inserted the point between the sole and heel. Suddenly the heel shot off revealing a small black polythene package which had been fitted tightly into the hollow.

"Have you done what I asked yet?" said the American.

For several seconds Gerald didn't know what to say. It was obvious what the package contained. It was also clear to him that he'd been set-up. The whole thing had been planned to entrap him.

"Gerald, are you still there?" The voice was anxious.

"Yes, I'm still here," said Gerald. "I think you're mad. Leave me out of this. I don't want to get involved. This stuff has nothing to do with me?"

"Sorry," said the voice on the other end of the line. "Number one, you are involved, and number two, it has a lot to do with you. Besides, I felt sure you'd appreciate the opportunity."

"Opportunity?"

"Sure, to make a lot of dough. I'll pay you £40,000 every month, and the shoes are free. There's no risk, I guarantee it."

"And what makes you so sure I'll agree."

"Come on, Gerald. You're broke, we've checked your financial status. You're up against it in a big way. This is a way out."

"I'm not that desperate," Gerald said sharply. "I'll make out."

The American's voice took on a harder tone. "No you won't, Gerald. One phone call to the drugs squad and they'll put you away for ten years – or more."

Gerald was silent for a moment. He was caught, and he knew it. Abe was right, he was desperate for cash and he did not want to lose Arlesford Hall. But drug dealing . . ? Then again, it was a way out. Did he really have any alternative?

"I can't say no, can I?" He said, half to himself but loud enough for Abe to pick it up.

"No, my old buddy," he said, "you can't."

"Okay, what happens now?" Gerald asked bitterly. His hand was shaking as he tried to light a cigarette, but it wouldn't light so he threw the lighter on the floor.

"You'll find one third of the shoes contain cocaine, all in false heels," Abe said. "Take them out. They're to be delivered to someone in Knightsbridge. You'll receive a phone call from this person in approximately ten minutes. Oh, and by the way, £40,000 has been credited to your bank account."

And that was all there was to it.

Since that day, five years ago, Gerald had taken delivery of a shipment of shoes every month. Any reservations or moral soul-searching he'd had earlier had long since evaporated. He now had to admit that the excitement, the intrigue, added spice to his life; it focused the mind wonderfully. Besides, he'd been successful. In a way it was all too easy.

This he reflected upon with some complacency as he entered Kensington Road and pulled up outside number 28. He lifted the briefcase off the back seat, glanced both ways to make sure no one was following his movements, then left the van and climbed the steps to the front door.

He rang the brass doorbell and waited. One, two, three, four seconds passed and then the door slowly opened, revealing a black nervous face.

"Hi, Gerald," the face said, as from somewhere below a hand reached out and took the case. "Thank you, man. See you next month."

And then the face was gone, the heavy door closed and Gerald heard the click of a padlock and the rustle of chains. It was the same every time. He never saw anything of the man behind the face, apart from the hand reaching out. But then it was a secretive business. He didn't need to know, and in fact, apart from a mild curiosity, had no particular desire to know.

He left the van at the hire company's offices and got a taxi back to his flat, but he didn't go in. Instead he opened the garage doors and backed out the Testarossa. Then he drove off to pick up Mary from her flat.

From the window of Gerald's flat, Hunaz Potra watched his quarry drive off. He'd been waiting for some time for Gerald to return. He clenched his fist in frustration and took a long, deep breath to calm himself. He picked up the revolver which he'd placed on the table by the window, then quickly left the room. Once in the street, he closed the door behind him and walked calmly away.

Chapter 23

Knightsbridge, London

Kilion Rastafaf checked the merchandise, weighed it, and frowned. He took a folded piece of paper out of his back pocket and spread it open on the desk by the telephone. He read the telephone number written down in red ink, and dialled. "Hello, man," he said. "Is this the Cuban Embassy?"

"It is," replied a polite voice. "How can we help you?"

"I wanna speak to Mr Hunaz Potra. It's urgent."

"Certainly, sir. I'll try his office. What name shall I say?"

"Tell him it's Kilion, he'll know."

The telephone went silent for a couple of minutes, then a quietly spoken man said, "I have contacted Mr Potra – just putting you through, sir."

"Hello, Hunaz Potra speaking."

"Hey, it's me, man – Kilion. I'm phoning to say I've checked the merchandise, and you know what? There's only 9.5 kilograms."

"Are you sure?" said Hunaz in a mildly surprised tone.

"Look, man, I'm sure, I'm sure. I've paid for 10 kilograms – I should get 10 kilograms."

"Yes, yes, I quite understand, Mr Rastafaf. I apologise," said Hunaz, trying to hide his irritation. "I'll arrange for the missing amount to be delivered this afternoon."

"Man, I don't like being taken in like this," he said, his confidence boosted by the conciliatory tone on the other end of the line. "Someone should pay for my inconvenience."

"I assure you, Mr Rastafaf, on my word of honour, that this problem will be dealt with quickly. It will not happen again."

But Rastafaf was not yet satisfied. "How long has this situation been going on, man? How long have I been taken?"

"To be honest," replied Hunaz, "I don't know, but on the next delivery you will receive 15 kilograms and only pay for the usual 10 kilograms."

"Okay," replied Rastafaf, "that sounds fine, but this business has worried my partners. I've been threatened, accused, man; it's been a very difficult situation."

"Tell your partners to ring me at the embassy today and I'll explain to them. You will not be compromised, I assure you."

"That's good, man," Rastafaf drawled, clearly relieved that he was not to be blamed for the losses. "I'll get them to ring you then."

"Very good." said Hunaz. "I trust we're still friends?"

"Sure," replied Rastafaf.

"Then I wish you good day." Hunaz replaced the receiver and sat pondering for a few moments, then he picked up the white telephone in front of him. This was his personal line. He quickly punched in the number and waited impatiently for the ringing tone.

After some time a husky American voice answered. "Senator Page."

"Senator, it's Hunaz Potra here. I'm still in London, and I've found a problem. It appears that only half the missing goods are accounted for this end. This I will deal with tomorrow."

"But I checked on everyone from my end," replied the senator hesitantly.

"No, my friend, not everyone."

"But you don't mean the mayor? I don't believe he'd do that."

"Look," said Hunaz, "the goods were still intact at the lake; it has to be the guys on the boat or the mayor."

"Well I can't believe it's the mayor," said the senator, "but I'll get on to it straight away."

"Wesley," Hunaz said in a stern voice, "this matter must be dealt with now, you understand?"

"Fine," replied the senator.

"This also means," Hunaz continued, "that we'll have to change the whole operation at the Inverness end. How we do that I don't yet know, though I have an idea, but in two weeks we've got to have a new system up and running."

"This idea of yours needs to be a good one."

"Wesley, what I have in mind is so simple, the person concerned won't even know."

"You going to tell me?"

"Not over the phone. Anyway, I have to talk to Jessica."

"Whatever you say."

"See you in Florida," said Hunaz, and the line went dead leaving Wesley to ponder on what the little man had in mind.

Chapter 24

Power Unit, Inverness

Betty Goddard entered the operation rooms at about 5.30 p.m. She was tired, her face strained and intense from overconcentration. The control panel looked like a jumbo jet's, with green and red lights flashing, innumerable dials flickering and an ever present buzz.

The power station had been fully operational now for five weeks and was running efficiently. In fact the company's first month's accounts suggested a yearly profit margin some 20% higher than originally thought. The main board of directors had met a few days before and were pleased with Wayne's report.

Betty's appointment (she had joined the team two weeks before) had enabled Claire and Wayne to have more time off together, and their lives had settled down to a routine. For the first time in months Wayne felt relaxed and pleased with his decision to move to Inverness.

They had taken a day off. They had left early and taken their small power boat out onto the lakes. Wayne had tried fishing for bass, but all he'd caught all day was a two-pounder; he was no great fisherman. They had anchored in one of the small coves in Lake Henderson, opened a bottle of champagne to go with the smoked salmon picnic and enjoyed the October sunshine. Later they made love and let the warm Florida sunshine soak into their naked bodies. Life was good.

As the afternoon waned they packed up and reluctantly made their way home.

As Wayne eased the boat onto the landing at the bottom of the garden, he could hear the telephone ringing in the house.

"Back to reality," Claire cried cheerfully. "I'll get it." She leapt out of the boat, charged along the landing stage into the house and grabbed the ringing phone.

Wayne had already secured the boat to the landing stage and was in the process of depositing its contents on the boardwalk when

Claire called from the open door, "Darling, it's Betty. She wants to speak to you."

"Can't you speak to her, Claire, I'm busy here?"

"I tried, but she insists it has to be you. She doesn't sound too happy."

Wayne was slightly annoyed at being disturbed on his day off, but Betty wouldn't have rung him unless it was something fairly urgent, so he made his way quickly to the phone. "Yes, Betty."

"I'm sorry to bother you on your day off," she said, "but I need to see you at the station urgently."

"Can't it wait until the morning? Surely it's not that urgent!"

"I'm truly sorry, Wayne," said Betty impatiently, "but no, it can't wait."

"But, what's the problem?"

"I can't tell you over the phone. You must come over now, please. Now!"

"Okay," said Wayne. "I'll be there in fifteen minutes."

Claire look hold of his arm. "You look worried," she said. "Whatever's the matter?"

"I don't know. She wouldn't say, but she sounded concerned and that's not like Betty. I'll have to go, I'm sorry. I'll be as quick as I can."

"Hey." Claire tugged at his sleeve. "Calm down, don't let this spoil a beautiful day. Do you want me to come?"

He kissed her affectionately on the tip of her nose. "No, don't worry, I'll see to it."

Wayne arrived at the power plant at 6.15 p.m. to find Betty, usually so calm, in a state of some anxiety. She did not greet him with her usual smile.

"What's the problem?" Wayne asked. "Things can't be as bad as you look."

"I hope you're right," said Betty tensely. "Christ, I hope you're right." She drew a deep breath and said, "It's the coolant water levels around the reactor. I think there's seepage."

Wayne's face froze. His muscles suddenly felt weak, his hands became moist and clammy and his stomach tightened. "It's only that bloody dial," he said falteringly, his mind hunting for excuses. "I've tried to get them to change it. They've confirmed it's not defective."

"It's not the dial," said Betty soberly. "I know about that." She paused momentarily and looked straight into Wayne's eyes. "Look,

I got suspicious today. I don't know why – intuition, who knows. I went down into the plant this morning and checked over the concrete casing. I found a hairline crack along the side. Oh, it's difficult to see, just above the ground slab level. There's no visible seepage. I checked with the Geiger counter. It shows no leak or activity, but there *is* a crack and it may extend well below ground." She paused and sighed deeply. Her eyes were red and she seemed very worried. "I've checked the water capacities on the computer based on the flow rates, and the water volume, according to my calculation, is down 2.3%. I've been ringing you all day but I got no answer. It's been driving me crazy not being able to get you, or talk to someone about it." She shook her head in despair and covered her face with her hands.

"Come on, don't cry," Wayne said with all the tenderness he could muster. "Show me the crack."

Betty brushed past him and opened the side door into the lower plant room. She switched on the lights and, taking a hand torch from its fixing on the wall, walked quickly to the far side of the room. Wayne followed.

At the section just above the slab level, where the concrete casing was exposed, Betty knelt down and turned on the flashlight.

"There, can you see it?" she said placing her middle finger over the crack. "It's about six inches long."

Wayne looked closely. "I can't see anything," he said and took some comfort in the possibility that Betty could have been mistaken. The crack sensors would have picked up any slight extension or movement of the casing, and the dials showed that everything was fine, but he had to be absolutely sure. "Give me the torch," he said to Betty. Kneeling on all fours he examined the area, indicated by Betty, thoroughly, but, much to his relief, found nothing amiss. 'Mistake,' he thought, 'but better safe than sorry.'

While he was carrying out his examination, Betty had left the room and had returned with a more powerful torch. She didn't speak, but knelt next to him and shone the stronger beam across the concrete. It was then that he saw it, a fine dark line, the faintest hairline crack like the sinew of a spider's web, probably no more than 1/1000 of an inch across, but it was a crack, there was no doubt about it.

"Have you checked the outfall pipe for flow and radioactive water?" he asked.

Betty nodded. "There is no active waste in the pipes or at the end of the discharge," she replied, "at least not according to the reading I took."

Wayne got wearily to his feet and began to pace the room, frequently running his fingers through his hair as if trying to stimulate the fibres of his brain, attempting to come to terms with what he feared most, or to find an answer, if there was an answer. He pushed open a door and entered the control area.

"I want to check the discharge pipe again," he said, turning to his assistant. "We must be absolutely sure."

Together they rechecked all the relevant dials and computer read-outs, but they came up with the same result: no radioactive water or discharge in either pipe or outlet.

"If there's no sign of coolant water or radioactivity in the discharge pipe or the plant," Wayne said, "then leakage must be taking place below the plant. The crack must widen underneath, below ground level. Damn! damn! I was never happy with that coolant level dial and print-out, always had a feeling something wasn't quite right. And those bloody people assured me that the dial was accurate. What were they playing at?" He realised that he was becoming agitated and losing his usual calm, so he closed his eyes and made a strong effort to compose himself. After a minute he said, "If there is seepage, it could have started as soon as the reactor was made operative – no, even before that, when we began to carry out the tests. My God, it could have been going on for weeks!"

"What shall we do?" Betty asked calmly.

"There's only one thing we can do," Wayne said incisively. "Shut the whole thing down."

"But we can't be sure," Betty said, alarmed at such a blunt and final end to all their work.

"No, we can't be sure, but we don't have to be. You know as well as I do that the slightest risk of a leak has to be taken seriously. Good heavens, radioactive water could be getting into the spring water system and entering the lake, or even into the drinking water boreholes."

Betty was all too well aware that what Wayne said was true. She slumped into a chair, a look of utter despair on her face.

"Okay, I'm going to ring the mayor," said Wayne abruptly. "He's managing director of the board. He can explain to the others why we're shutting down. Now, start computing the close-down programme."

Wayne dialled the mayor's number, but it was his wife who answered. She told him that her husband wasn't in, that he was at the factory, and gave Wayne the number. After several tries he eventually got through.

"Hello. It's Wayne Headbold," he said. "I've got some bad news. It concerns the plant." He went on to explain the situation and why he had to close down the plant immediately.

The mayor's reaction was a surprise. "Christ, son, you can't just shut it down. There are serious financial implications to consider here. Give me five minutes, I'll have to consult the rest of the board."

"Sir," Wayne said firmly, "we must do it immediately."

"I know, I know," replied the mayor, "but you said it's probably been like this for two months – or more. Hell, a few more minutes isn't going to make much difference. I need time to consult certain parties."

Wayne was silent.

"Wayne, are you still there?"

"Yes, I'm still here," Wayne said.

"Okay, look, just give me ten minutes, please. This is something that could affect the whole county. I know we'll have to close-down the plant. It's how it's announced to the citizens of Inverness and our investors that has to be considered; it has to be dealt with tactfully."

Wayne could sense that the mayor was panicking, not that he blamed him for that. "Okay," he said. "Ten minutes, but no more." He replaced the receiver.

Chapter 25

Leisure Industries, Inverness

Mayor Thompson punched in the number of the senator's car telephone and waited for the ringing tone. When the senator answered the mayor said, "Hi, Wesley, it's Abe. How long will it be before you get to my office?"

"Oh, about another thirty minutes," replied the senator. "You sound anxious, Abe. If you're worried about the missing cocaine, don't. I know you're not involved. We're dealing with the business tonight."

"No, it's not that," said the mayor. "There's another quite different problem that's just occurred. And, to be quite honest, I don't know how to deal with it."

"A serious problem?"

"Yes, I'm afraid so. Wayne Headbold wants to close-down the power plant. He thinks there's a crack in the concrete casing of the reactor, and it's leaking radioactive water."

"Fucking hell!" exclaimed the senator. "I don't believe this is happening. We've got enough on our plate at present without this. Damn!" He paused, and the tenor of his voice hardened. "Abe, listen. You know who our backers are on this project, so you'll know that closing it down is not an option. If we do, don't bank on retiring. Understand?"

"Wesley, please don't lecture me," said the mayor with annoyance. "I know what's involved."

"Then deal with it," said the senator sharply. "Who else knows about this?"

"As far as I know, only Headbold and his assistant, Betty."

"Right. Well, they mustn't be allowed to close the plant down. And they must be stopped from talking to anyone about this."

"What are you saying?" the mayor asked suspiciously.

"Abe, no one must know anything about this. Headbold and his assistant must never be allowed to talk; they must never have the opportunity to talk, if you see what I mean."

"I don't like what I'm hearing," the mayor said.

"Look, I'll be at your office as soon as I can, but I want these people sorted out quickly."

"But I can't! I can't!"

"Abe," said the senator in a tone that made the hairs on the mayor's neck jerk upright. "Put it like this, it's you or them. Make up your mind."

Mayor Thompson was now sweating, and it wasn't from the heat. His hands were trembling as if he'd had a sudden attack of Parkinson's disease, and he found that he had trouble swallowing; his throat had suddenly become dry. He replaced the telephone and sat quietly for a few moments in an attempt to get himself under some measure of control. He took a very deep breath, picked up the telephone and called Wayne Headbold.

"Ah, Wayne," he said as nonchalantly as he could. "Look, I've spoken to the chairman, Senator Page, and he agrees that we must close the plant, but we would like to meet you and Betty first to discuss how we are going to announce it to the county and the shareholders." He paused, his pulse racing, hoping that Wayne would agree without any fuss. But he needed a little more persuading. "Look," he continued, "the senator will be here at my office in about fifteen minutes. Why don't you leave one of your technicians in charge and both drive over here? You could be at my office by 7.30."

Wayne hesitated before answering. The man was a fool. Didn't he appreciate the seriousness of the situation? The plant had to be closed-down immediately. "But we're losing time," he said with urgency. "We must close-down – now."

"I know, I know," said the mayor, holding his temper in check. "But please try to understand our situation. Come over now. And by the way," he added, "have you told anyone else about this?"

"No," replied Wayne wearily, "I've told no one." He began to wish he'd never told the mayor, just shut the thing down and face the consequences afterwards. He was heartily tired of this silliness, these prevarications, and for what purpose? If driving over to the mayor's office was going to speed things up, then they'd have to go. "Okay," he finally said, "we'll be with you at 7.30, but we close-down the plant tonight, right?"

"Of course," replied the mayor with a relief that he hoped wasn't audible over the telephone. Had Headbold not agreed to come, he didn't quite know his next course of action. He took a little black notebook from his pocket, and ran his still shaking fingers along the telephone numbers until he found the Florida Haulage Company. He punched in the number and waited, nervously drumming his fingers on the desk. "Come on, come on, you bastard, answer the damn phone."

Eventually a voice said, "Florida Haulage."

It was a voice the mayor recognised. "Hi, Danny," he said cheerily. "I'm glad I caught you. It's Mayor Thompson."

"Oh." The voice on the other end of the line was hesitant. "If it's about that twenty grand I owe you, I'm trying to get it. I just need more time."

"Danny," the mayor said impatiently, "your time's run out. Have you got the cash or not?"

"No, man," was the sharp reply.

"Have you spoken to your father about your problem?" the mayor asked.

"Hell, you know I can't do that. He'd kill me," said Danny. There was real fear in his voice, which suited Mayor Thompson.

"Well, Danny," he said taking a long deep breath, "these guys you owe money to don't mess around."

Danny hesitated as if weighing up the partially veiled threat in the mayor's voice. At length he said, "I know, but what can I do? I'll do anything."

This was just what the mayor wanted to hear. "You could do me a big favour, Danny," he said. "I'll wipe the slate clean. I'll clear your debts and give you access to more white powder." He knew what Danny's answer would be; he could almost hear him clamouring to agree. Drug addicts like Danny made good foot soldiers; cocaine was a siren few of them could ignore.

"Yes," he said. "Whatever it is, I'll do it."

Chapter 26

Arlesford Hall, England

It was a beautiful September morning, the early orange glow of the sun flickering patterns of light on the surface of the swimming pool. Gerald Fitzgibbon strolled into the pool enclosure, a silk bathrobe draped around his naked frame, carrying a tray which contained coffee, two slices of lightly browned toast, a glass of orange juice and the *Sunday Times*. He placed the tray carefully on a cast iron Victorian conservatory table, retrieved the newspaper from between the orange juice and the toast rack, and settled back in his chair.

But today even the headlines, the usual catalogue of disasters, failed to hold his attention. His mind had slipped back to the previous evening when he had picked Mary up from her flat and they had driven out to Las Pacas disco, and had finished up at the hall making love in the swimming pool at about 2.30 in the morning. Perhaps, he thought with a little stab of guilt, that he was taking Mary too much for granted. She was always there when he wanted her, like an obedient dog. But last night seemed somehow different. Last night he'd felt real affection towards her. This frightened him, though he couldn't for the life of him think why. And this morning when he awoke to find her still sleeping beside him, an arm draped across his bare chest, he experienced a rare feeling of contentment.

But if Gerald had thought himself alone with Mary the previous night, he was mistaken. From the moment he had left to collect her, Hunaz Potra had been watching. He had followed them from the disco back to Arlesford Hall and had observed them from the cover of the shrubbery while they made love, and this morning he had returned. Gerald was under constant surveillance, and he suspected nothing.

He poured himself a coffee and ate the toast slowly. He perused the pages but nothing particular held his interest, and soon he rose and tugged at the silk cord around his waist, letting the robe slip from his body onto the floor. He stretched himself full height, taking in a great breath of air, expanding his chest. He felt good, and when he hit the water he swam vigorously to the far end, and then back again.

It was then that Hunaz began to move. He emerged from the bushes, crouching low. He carried a leather carpet bag, fairly capacious, and when he reached the side door of the pool enclosure he remained still. Gerald was in full stroke, his powerful legs and arms pumping through the water, totally unaware that he was being observed. At the near end of the pool, by the side door, he turned and began to swim back away from where Hunaz was crouching.

Quietly Hunaz opened the door, and moving low approached the edge of the pool. Cautiously he unzipped a corner of the leather bag and tipped its contents into the pool. Instantly the water came alive, as a long, thick sinewy body sunk and thrashed below the surface. The reptile was a good ten feet in length, battleship grey with a bluey tinge and it was almost as thick as a man's risk. *Dendroaspis polylepis*, the black mamba, one of the most dangerous snakes known to man. It could strike for 40% of its length, almost twice as far as the average snake, and its venom, secreted through a pair of large tubular fangs at the front its mouth, could excrete enough poison to kill ten men. It could move with great speed and, more importantly from Hunaz's point of view, it was quick to anger.

And it was angry now; the shock of the water had stung it into action. It was already only a few feet from the swimmer's receding back, and as Gerald turned at the far end of the pool, somersaulting beneath the water and pushing himself off with his feet, there was a collision of bodies. Gerald screamed as the snake struck, embedding its fangs in his neck. He tore at the whip-like body that thrashed around him, but the poison worked fast. The pain was intense. His mouth was full of water and vomit, his muscles weakened and then began to paralyse. Awful pains shot through his head and through his stomach. His vision blurred and his heart, always strong, thumped inside his chest like a sledgehammer. Yet Gerald still fought; he bit and clawed at the smooth rubbery coils until the end, and then he slipped below the surface, only to bob up again a few seconds later, blank, dead eyes wide open, staring at nothing. The body hung there in the water, rolling slightly.

Hunaz was pleased. So much could have gone wrong, but his plan had worked perfectly. He closed the door behind him as he left and made his way swiftly through the shrubbery back to his car, and drove as fast as he could to London.

Mary opened her eyes, stretched and looked about her. The bedside clock said eleven o'clock. She guessed Gerald was in the pool. "It will be nice to surprise him," she said to herself. She climbed out of bed and skipped down the stairs to the pool.

Opening the patio doors, she called, "Good morning, darling, sleep well . . .?" Her voice trailed off as she saw his lifeless body floating in the water. She clasped her hands to her mouth and sank to her knees. "No," she whispered. Then she screamed, "No! No!"

At twelve o'clock that same morning, Hunaz Potra boarded a British Airways jumbo at Heathrow, bound for Cuba. The stewardess showed him through to first class, and he settled back in his seat.

"Is there anything you require before take-off," the stewardess asked.

Hunaz hesitated for a moment, then he said, "Yes, champagne. I'll have a little celebration."

Chapter 27

San Remo Circle, Inverness

Claire was in the kitchen preparing supper. She glanced anxiously up at the clock on the kitchen wall. It was 7.30. Wayne was late. He should have been back half an hour earlier. She decided to ring the power plant. If he wasn't there soon, dinner would be ruined.

The technician, Tom, answered. He told her that Wayne and Betty had left in Wayne's car about half an hour before.

"Did they say where they were going?" Claire asked.

"No," said Tom hesitantly. "I did ask, but all Wayne said was that it was a personal matter and that they'd be back as soon as they could. That's all I can tell you – sorry."

"Okay, Tom, thanks anyway." Claire pressed the cancel button on the telephone. 'How strange,' she thought. 'It's not like Tom to be evasive. Does he know something that I don't?' She placed the phone on the table and returned to the kitchen in deep thought.

At the haulage depot Danny closed the door to the office and walked across the yard to where the articulated truck was parked. It was one of those huge vehicles with a front grill as big as a house. He reached up and opened the door and heaved himself up and into the driver's seat. For some minutes he sat motionless, staring through the huge high window, and then slowly he placed the keys in the ignition and started the engine. It came to life with a roar and the whole cab shook. It was a sound he had grown to love, the epitome of power. He depressed the clutch, pushed the lever into first gear, revved the engine and pulled away heading towards the highway.

Not too far away, and coming from the opposite direction, were Wayne Headbold and Betty. They were discussing the leakage and the effects on the community of closing-down the plant. After leaving the power station they had turned left just outside Inverness and

123

had taken the road which followed the country route along the edge of Lake Apopka.

Across the lake, Wayne could just see the power station as the sun set behind it. But he was in no mood for sightseeing. "It's a mess, Betty," he said, not taking his eyes off the road ahead. "A goddam mess."

Betty gave a little shrug of her shoulders, stared straight ahead and said nothing.

Meanwhile Danny had reached a T-junction and stopped the truck. He slipped it out of gear but kept the engine revs high.

The junction was at a corner curve where the road crossed over one of the canals linking Lake Apopka and Lake Henderson. The bridge at this intersection was constructed of concrete with a low parapet and no crash barriers.

Danny saw the white Chrysler coming around the bend some five hundred feet ahead. He could see the two occupants, a young woman and an older man, talking; the man was driving. He rammed the truck into first gear, revved the engine to a high pitch and, as the Chrysler approached the intersection, let out the clutch. The truck lurched forward right into the path of the oncoming car.

There was a loud thump, like the sound of a distant cannon, followed by the noise of shattering glass as truck and car collided. Sparks and metal splinters filled the air in a screaming cacophony of sound as the car, now on its side, was shunted towards the bridge. It struck the low parapet and hurtled into air. It spun as it dropped, turning over as if in slow motion until it hit the water. There was a red flash of flame, followed by an explosion, and fragments of searing metal scattered in every direction.

Betty and Wayne died instantly, their bodies torn and distorted under the force of the explosion and the intense heat. The water in the lake boiled and bubbled as remains landed on the surface sending clouds of steam into the air.

As the effects of the explosion subsided and the ripples of disturbance moved quietly to the sandy shoreline, an eerie silence descended. On the bridge above, the truck was skewed across the road, its nose embedded in one of the parapets, the front section of the cab caved in. Danny was still at the wheel. He did not move. There was a deep scarlet hole in the centre of his forehead where the rod supporting the sun visor had impacted, driving itself into his skull. His eyes were open, his face horribly distorted. His body still twitched; a trickle of blood ran slowly down his forehead over his cheekbones and, as it reached his lips, ebbed gently into his mouth.

Gordon Richardson was sitting in his garden when he saw the fireball at the far end of the lake and heard the explosions.

Senator Page and Mayor Thompson also saw the red glow over the lake from the mayor's office. Neither spoke. The senator's expression was cold, firm and tense; the mayor's one of profound shock.

After some seconds the senator spoke: "I think that takes care of one little problem," he said coolly.

The mayor remained rigid, his face white; and suddenly he began to sob, tears rolling down his rounded cheeks.

At home, Claire also heard the explosion and stopped what she was doing for a second. "Thunder," she said to herself. "We're in for a storm." Then she continued to prepare dinner. She was cooking something special, though wasn't sure Wayne deserved it, having not called her. He was clearly going to be late and she was still slightly concerned. She placed the lobster into the pot of boiling water, sprinkled salt into the pan and went into the living room to pour herself a gin and tonic. As she glanced across the lake there was a strange orange glow in the sky.

Chapter 28

Sugar Cane House, Inverness

Kevin O'Donnel was at home contemplating a steaming bowl of spaghetti bolognaise when the telephone rang. He dropped his fork. "Christ," he moaned, "can't even get time to eat – what a bloody job!" He lifted the telephone from the kitchen wall. "Sheriff O'Donnel," he snapped.

"Sir, it's me, Mark. I'm sorry to bother you, but it's bad news . . ."

"Well?" said the sheriff impatiently. "What is it?"

"There's been a serious road accident," explained the deputy. "Three fatalities on Lake Henderson Road."

"Local people?" asked the sheriff.

"I'm afraid so. Wayne Headbold, I believe, and a woman."

"My God!"

"And the third's Danny Goodyear."

"What in God's name happened?" the sheriff asked after some seconds.

"Well, it looks as if Danny came straight out onto the highway and didn't observe the stop sign. He hit the car side on and shunted it over the bridge into the lake."

"Right," said the sheriff, now fully alert. "I'm on my way. Keep the public away and organise Bud's boat. We'll have to recover the car."

"I've already done that," said the deputy. "We were unable to get hold of you earlier on. We have the two bodies, or what's left of them. I've placed them in Bud's lock-up garage."

"If it's that bad," said the sheriff, "how do you know it's Wayne?"

Mark hesitated. "I recognised what's left of his face."

When the sheriff arrived at the scene, Mark Wall had already set up a road block, and Deputy Jock Mackintosh was directing traffic away from the accident down a side road.

Mark moved a barrier back to let the sheriff's car through.

O'Donnel stopped next to the truck. It was skewed across the road, its front section caved in, its nearside mudguard bent and embedded in the front tyre. Danny was slumped over the steering wheel. Lucy Foster was in the cab about to examine the body.

Pieces of metal, fabric and tyres were strewn across the road and verges. The whole thing reminded him of his days in Vietnam, when they used to come across military vehicles that had been bombed by the Vietcong. In the middle of the highway was Wayne's black leather briefcase, the lid half hanging off. It was empty, its contents spread across the road.

O'Donnel could see his deputy by the edge of the bridge directing operations for the removal of the smashed car. He went over to him. "They didn't stand much of a chance," he said grimacing. "What a bloody mess."

Mark nodded. "I found what was left of the bodies floating near the bank, next to each other."

"You said you placed them in the garage?"

"That's right," replied the deputy taking a deep breath. He looked ill all of a sudden.

O'Donnel could see the nausea rising in his deputy's face. "Don't hold it back, son," he said.

Mark lunged for the bridge wall and vomited over the edge. "Sorry, sir," he said as he straightened up, wiping his mouth with his handkerchief.

The sheriff patted him on the shoulder. "It's okay," he said sympathetically. "It gets to us all sometimes."

The garage that contained the bodies was quite close, and as O'Donnel stepped into the building he could smell the stench of burnt flesh. He took off his hat, reached in his pocket for a handkerchief and held it over his nose and mouth. He turned on the light and raised the large sheet covering the remains. He was supposed to be used to this kind of thing, but these useless fatalities, even after years on the force still upset him; he would never get used to the horror of it all.

Betty's body was hardly recognisable. Her head was swollen and disfigured. Her hair had burnt off in the heat of the fire, leaving the top of her scalp charred and bloodied. Her left arm was missing and he could see the pink flesh and fragments of shattered bone where the arm had been torn off the body just below the elbow. The rest of her body was still partly clothed in a pink dress, now streaked with blood.

'What an awful waste,' he thought. Wayne's body was laid, like Betty's, face up. It was a dreadful sight, and hardly recognisable, though most of the structure of the face appeared to be intact. He looked to the side and stopped suddenly; the rear half of Wayne's skull and brain were missing. He closed his eyes and felt the bile rising in his own throat. 'At least,' he thought, 'they didn't suffer.'

He replaced the sheet, stepped outside and gulped in the clean fresh air. He needed to clear his head, compose himself.

He noticed Lucy Foster getting out of the cab by the roadside and went over to help her. "Hi," he said. "You okay?"

She nodded. "Yes, I'm okay, but I can't help thinking how life for all of us hangs by a mere thread waiting to snap," and she clicked her fingers.

"How did he die?" Kevin asked.

"Sun visor rod straight through the forehead," she said with a sigh. "He died instantly, thank God. He wasn't wearing a seat belt, must have shot forward under the impact, hitting the end of the visor with his head. He wouldn't have felt a thing."

"Can he be moved?" the sheriff asked.

"Yes," she replied leaning back against the truck, suddenly feeling exhausted. "I've done all I need to." She looked pale and vulnerable all of a sudden, not the patient professional he was familiar with.

"You know," he said dolefully, "sometimes I hate this job. I still get upset by what I have to deal with – death and destruction. The futility of it all. I suppose there's some cosmic reason behind it." He allowed himself a faint smile, as if lowering his guard was an embarrassment. "But, I couldn't do anything else, it's what I am. I'm plagued by this sense of duty, you see."

"So you're human after all, Sheriff." Lucy said with a wry smile. "Wonders never cease." She reached up and kissed him on the cheek. "You're okay," she said.

"Well that's as maybe," said the sheriff, feeling more embarrassed than ever. "Have you examined the bodies? Betty and Wayne's, I mean."

"Yes," said Lucy turning her face away from him. "Yes, what's left of them."

Deputy Wall, who had by this time recovered his composure, was coming towards them. "Can we remove the bodies, now?" he asked.

"Yes, of course," said Lucy. "I can't do any more here. Have you spoken to Claire yet?"

The sheriff glanced at Mark who shook his head. "No, not yet."

"Do you want me to do it?" asked Lucy.

"No," said the sheriff. "I'll speak to her, but I'd like you to come along, if that's all right."

"Of course," said Lucy.

"Right. Mark will take care of all the details and photographs. Let's go. I'll have to speak to Danny's father afterwards and contact Betty's next of kin, whoever they are. Oh, and Mark, get someone to drop Lucy's car off at her house."

They drove out to Claire's house in silence, both numbed by the sense of tragedy, by the incredulity of it, by the senselessness of it. They arrived at the house just as the orange Florida sun was disappearing in the west. All the lights in the house were on, and through the undrawn curtains they could see Claire working in the kitchen. The sound of romantic music drifted on the warm night air.

O'Donnel parked the car and they walked quickly up the front drive. Lucy rang the doorbell.

Claire called, "Is that you, darling? Forgotten your key again?" And then the door opened and she stood there, the welcoming smile draining from her face. "Why, Sheriff – Lucy – what . . . ?"

O'Donnel spoke first. "Claire, I'm terribly sorry – but can we come in. There's been an accident."

He took her arm gently and led her into the lounge. She sunk into a chair. She had gone numb; the sense of dread around her almost palpable.

"It's Wayne," said O'Donnel quietly, his throat tightening. "A tanker hit his car on the Henderson road. He died instantly."

At first Claire showed no response. She sat still, composed almost, her eyes fixed on a point somewhere beyond him, but her face was drained of colour; and then she closed her eyes and tears seeped through and down her cheeks. Lucy reached out and drew her close, holding her tightly as anguished sobs of pain and disbelief engulfed her.

O'Donnel felt inadequate. He touched Claire's shoulder lightly, compassionately. "Claire," he said, "I'm truly sorry." But there was no response, neither did he expect one. "I'll leave you for a while," he added, "there are things I need to attend to. Lucy will stay with you."

He was glad to get outside. He still had Danny Goodyear's parents to see, and that wouldn't be any easier; he had been their only child. And then there was Betty; he had to trace her next of kin. He shook his head. It wasn't just the act of death, he thought, the violence of that tragic moment, it was the vibrations it left behind, the grieving relatives – and friends – the shock of disbelief. It would change lives, alter perspectives, undermine faith. One had to be a cynic to ignore it all. He got into his car, turned on the ignition. He was a policeman, a professional; sentiment didn't come into it.

Chapter 29

Lake Henderson, Inverness

On the night of Wayne and Betty's death, Mayor Thompson had driven from the factory to the scene of the accident. Deputy Mark Wall saw his car approaching and beckoned him through the barrier. He told him what had happened. The mayor showed a great deal of concern and asked if there was anything he could do. Mark told him there wasn't and that everything that could be done was being done. This seemed to satisfy him. He nodded grimly, got back into his car and drove back to the factory where Senator Page was waiting for him. Mark thought he'd never seen a man looking so upset.

The mayor drove Senator Page to his house, and that night they locked themselves in the study and proceeded to get drunk on Southern Comfort and rye.

Next morning they woke to the sound of the mayor's wife, Marjorie, banging on the study door. "Abe!" she shouted. "Are you in there?"

The sound was painful to his head. He was slumped in his chair, his neck ached, his mouth felt dry. "Yeah, I'm here," he said weakly. "I'll be out in a minute."

By the sound of her voice she was none too pleased; he could almost see her shaking her head outside the door. This was not the first time he'd slept in his office, and his wife didn't like it.

Page, who was laid full length on the couch, opened his eyes painfully to the sound of Marjorie's banging. He felt bad. "What time is it?" he asked.

The mayor narrowed his eyes just enough to focus on the clock on the mantelpiece. "8.40," he said.

The senator got slowly to his feet, stretched, shook his head in an attempt to clear it, and staggered towards the bathroom.

The mayor stayed where he was, his mind preying on the accident and the part he had played, albeit unwillingly, in bringing it about. An enormous, mortifying sense of guilt, intensified by the after-effects of alcohol, swept over him. He didn't ever want to move from the safety of his seat; he wanted to stay where he was for ever, to sink into it, where nobody could touch him. There was the sound of the toilet flushing and the senator emerged, slamming the door behind him. Inside Abe Thompson's head the noise of that door slamming was intensified a hundred times. It made him sit up abruptly, back to reality, no escape through the armchair.

He fumbled with his crumpled shirt, eventually managing to tuck it into his trousers, and went upstairs to the bathroom. He stripped off his clothes, turned on the shower and began to scrub his soft, flabby body vigorously. He felt that if he scrubbed hard enough he could remove the guilt than clung to him like the morning dew outside. He knew that the killing of Wayne and Betty would haunt him for the rest of his life, his conscience was irreparably damned. In the privacy of his shower he felt like screaming, the water hitting the glass panel would drown the noise, but he wasn't sure – he might be heard, so instead he clamped his teeth against his bottom lip so that it bled, and the falling water turned red on his chest and tricked down to his toes.

He had no appetite for breakfast, though the senator, who appeared to be unaffected by the previous day's happenings, tucked into a mountain of ham and eggs as if he hadn't eaten for a week. Afterwards, Marjorie brought coffee to them on the patio overlooking the lake. She attributed her husband's low spirits to the aftermath of his drunken state, and had no sympathy for him.

When she had left, the senator dabbed his mouth with his napkin and said to Abe in a low voice, "We still have to deal with the problem of the missing cocaine. Now that I know you're not involved, Abe, there's no doubt that when the merchandise left the car and was thrown onto the boat at the lake, all 10 kilos were intact. I know that because I checked it myself."

"Are you suggesting that the stuff went missing between the shore and the factory?" Abe asked cautiously.

"That's exactly what I'm suggesting. Who picked up the merchandise from the lakeside?"

"Two local guys, Max Pace and Chuck Romford," Abe replied hollowly.

The senator thought for a moment, then said, "Have you seen any signs that either of them have come into money lately?"

'How the hell should I know?' the mayor thought to himself, but replied, "No, well, Max has a new car." It was the best he could do.

"Well, it's got to be one or both of them," the senator said. He leaned back in his chair and tapped his fingers nervously on the table. "Look, Abe," he said at length, "this business has got to be settled by tomorrow. We've lost too much time already."

"Well, how?" asked the mayor looking alarmed. He couldn't cope with any more violence.

"Ring them both up. Tell them I'm in town and want to go on a fishing trip. Say you want them to show me the best fishing holes. Offer them two hundred dollars each for the day, that should do it."

Abe couldn't see the point of it. "How will that tell us if they're guilty?" he asked.

"Once we're alone on the lake, I'll find out if they're guilty, believe me," the senator said coldly. "Now, please, would you telephone."

Reluctantly the mayor got up from his chair and went into the hall. He could feel the senator watching him through the glass doors. It was unnerving. He made the call and returned to the patio.

"That's okay," he said, "both men will be at the landing stage at twelve o'clock. I said we'd pick them up in my boat."

The senator looked pleased. "Good," he said nodding approval. A furtive smile spread across his face.

'Cunning bastard,' thought Abe. 'He seems to enjoy it; it's as if causing pain and fear to people turns him on.'

Marjorie had watched the two men through the kitchen window. There was something wrong, she could tell, and it sent a cold shiver down her spine. She moved out of view as the senator rose from the table to leave.

He walked across to his car which was parked on the lawn near the lake. He sat in the passenger side, picked up his mobile and hurriedly punched in a number.

"Good morning, Florida Power Company, how can we help you?" came the reply.

"This is Senator Page. I'd like to speak to director Dennis Camber. It's rather urgent."

"Just a moment, I'll check he's free." There was a click, and then silence for a few seconds. 'Slow,' he thought, 'always slow.' He began drumming his fingers along the front of the dashboard. 'Come on! Come on!'

"Good morning, Senator. How are you? Long time, no see." The hoarse voice of Dennis Camber was easy-going, relaxed. It was inappropriate to the senator's feelings, it was irritating, but he went along with it.

"I'm just fine," he said trying to contain his annoyance. "Look, I have a problem at the plant. My chief's been killed in a car accident. It was just terrible. But it's left me with no one in charge. I need someone to take it on, to run the plant, and I need them quickly, very quickly. Can you help?"

Camber noted the urgency in the voice, but said in his usually relaxed manner, "I'm sorry to hear about that, about the guy who was killed, I mean. Hell of a blow to his family."

"I know, I know, it's awful," said the senator trying to hide his impatience. "Look, I want somebody who'll do as he's told, if you understand my meaning."

"I think I do," said Camber after a long pause, "and I think I have just the guy. Name of John Critchley. He's a good engineer, but he has a problem . . ."

"What kind of problem?" He didn't want complications.

"Cocaine."

"Sounds perfect." The senator allowed himself a wry smile. "When can he start?"

"I'll have him at the plant by tonight," Camber said.

Chapter 30

San Remo Circle, Inverness

Lucy Foster stayed with Claire throughout the night. She had persuaded her into a stiff brandy after the sheriff had left. Claire had then gone to bed, but she hadn't slept much. She just lay there in the big double bed, eyes open, staring at the ceiling. And when eventually she closed her eyes, tears still lay on her cheeks. Lucy had pulled up a chair beside her and she, too, had eventually dropped off. When she awoke it was early morning, and the bed was empty. Crumpled sheets and a tear-stained pillow were the only signs that Claire had been lying there.

Lucy ran anxiously down the stairs to the kitchen, but Claire was not there. She rushed outside but still there was no sign; and then, moving towards the lake, she spotted her sitting cross-legged on the landing stage, staring out across the mirrored surface. There was no wind, the sky clear and deep; it appeared the world was at peace.

Lucy's first reaction was to run towards her, but her medical training held her back. Turning, she went back into the house, thinking that she would make some breakfast for them both. In the kitchen sat the remnants of the meal Claire had been busily preparing the previous night. Lucy set about clearing away. Then she went through the cupboards to find what there was for breakfast. She found enough to prepare a breakfast of waffles, toast, orange juice and strong coffee. She found a large wicker tray, laid everything out and carried it through to the garden. Claire was still sitting by the lake, and when Lucy approached her, she turned and smiled a sad thanks, thanks for just being there.

"I thought you could do with some breakfast," Lucy said with a nervous smile. "I think I've brought everything we need." She placed the tray on the landing stage and sat down next to Claire. Then she took off her sandals and dangled her feet in the cold water, sending rippled across the surface of the lake.

Some fifty feet offshore the old alligator stirred. Lying half

134

submerged he had sensed the movement of the ripples, and he waited expectantly for a further sign of approaching prey. He could see the two women on the landing.

"You know, it's funny," Claire said wistfully, "but yesterday, before you and the sheriff arrived, I was thanking God for everything I had; we'd been out on the lake all day, even made love." She hesitated and shook her head wearily. "Why? Oh Christ, why . . .?" She sighed and looked up at the clear blue sky as if searching for an answer. "I'm sorry," she murmured. "I'm making a fool of myself."

"Don't be silly," Lucy said. "Just remember I'm not only your doctor, I'm also your friend. You can rely on me. I mean that."

"Do you know something," Claire continued. "I know it's ridiculous, but what keeps going over and over in my mind is why he was on the Henderson road and what was Betty doing with him in the car? She was supposed to be on duty."

Lucy frowned. "I don't know the answer to that," she said, "and I didn't know Wayne that well, but in my job you learn to judge character, and I am sure he was not the sort of man to let you down. I'm sure that you were the only woman he loved. There must be some other explanation."

"She did telephone last night," Claire said. "I answered the call. She wouldn't speak to me. She said it was urgent – wanted Wayne."

"What was the problem?"

"He wouldn't say. After he'd spoken to Betty he went off – just went. There was something wrong, I know. He looked worried." Claire buried her face in her hands and began to sob again.

"Try to eat some breakfast," suggested Lucy soothingly. "It'll make you feel better."

Claire shook her head and sighed. "No, no, I'm really not hungry, thank you. I'd just like to sit here for a while, if you don't mind. I need to think."

Lucy was about to apologise and tell her she fully understood when the telephone in the house rang. She jumped up and ran across the lawn to answer it. It was Sheriff O'Donnel wanting to know how Claire was.

"She's as well as can be expected," said Lucy breathlessly. "She's still suffering from shock. It'll take time."

"Lucy, I know it's probably too early, but I need to talk to Claire soon. I have to find out why Wayne and Betty were on that road."

"Well it's no good asking her that," retorted Lucy sharply. "She'd like to know the answer herself."

"You've talked to her then?"

"We've had some conversation, but she's naturally still very upset.

She's also torturing herself thinking about Betty and her boyfriend in the car together."

"Well," said O'Donnel, "you never can tell. Two people working together – all the time. Get to know each other pretty well. Sexual chemistry and all that."

The implication in his voice irritated Lucy even more. If he really thought they were having an affair why didn't he just say it instead of making veiled insinuations. "I'm sorry, Kevin," she said forcibly, "but I cannot believe that Wayne would be unfaithful to Claire. I won't believe it."

"Okay, perhaps you're right. Don't let Claire dwell on it. I'll find out my own way. Oh, and by the way," he said in a softer tone, "thanks for staying up with Claire last night – beyond the call of duty."

"Oh, it's not duty. I wanted to. Look, I'm sorry I'm a bit snappy, but I'm feeling a little stressed out myself, and I have to stay with Claire for the time being, at least until I think she can be left on her own. Would you telephone the clinic and let them know?"

"Already done," said O'Donnel. "I telephoned your partner last night. He said to tell you he'll cover for as long as it takes."

"Thanks, I forgot to let him know – too much to think about last night."

"Right. Look, I'll speak to Claire later. You take care of yourself."

"I will, and thanks," said Lucy.

After she'd replaced the receiver, she stood by the telephone for a few moments thinking of Kevin O'Donnel, though why she did so, she didn't quite understand. For the most part she found him irritating with an unfortunate knack of saying the wrong thing at the wrong time, yet he was intriguing too, in a rough, somewhat blunt kind of way.

Suddenly the door flew open and Claire stood there, her face drawn and tense, her hands working nervously at the hem of her skirt. "Who was that on the phone?" she demanded to know in snatched syllables.

"It was the sheriff, Claire," Lucy said calmly. "He rang to see how you were."

"What did you say?"

"I said you were okay. You'll make it."

Claire stiffened, her eyes widening, and then she appeared to crumple, and dashed past Lucy into the bedroom where she flung herself onto the bed and gave way to a paroxysm of grief. The full horror of what had happened had finally sunk in, the numbness that nature permits had worn off. Lucy knew that Claire's grieving would run its course like a fever, and then die. Claire would then sleep, and when she awoke she would be calmer and at ease with herself.

Chapter 31

Lake Apopka, Inverness

By the time Senator Page and Mayor Thompson reached the landing stage it was 12.30. Max Pace and Chuck Romford were lounging about drinking from cans of beer; both men looked slightly drunk. As the boat approached they hurriedly collected up fishing rods and boxes of bait.

The mayor swung the boat slowly and skilfully alongside the landing stage and the two men jumped aboard.

"Gentlemen," he shouted above the roar of the engine, "this is Senator Page. I trust you two are going to find us some good fishing this afternoon."

"Sure thing," replied Pace, doing his best to sober up. "Make towards Alligator Island, there's a deep pool I know, usually has some big fish in it."

The boat pulled away and headed for the north of the lake. They passed Rastos dozing in his hammock by the shore. The sound of the boat woke him and he waved.

'If they're going fishing,' he mused, 'I hope they have more luck than me. I ain't caught nothing for days.' He chuckled to himself. 'It sure is strange. No fish – can't understand it.'

It was hot, the surface of the lake a mirror, reflecting the heat of the sun which blazed unhindered from a sky bereft of cloud. Herons perched in trees as if wilting from the heat. The mayor was sweating profusely, his head ached, his brain felt numb, he was unable to think with any semblance of clarity.

They rounded the bay and eased the boat towards the area Pace had indicated. For some time they fished but nobody caught anything. Pace and Romford were concerned. If nothing was caught they might not get paid, and the senator did not appear to be in the best of moods. They began to wonder why he'd wanted to come fishing. People that went fishing did so because they liked fishing.

After some time the mayor said, "Well, it doesn't look as though we're in luck today."

"I can't understand it," said Romford, shaking his head. "Only two weeks ago I took four fish over six pounds out of this hole. I don't get it." He lifted his baseball cap and scratched his sweaty forehead, and as he did so he cast a glance towards Senator Page.

It was at that precise moment that the senator moved. He lunged at Pace who was completely caught off his guard, and before he could speak he felt the cold muzzle of a Colt revolver rammed against his temple. The speed of the senator's actions even caught the mayor by surprise. Romford stood frozen to the spot.

"Now," said the senator quietly, "one false move from you, Romford, and your buddy is gone. Understand?"

Romford understood. The menace in the senator's voice was enough to convince him that this man meant what he said. He nodded quickly; the sweat trickled from under his hat and down the side of his face onto his craggy, unshaven neck.

"Now, on the deck," the senator ordered. "Feet and hands outstretched."

Romford dropped to the floor and laid out flat.

The senator nodded towards the mayor and told him to check for weapons.

The mayor lowered himself to his knees beside Romford's outstretched body. His hands were shaking. Nervously he went over the body feeling for weapons, but there were none. The mayor's shirt hung around his flabby body like a wet towel dropped in a swimming pool; it was saturated with sweat. He was frightened, very frightened. He wasn't cut out for this and wished he'd never got involved.

Addressing the two men in the same quiet, menacing tone, the senator said, "Let me make one thing quite clear, I know very well that you've been delivering a certain merchandise to the mayor's factory each month, but we've hit something of a problem." He paused and increased the pressure of the gun barrel against Pace's temple. "Now," he went on, "the problem is this: Every month this merchandise appears to be short by one kilo. I've looked into the matter of course, quite thoroughly in fact, and I've come to the conclusion that the only people who could possibly be causing this problem, are you two . . ."

Pace swallowed, with difficulty as his mouth was dry; Romford tried to claw his way through the deck.

Pace suddenly spoke up: "I don't know what you're taking about," he stammered. "We didn't know the bags contained cocaine."

"Who said anything about cocaine?" the senator said. "I certainly didn't. But I'll tell you something, my patience is running out." And with that he cocked the hammer of the Colt.

"Okay, okay!" Romford cried out. "Don't shoot him. I'll tell you where we put the stuff, but I swear we only got rid of half the stuff we stole. I swear it. The rest is still where we dumped it."

"Well," asked the senator, "where is that?"

"We – we dumped it in the lake near the power unit," Romford stammered.

The senator glanced at the mayor. "Abe," he said calmly, "there's a spare gun in my jacket over there. Would you get it, please?"

The mayor took the gun from the jacket and carefully and held it down by his side as if afraid it might go off.

"Abe, point the bloody thing at these two," the senator told him. "Don't just dangle it."

The mayor did as he was instructed, but his thoughts were in disarray. His hand was still shaking and he felt sick. For one brief moment of fancy he thought of turning the gun on the senator, but he knew he couldn't pull the trigger. 'What a bloody mess,' he thought.

"Abe! Cover him."

The mayor moved closer to Romford and held the gun barrel, unsteadily, close to his head.

"Now, Max," the senator said, "I'm going to let you get up, but slowly, mind. No false moves, just nice and easy." Slowly and deliberately he withdrew the barrel of the gun from Pace's temple, letting him rise. "Now," he said, "which way?"

Pace raised a dirty hand. "Over there to the west," he pointed. "You can just see the power unit from here."

As they passed close to the old alligator's den, the reptile stirred and opened its eyes. It was aware of the boat and moved ponderously towards the foreshore. It slid languidly into the water with hardly a ripple on the surface, and watched as the boat passed by.

The alligator was now totally dependent on its daily dose of sugar residue contained in the fish. The radioactive water had transformed it into a monster that feared nothing, least of all man. Its appetite was insatiable. Its problem, finding enough to eat. Over the past four weeks it had cleared out the bass from most areas of the bay; it needed a new source of nourishment. The old gator was now some twenty feet in length and its lower jaw, by some trick of nature had grown much bigger than its upper.

This had caused its teeth to desynchronise, resulting in a number of those in the top jaw puncturing the soft flesh in the lower. This caused the creature such intense pain when it closed its mouth, that it would thrash about in a frenzy whenever it fed.

It watched as the boat passed and then followed, gliding just below the surface, fifty feet to the rear. When the boat stopped at the drop-off point, the alligator moved closer until it was within fifteen feet of the stern.

The senator had dropped the throttle and the boat rolled slightly, water lapping its sides. "Can we be seen from the power unit?" he asked.

Romford shook his head. "No, I don't think so," he replied, slightly unsure of himself.

The mayor felt mildly relieved. 'If the cocaine's here,' he thought, 'then that will be the end of the matter. We could let these two go. They wouldn't dare double-cross. The senator has put the fear of God into them both.'

"Well?" the senator snapped, staring at Romford. "Where is it?"

"On the lake bottom," replied Romford nervously. "We dropped it there for safe keeping on block anchors so that we could retrieve it easily."

"Well – how do we get it? By praying?"

"Take the gaff," said Max Pace. "About six feet below the waterline you should hit a wire trace. Pull it up by the stem and just keep trawling it in. The dope's anchored to the line at varying depths."

Senator Page glanced towards the mayor without speaking. He grabbed hold of the long gaff, plunged it into the water and swept it along the side of the boat. He did this three times, his irritation increasing with each futile sweep, but no wire trace.

"It's not here," he snarled, his voice hardening. He was losing patience again.

"It must be, I swear," stammered Romford.

The senator made another and final sweep and suddenly the gaff jerked as it struck the trace. Slowly he hauled it up to the side of the boat and grabbed the wire with both hands, but it was too heavy a job for one man. He called to Max Pace to give him a hand, telling the mayor to keep him covered, and if he made a wrong move, to shoot Romford.

Pace took hold of the wire and began hauling.

The senator cast a cold glance at the man next to him. "I hope you haven't lied to me, boy," he said menacingly.

Max stayed silent. His reply came in the form of bunches of silver foil suddenly flashing in the water as the line came up, the foil snapping in the soft breeze that now fanned the surface of the lake. Aluminium foil, disfigured pieces of rubbish.

The senator's eyes narrowed; the skin across his cheekbones became taught and drained of colour. "You double-crossing bastards," he yelled, and grabbing Pace by the collar he flung him across the deck towards where Romford was cowering.

The senator had taken out his gun and was about to aim it at the two men when Mayor Thompson flung himself between them. It was a dangerous thing to do at that moment, and had the mayor thought about it too much, he'd never have done it.

"Look, Wesley," he stammered, "I think these guys are telling the truth. Someone's found the dope and taken it. These two have been set up."

"And what makes you so damned sure about that?" the senator asked, still in an ugly mood.

Mayor Thompson, appealing to common sense, replied, "Wesley, would they have brought us to this spot if they knew there was nothing here?"

The senator lowered his gun. "Okay, Abe, you've got a point," he said reflectively. "I'm going below, but if they move an inch, you know what to do."

"Wesley?"

"Kill them both."

Chapter 32

Inverness Rum Brewery

Peter Cooper was slowly manoeuvring the barge full of residue around the headland towards the power unit area, when he caught sight of the boat moored over the drop zone.

"Damnation!" he swore out loud. 'It must be fishermen. I'll have to pull back and wait,' he thought. 'They shouldn't be there – it's supposed to be out of bounds.'

He couldn't identify the boat as the light was fading, but he could make out three men aboard, though he couldn't see what they were doing. He pushed the rudder to the right and inched the boat into a reed bed so that he was out of sight of the intruders, and switched off the electric motor.

In the fading light the mayor glanced over towards the power unit. His mind was wandering; he couldn't stop thinking of the accident, of the mangled bodies of Wayne and Betty – people he had known, and he had been part of their misfortune. Guilt was a burden of intense pain that he carried always; sometimes he felt as if it were driving him insane.

Chuck Romford was watching the mayor intently. It was obvious to him that the man's mind was not on the job. His eyes kept wandering away, as if searching for something across the water – and with the senator still down below in the cabin – one chance he had, and once chance only.

He flung himself at the mayor with a courage driven by panic, one hand bunched into a fist that hammered into the side of the mayor's head and sent him reeling, the other reaching for the gun. But the blow had not been enough. The mayor was dazed by the sudden onslaught, but not out. Romford grabbed the mayor's arm, forcing it into the air, putting the weapon beyond reach, and for a brief moment both men were locked in a deadly embrace. Then Romford felt a hard pull on his shoulder, and as he turned towards this new threat, Senator Page shot him through the forehead at point blank range. The back of Romford's skull fragmented, and his body slumped on top of the mayor, who felt blood covering his chest, seeping across his white shirt and into his skin.

With a roar he flung the body aside. Bile rose in his throat and he vomited. "Christ!" he screamed, tears burning his eyes. "Christ! Oh Christ! There was no need to kill him. What have you done? What in Christ have you done!"

At that moment, Max Pace, realising that his own life now depended on swift action, made a charge for the side of the boat, but before he reached it a bullet hit him just above his left knee, sending him reeling backwards, screaming in agony. But his agony was short-lived as Senator Page aimed again at the squirming figure and put a bullet into his head. Pace died instantly, but his body twitched and writhed on the deck of the small boat for several awful minutes in a deepening mess of blood and gore before it lay still.

In the ensuing silence, which seemed to envelop the boat in a dark cloak, the mayor sank to his knees sobbing, his clothes and face still smeared with Romford's blood. "What a mess," he said, "What an awful, awful, bloody mess." Then he looked up to see the senator standing there above him, still holding the gun. "Why?" he questioned. "What have you done?"

For several seconds the senator gave no answer. He simply stood, rigidly staring at Pace's bloody body as if mesmerised by it. Then suddenly, as if someone had slapped his face, he seemed to snap back to reality and said almost briskly, "What have I done? I'll tell you what I've done. I've saved both our skins, that's what I've done. Now, Abe, pull yourself together, there's work to be done."

But Abe Thompson was in no mood for work. He had by now dragged himself across the deck and was wedged in a corner blubbering like a bullied schoolboy. Suddenly he felt the cold barrel of the Colt revolver against his neck. There was a click as the hammer was pulled back.

The mayor stopped crying and looked up to meet cold, grey eyes. "You wouldn't?" he stammered.

"Try me," the senator said. "We're both in this too deep, you and me. Now what I suggest you do is stop blubbering and give me a hand. It's your choice, Abe – your choice." It was said with such cool menace that the mayor was in no doubt as to the consequences if he didn't comply.

"Okay, okay. Okay, Wesley, I'm with you," he said struggling to his feet, though at first he didn't think his legs would hold him. Like the rest of him they were shaking.

The senator looked about him, assessing the situation. After some seconds he said, "Right, now, we can't take these two back to shore, so we'll have to dump them here in the lake. Do you think anyone will have heard the shots, Abe?"

The mayor shook his head. "If they have they'll think it's hunters," he said shakily.

"Right," the senator said again, as if he'd just thought of a bright idea, which he had. "We'll use the trace line. Tie the bodies to the trace line and lower away with the anchor blocks at one end. Problem solved. No one will ever find them. Good idea?"

He was appealing to the mayor, who simply nodded wearily, although he thought it a bad idea. Anything to do with Wesley Page was a bad idea, but he was too frightened to say so.

"Come on then, let's get a move on."

Securing the two bodies to the trace line was not an easy job, particularly when they were slippery with blood, but eventually they succeeded and the bodies disappeared into the depths, secured fast to the trace line and weighed down with the anchor block.

They stood and watched the receding line in silence. A strange, uneasy calm descended on the boat, even the senator appeared effected by it. The mayor sank to the deck, crossed his legs beneath him and lowered his head into his hands. Neither man spoke. The senator still stood, as if in a trance, his eyes fixed on the dark water.

After some time Mayor Thompson rose wearily, unbuttoned his blood-soaked shirt and threw it on the deck. A change had come over him. He felt differently. Fear had given way to a kind of resignation, an acceptance of the obvious fact that his soul was now brutalised beyond redemption. He was an outcast in the eyes of God, in the eyes of his fellow man. He no longer cared what happened to him. His life was blighted beyond any hope of salvation. He started the Johnson motor, pulled up the anchor and eased the boat slowly around, glancing into the water as he did so. The bodies by now were on the bottom of the lake. 'Food for the fishes,' he thought impassionately.

He glanced at the blood-stained deck, and suddenly felt a surge of anger. He pulled both throttle levers back to their maximum, raising the bow of the launch high in the water, and throwing the senator off his feet, so that he sprawled on the deck, staining his yellow shirt and grey slacks with the congealing blood of his two victims.

"For Christ's sake, slow down!" he shouted at the mayor.

But Abe Thompson took no notice and kept the throttles pulled far back.

The boat raced across the lake, past Peter Cooper's concealed position in the reed beds. He'd heard the shots but had seen nothing. He assumed there were hunters about. He decided, therefore, that it was too big a risk to dump the residue that night as he was bound to be seen, so as soon as the launch was out of sight, he eased the boat out of the reeds and headed back to the factory, where he covered the barge with a tarpaulin. He then went to Murphy's Bar.

After they had reached the landing stage and secured the launch, the senator and Mayor Thompson stripped off their clothes down to their undershorts and placed the stained clothing in the lower deck next to the engine room.

As the senator stepped off the boat he turned to the mayor who was busy locking the door to the cabin. "Burn it," he said.

"What?" enquired the mayor.

"You heard. Burn it. We can't take any risk."

"Do you realise how much this cost?" said the mayor in a half-hearted attempt to argue.

"I don't give a damn how much it cost," the senator said angrily. "Just burn it."

"Well, I can't do it here," said the mayor. "I'll have to tow her down one of the old channels, miles from anywhere."

"Tow it where you like," the senator said, "but get on with it. I'm going to shower and change. I must ring Cuba," and with that he disappeared into the dark deserted factory.

Mayor Thompson walked across the landing, unhooked a small fishing punt from the edge of a pontoon, pulled it round to the launch and tied it to the stern.

He climbed aboard the launch, started the engine and headed off towards a secluded deep-water pool that he knew.

When he reached his destination, he laid down the anchor, dowsed the deck in petrol and climbed into the punt. He started the outboard after several pulls and then let it idle. He was sweating, even though all he had on were boxer shorts. Reaching from the boat, he took a handful of dry brown reeds and twisted them into a tight, stiff torch. With a lighter, which he always kept in the boat, he lit the torch. The reeds were so dry that they instantly caught alight, and he tossed the flaming mass onto the deck of the cruiser. There was a sudden whoosh of flame which ran across the length of the deck and then quickly took hold. The air was full of petrol fumes. He rammed the outboard onto full power in order to distance himself from the launch as quickly as possible.

Even as he began to move away, an explosion ripped through the open door to the lower cabin, and the launch began to sink. By the time he was two hundred feet away she was almost gone. He turned just in time to see her stern disappearing below the water, and seconds later there was nothing there.

Back at the factory he telephoned the Inverness Police Department and informed them that his launch had disappeared from its moorings.

Chapter 33

Mitcham Creek, Inverness

Gordon Richardson woke on Saturday morning with his alarm bleating, ping, ping, into his right ear. He reached out in the darkness, as if by instinct, and dropped his hand onto the red button. He rubbed his eyes and sighed.

Sheila stirred for a brief moment, moaned and then dropped back into an alcohol-induced sleep. He glanced down at her as he sat back against the bed headboard. She had aged in the last three months. Her once smooth olive skin was now pale and taught and dark rings showed beneath her puffed red eyelids. Even in sleep she was not at peace with herself; her eyelids kept on flickering and her head occasionally jerked from side to side with some inner torment.

Over the past few weeks things had deteriorated between them. All she seemed to want to do was lie in bed until noon, and when she rose it was to pour herself a large gin and tonic and go and sit with it by the lakeside, where, throughout the rest of the day, she would drink herself into a drunken stupor.

Every evening when he arrived home from the gallery, she was there with a glass in her hand, too inebriated even to greet him. They seldom spoke, and on the odd occasion when she was actually sober, their conversation was restricted to one word syllables. They never made love; she would never permit him to become that intimate. To her he appeared not to exist.

Occasionally she would call out in her dreams, "Julian! Julian! Please forgive me!"

It was disturbing, and it baffled him. Why should she call out their son's name? And why was she asking for forgiveness? Why was she blaming herself all the time for Julian's death? He had died in an accident. There was no blame.

He reached out and touched her cheek, but she turned her head away, and raised her hand against his defensively. Every night was the same.

It was 7.30 a.m. before Gordon was dressed and breakfasted. Before he left the house he opened the bedroom door and whispered, "Sheila, I'm going now. Don't forget, I'll see you at the gallery at 5.30 – for the party."

His wife responded with a faint groan and turned away from him.

"Sheila, did you hear me?"

"I hear you," she murmured.

"You'll be there, then? You promise you'll come. I need you there."

"Shut the door behind you – PLEASE."

He closed his eyes. 'Why does it always have to be like this?' he thought. 'If she could only stay sober for one day.'

He closed the door behind him. He needed fresh air, so he made his way down to the lake. He felt frustrated, perplexed, even angry. The gentle lapping of the water on the white sandy beach subdued much of it, but it still festered beneath the surface. He noticed Sheila's chair, where she had left it the night before, and nearby two empty gin bottles half hidden by a wild rubber plant. He bent down and picked them up, and hurled them as far as he could into the lake.

Just offshore the old alligator was resting on the surface. It had been hunting all night and had only managed to feed on a couple of bass and one stray otter. It had been a poor night's work and it was still hungry.

The impact of the bottles on the surface of the water had aroused its attention, and it moved towards them, grabbing one of the bottles and crushing it between its jaws. The result of this was a mouthful of shattered glass, a thousand jagged particles of pain that bit into the soft tissue of its mouth. In an effort to free itself from the torment, it stretched its jaws and rolled over on the surface of the water, and as it did so the water turned red.

Gordon returned to the house, and ten minutes later was driving down the highway towards the gallery. He loved going there, loved the pictures, all now carefully positioned on the walls. He allowed himself a brief moment of contemplation. Looking at them eased his tension, the colour, texture, mood of a picture had a soothing effect. And when he moved the pictures around, into different areas of the gallery, each one reacted differently when hung in its new position. Some pictures showed better in a soft light, others in a stronger one. He never managed to get it just right.

His thoughts were disturbed by a knock on the door, and there was Margaret Cooper, her hands full of boxes. She was early. "I couldn't sleep," she explained, "so I popped into the deli on my way to pick up your order for sandwiches and other things."

"Well, thank you," said Gordon. "That's kind of you."

"Oh, that's okay," she said breezily dropping the boxes onto the table. "All in a day's work."

Margaret had been working in the gallery for two weeks, and it was only now that Gordon realised how pretty she was. Her features were soft and round, which gave her a cheeky look, and her light blonde hair hung down over her shoulders like a horse's mane. She had bright, light-blue eyes.

"I'm looking forward to this evening," she said, her face partly hidden beneath her blonde fringe. "But it's a pity about the accident – makes you feel guilty enjoying yourself."

Gordon nodded. He felt guilty, too. "I know what you mean," he said, "but it's too late to change the date now, everything's organised."

Chapter 34

Inverness Police Department

Following the accident in which Betty and Wayne had died, Sheriff O'Donnel had conducted intensive interviews with everyone close to them, but he could find no logical explanation as to why the two of them should have been together on the Lake Henderson road that evening.

What was even stranger was the fact that Danny Goodyear, the driver of the truck, was supposed to have been taking his girlfriend out to the local bar that night, but he'd never turned up at 6.30 to pick her up as planned.

O'Donnel had interviewed Danny's father, who was in deep shock over his son's death. He could not or would not give a reason why his son had been driving the truck that evening.

Claire had been unable to give an explanation. Yes, she confirmed that Wayne had taken a phone call from Betty, and in response to that had left for the plant in a hurry, and without telling her anything. And, yes, he had looked concerned, but not unduly so.

Tom, the technician, had also confirmed that Wayne had called at the plant at around 6 p.m. where Betty had met him, and they had entered into a close discussion. Wayne had then made a couple of telephone calls after which the two of them had left the plant together.

Even Claire had to admit that everything did rather point to an affair. On reflection, she thought, Wayne had practically begged Betty to take the job at the plant.

Sheriff O'Donnel had only known Wayne and Betty for a few months. He felt he was a good judge of character, and in his own mind he did not believe that they were lovers, and had told Claire so, but in her confused state of mind, Claire would not be reassured. Her recurring nightmare was that her boyfriend and Betty were having an affair.

In the middle of his investigations, Sheriff O'Donnel received a telephone call from Chuck Romford's mother. She told the sheriff that her son and Max Pace had gone fishing together some days ago, and hadn't returned. She was very worried.

The sheriff, while noting her concern, reminded her that this sort of thing had happened before. On a number of previous occasions they had both arrived home looking like a couple of tramps after a drunken binge in Orlando or Tampa, and once they had spent a whole week away living it up in Miami. The sheriff had suggested they wait a little longer before he filed a missing persons report, to which May Romford agreed.

At around 1.00 p.m. on Saturday the sheriff returned to his office with the post-mortem results. Wayne's body contained some traces of alcohol, but well within the proscribed limits, whilst Betty's showed negative. The report on Danny, however, indicated that he had taken cocaine just a few hours prior to the accident. It seemed pretty certain that drugs were to blame.

The sheriff leaned his elbows on the desk and sunk his head in his hands. He felt tired, washed out. He couldn't get the accident off his mind. It was a bad one. He felt it could have been avoided. A kid on drugs in charge of a ten-ton truck! Lethal combination!

He heard the door behind him open and he turned to find Lucy Foster standing there.

"What have you been reading?" Dr Foster asked.

"Oh, the post-mortem reports," he said. "It appears young Danny had been on drugs."

"Ah! And are you going to keep this quiet as you did with Christy?" she asked with a tinge of sarcasm.

The sheriff thought about this, then said, "In that situation I'm afraid I have to, but I swear to you there was ample reason. Sometime I'll explain it all to you. That I promise."

Lucy stood looking at him, not overly convinced by what he had said, but willing to give him the benefit of the doubt. "Okay," she said, "I'll accept that."

"Grateful thanks," he said, meeting her eyes. "You look a bit washed out."

"I am," Lucy replied. "I've just left Claire. She's sleeping at the moment, and she's much better. At least I think she can cope on her own now. So tonight I'm going to sleep in my own bed."

"What about long-term?" the sheriff asked. "Will she be okay?"

Lucy shrugged her shoulders. "Who can say?" she said, faintly irritated by questions she could not possibly answer. "Eventually she'll come to terms with Wayne's death. She's not the only person to lose a boyfriend." She sighed and rubbed her forehead. "I'm sorry," she said wearily. "It's just that I'm tired and I feel so useless."

"I understand," the sheriff said sympathetically. He got up from his chair. "Come here," he said.

Without really thinking, Lucy obeyed.

"Now turn around."

She did so and O'Donnel gently massaged her shoulders. In spite of his large hands his touch was tender and she leaned back against him. "Hmm, that feels good," she murmured, and then she laughed and closed her eyes.

O'Donnel kissed her softly on the cheek. She didn't pull away. He kissed her again and held her tight. There was real tenderness in his embrace, and Lucy felt a warm and rare sense of calm.

"Dinner tonight?" he whispered. Then, without waiting for a reply, he said, "Of course, I forgot, there's the gallery opening tonight. We could go to that together."

Lucy thought for a moment, then said, "Fine. I'd like that, but I'd better first check that Claire will be okay on her own tonight. I can ring you later and let you know. Now I really must get back."

"If it helps," O'Donnel said, "we could drop in on Claire after we've been to the gallery – make sure she's okay."

"That'll be nice," she said. At the door she turned and added, "I'll ring you later, and thanks."

Chapter 35

The Gallery, Inverness

Gordon glanced at his watch. It was five o'clock. Everything was almost ready, the food and drinks laid out on the tables, glasses standing ready on silver trays. The caterers were adding the final touches.

Margaret had gone home to get changed. She returned in a pretty flowered pastel-coloured dress, which Gordon thought did wonders for her slim figure and small, firm breasts. She was fussing around like a mother hen.

He checked his watch again. He felt unnecessarily nervous. It was only fifteen minutes before the guests were due to arrive and there was still no sign of Sheila. In his office he picked up the phone and dialled home. He knew from past experience that if his wife had been down by the lake drinking all day, it would take a while for her to answer, so he let it ring for longer than usual.

Eventually, a husky voice drawled, "Hello? Gerald, is that you?"

At first he didn't answer. "It's Gordon, not Gerald," he snapped. "What the hell are you doing there? And why did you call me Gerald?"

There was an embarrassed silence on the end of the telephone.

"Look," he said irritably, "the party starts in ten minutes; I need you here. We'll discuss Gerald later."

"Unfortunately, my dear Gordon," she replied, scornfully slipping over her words, "I do not think I will be available today. I'm not feeling very well."

"You mean you're too damn drunk. Just for once couldn't you have stayed sober! This evening's important to me. You know that."

"It was very important to *me*, my dear, that I got drunk." This she appeared to find amusing as she began to giggle.

He knew there was no further point in trying to persuade her, besides which it was no good if she arrived drunk. He slammed the phone down. He was angry and disappointed. 'Just this once,' he thought, 'she could have stayed sober for me.'

He sat at his desk for a while to calm his nerves, then he adjusted his tie and went back into the gallery, trying to look more relaxed and confident than he felt.

He told Margaret that his wife would not be coming, that she was unwell.

Margaret looked down at the carpet. She knew what unwell meant. "I'm sorry," she said. "Perhaps I'd better get you a drink."

"No," he said hesitantly. "You have one."

"It'll help you relax," Margaret said.

"Mmm. Perhaps. Glass of white, then," he said.

Margaret returned a few moments later with two glasses. "Here's to a successful show," she said raising her glass.

"To a successful show," Gordon replied, raising his own.

After Gordon had slammed down the phone, Sheila had held it to her ear for a few seconds. It made such a horrid noise, the ringing tone buzzing in her head. Her hand began to shake violently. She tried to replace the receiver, but instead missed the table and sent the whole thing clattering to the floor.

'Oh,' she thought, 'poor Gordon. He won't be able to ring me. I must put it back.' She began to giggle again, knelt on the floor and purposefully pushed the telephone under the settee, patting it as she did so. "There, you'll be safe there," she said to herself. With difficulty she managed to get to her feet, her long black hair covering her bloated face, and staggered through the lounge out into the garden, eventually flopping down like a sack into the chair that stood beside the lake.

Reaching beneath the seat she groped around for the bottle of gin she knew was hidden there. Finding it, she unscrewed the top with shaking hands and raised the bottle to her lips. She swallowed thirstily as if it was lemonade, and as she withdrew the bottle from her lips, neat gin ran down her chin and onto her chest, wetting her bathing costume.

"Oh, dear!" she exclaimed aloud. "I'm all wet and sticky. I'll have to wash it off." She tried to raise herself but fell back into the chair. She couldn't get her balance, her arms felt like putty. She tried again, this time holding tightly onto the arms of the chair, and gradually raised her body to a standing position. She then staggered towards the lake edge.

As she reached the shoreline, she dropped onto her hands and knees and crawled to the water's edge. She cupped some water in her hands and tried to wash the gin off her swimsuit. After a few moments she lay back, exhausted, too drunk for further effort, and began to doze, the warm water of the lake lapping her slim thighs.

Just offshore the old alligator, still in pain, was lying quietly below the surface of the water. A few days before, when scavenging, it had come across the bodies attached to the wire trace. Human flesh had never before been a part of its diet, but it devoured the remains, crushing the decaying meat and bones into a mulch. Now, lying motionless fifty feet offshore, it became aware of vibrations in the water. Sheila was awake, splashing herself again to rid her bathing costume of the gin stains. The alligator could make out a dark form by the water's edge, sometimes still, sometimes moving. With caution it moved slowly, like an old gnarled log drifting on the tide, towards the disturbance.

Sheila was now splashing around, laughing and shouting out loud. "To hell with you, Gordon! To hell with you!" she yelled at the sky.

The alligator increased its speed, excited by the flurry of movement. It was now heading at full bore towards the disturbance, making its own waves.

In her drunken state, Sheila vaguely felt the increasing disturbance in the shallow water and looked up scanning the lake for signs of a boat, but there was no boat.

The alligator was now within fifteen feet of the woman, its orange eyes fixed on its prey. It now increased its speed and shot towards her. She saw it at the last moment, screamed as she turned, clawing at the sand in a frenzy. She tried to stand, but staggered back, and as she rose the alligator was upon her. With one swift movement its huge jaws closed on Sheila's trailing leg. She screamed out in pain and clawed at the sand, but he dragged her down into the water beyond the shoreline. In an heroic effort she lunged for a half submerged tree root, but the force of the assault wrenched her fingers from their sockets. Then her body suddenly went limp, bubbles exploded from her open mouth, her eyes were wide open, transfixed, and then she was gone.

A neighbour, Mr Jones, heard the screams but took little notice; he'd heard her before when she was drunk shouting and staggering around the garden. He felt sorry for her husband. 'She is certainly fighting her demons tonight,' he thought.

The alligator did not relinquish the body until it was back under cover. It dragged the broken and battered corpse deep into its hole in the bank. The old alligator was still in pain but it wrenched large chunks from the body in a ravenous fury. For the second time it had feasted on human flesh.

Chapter 36

The Gallery, Inverness

The guest list for Gordon's opening party at the gallery read like a 'Who's Who of Citrus County', in no small part thanks to Mayor Thompson. Sixty or more of the richest and most influential people in the county were gathered in the gallery on that warm Saturday evening.

Senator Page and his wife arrived about seven o'clock with Jessica Larimer and her beautiful daughter, Jane. Jessica was accompanied by a dark-skinned Latin American who introduced himself as Hunaz Potra, Minister of Tourism for Cuba.

Gordon felt honoured by the presence of these dignitaries and he thanked the mayor openly for his assistance.

Margaret had been distributing brochures and a glass of champagne to each of the guests on arrival. Gordon was relieved that many of them appeared genuinely interested in the pictures, but he was under no illusions. The majority of them had come because they felt it necessary to be seen to be there, and no doubt there were those who followed the champagne trail wherever it led. How many pictures he would actually sell remained to be seen. Surprisingly, by 7.30 he had actually sold two.

Among the guests he noticed Macceffy from customs and excise in Orlando. Macceffy had not been invited. What was even more irritating was that he had arrived with Jean Manley on his arm. He hadn't seen Jean for a couple of weeks, but he felt a tinge of resentment, even jealously. Unjustified, of course, as he had no claim on her, but seeing her with rat face rather irked him.

Jean saw him and nodded her head in recognition, but instead of coming over to say hello, she left Macceffy and went over to talk to Senator Page, while Macceffy, much to Gordon's displeasure, made a beeline for him.

"Mr Richardson, this is a pleasure," he said holding out his hand.

"We haven't spoken for a while. How are you?" He had a self-satisfied look about him, like a well-fed tabby. Not appealing.

"I'm okay," Gordon replied, his eyes on Jean at the far side of the room.

Macceffy looked about him. "Well, it looks as if you've managed to get all your pictures released without any problem," he said.

Gordon looked straight into Macceffy's eyes. "Not without difficulty," he replied cuttingly. "It was also expensive – unnecessarily so."

Macceffy lifted his cigar to his mouth, took a long, purposeful draw and exhaled so that Gordon found himself immersed in smoke. "You will excuse me," he said, turning away. "I must have a quiet word with Senator Page."

'Horrid little rat,' Gordon thought, and wondered what possible business he had with the senator. He couldn't help noticing that they greeted each other as old friends.

His eyes fell on Jean Manley again. She was now in conversation with Dr Foster and the sheriff. He was just about to go and join them when there was a light tap on his shoulder. He turned to find himself face-to-face with Jessica Larimer.

"Mr Richardson," she said in perfect public school English. "I've been admiring the Munnings – *Horses at a Fair*, I think it's called."

"Ah, yes," Gordon said, forgetting Jean Manley for the moment. "Remarkable picture. I've owned it for – must be fifteen years. Part of me. The whole thing reminds me so much of England on a hot summer's day – green meadows, blue sky with those fluffy clouds, and the horses. Wonderful, really."

He realised he was becoming almost sentimental, not good for an art dealer.

"But I cannot find it in the catalogue," she said with a tone of mild exasperation.

"No. It's not for sale, actually," he explained.

"Oh." A whisper of a smile fanned her face. "May I call you Gordon?" she asked.

"Of course."

"You know, Gordon, everything has its price."

"Not this picture," he replied firmly.

"But, Gordon," she said with a firmness that rather surprised him, "I'm used to having the best, and this picture is the only one in the exhibition I want."

"Sorry," he said again, shrugging his shoulders as if it wasn't his fault, "but it's not for sale."

She remained looking at him so that he couldn't avoid her face, and that face had determination written all over it. A very attractive woman, he thought. Intelligent, sophisticated. A woman who would find it difficult to take no for an answer.

"Come now, Gordon," she cajoled. "I'm sure that half a million dollars could change your mind. I would like so much to hang it in my Knightsbridge apartment." She watched his expression change from one of resistance to one of malleability, and then added, "You could say I'd be returning it to its rightful country." It was an appeal to his sense of patriotism, but it wasn't going to work with him. "Surely that's where it belongs – back in England?" she persisted.

He smiled. 'Good try,' he thought. 'Rich and used to getting her own way.' But he really didn't want to part with the picture. In fact he wished he hadn't been so vain as to hang it, when he had no intention of selling it.

"Seven hundred thousand dollars, then," she said abruptly. "That's my final offer."

Her persistence and the magnitude of the offer, it had to be admitted, had caught him off guard. Seven hundred thousand dollars was a lot of money. With that kind of money in the bank he'd be financially secure. He glanced at the painting as if asking for divine help. But it was something he knew he had to decide on his own, not that the actual decision was that difficult.

"Okay, Mrs Larimer," he said with a deep exhalation of breath. "You've bought yourself a Munnings."

Then she did something he hadn't expected. She leaned across and kissed him on the cheek. "Sealed with a kiss," she said with mock shyness, and then she laughed. "You see, I always get what I want. Now, perhaps we could discuss the details in your office after the party?"

Gordon nodded. "As you wish," he said. "I'll look forward to it."

He watched her as she left, walking purposefully across the room without a second glance, hips swinging, back straight. 'Real class,' he thought, 'and what a body.' It made him think of Sheila when she was younger.

Remembering his wife, he made his way to the office and closed the door behind him. He dialled home and, as before, he let the number ring for several minutes, but no one answered. "Where the hell is she?" he said out loud.

"I'm here, darling."

He turned to see Jean Manley standing in the doorway. All he could say was, "It's good to see you."

"You don't *sound* glad to see me," she said in a hurt tone that was clearly exaggerated.

"You caught me off guard," he said. "Besides, I have the distinct feeling that you've been avoiding me these last couple of weeks."

She didn't answer, but closed the door behind her and approached the desk, behind which he was standing. The movement of her body, the bewitching way she walked with a slight coquettish tilting of the head, eyes lowered beneath deep eyelashes, was disturbingly erotic, as it was intended to be. It had the desired effect. Jean Manley had the ability to send his blood pumping through his veins at a furious rate, particularly in the region of his loins. But he remained behind his desk as she stopped short on the other side.

"Why did you bring Macceffy with you?" he asked, searching her eyes.

"Him?" she replied dismissively. "The senator asked me to. Why? Are you jealous?"

"Of course not," he said quickly. Then he thought about it. "Well, yes, perhaps I am a little bit," he said more softly. Then he added, "But you know I don't like him. Anyway, he wasn't invited."

Jean averted her eyes, ran a finger along the polished surface of the desk. "But if it wasn't for your visit to see him that day, we wouldn't have met."

He smiled. "That's true, but he's still a rat."

Jean leaned across the desk, took hold of his tie, drew him towards her and kissed him fully on the lips.

Suddenly there was a knock on the door. Gordon cleared his throat, straightened his tie and said, "Come in."

Margaret burst into the room. "Gordon, the mayor...." She stopped mid-sentence as she took in the situation. "Oh! I'm sorry. I'm disturbing . . ."

"It's okay, Margaret. This lady and I were just discussing one of the paintings. What's the problem?"

"There's no problem," Margaret said. "Mayor Thompson is interested in the Duckworth. I thought it best if you spoke to him yourself."

"Right," he said. "I'll be with you in a few seconds."

Jean interrupted. "Mr Richardson, please don't let me hold you up. We could discuss the picture later?"

Gordon nodded. "Of course, Miss Manley. That would be fine. Now, Margaret, we'd better go and speak to the mayor before he cools off."

Back in the gallery, Mayor Thompson was admiring the painting.

It was a particularly fine work by Duckworth of Greta Garbo, and Gordon had bought it against stiff competition.

"Stunning, don't you think, Mayor?" Gordon said as he approached.

The mayor nodded in agreement. "Fine indeed," he said, "but the price on the ticket's a bit steep."

Gordon laughed. "The best, Mayor, is always expensive. I can show you something cheaper?"

It was a bluff of course, but with men of high ambition and social climbers it was sometimes known to work. He wasn't sure into which category the mayor fitted, though he doubted, on a mayor's pay, if he could afford it, which was why he took the risk. He was therefore surprised when the mayor persisted.

"Tell me more about it," he said.

So Gordon did. "Royal Academy exhibit, acclaimed by the critics as amongst the artist's finest works, wonderful condition, 'glowing' [pictures were always 'glowing' when you had to sell them, usually drab when you were buying], altogether a very fine picture. It's always been one of my favourites. I've had it in my own collection for several years."

The mayor continued to nod his approval without taking his eyes off the canvas, as if agreeing with every word Gordon spoke. It was a good sign.

It was an even better sign when the mayor mentioned money for the second time. "Sixty thousand dollars is a lot. Do you think it's a good investment?"

"As good as you'll get," Gordon told him. And, as if to drive the nail home, he added, "The finest pictures always hold their value."

That seemed to be the clincher, because the mayor said triumphantly, "What the hell. I'll have it!"

Feeling mightily pleased with himself, Gordon went to get a red sticker. But he couldn't help wondering how Thompson could get that kind of money. Every time they'd discussed business, he'd complained about the lack of it, how bad things were, and here he was spending sixty grand almost on a whim.

He returned and stuck the little red dot on the label and shook the mayor's hand. The mayor seemed particularly pleased with himself. Puffing away at his big cigar and with his stout figure, he seemed to exemplify the successful businessman, and wanted everyone in the gallery to know it.

Gordon thought that at one point the man was going to announce to the gallery en masse that he'd just become the owner of a sixty thousand dollar picture, but much to Gordon's relief he confined himself to puffing and strutting.

Gordon's attention was suddenly drawn to a noise at the door and turned to see Peter Cooper push his way into the gallery carrying a crate of Inverness Rum. He was smiling, his face was red, he was a little drunk.

He lugged the crate to the centre of the room, plonked it down and climbed on top of it like a soapbox orator about to hold forth, which he did. "Ladies and gentlemen!" He was swaying slightly and he held his hands in the air for silence. It had the desired effect as people in the room stopped talking to watch an inebriated Peter Cooper make a fool of himself. "Ladies and gentlemen," he repeated.

"You've already said that," his sister, who was standing by his side, reminded him in a whisper.

"Ah! Right! Now listen you all. I have fantastic news. What I have done," he announced with an extravagant gesture, "is sold the brewery." He waited for this staggering fact to sink in before continuing. "That's right. Sold it – to a Japanese company, no less." He took a deep breath to steady himself. "They love rum, you see. And they say they are going to increase production. And do you know how much by? By 100% over the next twelve months. Isn't that absolutely wonderful?" He was still unsteady, and his voice was slurred, but he managed to keep his feet. "Hong Kong, Japan, England – export everywhere. And they tell me. Wait for it – wait for it. They tell me they're going to build a new two million bucks extension, which means they will employ a further one hundred operatives." He threw his hands into the air as if to encompass the applause, and he wasn't too disappointed, as the whole gathering applauded. They pulled him from his soapbox, shook his hand and patted him on the back. The champagne corks popped, and everyone drank a toast to Peter Cooper and the Japanese nation.

One of the first with congratulations was Jimmy Clark, the bank manager. "Glad you've pulled through," he said with a tinge of sarcasm, which Peter, even in his faintly abused state, picked up on straight away.

He leaned across at Clark and shouted in his ear, "And no thanks to you, you cocksucking son of a bitch. I'm going to payoff every dollar I owe you in the morning – first thing, so you can stay out of my life and stick your overdraft up your fat arse!"

Jimmy Clark turned bright purple and his hands at his sides balled into fists. He was struggling to keep a smile on his face. Perspiration ran down his fat, pink cheeks. Summoning up all his mental strength he said, "See you tomorrow, Peter," and turned to leave, but Peter Cooper was in full vocal swing.

"You sure will," he shouted provicatingly and loud enough for everyone to hear. "Do you know, everyone, this leach almost made me close the factory."

"Not me," Jimmy Clark broke in. "It was head office."

Most of the guests in the room were now giving the two protagonists, for that is what they were fast becoming, their full attention. Everyone, it seemed, loved a fight.

Gordon, sensing the tension, went over the Peter Cooper and placed his hand on his shoulder. "Right," he said in a jovial manner, "now that you have money, let's see if we can find a nice picture for you to spend it on."

And with that he guided Cooper across the room, away from Jimmy Clark, who collected his coat and quickly left. As he reached the door he looked back, catching Cooper's eye. He wasn't going to forget the humiliation to which he'd just been subjected.

Chapter 37

The Gallery, Inverness

The last of the guests finally left the gallery at around two in the morning. Gordon was sitting in his office. He had just picked up the telephone to check on his wife when the door opened and Jessica Larimer entered. Without speaking she walked over to the desk and placed a cheque for $700,000 in front of him. As Gordon went to pick it up, she snatched it away from him, and waved it playfully in front of his eyes.

"I'm giving you this cheque in payment for the Munnings on two conditions," she said pointedly. "Firstly, you are to bring the picture to my house on Monday. And secondly," and here she hesitated. "Secondly, you will deliver it in person to my flat in Knightsbridge." Gordon opened his mouth to say something but she stopped him with an upturned palm. "Don't worry," she said, "I will pay all expenses."

Put like that, Gordon couldn't really object. A few days in England, all paid for, couldn't be bad. "Okay," he said. "That's a deal."

Mrs Larimer looked pleased with herself. She reached out a slender, manicured hand and slipped the cheque down the front of Gordon's unbuttoned shirt. It was an erotically provocative move, immediately followed by a kiss. Gordon reacted instinctively by reaching out and pulling her towards him, but Jessica had teased enough and she placed her hands firmly on his chest, forcing herself away from his embrace.

"I'll see you Monday evening," she whispered, "and don't be late."

With that she swept out of the room. Through the open door he noticed her collect her daughter and they left together a few seconds later.

Gordon looked down at his glass. It was empty. He walked through the gallery, snatched up a whisky bottle and poured himself another drink. He sauntered to the window. The moon was bright and he could make out one or two hangers-on still getting into their cars. And then to his surprised he saw Jean Manley. She was accompanied by the sheriff and Lucy. 'What the hell,' he thought, 'is she doing with him?' He went to the front door and wrenched it open. "Jean!" he called. She turned and for a second he thought she wasn't going to acknowledge him. Then she waved.

The sheriff then eased her into the car. "Thanks for the evening," the sheriff called through the night air. "Enjoyed it." And then he ducked into the driver's seat and they were gone.

Perplexed, unable to fathom this turn of events, he stared once more into his glass as if the answer were to be found there. Clearly it wasn't. He gulped down the whisky in one go, shook his head in a vain attempt to clear it, and thought he'd better ring his wife. But Sheila failed to answer, and he assumed, with a sense of foreboding, that she was drunk again. He decided to make for home.

Chapter 38

Mitcham Creek, Inverness

As he pulled off the highway, Gordon could make out the house lights blazing like beacons through the night. 'Christ!' he thought, 'I suppose she's fallen asleep on the couch again.'

He stopped the car in front of the garage, and sat still for a moment or two to relax. He was in no mood to face his wife; he didn't want an argument, had no stomach for an abusive tirade that he was sure would come at him. As he approached the front door he glanced across to the pool; the lights were still on over the patio but there was no sign of Sheila. He went back to the house. The television was on and several magazines were laid out on the floor. He picked up the remote control, pressed the red button and the television died, leaving an eerie silence. A light breeze fanned through an open window, but still the air felt humid, sticky.

Increasingly concerned, he wandered into the bedroom, the dressing room, bathroom, guest room and finally the kitchen, but Sheila was nowhere to be seen. He ran through the utility room and opened the door to the garage. Sheila's car was still there. He placed his hand on the bonnet, it was cold. Sheila never went out without the car – she hated walking. What in God's name had happened to her?

Now, desperately concerned, he hurried back into the house calling her name. He reached the kitchen and searched through all the cupboards looking for a flashlight. Eventually he located a torch on a bottom shelf and ran out onto the patio. He scanned the torch beam around the garden, but still no sign.

Making his way towards the lake, he methodically flashed the light into the bushes as he passed, just in case.

At the edge of the lake he found her sunlounger, also her multicoloured towel. It was lying on the ground next to a half empty bottle of gin and an upturned crystal tumbler. He shone the torch along the lake edge and then out across the lake. In the darkness, beyond the torch's beam he did not notice a small object hanging from a gnarled tree root. It was rocking in the night breeze. It was red, a manicured nail with pink skin attached. It was Sheila's forefinger.

As Gordon gazed out across the water, he felt an overwhelming sense of dread. He was not a fatalist by nature, but there was something desperately wrong, something tragically wrong, his wife had disappeared without a trace. There was no sign of her having left. It was almost as if she had been whisked away into the ether, kidnapped by some alien force. He shrugged off such fanciful thoughts.

He ran back to the house, went through every room all over again, but he knew she wasn't there. Now he knew something had happened, and he had an awful feeling that whatever it was, whatever had caused the disappearance, would not give up its secret.

In a state of deepening despair he went into the lounge and slumped down on the settee. He didn't know what to do. He thought of telephoning all those living nearby to ask if they had seen her, or anybody in the vicinity behaving strangely, but it was 3.30 a.m.

He decided to make one more traverse of the garden, but it was all to no avail. He wondered vaguely if she were wandering around drunk somewhere far beyond the house, so he jumped into the car and drove slowly along the drive and onto the road. Checking left and right in the darkness, he joined the main highway. He knew it was hopeless, even if she were laid out somewhere sleeping it off, he would not find her. There was nothing he could do until morning.

He reached the court house in the town centre, before reluctantly turning the car round and heading back home, but sleep was coming on so he pulled off the highway, stopped the engine and fell into a disturbed sleep. He dreamed he was searching for his wife, but in place of Sheila's face was Jean Manley's. In his dream he searched every inch of Florida, from Miami to Orlando, showing the picture of Jean's face to anyone who would look or listen. But people looked at him strangely, some simply walked away, others shook their heads, and some asked for the girl's telephone number. He awoke suddenly; his shirt was wet with perspiration, the morning sun was blazing through the windscreen onto his face. He raised a hand to shield his eyes. Someone was tapping on the window. It was Sheriff O'Donnel, who looked concerned.

Gordon wound down the window and told him what had happened.

"She's bound to turn up," the sheriff said almost dismissively. And when Gordon raised an eyebrow, the sheriff continued. "Look, Gordon, the whole town knows Sheila has a drink problem, and she's not the only one in this town. She may have bunked down at a friend's house to sleep it off. She's probably back home now. Your best bet is to get back quickly."

Gordon nodded. "I guess you're right," he sighed. "Thanks for your help, Sheriff."

He parked outside the house with an overwhelming sense of guilt. He hadn't been much help to his wife in her time of need, hadn't given her the attention she craved, he'd been too wrapped up with the business, not to mention Jean Manley. Well, he'd make a fresh start, do his damnedest to help her get better.

He pushed open the front door and and called out, "Sheila, it's me – Gordon." His voice echoed through the house to be met by an empty silence. It was strange, he thought, how the absense of one person left this void of quiet stillness, like the emptiness of a tomb. And it was then that he knew his wife was dead, and that he would never see her again. The realisation came to him with a coldness that caused him to wrap his arms around himself. He lowered himself into a chair in an effort to make sense of the alien thoughts that were crowding in upon him.

Chapter 39

Bass Lodge, Inverness

Rastos Nokes rolled over in bed in a futile attempt to ignore the clatter, like pebbles revolving in a tin bucket, of the alarm clock. He grunted and reached out to turn on the small bedside lamp, then flopped onto his back again, making the old bed shake and creak. He glanced at the alarm clock, it was 5.30 a.m. He reached out a big hand and stopped the noise. "Rise and shine, Gertrude! Rise and shine!"

The black Labrador, lying on the carpet next to the bed, shook her head and struggled unsteadily to her feet. She was an old dog and her limbs were beginning to feel the effects of arthritis.

Rastos swung his legs over the edge of the bed and cupped Gertrude's big head in his hands. Doleful eyes looked up at him. "It takes you longer each morning to get off that carpet," he chuckled, rubbing her ears. "Just like me, getting old and senile. Never mind, we've still got each other." The old dog wagged her tail and shuffled after him into the kitchen.

Gertrude had been with Rastos for sixteen years. She'd been given to him as a fiftieth birthday present by an old friend, Tom Crouch. Tom had told him that the dog would be company for him in his old age, and that's how it had turned out. They ate, slept and fished together. They knew each other's minds. Rastos didn't need human companionship, he had Gertrude. He poured himself a cup of coffee, filled Gertrude's dish with milk, and the two sat drinking, friends together.

When they had finished, the old man took his work jeans and sweatshirt from the back of a chair and dressed. He looked at his watch. Time was getting on. "Come on, old girl," he said to the dog, who understood every word. "Time for your walk. We have to be at the dock at 7.30. We've got important clients from Orlando today who want to catch bass. Hear that? Bass. Some hope!"

The dog had finished her drink and she was now standing at the kitchen door waiting to go.

"Okay, okay, I'm coming. I move slowly nowadays, dog. Just remember that, it prolongs your life."

The dog barked as Rastos opened the door and let her out. She ran stiffly down the garden towards the lake edge. Rastos followed and was soon standing on the sandy beach scanning the water.

The lake was like a huge mirror, reflecting the clear blue sky. The sun had already risen in the east and he could feel its soft gentle heat upon his face. "My, oh my, Gertrude," he said out loud, "this is going to be a wonderful day. Too warm for catching bass, mind you, but a wonderful day nevertheless."

The Labrador was sitting looking up at him with big languid eyes waiting for something.

"Okay – go!" said Rastos, "but only fifteen minutes, mind."

Every morning for the past ten years, man and dog had taken an early morning swim together, though lately Rastos had felt it was too much effort for him. Gertrude, however, was still keen, so he let her go out on her own.

She was a good swimmer. He watched her as she swam straight out and into deeper water. When she was about seventy feet off shore she turned to make sure Rastos was still watching. She'd gone out far enough now, so Rastos beckoned her in with a wave of his hand. She knew the signal and responded immediately, paddling towards the shore.

Some twenty feet beyond the swimming dog, the alligator was lying on the lake bottom, partly submerged in sand. After snatching Sheila it had carried her mutilated body across the lake to his den. Later that night, it had dragged parts of her dismembered body back across the lake and had buried it in a deep hole on the lake bed, just offshore from Rastos's house. It would return to this later to feed as soon as the body had begun to putrefy. Now, as it lay there, it picked up the vibrations of the swimming dog, and moved silently towards it, remaining submerged until it was beneath the dog, and then it struck.

Rastos had been watching Gertrude coming fast towards him, when suddenly she had vanished. It had happened so fast, with hardly a ripple on the water, that Rastos stood disbelieving. He closed his eyes, then opened them again, but the surface of the lake remained calm, without a sign of Gertrude. In desperation he called her name and ran into the lake. As soon as he was out of his depth he began to swim. When he reached the spot where he had last seen Gertrude he trod water. He called her name again and again but there was no sign, so he dived. He went as deep as he could, reaching out with his hands, but there was nothing.

By now the old alligator was fifty feet away. Blood was flowing from Gertrude's mangled body, leaving a red stain on the surface of the water like an oil slick. But Rastos didn't notice, his eyes were clouded by tears. He swam slowly back to the shore, knowing that Gertrude was gone. A great weariness descended on him, clawed at his heart, and by the time he reached the beach he had no strength left. He sank down onto the sand and wept.

Chapter 40

Alligator Island, Inverness

It was late afternoon as Gordon drove along Highway 49 by the edge of Little Lake Henderson. The day was hot and humid with the odd rumble of thunder not too far away. He glanced across at Alligator Island on the far side of the lake. Above it hung a grey cloud, behind which larger clouds were banking up. Very soon the deep blue of the sky would be claimed by storm clouds. Even as he watched a flash of lightning fractured the calm. The lightning so captured his attention that he failed to notice the stop sign until he was nearly on it. He braked hard and a tanker swept before him and away. It was a close thing. His concentration was not what it should have been. He hadn't slept more than a few fretful hours since Sheila's disappearance, and he felt weary, worn down by worry. There had been no news, no clues, nothing. He looked both ways and eased the car onto the main highway and headed towards The White House on Alligator Island.

On the Sunday following Sheila's disappearance he had spent the whole day checking the local beer halls, cinemas, shopping malls, anywhere in fact that Sheila might have visited, no matter however remotely unlikely. He had even taken the boat out onto the lake, searching along the water's edge amongst the reed beds. On Sunday evening, as the night drew in, he fancied he saw something floating in the water near the island itself, but it turned out to be nothing more than a rotted tree trunk. On the Monday he'd called in at the sheriff's office, but there was no news. The sheriff was as baffled as he was.

He tried to concentrate on the road ahead, but his mind seemed unable to concentrate on one single thing. He still hadn't made contact with the children, and he wondered what he would tell them: That their mother had simply disappeared, couldn't be found? That she was dead? No, he couldn't bring himself to think that, let alone say it. No body had turned up, there had been no sign of a struggle, no sign of anything. Would the children blame him for her disappearance?

Gordon slowed the car as he approached the iron gates, and they opened automatically. He drove on through, passing a guard seated in a wicker chair with an umbrella for a shade. He didn't stir, so Gordon assumed they'd been forewarned of his visit, but the guard watched him closely.

He parked in front of the sweeping steps that led up to the front door. The doors were made of walnut, inlaid with Lalique panels depicting scantily clad women. He got out of the car and unlocked the boot. He could feel he was still being watched. As he lifted the picture out into the sunlight he noticed someone coming down the steps towards him.

"Good afternoon, sir. May I take that from you?" The butler was English with a perfect Oxford accent, though perhaps a little affectatious.

Gordon lowered the picture carefully as Dobson waved a finger towards the house. A young man in a red and white striped shirt, scarlet trousers and white gloves, came tripping down the steps.

"Nigel," said Dobson, "carefully retrieve the picture from the boot and transport it to the lounge." Then, turning to Gordon, he said, "Mrs Larimer will see you there, sir."

"Thank you," Gordon said and stepped aside to let Nigel lift the picture from the boot.

This he did with great care, clearly overwhelmed by his responsibility. He carried it in front of him cautiously, like a waiter with a tray of crystal.

Gordon followed and was ushered by Dobson through a pair of enormous doors into a circular hall of colonial splendour with great fluted columns reaching up to a decorated ceiling depicting nymphs and angels. On the floor lay an oval mid-fourteenth-century Byzantine rug. Expensive furniture adorned the perimeter. Just three pictures hung in the hall, but what pictures they were – a Cezanne, a Monet and a Picasso. He looked closer. In each of the paintings something was not quite true, not right – the colour, the brush strokes, the quality wasn't there. The pictures were forgeries, good copies admittedly, but they were not what they appeared to be.

Dobson, who was standing by the door, coughed politely. "Sir, Mrs Larimer can see you now – if you will follow me."

The room they now entered was, like the hall, oval in shape and adorned with rich Chinese carpets and early English furniture. There were a number of paintings which, as far as he could see from little more than a cursory glance, were original.

Mrs Larimer was seated on a silk-clad armchair gazing out across manicured lawns towards the lake. She appeared to take no notice of the picture, although Dobson had propped it up on an easel near the fireplace.

As Gordon approached she stood to greet him. She was dressed in a pink mini-skirted dress with a plunging neckline, the darkness of her nipples showing hard up against the smooth silk cloth.

"That will be all, Dobson," she said to the butler. "We will require tea on the patio in ten minutes. I will ring if I need you before that."

When they were alone, she held her hand towards him, and as Gordon moved to take it, she drew him towards her and kissed him gently on the mouth. "Welcome to Alligator Island," she whispered in his ear. "Now, come and sit next to me for a moment," and she led him to the settee, holding his hand tight. As they sat down he could feel her slim thighs against his leg.

Slowly she crossed her legs and the silk skirt ruffled and shifted upwards exposing her lean, brown suntanned thighs.

"Mr Richardson," she purred, "I hear you have a reputation as a ladies' man – is that true?"

"I can't think where you heard that," he replied, "but it's not true."

"Gordon," she whispered sexily, "I believe you, but it won't save you. I've been waiting since Saturday." She slid her hand across his waist and gently and purposefully held the inside of his leg.

Gordon felt passion stir, his penis began to expand, pressing against her hand. Gently she moved her forefinger and stroked his hardness against the taught cloth of his trousers. He felt the surge of desire filling him and he reached out for her, but as he did so her mood changed.

She stiffened and slid her hand away. Then she sat upright, brushed her dress down and said trimly, "This won't do. We have business to discuss."

Gordon shifted in his seat, the wave of passion quickly dying. He cleared his throat. "You asked me to deliver the picture and discuss shipping it to London," he said as impassively as he could in the circumstances.

"So I did," she said as though the very reason for his visit had slipped her mind. "Yes, yes, of course." She smiled. "Now, I've made arrangements for you to fly out with the picture on Thursday, on Virgin flight 0162. It leaves at 6.00 p.m. You'll be in London at about 7.30 in the morning. Is that okay?"

He was impressed by her sudden recall coming on the heels of such a lapse of memory. But no, it wasn't okay. He shook his head, "Fine under normal circumstances," he told her, "but at the moment I've got serious family problems, and they have to be dealt with straight away."

"Yes, I've heard," she broke in impatiently, "but you can't help your wife by just hanging around here. She'll turn up sooner or later, when she sobers up."

Gordon felt a stab of anger. Who was she to talk to him like that? Denigrate his wife.

He stood up to go. He wanted none of her, he was fed up with the whole thing, but she put a restraining hand on his arm. "Please don't go," she begged. "I'm sorry. I didn't mean to make you angry. It was foolish of me, but there really is nothing more you can do here. A break would do you good."

God, she was a cool character, he thought. She said before she always got her way and she was about to get it again. He shrugged his shoulders. "Okay," he said. "You're probably right, but I don't know why it's so important for me to accompany the picture. It's simple enough to ship it direct."

A mischievous smile passed across her face. She sank into an easy chair and crossed her long legs so that her short skirt exposed more of her thigh. "All right," she said. "It's no big deal, but I though it would be nice if we could spend a day or two together in London, just seeing the sights."

She was appealing to his sense of adventure, whilst at the same time challenging his pride. She was a cagey one all right, and she knew it. All he could think of at that moment were those thighs, he couldn't take his eyes off them.

"Gordon?"

"Ah, of course," he said tearing he eyes away. "I submit. I surrender. But how long are you planning to stay in England?" he asked.

"Well," she said with mock coyness, "that depends on how good you are."

At that point there was a polite tap on the door and, after the mandatory pause, Dobson entered. "Madame," he said pompously, "I have taken the liberty of laying out tea on the patio as you instructed."

"Thank you, Dobson," Mrs Larimer said. She then rose, smoothing her skirt so that Gordon could hear the crackle of skin against silk, and said coyly, "Please follow me."

The patio was suitably impressive with stone steps on all sides, the level raised above the lawn by about five feet.

Dobson had laid the tea and sandwiches in the shade beneath a Victorian wrought iron gazebo, which was richly adorned with exquisite ironwork depicting English roses and crowns.

"That will be all, Dobson," Mrs Larimer said.

"This is a beautiful piece of work," he said admiringly, running his fingers across the fine fretwork of a rose. "Where on earth did you get it?"

"I found it in a house sale near Petworth," she told him. "I had it shipped out last month. I'm glad you like it. I think it's rather magnificent."

"You were lucky to get an export licence," he remarked. "They don't like parting with things as good as this without a fight."

"I have a friend," she said mischievously.

"And what about the export licence for the Munnings?" he asked.

Instead of replying she picked up a porcelain handbell from the table and rang it vigorously. A few seconds later Dobson appeared.

"Madam, you rang?" he asked, stating the obvious.

"Dobson, there's an envelope marked Munnings on the dressing table in my bedroom, would you please fetch it."

"Certainly, Madame," said Dobson, and he disappeared as quickly as he had arrived.

For such a big man, Gordon thought, he was very quick on his feet. He began to think ahead to London. This woman excited him as no woman had before; she was quick to arouse his most basic instincts. If she was flirting with him now, he was a willing party to the dalliance.

"Can we be alone for a while?" he said to her.

"Certainly not, Mr Richardson," she replied roguishly. "This is my home! What can you be thinking! Anyway," she added lowering her eyes, "your time will come – in London."

She was a teaser, a woman skilled in the game of seduction. It made her that much more desirable.

She poured the tea. "Milk and sugar?" she asked.

"Just milk," he replied unable to take his eyes off her.

As she handed him the cup their fingers touched; it was the faintest whisper of a touch, yet it aroused in him an almost feverish desire that he fought to control.

If that brief contact had aroused her, too, she made no show of it. Her mind seemed to be on other things. She sat up stiffly and said, "Now to business. As I said earlier, all the papers are in order. You will keep the picture next to you on the plane. I have reserved a seat next to yours for this purpose."

"The picture has its own seat?"

"Gordon, I have just paid you a lot of money for this picture. I do not want to take the risk of losing it or having it stolen."

"Is that all it means to you – an investment?"

"Gordon, quite frankly I don't give a damn about the picture, but my husband, he likes to make sound investments, and he believes the Munnings is a good buy."

"A man of good commercial sense," Gordon heard himself saying.

"I've always thought so," she said with an edge of tetchiness to her voice. "Look, just accept what I'm saying, you must keep the picture with you at all times."

"What if I go to the loo?"

"Then take it with you," she said, smiling.

"I'll guard it with my life," he said, placing his hand on his heart, "if it's so important to you."

"My husband will be forever thankful. Ah, Dobson."

The butler had appeared carrying a large brown envelope which he handed to Mrs Larimer. Whilst this had been going on, Gordon's attention had been drawn down to the garden where he noticed two men some distance away in conversation with one another. He fancied one of them was Senator Page, while the other, a small swarthy man, he couldn't quite put a name to. And then he remembered, it was the Minister of Tourism for Cuba who had accompanied Jessica Larimer to the party. He briefly wondered what they were both doing there, but then Mrs Larimer interrupted his thoughts.

"Here you are," she said, handing him the envelope. "There's everything here that you need – papers, flight tickets and your reservation at the Dorchester for four nights."

He took the envelope and slipped it into his shirt pocket. "I'd better take the picture back with me now and have it wrapped up," he said.

As he went to take it from the easel she stopped him and said, "No, that's okay, I'll have it wrapped here and deliver it to the gallery on Wednesday afternoon. I'm sure that's best."

"Up to you," Gordon said, "but packing comes with the price."

She ignored that and said, "Now, when you get to London you'll be met by my chauffeur. He will take you directly to my flat in Bayswater Road where my sister, Trisha, will be waiting for you. You don't need to enter the house, just hand the picture over to her. She'll unwrap it and hang it up. I don't want to bother you with all that."

"No bother," he said.

She smiled. "No. It's all organised," she said with a flurry of her hands. "The quicker the picture's delivered the more time we shall have together." She paused. "So, I'll meet you at the Dorchester on Friday evening at nine o'clock – in the long bar, if that's all right with you?"

"Fine," he said somewhat overcome.

Dobson appeared again and Mrs Larimer rose. "Dobson," she said, "Mr Richardson is just about to leave. Would you show him to his car, please."

Gordon was caught unawares. His tea would have to remain, untouched and cold. He rose from his chair and, before he knew it, had shaken Jessica Larimer's hand and was being escorted by Dobson toward the door and to his car.

He glanced back as he left to capture a quick glimpse of Mrs Larimer, but she was no longer seated on the patio, but was walking quickly across the lawn towards the two men he had seen talking.

Chapter 41

San Remo Circle, Inverness

Two weeks had passed since Wayne's death. During that time the numbness that nature provides as a shock absorber to tragedy had worn off, and Claire had felt the full force of his loss. She moped around the house in a mood of dark despair. She missed Wayne more than she could ever have imagined, and when she awoke in the mornings she still expected to find him there beside her. If she cried, she cried inside, the hurt had gone too deep to surface.

The joint funeral was held at the local Baptist church. There weren't many mourners, which would have suited both of them as neither liked any fuss. Wayne's mother came down from Texas. Lucy, the sheriff and several colleagues from the power station, including Tom, stood by the graveside. Claire and Tom held one another's hands for comfort.

After the funeral it was Lucy who suggested to Claire that it might help if she returned to work, perhaps on a part-time basis. It might help her to adjust to a life without Wayne, she told her. At first Claire was unsure. Her confidence had been damaged and she was not convinced that she was capable of doing anything of use, but Lucy persevered, and eventually persuaded Claire to see Mr Critchley, the new engineer at the power station. Critchley was understanding and seemed pleased that Claire wished to return to work. It was agreed that she would start on the Wednesday morning.

Claire arrived back at work on the appointed day feeling very unsure of herself. She noticed before she got out of the car that her palms were sweating. She lowered her head onto the steering wheel, gripping it tightly with both hands in a spasm of fear and uncertainty. Wayne had left her alone and she was not sure if she could cope. She remained sitting there, her mind in deep conflict, for several minutes, before she felt calm enough and in control enough to face the world outside.

She need not have worried. Everyone in the control room welcomed her with such genuine warmth that she immediately began to feel more confident.

"We need you here," said Tom. "Mr Critchley's an easy-going boss but, if you want my opinion, he's no expert. And it's an expert we need," he added knowingly.

Tom showed her the log sheets and electricity power readings for the last few weeks, and Claire settled back at her desk absorbing the information and data. As she worked through that morning she glanced up several times. Each time she noticed Tom and Mr Critchley watching her.

At about 2.30 p.m. Mr Critchley received a phone call. When he replaced the receiver she thought he looked worried. He told her that he had to go out for an hour, and wondered if she would be okay. He seemed nervous and on edge. Claire put it down to him being embarrassed, having to leave her in charge on her first day back, but she assured him that she would be fine.

After Mr Critchley had left, Claire noticed that Tom was agitated. He was hovering around in the vicinity of her desk as if he wanted to tell her something, but was embarrassed to do so.

"Tom," she said at length, putting down her pen and looking up at him over her glasses, "what is it?"

"Claire, I need to talk to you," he stammered. "I know it's your first day back, and I'm sorry, but . . ."

"But what? Tom, I don't think I can quite cope with being an Agony Aunt at the moment."

"No, no, it's nothing like that. But, well, if you don't feel up to talking to me right now, I'll understand."

"Tom," said Claire firmly. "What have you to tell me?"

Tom glanced down at the floor. "Well, it's like this. Of course I don't know the station as well as you and Wayne, but, but I think there may be a problem. The trouble is I've no proof."

"Proof of what?"

"Claire, there's a leakage of contaminated water from the reactor."

Claire's face paled and her glasses slipped down to the edge of her petite nose. "Do you know what you're saying?" she asked calmly, though her pulse had begun to race.

"Of course I do," said Tom. "The trouble is I can't prove anything, and anyway, how can I speak to Mr Critchley about it – he's the senator's man. You're the only one I can trust, there's no one else. You know the plant, you helped design it."

Claire was trying to keep herself calm, but her stomach was

churning. She didn't want to believe what she was hearing. "What exactly have you discovered?" she asked.

Knowing that he had a willing ear, Tom relaxed a little. "Well," he said, "you remember the dials and the computer read-outs on the water level in the casings that we've always been told were OK?"

Claire nodded. "Yes. Wayne had a report from Computer Aided Electronics just before he . . ." She stopped in mid-sentence. "Just before he died."

"Yes, I know he did," said Tom. "But in the last few weeks the readings have got worse. When Mr Critchley arrived I mentioned the faulty readings to him, but he said they'd all been rechecked. Then new dials were fitted one weekend when I was away."

"So?" said Claire, "that seems logical. They did need replacing. I knew that."

"Perhaps," said Tom, "but I was suspicious. So last week I bypassed the system by reprogramming the computer to print-out the water levels on a separate database in my office. I've carefully checked all the tabulated results over the past week." He stopped and drew a long breath. Then he said, choosing his words carefully, "The readings show a loss of contaminated water of 1,000 gallons a day."

"But that's ridiculous," said Claire. "The reactor would begin to overheat."

Tom shook his head. "Not if the water levels were topped up on a daily basis."

"But there's only one person who could do that."

"Quite," Tom replied. "And I'll tell you something else, he always stays behind each night when everybody's left, and it doesn't matter how late."

"Perhaps he's just conscientious," said Claire, feeling more uneasy by the minute. "These are serious accusations. Have you talked to Critchley?"

"No, I haven't," replied Tom firmly. "I don't trust him. For that matter there are a lot of people I wouldn't trust. If this plant were to close the whole community would face financial ruin, and I can name at least four local businessmen who wouldn't take kindly to that."

Claire was becoming confused. "Look. Wayne mentioned the problem with the dials. He was worried – I know."

Tom drew a deep breath. "Claire, there is one more thing I have to tell you. I'm sorry, you're going to hate me for it, but I was so frightened." He paused for a moment. "On the night Wayne died,

Betty telephoned him at home."

"I know that," replied Claire, "but what has that got to do with the plant? Everyone assumed they were having an affair," she added bitterly.

"Claire, that's ridiculous. It's not true. Betty rang Wayne to tell him that she suspected the plant was leaking radioactive water. They were both on the way to see the mayor when the accident happened."

Claire was silent. There were so many things going through her mind she could not assimilate them all. After a few moments she said, "Tom, do you know what you're suggesting?"

Tom coughed, and for a moment he held back his fears. "I'm not suggesting anything," he said. "I just don't know."

Claire felt a strange sense of calm. She had no idea why, but she felt in charge of herself for the first time since the accident. "How do you know they were on their way to see the mayor when the accident happened?" she asked quietly.

"I listened into their conversation. I was in the office next door. I was jealous, I suppose. I thought they were more than just friends. I was wrong."

Claire felt her eyes wet. She rose from her chair and drew Tom towards her, and they held each other tight. "Why didn't you tell the sheriff?" she whispered.

"Who could I trust?" Tom said. "I could be next – or you."

Chapter 42

Mitcham Creek, Inverness

Gordon slowly replaced the telephone; he heard the click and the long buzz as the line was cut off. He had just telephoned Neil at the hotel to let him know that his mother was missing. Neil had offered to drive up from Miami, but Gordon had persuaded him not to come, saying that he would telephone him as soon as there was any news. Besides, he had added, Neil should stay at the hotel just in case his mother turned up there.

Gordon tried to make contact with Emily, to no avail. He'd telephoned the base at Portsmouth, only to be told firmly by a no-nonsense woman officer that the *Ark Royal* was on manoeuvres. She had asked, almost as an afterthought, if his call was a matter of life or death.

"It could be," Gordon said. "I need to speak to her."

"Well, sir," the woman had said, "could I suggest you leave a message and I will ensure that it gets through to Lieutenant Richardson as soon as she's back in port."

Gordon thanked her and left his telephone number with a message to ring him.

He rang Faye at the university and explained the situation. They agreed to meet at the Dorchester on Friday evening when he would be in London. He replaced the receiver and thought for a moment about the mess he'd made of things. He'd been a lousy father, and a worse husband. He felt a grievous sense of remorse, or was he simply feeling sorry for himself? He really didn't know.

Next he rang the sheriff's office.

Deputy Wall answered the call. "Hi there, Mr Richardson, how you doing?" he drawled. "No, the sheriff's not in. He's out on the lake – human remains." And then he hesitated and his voice lost its chirpiness. "A body's been found on the shoreline near the power unit. He'll be away some time, I guess."

Gordon's pulse was racing. A body in the lake? It's what he had feared. "It could be my wife," he said falteringly.

"No, sir," the deputy assured him. "The torso's that of a male."

"Thank God," Gordon whispered to himself. "Is there any news regarding my wife?" he asked.

"If there was any news, sir, we would have telephoned you."

"Yes, I know, of course. It's not knowing that's the hardest part."

"Look, Mr Richardson," the deputy said, trying to chose his words carefully, "don't worry, she'll turn up. I know it."

"Thanks for your help," said Gordon, and slowly put down the receiver. In spite of Mark Wall's comforting words, he knew differently. He knew she was dead. Anger, frustration and despair spun their heady mix and he cried out, "Dead! She's dead!" and the words, as if taunting him, echoed around the empty house.

Chapter 43

Lake Henderson, Inverness

Sheriff O'Donnel stood by the lake shore with Rastos Nokes looking down at the bloated human remains.

"There's no doubt about it," he said, "the arm belongs to Chuck Romford. I recognise the tattoo, see, a bald eagle. That's his arm all right."

Rastos nodded toward another body lying several feet away. "What about the other one?" he asked, turning away as he felt the nausea rise from his stomach.

The sheriff scratched his head. "Who knows. It could be Max Pace. Right size, but it's hard to tell from what's left. I'd better get on to the morgue. I need an autopsy." He went over to his car, reached in for the phone and clicked the switch. "Mark, is that you?"

"Yes, Sheriff."

"Look, we've got what's left of two bodies – not one, *two*. I want you to get onto the morgue, ask them to send an ambulance as soon as possible, and warn them they're in pieces."

"I'll get right on it now," replied Mark.

"Oh, and I nearly forgot," the sheriff added, "contact Doc Mortimer. I need a report from him as to the cause of death, if possible within the next twenty-four hours. You get that?"

"Will do," replied Mark.

O'Donnel replaced the phone and walked back to Rastos on the beach. "How did you come to find them?" he asked.

Rastos told him he came across the bodies while he was out looking for his dog.

"Your dog?" queried the sheriff.

"That's right." said Rastos gravely. "She just disappeared while swimming out there, opposite the house."

"You mean she drowned, ran off, what?"

"As I said," Rastos told him, his eyes beginning to fill with tears, "she just disappeared. One second she was swimming, the next she was gone. Just disappeared."

The sheriff looked down at his boots, distressed by the old man's anguish. After a short silence he asked, "What's your theory, then?"

"I think the gator took her," the old man replied quickly.

"What, the one over by the brewery? But he's been around for years. He doesn't bother anyone."

"I know," said Rastos, "but I've got this feeling about him."

The sheriff hesitated for a moment, trying to make sense of all this. "You know, Rastos," he said at length, "if what you say is true, then something very strange is going on here."

"Well," Rastos said vaguely, "things have changed in the lake over the past few months."

"What the hell do you mean by that?" the sheriff asked in a tone bordering on frustration.

Rastos hesitated. Then he said, "Well, firstly the bass. A couple of months ago they were taking anything you threw at them. Fish were being taken out over fifteen pounds, and then gradually within a few weeks, no fish, no bites, nothing. I've tried every spot I know."

"But that's not unusual," the sheriff said. "Sometimes fish don't feed."

"Maybe for a few days," said Rastos, "but not for two weeks. Besides, folks are catching plenty of fish on Lake Touissa. No, something's definitely wrong."

O'Donnel cast a worried look out across the water. Questions needed answers, and he didn't have them. "Perhaps," he said, "there's been a poison discharged somewhere, killed the fish." It was a wild hypothesis he knew, but what else could it be?

"No carcasses," Rastos pointed out. "Nothing. No, that can't be the answer."

"Any other ideas?" the sheriff asked.

"Well, there is one," Rastos said hesitating, "but you won't like it. I think all the fish have been taken by the alligator."

"But that's ridiculous!" the sheriff scoffed. "No gator could eat all the fish in the lake, certainly not within the space of a few months."

"I know it sounds incredible," said Rastos nodding his head, "but that's the only explanation I can give. I saw that old gator for a moment a few weeks back, off Alligator Island, and the old guy seemed to me to be at least fifteen feet long."

The sheriff chewed vigorously on his gum. "Well, that's not *that* unusual, surely. Alligators have been know in this area to grow up to twenty feet."

"That was years ago," Rastos explained. "That old gator was

only twelve feet long last year when I saw him. Alligators grow only a few inches a year when they get over ten feet or so. This old boy, he's grown three feet in just a few months."

"Maybe you were mistaken," said the sheriff. What he was hearing was beyond logic.

Rastos looked at the sheriff and their eyes met.

"Okay," said the sheriff, raising his hands. "Okay, so the gator's putting on weight, but what the hell do we do now? If it's taken dogs, humans could be next." He stopped as his eyes fell once again on the two bodies. He took a deep breath and looked across at Rastos. "You think he's done that already, huh? These two were just an aperitif. Is that what you think?"

Rastos fidgeted with a stick in the sand. "Well, it's a possibility. Something chopped these two up and took my dog. If that old boy's eaten all the fish, and there's no food left, and come to think of it, I ain't seen many turtles around lately, well you put two and two together."

O'Donnel took a long, deep breath. "If you're right," he said, "we've got to kill this monster now. Where the hell do we find him?"

"Can't be sure," Rastos replied, "but he has a den over on the beach there." He pointed in the direction of the power unit and brewery.

"Well, let's go look," said the sheriff with a sense of urgency.

"It's a no-go area," Rastos reminded him.

"Fuck that! I can go where I damn well like," exclaimed the sheriff. "Let's get back to your place and get the boat. I want this thing dealt with now. Let's go." As he spoke two ambulances screeched to a stop by the roadside. The sheriff went over and gave instructions to the two orderlies. "Take care when lifting the remains," he told them. "And get them to the doc as soon as possible. I want a report in twenty-four hours."

It was some forty minutes later when Rastos and the sheriff eased the boat onto the shore near the power unit.

Claire was gazing out of the window in her office when she noticed the boat in the restricted area. She telephoned the sheriff's office only to be told by Mark Wall that he knew all about it; the sheriff was on board with Rastos Nokes.

Claire was puzzled. "What's he doing in a restricted area?" she asked.

"I don't know," replied the deputy. "All I know is that the sheriff was following up his investigations regarding a body found on the beach today."

"Oh," said Claire, more puzzled than ever.

Chapter 44

Lake Apopka, Inverness

The bottom of the boat made a high-pitched grating sound as it slid onto the beach. Both men were sweating profusely. They hesitated at the water's edge, looking for any sign of the alligator. There was none.

O'Donnel was the first to jump clear of the boat onto dry land, taking his Magnum out of its holster as he did so.

Rastos moved to the centre of the boat, lifted a hatch and, with his strong arms, began pulling up a fishing net from below.

The sheriff turned his head. "What the hell's that for?" he asked.

"Just in case," explained Rastos. "He might be in there. We can stretch this across the entrance. It won't hold him, but he'll get in one hell of a tangle."

"Good idea," said the sheriff. "Do we have a torch?"

Rastos patted his stomach where a big black torch was sandwiched between his crocodile belt and his enormous paunch.

The sheriff nodded. "Now, where exactly is this den?"

"Just ten feet to the left," Rastos told him. "You can just see the entrance under that old tree. Look, this is where he lays out in the heat of the day – see the hollow?"

O'Donnel squinted. "Well he ain't there," he said.

Rastos shrugged. "If he ain't, he ain't. He's certainly not in the water around here," he added.

"How do you know that?"

Rastos didn't reply. The sheriff smiled nervously; trickles of sweat rolled down over his cheek to the edges of his mouth. He wiped away the globules with his forefinger. It was hot – hot and humid, with no wind, and an ominous silence, broken only by the constant buzzing of crickets. Cautiously the two men approached the entrance to the den.

Rastos took the torch from his belt and aimed a beam of light into the darkness. O'Donnel stood by, gun ready cocked, aiming at the dark entrance.

Rastos eased himself closer until he was able to scan the beam deep into the den. The stench of rotting flesh assailed his nostrils. It was so powerful that his stomach immediately reacted. Turning away he retched violently, regurgitated his breakfast.

O'Donnel didn't move. He expected the monster to come charging out of the hole at any second.

Rastos wiped his mouth on his sleeve. "Jesus Christ! What a stench." Then he looked up at O'Donnel, standing like a statue, legs planted apart, gun aimed at entrance. "It's okay," he said. "He's not in there – you can relax."

"Are you sure?"

"Yes, I'm sure."

The sheriff relaxed his grip on the gun and his arm dropped to his side, but he kept the gun in his hand. "Will he be back?" he asked.

"Can't say," said Rastos. "He must be out hunting. Alligators relax during the day, absorb the sun. They hunt at night."

"This guy's not acting normal then?"

"Appears that way," replied Rastos.

"We'd better look at that den more closely," the sheriff said. "See what's in there."

Rastos nodded. "Won't be a pleasant experience," he said. "But should be okay. Be warned, though, the stench is horrible."

"I did notice," the sheriff said, nodding towards the remains of Rastos's breakfast now festering on the sand. "Right, we'd better get in there."

Crouching low, Rastos led the way with the flashlight. O'Donnel followed, and as he did so he caught the full force of the stench which stopped him like a wall.

"You okay?" asked Rastos.

The sheriff swallowed hard, though he could feel the bile rising in his throat. "If I didn't know better," he said, "I'd say that was rotting human flesh."

Rastos said nothing. They both knew what the other was thinking.

They moved in deeper, hunched up. The beam of light caught something white and red in the far corner. It looked like a pile of old sticks and paper. O'Donnel nudged the old man, and when they were a few feet away, Rastos focused the torch beam directly at the pile of debris. Both men froze in horror. The tangled mess upon the ground was decomposed human flesh and bone.

O'Donnel could clearly make out part of a hand, and beside it lay a section of a rib cage, with torn pieces of black silk pulled tight across it, as if its owner still clung desperately to one last earthly possession. Beside them lay the hind leg of some animal.

Rastos was the first to speak. "And that's what's left of my dog," he said in a wavering voice.

O'Donnel was more concerned about the human tragedy than about a dog. "We've got to get out of here," he said. "We've no time to lose. We have to find this monster quickly, before it takes someone else." Rastos still had his eyes on the remains of the dog. "Snap out of it, man," the sheriff said angrily. "I know you were fond of your dog, but we have more pressing problems. We need a search party out on the lake, and we need surveillance on this place round the clock. What about the mess?" he said, thinking out loud.

"We leave it," said Rastos grimly, "in case he comes back."

Chapter 45

The Gallery, Inverness

It was Wednesday morning. Gordon was on the telephone discussing a Rembrandt with a Bond Street dealer, when through the gallery window he saw a blue Rolls-Royce Corniche pull up outside. He recognised it as the Rolls Sheriff O'Donnel had been driving in Orlando, but now it was being driven by Dobson. He motioned to Margaret to open the door.

Dobson came into the gallery carrying a brown paper package. "Your painting, sir," he said, placing it against the wall. "Mrs Larimer, sir, asked me to remind you to take good care of it. She is worried that the frame might get broken."

"I understand," said Gordon, playing along with the charade. "Tell Mrs Larimer not to worry. I have my instructions in the envelope, remember?" And he patted the breast pocket of his suit.

"Of course, sir. Safe journey, sir." The butler smiled weakly, turned and left the gallery.

'Pompous ass,' thought Gordon. But he did rather wonder at all this secrecy. The Munnings might be expensive, and he understood their caution, but all this fuss over safety was a bit much. But then, millionaires had strange foibles. Besides, why should he worry, he'd been paid, and if they wanted to give him a free trip to London, that was fine with him. He glanced at his watch, it was 11.30 a.m. He would have to leave by 3.00 p.m. to catch the 6.00 p.m. flight.

He decided to check with the sheriff's office to see if there was any news, but there wasn't. He told Mark Wall that he was going to London for a few days, and left him his number at the Dorchester.

He left the gallery in Margaret's capable hands and told her that he'd be back on Monday, but that he'd call at the house before he left. She told him not to worry, and that if there was any news of his wife, she'd phone.

Just as he was about to leave the door opened and in marched

Jean Manley. She was accompanied by a rather dour-looking thick-set man in a light-grey crumpled suit. The man had a moon-like face with a scar running the length of his left cheek, and he looked irritable. Dark sweat stains showed under his armpits. Not a pleasant-looking character, Gordon remembered thinking. Jean looked worried.

"An unexpected pleasure," Gordon said.

But she didn't answer. Instead, with her companion she swept through the gallery and into Gordon's office. Margaret made a move to intercept them but she was brushed aside. Gordon, angry at this sudden imposition, followed. Once inside his office he closed the door behind them and demanded to know what they thought they were doing.

Jean looked glum and said nothing. Her companion, on the other hand, turned to Gordon and, holding up a badge in front of him, said, "FBI Narcotics Squad. Commissioner Brown."

For once in his life Gordon was speechless. He wanted to say something, to protest even, but nothing came out.

The man said, "It would help a great deal, Mr Richardson, if you do exactly what I tell you. The first thing is to ask your assistant to leave."

Gordon felt a need to argue, but the authority in the man's voice compelled obedience. He left the office quickly and called Margaret. He told her something had come up that he needed to deal with right away, and to take an early lunch.

"But I wasn't planning to take a break at all today," she said. "You weren't going to be here."

"Margaret," he repeated with a touch of irritation, "what's come up is important. I have to discuss things with these two people. Please."

"Okay, if you're sure," she said nervously.

"I'll see you in one hour."

She mumbled something, then collected her bag and left.

Gordon flipped the sign to 'Gallery Closed', locked the door and returned to his office. They were both sitting in front of his desk so he walked behind it, which gave him a territorial advantage, and demanded, in the most commanding tone he could muster, to know what was going on.

Jean cast a nervous glance at the commissioner. He said nothing but gave a little nod; clearly permission for her to continue.

She looked unsure of herself, as if this was something she didn't want to do. She hesitated for some moments, and then she said, "Gordon, I'd better explain. I'm not what you think I am."

"What on earth do you mean?"

"I'm an FBI agent on the drug squad. I've been working undercover for the past eighteen months – on a project."

"Christ!" That for the moment was all Gordon could think of saying as his mind grappled with the enormity of her words. After some seconds he managed enunciate something more relevant. "You mean everything that happened, the meeting on the plane, your job at customs and excise, our friendship, it was all contrived, planned, right down to our relationship?" By this time his voice had increased in volume as disbelief gave way to anger.

Jean had her eyes fixed to the desk top, her long fingers playing at the leather nervously. "Gordon – I'm sorry," she said softly.

"Bitch," cried Gordon in a rage, and raised his right arm to strike the woman opposite. But the blow never landed. A hand shot up clamping his wrist in a vice-like grip, tight, secure, rigid.

"Settle down," growled the commissioner. "I don't want to hurt you." The scarred cheek was close to Gordon's face, and the brown eyes burned deep into his own.

Gordon nodded, his body relaxed and the commissioner released his grip.

Jean said nothing. Throughout the incident she had sat in her chair, rigid like a tailor's dummy, but now, as he sat back in his chair massaging his wrist, she spoke: "Gordon, I *am* sorry. Originally it was just a job – part of the plan." She glanced at the commissioner. "But it wasn't like that later on. That's why I cooled things off. I know you'll never understand, but I would like you to know that I did . . ." She hesitated for a second. "I *do* feel some affection for you, but I had to see this operation through to the end." She glanced nervously at the commissioner again.

"What are you talking about?" asked Gordon. "What operation?"

The commissioner looked at his watch. "It won't be easy in the time we have," he said, "but I'll try to explain. Don't interrupt – just listen. Some years ago we heard from one of our contacts in Cuba that drugs were being laundered through Cuba from Columbia on a large scale. These drugs eventually arrived in Florida by way of St Petersburg, where they were distributed. Half the drugs were destined for consumption in Florida and Georgia, but the rest, to the best of our knowledge, moved through Inverness and on to England."

"But what's this all got to do with me?" Gordon broke in angrily.

"I said no interruptions," the commissioner said sharply. "The point is that we were interested in you. We thought you might be involved." He paused for a moment to let his words sink in.

Gordon reacted with disbelief. "Christ, I know nothing about drugs! Or drug dealers! I know no one who might be remotely involved in something like this. The whole assumption is ridiculous."

"Do you know someone by the name of Gerald Fitzgibbon?" the commissioner asked, ignoring Gordon's denials.

"Why, yes, he's a good friend of mine," Gordon said. "He has a shoe shop in Bond Street. Why do you ask?"

"He's the main distributor in London. He has been for the past five years."

"I don't believe you," Gordon said. "You've got the wrong man."

Jean said, "It's true, Gordon, but there's something else. He was murdered two weeks ago – found dead in his swimming pool. He appeared to have died from a snake bite."

The colour drained from Gordon's face. He felt dizzy, confused. "What made you think I was involved?" he asked.

"Well, for one thing," said the commissioner, "you'd just sold your art business in Portsmouth and moved to Inverness. Quite a coincidence, don't you think?"

Gordon rubbed his face nervously, his cheeks felt hot and moist. "I see what you mean," he conceded, "but I swear to you I knew nothing about Gerald's involvement in drugs."

"We know," replied the commissioner, "but we had to be sure."

"So to be sure," said Gordon with a hint of sarcasm, "you put Miss Jean here onto me. Damn you, Jean, how could you?" But when he looked at her, her eyes held steady. What he was seeing was professionalism; hard, cold professionalism. He looked away mortified.

The commissioner continued: "There are others of your acquaintance – Senator Page, Mayor Thompson, Mrs Larimer, Mr Macceffy and the Cuban Minister for Tourism, Hunaz Potra – at least, that's the list so far."

Gordon swallowed hard. "Why should I believe you after the way you've set me up?" And then he suddenly thought of something. "My God, that's why Sheila's disappeared, they have her as a hostage. She was a friend of Gerald's."

"Look," said the commissioner calmly, "your wife's disappearance has nothing to do with this matter. We checked that out very carefully."

"The sheriff. You must have talked to him. Does he know about all this?"

"The sheriff's one of our agents," said the commissioner. "I sent him up here to keep an eye on the situation."

"But he can't be. I saw him with Macceffy in Orlando."

The FBI man looked across at Jean Manley. "Yes, we know," he said. "He's a double agent. They all think he's involved. They trust him, but I assure you he's on our side."

Gordon sat motionless for a moment trying to rationalise the situation. "Please," he said, tossing an angry glance at Jean, "you said I'm not involved, then why are you here in my office with her?"

"Because you've just become involved – a few minutes ago."

"I'm sorry, I still don't understand. I'm not involved."

The commissioner got up from his chair. "Let me show you something," he said. He opened the door of the office and went into the gallery where he picked up the brown paper package containing the Munnings.

"Sorry," said Gordon, "that's just a picture. I'm taking it to London for a client."

"Have you opened it?" The commissioner asked.

"Of course not. I was told not to disturb it. I have instructions to deliver it my client's sister in London."

"Mrs Larimer's sister?"

"Yes, that's right, but how did you know?"

"Mrs Larimer has no sister. For that matter she has no husband either. She has a lover, Hunaz Potra. It might explain a few things."

Gordon was feeling desperately out of his depth. He didn't know whether to believe what he was hearing or not. Everybody he knew, it seemed, was involved in the drugs racket. "But how are the senator and the mayor involved?" he asked.

"Both act as receivers," Jean explained. "The senator in St Petersburg; the mayor in Inverness."

"It's all a bad dream."

"It's no dream, believe me," said the commissioner. "So far at least five men have lost their lives, two of them my undercover agents."

Gordon's shoulders drooped. He felt wiped out, sapped of strength, the way he felt after a heavy drinking session. "What do you want from me?" he asked.

"I want you to deliver this picture as planned," the commissioner said.

"Why this picture?"

"The frame has been packed with drugs," Jean told him.

"Then you must be mad," Gordon stammered, fixing his eyes on the woman opposite. "I don't want to get involved."

"Gordon," said Jean with a firmness that surprised him, "whether you like it or not, you *are* involved. We've got to nail these people, and you're the only person who can do it."

"Oh, no, no," said Gordon. "None of the things you've said affects me in any way."

"I'm afraid they do," said Jean. "Your wife has been taking cocaine for at least two years – maybe more."

"That's not true. She may have been having problems, but cocaine isn't one of them."

The commissioner tossed a small package containing white powder onto the desk. "We found this in your bedroom, hidden behind one of the pictures," he said. "If it isn't your wife's, it must be yours."

Gordon felt numb. He was angry at the way they had infringed his liberty, upset and confused at what they had found.

"We need your help, Mr Richardson," the commissioner said.

To this Gordon made no reply, which the commissioner took as a refusal.

"If you don't help us, I'll charge you with possession and trafficking."

Still no response.

"Mr Richardson, you have no choice." And then he softened his tone. "Help us for your wife's sake and thousands like her. We have to fight these people, and we have to get the men at the top; not the little guys, but the ones who really profit and make millions out of other people's misery."

Gordon was staring at the woman across the desk, looking for some form of contact, but there was none. Jean avoided eye contact. She was doing her job, that was all. The only interest she had ever had in him was as a small link in a big chain. The end of which was probably a bullet in the back. But he only had himself to blame. He'd gone for her like a dog on heat.

"Okay," he said submissively. "What do you want me to do?"

The commissioner looked distinctly relieved. "Good," he said. "Do as we said; deliver the package. However, there will be one difference. The drugs will be replaced with baking powder."

Gordon swallowed hard. "You must be mad," he exclaimed. "If they find out they'll kill me!"

"Not right away," the commissioner said, with a chink of a smile playing at the corners of his eyes. "They'll want to keep you alive until they find out what you've done with the cocaine."

"Oh, great! And then they'll kill me?"

"The commissioner's joking," Jean broke in earnestly. "We have contingency plans. You are supposed to stay in London until Friday, and you're booked to return on BA flight 138, accompanied by Mrs Larimer. Is that correct?"

Gordon nodded. Their intelligence gathering was impressive. 'But how do they know all of this?' he wondered.

Jean Manly wasn't finished. "But you're not coming back on that flight," she told him. "You're booked in on the Thursday morning flight under the name of Fredrickson." She took a passport out of her handbag and handed it to him, and by way of reassurance added, "And by the time they find the drugs have gone missing, you will be back in Inverness."

Commissioner Brown said, "I'll have the house under surveillance by my agents when you get back, and your phone will be tapped. There will be no way they can get to you – until we want them to."

"What the hell do you mean by that?"

"I want you to arrange a meeting with them. Tell them all you know. Insist that all parties – Senator Page, the mayor, Hunaz, are all present."

"You've missed one out," Gordon pointed out with a touch sarcasm. "Mrs Larimer."

"We'll take care of her," the commissioner replied bluntly. "Her flight will be delayed in London. Don't worry." He walked over to the window, drew a blind back a few inches and made a signal.

A few seconds later two men entered the gallery at the rear carrying a bag of tools. They unwrapped the picture and placed it face down on the carpet. Then they began to lever away the back of the frame, which came away easily to reveal a number of small packages. Gordon was mesmerised.

"About three million dollars worth," the commissioner said, reading his thoughts.

The two men deposited the packages in a black holdall and replaced them with identical bags. To Gordon the contents were indistinguishable from one another, though one was the cause of appalling misery, whilst the other was used to bake cakes.

Chapter 46

Power Unit, Inverness

By Wednesday evening, Claire had analysed the data provided by Tom from his own computer assessment. She sat at her desk, her head cupped in her hands. There was no doubt in her mind that radioactive water was escaping from the plant.

She buzzed Tom on the internal phone. "Tom, it's me," she said wearily. "You're right. I agree with your findings, but we need to know how the water in the casing is escaping." And then a thought struck her and she said, "Just supposing that Wayne and Betty had discovered where the leak was, and were on their way to report to the mayor. Do you think – do you think they could have been murdered?" She found it difficult to say the word, but now that she had, she almost felt a sense of relief.

Tom was silent.

"Tom, are you still there?"

"In my opinion, Claire," Tom replied after some hesitation, "that is exactly what happened."

Claire hadn't somehow expected such ready confirmation. Tom's uncompromising words brought tears to her eyes, and suddenly she could control herself no longer and broke down in a fit of crying.

Tom came rushing round to comfort her.

"You're right," she confided between sobs. "There's no one we can trust if the mayor's involved. Who can we turn to?"

Tom couldn't answer that, but he squeezed her hand a little tighter, and after a few minutes she began to rally.

"Tom," she said, "we must think how the water's escaping."

"I know how it's escaping," he said. "I found it on Friday. The outer concrete casing's cracked. It's hard to spot, but it's there."

"Are you sure?"

"Absolutely. I checked it again today. The cracks are getting wider. I've calibrated the movements through the computer."

"If the loss is through the casing," said Claire, feeling her stomach tighten, "then the contaminated water could be leaking into the lake."

Tom simply shrugged his shoulders and said nothing, but he looked suddenly pale.

The enormity of the implication was obvious, and the seriousness of the problems which now faced them shook Claire into action. She was suddenly the seasoned professional, her mind clear again. "Have you checked the lake for any signs of contamination, particularly at the end of the outfall pipe?" she asked Tom.

Tom replied that he had, but that he had found no sign of radioactivity.

Claire thought for a moment, tapping her pen on the desk. "That's not so surprising," she said. "The radioactive water could be seeping into one of the underwater springs and entering the lake some distance away. We'll have to survey the whole lake area. Can we get hold of a boat?"

"Give me ten minutes," Tom said. "Meet you at the landing stage," and with that he was gone.

Claire sat in silence for several minutes to put her confused thoughts into some kind of order, then she picked up her coat and went to meet Tom who was already waiting at the landing stage. As she approached she could hear the putt, putt, of an engine, and once she was aboard, Tom gently opened the throttle and eased the launch out into the lake.

In the cabin, Claire found a detailed map of the lake and spread it out on the table. The map showed eight possible spring locations on the lake bed, all of them flowing outlets. The nearest one was about fifty feet offshore, so they decided to begin there.

When they were on station, Tom dropped the engine to idle and Claire gently lowered the Geiger counter into the clear water. There was no reaction.

"Looks okay," said Tom.

Claire nodded. "We'll move onto the next one," she said pointing north-east in the direction of the brewery. Tom throttled up, and Claire repeated the operation at the next location. That, too, was negative.

At the third location, Claire lowered the counter and there was an immediate reaction, a strong buzz; the counter registered a high level of radioactive contamination. As the instrument went deeper so the buzz became louder. Claire looked across at Tom, but neither spoke. She signalled to move off station slowly, but even as they moved away the counter registered high levels of radiation.

"My God," said Tom. "Most of the lake could be affected."

Over the next two hours they checked a large section of the lake and found various ranges of contaminated water. The conclusions were obvious, the whole lake, and in all probability the town's water supply, was contaminated. The most drastic action was needed.

"We've got to close-down the unit immediately and notify the authorities," Claire said.

Tom frowned. "Which authorities? It seems to me there's no one we can trust."

"I'll talk to Lucy," said Claire. "She seems to know everybody, at least she may know someone actually trustworthy we can talk to."

Tom turned the boat.

"Not that way," Claire said. "Head across the lake to Lucy's house. We've no time to lose. When we get there take Lucy's car and drive straight to the plant, and don't stop for anybody."

It took them less than ten minutes to reach Lucy's landing, and as Claire helped Tom secure the boat, Lucy, hearing the noise, came out to meet them. She could see they were both agitated and that this was no casual visit.

"What's wrong?" she asked.

"Just about everything," replied Claire. "Please, can we talk inside?"

"Sure," said Lucy and led the way through into the lounge.

"Oh, Lucy," said Claire, "can Tom borrow your car? It's very urgent."

"The keys are in the ignition," Lucy told her, but even as she said it she heard the roar of her car engine and tires spinning in gravel. "My word, he is in a hurry," was all she could say.

In the following fifteen minutes, Claire told Lucy the whole story, adding that she was now convinced that Betty and Wayne had been murdered.

At first Lucy had refused to believe her. She knew how desperately depressed Claire had become over Wayne's death. Her present paranoia could well be a symptom of her state of mind. "Are you sure of your facts, Claire?" she asked cautiously.

Claire, reading the sign of doubt on Lucy's face, said, "Lucy, I'm not making this up, and I'm quite rational. What I'm telling you is the truth. Tom can vouch for that. The important thing is for us to shut down the plant, which is why Tom has taken your car. We must put the matter in the hands of the proper authorities, but we have no way of knowing who those authorities now are, since it appears so many of our upstanding public servants are mixed up in this."

Lucy's initial scepticism had crumbled. She knew Claire to be intelligent and passionately honest. She could not possibly be making all of this up. "There's only one person I can think of," she told Claire, "and that's Kevin."

"But I thought you and the sheriff didn't get on," Claire said.

"Having our differences is one thing," Lucy said, "trusting someone is quite another. And I do trust Kevin O'Donnel."

Claire nodded. "Okay, then let's go."

"No," Lucy said, placing a restraining hand on Claire's arm. "I'll phone him, ask him to come here. It's better that way."

"Whatever you think," Claire said. "And, by the way, thanks. I don't know what I would have done if you weren't here."

Lucy telephoned the station, but they said the sheriff was out on the lake. She told them it was of the utmost urgency, so they said they would try him on his mobile phone.

Meanwhile, Claire was worrying about Tom. Had he got to the plant safely? She began to rebuke herself for not going with him. There was nothing they could do for the moment but wait.

Chapter 47

Orlando, Florida – London, England

Gordon arrived at Orlando Airport at around 4.30 p.m. He parked his car in the long-stay car park and hailed a porter to carry his luggage, including the packaged painting, to the Virgin first-class check-in.

The tall blonde in the peaked Virgin Airlines cap behind the check-in desk took his passport and the brown envelope without the courtesy of looking up. This irritated him. He asked her if there was a problem.

"No problem," she said and raised her eyes to meet his. It was Jean Manley. "Everything here is in order, sir," she continued officiously with no sign of recognition, and handed him his passport and an envelope. "Please proceed to the first-class lounge. Your flight will be departing in forty minutes."

Nothing surprised him any more, he had to concede. These people were everywhere. 'They'll be popping out of manholes next,' he ruminated, and decided that Jean Manley had become an automation. She no longer had any normal feelings. If top brass pulled the right strings she'd dance. He reclined his head slightly and smiled broadly. "Thank you," he said, then picked up the picture and went to the departure lounge, where he ordered a large gin and tonic and spent the forty minutes wondering why all the world's most beautiful young women become barmaids.

The flight went without a hitch, and at customs he walked boldly through the green channel carrying the picture with all the confidence of a man protected by the law.

As he left the departure lounge, a black man stepped in front of him. "Mr Richardson?"

"That's me?" he replied, stepping back, and noticing that the man was wearing a chauffeur's uniform.

"Mrs Larimer, sir, asked me to take you to her sister in Knightsbridge."

Gordon hesitated. "What's Mrs Larimer's sister's address?" he asked.

"Number two, Blenheim Palace Road, sir," he replied.

Thirty-five minutes later the Bentley pulled up at a smart four-storey town house in Knightsbridge. The car's central locking system ensured that he was imprisoned in the back seat with his picture for the total duration of the journey, something that had not escaped his notice. Though he had to admit, the same system operated in taxis, he wondered briefly if many people actually realised that.

The chauffeur waited for him as he rang the bell. A minute later the door was opened by an elderly butler. It was Dobson.

"Mr Richardson. Good to see you again," he said with an almost genuine feeling of warmth. "How can I help you, sir?"

Gordon lifted up the package. "For Mrs Travers, from Florida."

"Oh, yes, sir, Mrs Travers is expecting it. May I take it?"

"Bit difficult," said Gordon, feeling slightly embarrassed, "but I have strict orders to hand this package to Mrs Travers personally."

Dobson looked slightly ruffled. "Just one moment, sir," he said and disappeared, closing the door behind him.

After a wait of approximately five minutes it opened again, and this time the aged butler had turned into a raven-haired twenty-something.

"I'm Mrs Travers," the woman said disarmingly. "You have something for me?"

Gordon passed the picture over to her. As he did so he glanced over her shoulder into the entrance hall, which looked rather grand. Although it was dark, he just caught a glimpse of another woman on the staircase, about halfway up. She reminded him of Mrs Larimer.

"Is there anything else?" the woman asked.

"Oh, no, I'm sorry. No, there's nothing." He turned and went down the steps to the waiting Bentley, but he could feel her eyes following him. At the bottom of the steps he turned, and as he did so the door closed with a click.

"Where to now?" the chauffeur asked.

"The Dorchester," replied Gordon.

As they sped through the London streets he began to feel uneasy. He was sure the woman on the staircase was Mrs Larimer. If that was the case how long had she been there, and why didn't she greet him at the door? Did it mean that she was suspicious? Questions without answers. He wanted at that moment to get back to Florida as quickly as he could.

When they reached the hotel he dismissed the chauffeur with a

£50 tip and told him he wouldn't be needing him any more. At first the man looked puzzled, but then shrugged and went on his way.

Gordon booked into his room, and after he'd freshened up, he sat on the edge of the bed and took from his pocket the envelope that Jean Manley had given him at the airport. It was a letter in his own handwriting, or rather a forgery of his handwriting. He read it carefully. The letter explained that he, Gordon Richardson, had removed the cocaine from inside the picture frame. That he was aware Senator Page, Mayor Thompson and Hunaz Potra were involved in the drugs operation, and requested that he meet with all three. He demanded two million dollars for the return of the cocaine. He read the letter again. By this time his hand was shaking, as what he was holding amounted to his death warrant.

He went to the phone, dialled reception and requested a taxi. He told the receptionist that it was urgent, he had to leave immediately.

Five minutes later the receptionist rang to say his taxi was waiting. He grabbed his bags and hurried to the lift. His forehead was damp with perspiration and he realised, without a great deal of surprise, that his pulse was racing. It almost went into orbit when the door of the lift opened and who should be facing him but Mrs Larimer's chauffeur. Gordon's jaws lost their ability to close his mouth, and for a few awful seconds he thought he was about to die. It was only when the man spoke that his brain clicked in again and he became capable of rational thought.

"Don't panic, sir, I'm on your side," the man said. "I'm taking you to the airport."

At reception, Gordon asked for his bill, only to be told that it had already been paid. He took the white envelope out of his pocket and asked the receptionist to give it Mrs Larimer, who was due to arrive about noon. Then he followed the chauffeur to the car. As soon as he had settled into the folds of expensive leather he began to relax.

The chauffeur cast a glance at him through the driver's mirror. "Don't worry, you'll be back in Florida soon, sir," he told him.

Gordon closed his eyes and a great sense of relief washed over him. At last he felt safe, a guardian angel was in the front seat. By the way," he asked, almost cheerfully, "what's your name?"

"You don't need to know that, sir," he replied in a much cooler tone. "Names aren't important."

Gordon felt a chill along his spine. Suddenly the leather seat became less comfortable. He cast a glance at the door locks; they were all closed down.

At the airport he rang Faye and told her he had to go back to Florida immediately.

Chapter 48

Power Unit, Inverness

Tom roared to a halt outside the power station's main entrance and bolted up the steps, through the main doors and along the corridor, ignoring the shocked receptionist at the desk.

Critchley turned as Tom burst into the control room.

"We've got a problem with the reactor!" Tom cried. "Contaminated water's leaking throughout the casing. We have to close down – immediately!"

Critchley's eyes widened in disbelief. "No! No, you can't do that! The mayor won't allow that."

"We don't have a choice," Tom told him. "We have to shut it down."

"Of course we have a choice," Critchley said defiantly. "We just leave things as they are. No one will ever know."

Tom was furious. "I'll know," he shouted at Critchley, leaning across his desk, "and so will all those poor bastards we've poisoned with radioactivity."

Critchley wasn't going to have his authority challenged. He looked Tom directly in the eye and said, "I said, no, and I mean, no!"

But Tom knew Critchley for what he was, a yes-man whose authority was only as good as the strong men behind him, and at this moment the back-up team was distinctly absent. Tom spun around and made a rush for the control panel on the far side of the room.

Critchley began to shake. He stood up, his fists pressed hard into the desk top, his face flushed red with a venomous mix of anger, fear and frustration. One hand dropped to the drawer of his desk, pulling it open slowly. He fumbled inside the drawer until his hand closed on the revolver.

Then, holding it tightly, he stepped from behind his desk and approached his errant assistant. Tom had his back to Critchley and was feverishly programming the computer for close-down. He just needed a few more moments, but he never got them. The bullet struck him at the base of the neck, blowing the back of his head away. His body crashed against the computer and slid to the floor.

For a few brief moments Critchley stared down at the body with resigned disbelief, then dropping the gun he turned his attention to the computer and cancelled Tom's instructions. Stepping back, he bent down to retrieve the weapon, and as he did so he reached out a trembling hand and touched the body as if unsure as to quite what he had done. Then realisation seemed to strike him and he recoiled, backing away with the helplessness of a frightened child. He staggered across the room and slumped into his chair. There was a deadness about his eyes as if the sparkle of life had left him too, and was receding through his skull. He gazed at the gun in his hand as if through an alcoholic daze, then slowly raised it to his temple, closed his eyes and pulled the trigger.

Chapter 49

Inverness Police Department

Sheriff O'Donnel entered his office wearing dark sunglasses, and without speaking walked across to his desk and collapsed into his chair. Mark Wall knew something was wrong. The sheriff's face looked ashen, not bronzed as usual and there were beads of perspiration on his forehead; his black shirt was plastered to his body with sweat, and when, after some minutes, he spoke, his voice sounded weary.

"It's not good news, Mark," he said rubbing tired eyes. "We've got a real problem on our hands. That old alligator's a man-killer – there's no doubt about it."

"But alligators aren't man-eaters," said Mark incredulously, "at least not those round here. For one thing we're not part of their food chain, and for another they've taken thousands of years to evolve. Things change slowly in their world, Sheriff."

"That may be the case," said O'Donnel. "At least that may be the logic of it, but I've seen evidence to the contrary, and what's more some of the evidence, I'm afraid to say, could be the remains of Sheila Richardson."

Mark Wall took in a deep breath and exhaled slowly. "Christ!" he said.

For a few seconds neither of them spoke, then O'Donnel rose from his chair, removed his sunglasses and stretched his big frame. "Right," he said decisively, "this is what we're going to do." He then went on to explain. "I've placed two officers at the gator's den over on the lake, just in case it returns. Rastos Nokes is gathering up all the people with boats he can muster to form search parties to check all the lakes in the area. Mark, you get word out on the local radio and TV stations that no one – and I mean no one – swims, water skis, fishes or goes near the lakes until further notice."

"But what reason do I give?" asked the deputy.

"Think of something, Mark, you're good at that."

Mark thought for a moment. "Like – I'll tell them we've found a highly virulent mosquito that's a potential killer. That'll stop them."

"Something more original."

"Can't think."

"Okay, this is what you tell them. Say there's been a chemical leak from the old leather factory – discoloured the water, nothing serious, but it has to be investigated."

"Do you think they'll buy that, Sheriff? That factory's been closed for nigh on ten years."

"I well know that," O'Donnel said sharply. "Tell them one of the old tanning tanks has ruptured. Say it will be at least a couple of days, maybe longer, before we can give the all-clear. Now get on with it. Oh, and by the way, just so as we sound more convincing, put a couple of officers up there on the old gates."

"Okay," Mark said. "Is that all?"

"Not quite. I want every available officer searching the backwaters, lakes, everywhere, for that crazed gator. Cancel all leave – and, Mark, make sure that all our people search in pairs and are armed with hunting rifles."

"I'll need the keys to the armoury," Mark said.

The sheriff unclipped a bunch of keys from his belt and tossed them over to his deputy.

As Mark left he remembered something and turned back to the sheriff. "I nearly forgot," he said. "There was a message for you from Dr Foster. She said could you call over. It sounded urgent."

"I don't have time for this," O'Donnel said irritably. "I'll call over later."

"Sheriff," Mark persisted, "she did sound distressed when she called, which is a bit unlike her, and that was about two hours ago."

O'Donnel raised his hand in compliance. "Okay! Okay! I'll call in a few minutes. Now, move your ass, you've a lot of things to do. And by the way, Mark, don't say a word about a man-eater to the men. Just say it's killing dogs and wildfowl and needs to be stopped before it goes further. But make sure they know that this thing could be dangerous. I should think that most of them will put two and two together anyway. It's supposed to be about fifteen feet long, so make sure that they only kill anything that looks to be over ten feet; I don't want to wipe out the entire local alligator population."

"I'm on to it," Mark said, grabbing his coat.

The next two hours were hectic. O'Donnel's office was the centre of operations, and police officers were coming and going continuously. He had men patrolling the lake and searching the foreshore. There were several sightings, all of which turned out to be false alarms. Some alligators were shot and Rastos was called in to inspect the corpses, but none was large enough to be the one they were after.

In all the commotion Sheriff O'Donnel forgot to phone Lucy.

For her part, Lucy had tried again and again to get through to the sheriff's office, but the line was always busy, and then she and Claire had heard on the radio about the leak from the tanning factory, and they had wondered at the irony of it.

"Damn! He's tied up with this other business," said Claire, "but he's got to listen to us. Compared with this thing, the tanning factory leak's an irrelevance."

"We can't wait here," said Lucy defiantly. "If Mohammed won't come to the mountain, then the mountain will have to go to Mohammed. Let's go and see him."

"Wait," Claire said. "I want to phone Tom before we go. He should have started the close-down programme by now." She picked up the telephone and dialled his number but there was no answer. After the third attempt she tried Reception.

The receptionist sounded nervous when she answered.

"Sarah, it's Claire. What's the matter? Your voice sounds strange. Can I speak to Tom?"

There was complete silence.

"Sarah, are you there? It's me – Claire."

After a few moments the voice came on line again. This time it sounded terrified and on the edge of tears. "I'm sorry. I can't put you through to Tom. He's dead! Mr Critchley shot him – and then," she sobbed, "he shot himself."

Claire dropped the receiver and slumped against the wall, her face a pallid white.

Lucy reached her just in time to stop her from falling over. "Claire, what's wrong?" She shook her gently.

"It's Tom," she replied in a shaky voice. "Tom's dead."

Lucy grabbed the phone. "Sarah, this is Dr Foster. Stay where you are. I'll be right over. Have you phoned the police?"

"Yes," replied Sarah between sobs. "The sheriff's on his way."

Chapter 50

Orlando Airport

Gordon Richardson touched down at Orlando Airport at 6.00 p.m. Throughout the flight he had sat next to a young man who spent the entire time either looking out through the window or engrossed in his book. Gordon had taken a stab at conversation, but there had been no response, so that now, as the plane touched down and Gordon was about to get up, the young man grasped his arm and in a low voice said, "Mr Richardson, my name's Guy Roberts, I'm with the FBI. I'd appreciate it if you follow me closely when we disembark."

'Another guardian angel,' Gordon couldn't help thinking.

On the tarmac, Jean Manley was waiting beside a Cadillac with blacked-out windows. "Well done," she said, opening a door. "We'll make an agent of you yet."

"You must be joking," Gordon said. "When this is all over I plan to distance myself from the FBI and its drug squad as fast as my little legs will carry me."

Jean smiled. "We'll see," she said and settled back in the seat next to him so that her perfume assailed his nostrils, and her very nearness sent his heart into the familiar pounding rhythm. He resented having been used, drawn into this undercover world, but Jean Manley's close presence was fast softening the hard edges. How long he could resist, he wasn't quite sure. He felt his loins tighten. He wanted her even then.

It was around 8.00 p.m. when the Cadillac drew up at his house. As he opened the door he could hear the telephone ringing.

Jean put a restraining hand on his shoulder. "Be careful," she said. "Remember who you're dealing with. If it's Mrs Larimer, tell her you have the cocaine in a safe place and you want to meet."

Gordon nodded nervously.

She continued: "Tell her that you want to meet the senator, the mayor and Hunaz. If they don't comply, say the deal's off."

At that point the telephone ceased ringing.

Jean smiled knowingly. "Don't worry," she said, "she'll ring back."

Chapter 51

Power Unit, Inverness

By the time Lucy and Claire arrived at the power station the car park was filled with police cars, their blue lights flashing in the fading light.

As the two women approached the gate house, Deputy Wall stepped out with his hand up. He peered into the car, he was looking nervous and ill at ease. "Hi, Lucy, Claire. It's bad," he said. "The sheriff could do with your help."

"Where is he, Mark?"

"He's over by Tom's office, but you'd better get there quick."

Lucy was out of the car the instant it pulled up at the main entrance. Grabbing her doctor's bag, she and Claire hurried along the corridor towards Tom's office. They almost bumped into Sheriff O'Donnel who was trying to comfort a very weepy Sarah.

"Lucy, thank God you're here," he said with relief. "My office has been ringing your home, but there was never any reply."

"Is it true that Tom's dead?" Lucy asked breathlessly.

The sheriff nodded. "Killed instantly." He looked at Claire and added, "If it's any consolation, he didn't feel a thing."

Lucy asked, "What about Critchley?"

"Still alive – just about," the sheriff said. "The medics are with him now. They might need your help."

"Where is he?"

"Slumped behind his desk."

Lucy glanced at Claire whose face had drained of colour. "Will you be all right?" she asked.

Claire nodded, but Lucy could see that her friend had slipped back into mild shock. Coming so soon after Wayne's death this was almost too much.

Claire followed behind Lucy as they entered Critchley's office. To the right was the door to the control room where Tom lay dead.

Claire turned towards it, but O'Donnel stopped her. "I'm sorry, Claire," he said firmly, "but you can't go in there."

She struggled against him but he held her firmly in his strong arms, and she collapsed into them, sobbing against his chest. All of her new-found strength and confidence had vanished; she was vulnerable all over again.

O'Donnel held her tight for a few moments until a policewoman arrived. "Look after her," he said softly, "and don't leave her alone."

At that moment, Lucy Foster was battling to save a man's life, a man who in the last half hour she had begun to hate, but she was a professional, and her job was to save life – any life.

"Will he live?" asked the sheriff from the half open doorway. The question was delivered in a sombre tone, as if the answer was of no matter one way or the other.

Lucy nodded. "Probably," she replied, "but he'll never be a pretty sight."

In the control room the medics were placing Tom's limp body in a plastic coffin which they would then seal. The sheriff watched them going about their duties with a sense of profound distress. Depression was not an affliction from which he suffered, but these deaths, violent deaths of people with whom he had more than a passing acquaintance, had disturbed him more than he would like to admit.

One of the medics looked up at him and their eyes met. There was a hint of compassion in those eyes, yet, strangely there was something else there, conversely, almost an indifference, an acceptance, a look that didn't quite connect with reality, as if this body with its head blown away, the kind of thing that he had to deal with every day of his life, was not out of the ordinary, a chore, nothing more, a job to be done and forgotten by tea time; a soldier burying his dead on the battlefield, brutalised by the horror that had become commonplace.

O'Donnel signalled for him to take the body to the waiting ambulance.

Still in a mood of morbid contemplation, the sheriff went to see how Claire was getting on. She was lying down in the rest room, talking to the policewoman. When she saw him she raised herself on one elbow.

"Please don't get up," O'Donnel said, sitting down on the end of the bed. "Look, Claire, this might not be the right time, but I have to get to the bottom of all this – this, tragedy." He was fumbling for words and felt uncomfortable. He shifted his seat. "Claire, you knew these people, both of them, one of them well, you worked with them. What I'm asking is – why? What happened here? What happened to make it happen?"

Claire's eyes glazed over. She didn't blink. She looked at him as if she were in a trance, and then she said, "Lucy and I were trying to contact you. We left a message. Didn't you get the message?" Her voice was raised to an accusing pitch.

"Yes," O'Donnel said, "I did get the message, but I was tied up with the pollution scare out on the lake. I was going to ring as soon as I could; I guessed it could wait."

Claire turned on him shaking with anger. "You guessed it could wait! Oh, yes, it *did* wait. And now Tom's dead. He's dead because you – thought – it – could – wait!" She buried her face in her hands sobbing and fell back onto the bed.

O'Donnel reached a comforting hand towards her, but Claire recoiled.

"Stay away from me!" she cried. "Go to hell!"

Chapter 52

Lake Henderson, Inverness

Rastos had been searching the beaches and alligator holes systematically for the past three hours. There had been no sign of the old alligator; he had found nothing. It was either lying low in the undergrowth somewhere or had moved to another lake.

On several occasions he had been called by officers to examine alligators they'd shot, but none was old enough or big enough. He had radioed the two officers who were guarding the alligator's den, but they reported having seen nothing. They both sounded nervous.

It was now early evening and Rastos was traversing the northern section of Lake Henderson. Officer Dawson, who had been accompanying him throughout the day, had been called away, and now he was alone. He turned his eyes towards the rim of sky to the west. Dark stormclouds were rolling in; he could already smell the rain, and feel the strengthening wind on his cheeks. In a few minutes the storm would be upon him. There was a deep roll of thunder and the sky suddenly darkened and was split by a flash of lightning that illuminated the horizon like a New Year's Eve fireworks display.

"It's going to a big one," he said to himself. "Better find cover and quick. You won't mind, old girl, if I run for cover. You're down there at the bottom somewhere, and I know you're watching me. I miss you, dog."

Another crack of thunder ripped though the air and the rain began to sheet down. He opened the throttle full out and raced for cover.

It took him only a few minutes to reach the safe cover of the bridge, but by that time he was soaked to the skin, his clothes hanging loose and wet from his huge frame. He swung the boat alongside one of the old timber support piles and tied up. The wind was now gusting, and as he stepped out onto the bank it knocked him half over, and he had to scramble through the mud to firmer ground before he could stand. White foam was flying off the tops of the waves; the water angry, seething, running before the storm. Rastos staggered further up the bank, where among some tall grass he dropped down beside a rotted trunk, which afforded some cover from the storm.

But amidst the frenzy of the storm, Rastos's movements had not gone unnoticed. The alligator stirred as it lay in the hole overhanging the foundations of the bridge. Its hideaway could not be seen from the lake or from the road as it was concealed by heavy reeds. It was hungry. It could sense live prey, and it began to move. Any sound it may have made as it slipped into the water was downed by the storm. It swam slowly, without a sound, until it came to within a few feet of the bank, beyond which Rastos lay in the grass against the tree, his eyes closed, waiting out the storm. He was unaware of the two orange eyes that watched him intently from the foaming water.

Very slowly, with quiet stealth, the great armoured head emerged from the lake, eyes fixed upon the figure by the log, like a spider fixed upon a fly. A matter of yards separated hunter from its prey, but that distance could be closed within seconds.

Suddenly, the hunter made its rush, its great tail propelling it from the water with frightening speed. It was then that Rastos saw it, the nose, the jaws, the great bulk of pre-history bearing down upon him with terrifying intensity. Rastos flung himself aside, but it was too late. The alligator lunged at him fastening its jaws onto his leg. There was the crunch of bone and Rastos screamed as his leg was torn from his body. The alligator flung its head from side to side, champing at the severed limb, and it was then that Rastos rolled away, and by some superhuman effort scrambled through the grass, dragging his severed body, screaming in pain and fear. Terror drove him on. He reached a low bank and scrambled over it, then through a fence and on again, numbed now but propelled by the urge to live, until he hit wet tarmac and the screech of brakes and the flashing of lights and men's voices.

By the time the ambulance got to him, Rastos was unconscious, but alive.

Chapter 53

Mitcham Creek, Inverness

It was just after ten o'clock in the evening when the telephone rang. Anxiously Gordon looked at Jean Manley for instructions.

She nodded. "Okay, answer it. I think you've made her wait long enough. Just let me check that the recording equipment's working." She picked up her mobile. "Commissioner, have you got the call?"

"All systems go," he said.

Jean pointed to the phone. "Pick it up," she told Gordon.

Gordon's hand was shaking, he could feel the sweat making its way down the nape of his neck. Taking a deep breath he picked up the telephone. "Hello," he said as authoritatively as he could.

"Hi, Dad, it's me," said a nervous voice. "Just thought I'd ring to see if there was any news of Mum?"

Gordon clamped his hand over the receiver. "It's my daughter, Faye," he said. "What shall I do?"

Jean looked agitated. "Get rid of her quick. Do it now."

Gordon removed his hand from the mouthpiece.

"Dad, are you still there? Are you okay?"

"Yes, I'm okay, darling, it's just that I have a client with me at the moment. It's a little awkward. No, I'm afraid there's no news about your mother." He hesitated. "Look, are you at home? I'll ring you later."

"Dad," said Faye anxiously, "are you sure you're okay?"

"Yes, I'm fine. I'll ring back later." Before she had a chance to say any more he replaced the receiver. He knew Faye would be upset, and he immediately regretted cutting her off. Jean was looking at him with raised eyebrows, and then the phone rang once again. Gordon grabbed it. "I said I'd ring you back, Faye." But it wasn't Faye.

"Mr Richardson? It's Mrs Larimer." There was a long pause. "What the hell do you think you're playing at?" She went on: "Do

216

you want to get yourself killed?" To neither of these questions did she wait for an answer but continued with a controlled anger. "Where's the merchandise? Your note said that you wanted to trade. I must warn you that the people with whom you are dealing are very annoyed. You've cost them three million dollars and wrecked their reputations."

Gordon said nothing. He clamped his hand over the receiver and looked to Jean for direction.

"Keep her talking," Jean whispered. "Don't lose her."

He took his hand from the mouthpiece and what he got was an expletive followed by, "Don't start playing games with me."

The voice had changed, it was harsh, with a slight tinge of a northern accent, quite unlike the refined vowels of its previous incarnation, that of an English public school educated blue stocking. 'Good actress,' he thought.

"I'm not playing games with you, Mrs Larimer," he said, "if that indeed is your name. I meant what I said." He caught Jean's eye. He was doing okay. "You were using me," he continued. "If I'd have been caught I'd be looking at twenty years."

"Don't waste time," she barked down the phone. "Where have you hidden it?"

"It's in a safe place," he assured her.

"You're a fool!"

"Not such a fool," he replied. "I know who's involved in this operation."

For a few seconds the end of the line went quiet, but he could hear heavy breathing – he'd caught her off balance. And then in a soft, though unconvincing voice, she said, "You're bluffing."

"No bluff. Try these for starters." He rolled off the names: "Senator Page, Mayor Thompson, Hunaz Potra and Macceffy, the customs chief."

There was another silence, longer this time, but he could hear whispering. She was talking to someone, then a man's voice came on line. It belonged to a Latin American and it carried a cadence that made the hairs on the back of Gordon's neck stiffen.

"Mr Richardson, this is Hunaz Potra. I think you are trying to be a little too clever. Tell me frankly what you want from us."

"You know what I want," Gordon said, trying to gain control of his voice. "It's in the letter to Mrs Larimer. I want two million dollars, as well as a share in the action."

"But, Mr Richardson, that is absurd," Potra said in the same coolly controlled voice that barely veiled his intense irritation. "Two million is not possible." He hesitated. "Perhaps one million, but that's as far as we go."

It was then that Gordon realised he had control of the situation. They took him seriously and they were willing to bargain. He was now sure that he could actually get them together, and then his part in all of this would be over. "Two million's the deal," he said firmly. "Take it or leave it."

This time there was a longer pause. He was sure he could hear whispering and a woman's angry voice in the background. Then Potra was back on. "I'll have to ring you back in a few moments," he said.

"There's one other thing," Gordon broke in. "I want all of us to meet here in Florida. I'll hand over the stuff then."

"All of us, Mr Richardson? What is that supposed to mean? Who is 'all of us'?"

Gordon said, "Page, Thompson, Macceffy, Mrs Larimer and your good self."

"That's impossible."

This time Gordon didn't wait but calmly replaced the receiver. He glanced down at his hands – they were steady. He was still in control. The ball was in their court. They would have to come to him now.

Jean, whose eyes had never left him, said, "You did well." Then she punched in a number on her mobile. "Commissioner, did you get all that?"

"Positive," the commissioner replied. "We're playing back the tapes now; all is okay so far."

She turned back to Gordon. "When he rings back," she said, "he'll want to close the deal. He'll probably tell you where they want to meet. Before you okay it, I want to check it on the map."

Gordon nodded, but he was concerned for his life. "They could just kill me," he said, "and write the whole thing off."

"They won't do that," said Jean with a whisper of a smile, which he thought was totally unjustified in the present situation, unless they actually thought that his likely death was cause for mirth.

"Why not?"

"They want the merchandise back. For one thing, it's worth an enormous amount of money, and for another, if they don't get it back, every petty crook they employ will be doing a runner with the stuff. Besides, they're professionals." She paused and thought for a moment. Then she said, as if putting thoughts into words, "There is just a chance they might try something later. No, by that time we'll have them all locked away."

Gordon immediately picked up on this. "You don't seem that certain," he said anxiously. "What about their friends? They might have avenging ones."

Jean gave a little shrug of the shoulders. "You'll have a new name, a new identity, and protection. You should be okay."

"Should, doesn't sound convincing," he said. At that point the phone rang, and he grabbed the receiver.

It was Hunaz Potra. "Okay, Mr Richardson," he said sharply. "I will speak to the other parties and ring you back in one hour."

"It must be *all* the parties," Gordon reiterated firmly, "or the deal's off. I want to meet you all. I have to protect myself, Mr Potra."

"You don't trust us?"

"No."

"You're very cynical for a beginner, Mr Richardson," Potra said. "One hour." The phone went dead.

Gordon glanced at Jean. "Was I okay? Was I convincing enough?"

"You were fine, just fine," she said. "I'm sure the commissioner will be pleased."

"I don't want praise from him," Gordon retorted.

Jean smiled. It was the kind of smile he remembered. Not a sardonic smile full of cynicism, but one approaching warmth.

"Look," she said, moving towards him, "don't feel too bad about me. If it helps, I'm genuinely fond of you, and I can assure you that's unusual."

"You're a bloody good actress," he said. "You took me in."

"Perhaps that's what you wanted," she said coquettishly. "Just think about that."

Chapter 54

Power Unit, Inverness

Lucy emerged from the control room with a haggard look on her face. What with Claire and these two deaths, and the problem with the radioactive leak, which was still known only to Claire and herself, she felt as if she were still in medical school, worn out by long hours on the wards.

She met O'Donnel in the corridor.

"How is he?" he asked.

"There's nothing we can do for him now," Lucy replied. "He'll live, but his face will make him wish he hadn't. By the way, how's Claire?"

O'Donnel said, "She's okay, I guess, but I think she blames me for Tom's death. She says I should have called around to the house as soon as I got your message."

"She's right," Lucy said, "but you already know that."

"I guess so. But there was an emergency."

"The pollution from the tanning factory, you mean?"

"No, I lied about that," said the sheriff. "There was no pollution. What I meant was . . ."

But Lucy broke in before he could finish. "There *is* pollution," she said indignantly. "That's what Claire and I wanted to talk to you about. The cooling water in the nuclear reactor is leaking. Do you know what that means? It means that the lake is radioactive." She took a deep breath to calm herself. "Tom was coming back here to close the plant down. That's why Critchley shot him, and then tried to kill himself."

"Jesus! But why didn't you keep phoning me?"

"I did phone, several times, damn it! You weren't there. When we really needed you, you were playing boyish games out on the lake."

"We were *not* playing boyish games."

"Okay, okay, but something has to be done."

"I need to know more," the sheriff said.

"Claire will tell you all," said Lucy, "but we don't have much time."

From Claire, O'Donnel learned the whole story, but on Claire and Lucy's insistence that the plant be closed down immediately, he was reluctant.

Claire was angry. She was beginning to see the sheriff as the unacceptable face of officialdom, the one that dragged its heels. "You're mad," she cried. "We've told you everything. You know the problem. That lake is becoming more radioactive with every minute, and you're going to do nothing!"

"Now hold on there, Claire," the sheriff said calmly. "Getting excited is not going to solve the problem. I know how you feel, but the worst thing we can do now is to set off a panic reaction. Of course the plant has to be closed down, but I don't want anyone to know why. I've already put out an open pollution warning and that was nothing but a cover."

"Cover?" they both said in unison.

"An alligator's developed a taste for people. We found a body, or what was left of one. We couldn't have everyone with a gun in the neighbourhood out hunting alligators or we'd wipe out the species, but we had to close the lake off, hence the pollution story."

"Well, at least it's closed off," said Lucy.

"Yes, but that doesn't solve the big one," Claire remarked. "If this thing gets into the water supply . . ."

"I'm mindful of that," the sheriff said sharply.

"Then I'm going to close it," Claire announced. "I'll have to notify the main power station at Pine Island that we've got a technical fault and that we have to decommission the plant for a week."

"Why do you have to do that?" the sheriff asked.

"Because they will have to supply stand-by power whilst the plant's out of commission. The town still needs an electricity supply."

"Will that be a problem?"

Claire shook her head. "Just one phone call and two switches." Then she thought for a moment and her face clouded. "Who's going to tell the mayor we're closing down," she asked.

"Don't worry about that," said O'Donnel. "I'll take care of the mayor. I'll also leave four of my men at the plant with you to stop anyone interfering."

When Claire had gone, O'Donnel took Lucy by the arm. "This mess rather complicates another operation that we have going on at the moment," he told her, "and I don't mean the alligator one. Look, before I go on I have to make a phone call. I'll be a couple of minutes."

Lucy nodded, but wondered what could be more important that

the present crisis. "I'll make some coffee," she said.

O'Donnel telephoned Commissioner Brown from the privacy of his patrol car and told him the situation.

The commissioner reacted with a few well-chosen expletives. "Goddamit, Kevin," he exclaimed, this could jeopardise our whole operation. You can't tell Thompson that you're going to close the plant. He's in this shit as deep as the others. If he gets a sniff of this, they'll go to earth, every one of them."

"Well it's not something you can keep *that* secret," the sheriff pointed out. "People are going to soon know if the plant closes. The mayor's not that much of a fool."

"You can't delay?"

"No."

Public safety was the priority. That took precedence and O'Donnel slightly resented the commissioner's insinuation that it didn't.

"Leave it with me," he said. "I'll come up with something."

"Okay, but keep in close touch." Commissioner Brown had faith in O'Donnel. He'd known him for a long time and he fully trusted his judgement, even if at times the sheriff was abrasive and tended to take matters into his own hands.

O'Donnel slowly replaced the phone. Running through his mind was the realisation that he was the piggy in the middle, trying to juggle the demands of two opposing sides. At the moment the balls were in the air.

He found Claire in the control room preparing to close down the plant. O'Donnel needed a delaying tactic. "Have you phoned the power plant at Pine Island yet?" he asked.

"Not yet," Claire replied.

"Good, because I need to talk to you both."

"But I must close down . . ."

"Please, Claire. I want to explain something to both of you. It'll take a few minutes only."

Claire sighed. "Okay," she said, "if you insist. I'll get Lucy."

When both women were in the room, O'Donnel asked them to sit down, and he began: "What I'm about to tell you is for your ears only. It mustn't go beyond this room. Is that clear?"

Both women nodded, though Claire looked sullen. He was just about to continue when Mark Wall charged in through the door.

O'Donnel rounded on him angrily. "Jesus! Don't you ever knock," he barked.

"Sorry, Sheriff, but I have to talk to you urgently – right now."

"Does it have to be this minute?"

"It does."

"Forgive me ladies," O'Donnel said.

When they were alone, Mark Wall said, "It's Rastos Nokes. He's lost one of his legs."

"Lost one of his legs? What's that supposed to mean?"

"Just what I said," the deputy reiterated calmly. "He was found down by Henderson Bridge, lying in the road with his right leg missing – torn off, by all accounts. He was found by a passing motorist."

The sheriff massaged his forehead with his fingers, as he was in the habit of doing when things began to get him down. "Have you seen him?" he asked.

"No," replied Wall. "They've taken him to Rutland Hospital."

"Shit! Look, get down there right away and find out exactly what happened, and get someone to search around the area where he was found. And, Mark," he added, "tell them to be careful; the alligator might still be around."

"Sheriff," Deputy Wall said, "I thought you might want to deal with that matter yourself, seeing as you've been so involved, and all."

"No, Mark. I've got a murder here, as well as a possible suicide. You deal with it."

"Okay," Wall said. "I'll ring you as soon as I have something."

When his deputy had left, O'Donnel went back to the control room where he found Claire just about to pick up the telephone. She had a determined look on her face. O'Donnel asked her who she was phoning.

"The power station on Pine Island," she told him.

He reached across and took the telephone out of her hands. Claire bristled and was about to protest, but O'Donnel stopped her. "I want to speak to you before you phone anyone," he said. "It's important. Now, please can we resume. I'll be as quick as I can."

O'Donnel then told the story of how five years before he had been seconded to the FBI Narcotics Department, and sent to Inverness in order to investigate a drugs cartel that was thought to be operating from Clearwater through Inverness, and from there throughout Europe, including England. It turned out that a number of important dignitaries were involved, including the mayor and Senator Page.

He glanced at the two women expecting surprise, but Claire said, "We know about the mayor, or at least Tom suspected he was involved. Others, too, but he wasn't sure. That is why we didn't know who to trust and why we tried to contact you."

The sheriff nodded. "Well, Tom's hunch was right. The money from the drug-running activities of the mayor and his senator buddy went to finance the new power plant and a number of other major projects around the town."

"But why the mayor?" broke in Lucy. "He seemed pretty harmless. I always thought he loved this town."

"I'm sure he does, or rather did, but his business, we discovered, has been in trouble for years. The bank was about to foreclose, so he borrowed from the drugs people, and from then on he just dug himself into a great pit that simply got bigger. As for the senator, he just does it to support his lifestyle; he liked to be rich and famous."

"Okay," said Claire, "but what has this to do with not closing down the plant?"

"Claire, we have just managed to get all the main players into a corner, and we're ready to hook and reel them in – big operation. Now, if the mayor hears about you shutting the plant down, it would scupper all our plans. They'd close ranks immediately. It could jeopardise our whole five-year operation. Now do you understand?"

"But surely public safety comes first," said Lucy.

"I agree," replied the sheriff. "And if there is no other way, we shall have to close-down and wind-up our operation and all that it means. I just wanted to tell you this in case there was an alternative, but I know now there is not. As you say, Lucy, public safety must come first."

The two women remained silent. Then Lucy said, "I'm beginning to understand about a lot of things now. Your attitude when Christy died for one thing."

"That's right. I couldn't afford to blow our cover. I was sorry for it, but the operation was getting to a critical stage, and I couldn't jeopardise it. These people have to be stopped. If we fail we put generations of kids at risk; people like Christy, for one thing."

Lucy glanced at Claire for help. The sheriff was convincing, and he was right. "What are you going to do?" she asked Claire. "Whichever way you decide someone's going to be hurt."

Claire said nothing. She got up from her seat and went over to the computer panel. Reaching down she pulled out a wad of design manuals and plans.

"Claire?"

O'Donnel turned to Lucy and placed his index finger to his lips. Lucy remained silent.

After a few moments, Claire turned to face them. "I think I have the answer," she said. "But it won't be strictly legal."

"We'll let it go this time," the sheriff said with a faint smile. "What's the plan?"

"I could steal power from the main supply at Pine Island. We could then close the plant down and pretend that all elements were functioning as normal. No one would know the difference."

"How long?" asked the sheriff.

"Two days," replied Claire, "maybe a week before they find out."

"But can it be done?" questioned Lucy anxiously.

"Well, there are two standby power supplies through to the main power station. One that goes directly back to the computer terminals at Pine Island, but the other is not programmed into the computer, we never got round to completing the link."

"But that's no good," interrupted O'Donnel. "If there's no link, there's no power."

"That's not quite true," replied Claire. "I could make the link at our end and divert the power, but I will need to introduce a virus into the computer at Pine Island to keep them occupied while we steal their power."

"Well what are we waiting for!" exclaimed Lucy. "Claire, you're a genius."

"Hold on," said Claire with a note of caution, "there's still a problem. I first have to crack the code to get into their computer, and that could take days – weeks even."

Lucy's enthusiasm took a sudden dive, and she sunk into a chair.

O'Donnel scratched his head. Suddenly he seemed to have an idea. "Back in a moment," he said. He left the room and made his way along the corridor and out into the sunlight. Reaching his car he climbed into the front seat and picked up the phone. It was the commissioner who answered.

"I think we've solved the problem," O'Donnel said, "but I need a big favour, and this one will have to come right from the top with no explanations. It's the only chance we've got."

"What do you want?" the commissioner asked.

"I need the access code to the computer at the power station on Pine Island."

There was an escape of breath down the phone. "Hell, Kevin, that's a tall order – how long have we got?"

"I'd say about thirty minutes. After that we start to close-down the plant here."

"I'll be back as soon as I can," the commissioner said. "Well done."

"Just get that code." said the sheriff.

"Oh, I'll get it," came the reply. "Don't you worry about that."

Chapter 55

Mitcham Creek, Inverness

Gordon sat in his armchair trying to concentrate on the Channel 28 big bass review, but it was useless, his mind wasn't on it. He got up and went to the window where he could see across the lawns to the lake.

Jean had left a little earlier and the commissioner had taken her place. The sun was setting in the west, casting deep purple shadows across the landscape. Normally he would have gone outside on an evening like this to watch the changing patterns of light and colour mingling with the coming darkness, but tonight he was preoccupied with more worldly matters. He was waiting for the phone to ring.

Commissioner Brown, aware of Gordon's anxiety, said, "He'll ring soon. Potra has a lot of things to organise, and don't forget, as far as we know he might still be in London."

"That doesn't help me," said Gordon nervously. "They said they'd ring an hour ago."

The commissioner remained silent, apparently unperturbed. He was watching the television.

Then, as if guilty at having kept them so long, the telephone rang. Gordon moved across the room quickly and snatched it up. The commissioner was about to tell him to take his time, but it was too late.

"Gordon Richardson."

"Mr Richardson. I hope you enjoyed your wait." It was the Latin voice again, heavy with contempt.

"No problem," Gordon replied. "I was lying out by the pool watching the sunset."

"Very good, but I suggest you enjoy it while you can, because if this escapade of yours goes wrong, you're a dead man." There was no change in the sober tone of voice, but there was no denying the menace lying beneath.

Gordon took a deep breath. "Look," he said, "it was Mrs Larimer who involved me in this business in the first place. I just want my dues." As soon as he'd finished he knew he shouldn't have said what he did. It showed a sign of weakness on his part and sent the wrong message to the other side.

The commissioner clearly thought so too, as he raised his eyebrows a fraction, a mild note of disapproval.

"Quite," Potra said in a patronising tone, "but where's the merchandise?"

"All in good time," Gordon said. "You'll get it back when the deal's closed."

There was a brief hesitation on the other end of the line, then: "The meeting you requested. It is arranged for seven o'clock tomorrow evening. There will be four of us present, the senator, the mayor, Macceffy and myself. We will bring the money – you make sure you have the goods."

"Not so fast. Surely you don't believe I'll bring the stuff to the meeting. That would be foolish. But I'll tell you where it is."

Potra's voice changed. All pretence of the faint thread of cordiality had gone. "You bring the powder with you, or no deal." he snarled. "I'll telephone your gallery tomorrow morning at 11.00 a.m. precisely. I will then give you the location for our meeting." And with that he hung up.

"Well done," said the commissioner. "You got through that okay."

Gordon frowned. "Why do you think they want to telephone me at the gallery?" he asked.

"I'll tell you why," replied the commissioner. "It's because they'll be watching the place from now until tomorrow evening, just to make sure you're legit." He paused for a moment. "They've probably already tapped your phone – all your phones. You've got to remember these guys are professionals, they're going to make sure 100% that no one else is involved."

"Well, how are you going to case the location for the meeting?" Gordon queried, feeling somewhat vulnerable.

"We won't be able to," the commissioner said matter-of-factly. "We'll have to play it by ear."

Gordon felt a chill down the length of his spine. They were playing with his life, and they didn't give a damn. "I can't go through with it," he said suddenly.

The commissioner cast a look in his direction. "You'll go through with it," he said. "If you don't they'll kill you." He picked up his mobile and punched in a number. "Jean, did you get the whole conversation?"

227

"Positive. Just rewinding now."

"Okay, close-down for now. Oh, and can you come over here. Your friend, Gordon, is in need of a little company. He's feeling unprotected."

"I don't need her here," Gordon said with irritation. "I'll be okay on my own."

The commissioner turned to face him. "Mr Richardson, I don't give a fuck what you think– I want you protected. This surveillance has taken five years and cost nearly ten million bucks, and a slime head like you is not going to fuck it up – so, you have protection. Anyway, you like Miss Manley and she, for some unknown reason, seems to have the hots for you."

"She's a bitch."

"Naughty, naughty. You know you don't mean that."

Chapter 56

Power Unit, Inverness

Sheriff Kevin O'Donnel was sat in his car when the phone rang. It was Commissioner Brown with the code.

O'Donnel thanked him.

"We'll get on to it right away," he told the sheriff.

"No, we don't need to tell anyone. We can close the power plant down and carry on as though everything is functioning as normal, but we only have a few days."

He replaced the receiver and hurried over to the plant. Claire was busy programming as he burst through the door.

"Do you have it?"

"Got it," O'Donnel said, handing her the piece of paper.

She stared at it almost disbelievingly for a few seconds, then went into action. She pressed several key modes and the screen flashed up. 'Please Confirm Key Code' it said.

Claire put in 'Pelican0I842Eagle'. The computer buzzed for a few seconds then acknowledged.

"We're in," she said excitedly. "Just a little longer and we'll be locked into the Pine Island power source."

"It's that easy?" O'Donnel said.

"If you know what you're doing," said Claire, without taking her eyes off the screen, "it's that easy."

"I never could understand those machines," said O'Donnel.

"Got work to do, Sheriff," Claire told him impatiently. "Out, out, out."

"I'll go find Lucy," he said.

As he entered the rest room the lights dimmed for a second and then normal power resumed. He heard Claire cry out, "Yes!"

"Clever girl," he said to himself. "Clever girl." He glanced down at Lucy, fast asleep on the couch, her legs pulled up to her chest in the foetal position. He allowed himself a smile and leant over and kissed her on the forehead. Then he left her to her dreams and returned to his car, where his telephone was already buzzing.

"Sheriff, are you there?" It was Mark Wall.

"Mark – any news?"

"No, Rastos is still unconscious. It could be days before he recovers. I've talked to Doctor Hawkins. He says there is no doubt that the injuries were caused by an alligator, or something similar."

O'Donnel wondered what else 'similar' there could be in the lake. He said, "Have you searched the area where Rastos was found?"

"Yes, and everywhere else, no signs, no clues, nothing. The big feller's simply disappeared."

"What about his old den?"

"Negative," replied the deputy.

O'Donnel swore beneath his breath. He never thought it would be so difficult to find one single alligator. "Are you making sure that no one goes near the lakes?"

"Sure, as far as possible. One or two people, mainly fishermen, have ignored the warning, but we've stopped them and sent them home. Oh, and by the way, Sheriff, the mayor's been trying to get hold of you."

"Has he indeed! What did he want?"

"He didn't say."

"I bet the son of a bitch is trying to find out what's going on. Well he'll get nothing from me, except a nail in his coffin when the time comes." He picked up his mobile and phoned the mayor's office. The mayor was out, so he left a message to say he'd called.

Chapter 57

Power Unit, Inverness

It was about nine o'clock in the evening when Mayor Thompson drove into the parking lot at the power station.

Watching through the rest room window, Sheriff O'Donnel saw the car pull up. He instantly recognised the black Cadillac with the gold-plated mascot. 'Bad taste,' he thought, but then it went with the man. He looked at his watch. Time was running on. He seemed to have been waiting for an age. He went to meet the mayor at reception.

The mayor, his tubby face covered in perspiration as usual, had his hand thrust forward. "Hello, Sheriff," he said solemnly. "I heard on the radio about the killing. I've been down in St Petersburg at a meeting. Tried to make contact with your office, but couldn't catch you in. Sad business."

"Sure is," said the sheriff.

"Any motive?"

"None that I'm aware of. This guy Critchley had only been here for six weeks. Do you know where he came from?"

"I do not," the mayor said with a perceptible tightening of his brow, which O'Donnel registered as a lie. "He was recommended to the board by a friend of Senator Page. He had the experience and the necessary credentials. And, of course, following that terrible tragedy with Wayne and Betty, we were desperate to find someone." He caught the sheriff's eyes as he said this, and he must have read doubt in them, for he quickly shifted his gaze to the wall beyond.

It was something O'Donnel had always noted about Mayor Thompson, you could never hold his gaze, his eyes were always roving, left, right, somewhere beyond, thinking of other things as he spoke to you. O'Donnel didn't like men with that tendency.

"Did Tom die instantly?" the mayor asked.

The sheriff nodded.

"What about Critchley?"

"Still alive – just. Half his face was blown away, but they say he'll live."

"Which hospital is he at? Rutlands?"

Again the sheriff nodded. Rutlands was the nearest hospital. They had a special until there to deal with gunshot wounds, so he wasn't giving away any secrets.

"Have you been able to speak to him yet?"

"No. It'll be weeks before they'll know if he'll be able to speak at all."

The mayor sighed and shook his head. "Sad, sad business. I mean, why would Critchley want to kill Tom? It just don't make sense."

O'Donnel said nothing, though beneath his civil exterior he would have liked to take Mayor Thompson by the scruff of the neck and shake a confession out of him.

But the mayor wasn't finished yet. "Who's looking after the plant?" he asked.

"Claire," the sheriff replied cautiously.

"Is she okay? It must have been a great shock to her, especially after Wayne's death."

"She's a little cut up," the sheriff said, "but she seems to be coping at the moment."

"Do you think I could speak to her for a few moments?" the mayor asked warily. "There are some things about the plant I need to talk to her about."

O'Donnel baulked. The last thing he wanted was to throw the mayor and Claire together, though he knew Claire could be depended upon to give nothing away, besides which he had no authority to stop him. "She's in the control room," he said.

Claire heard the door open and turned, thinking it was Lucy. Her expression changed when she saw who it was, and her pulse rate increased.

"Oh, there you are, Claire," the mayor said smoothly. "How are you coping? It must have been a great shock to lose Tom, and so near to Wayne's death."

Claire didn't answer. She was trying to stay calm, though a mix of fear and anger was working its way to the surface. She concentrated on punching numbers into the computer.

The mayor came closer. "How do you think you can cope on your own?" he asked her.

"Perfectly well, thank you," she replied sharply.

"Claire," he persisted, "I don't want to sound as if I'm interfering,

232

but I do think that you need assistance here, and quickly. Look, I'll see what can be done."

It was then that Claire turned to face him, her face flushed with anger which overrode her fear. "Mr Mayor," she said shaking. "I do not need any help. I can manage this job quite well on my own. And if I should need assistance at any time, then I can call on Ted and Nancy. They're qualified technicians – they can help me."

The mayor opened his mouth to protest, but Claire cut him short.

"The last choice of a manager was a big help," she went on. "He just killed my friend."

"Surely," the mayor blustered, "you're not blaming me because some screwball lost his head?"

Claire stopped short of giving him an answer to that. She had to be careful and she suddenly realised that the police department were investigating this man and his cronies, and that was a situation she did not want to jeopardise, so instead of giving further vent to her anger she drew a deep breath and said wearily, "I'm sorry, I didn't mean that. Let's leave things as they are for a few days – then we can discuss it."

The mayor nodded. "That's reasonable," he said. "Let's say three days. After that we'll talk about getting you some assistance."

Claire didn't appear to hear him as she had turned her attention back to the control panel. He thought about repeating what he had said, more forcibly this time, but then thought better of it. She'd come to heel eventually, he thought to himself. He turned and left the control room, closing the door firmly behind him.

Claire heard the door click shut but didn't look up. She was relieved that he'd gone, but more than that she was gratified that she'd conquered her fear and stood up to him. She hated the man with a deep loathing and was determined to keep control of herself, and of the situation at the plant. The mayor would not bend her to his will as he had done others, and he needed her, there was no one else who understood the system. As long as she was in charge, she felt nothing could hurt her.

The mayor acknowledged the sheriff as he passed through reception, but didn't stop, he was in no mood. "Can't stop," he said. "Things I need to do."

Chapter 58

Mitcham Creek, Inverness

Gordon was alone on the porch when the doorbell rang. Over the past few days he had become apprehensive about anyone coming to his house unannounced.

Cautiously he went to the door, but before opening it he asked, "Who is it?" The reply surprised him.

"It's me, Jean."

For some seconds he was unsure what to do, but his dilemma soon passed. He turned the latch, and as Jean Manley entered he turned his back on her and went back to his seat on the patio.

Jean slammed the door behind her. "It's good of you to make me so welcome," she shouted angrily at his receding back, but he didn't answer. "Where's the bathroom?" she demanded to know.

"Guest bedroom, first on the left," he called and left her it find her own way.

"Thanks," she said.

Twenty minutes later, as Gordon was pouring himself a double Scotch and soda, she emerged from the bedroom. She looked stunning. She'd changed into a short, tight-fitting black dress which clung to her naked body like wet silk. Long hair cascaded over her shoulders, brushing her nipples tight up against the material. In the half light she looked unreal, like some goddess from antiquity. She was wearing black stockings and, as she moved towards him, he could see the lower section of her suntanned thighs above the edge of the stocking tops, and by the way the skimpy skirt hung around her thighs he knew she wore no panties.

Their eyes met as she moved closer, and held the focus. He could feel his penis begin to harden. God he wanted her. He offered her a gin and tonic and she took it from him, her eyes not leaving his. Their fingers touched and she lowered her head and kissed his hand.

Then slowly she placed the glass on the table and eased him back onto the settee. Lifting her skirt slightly she crouched on his lap and with long, slim hands felt for his zip, slowly pulled it down and slipped her hand into his underpants, grasping his erect penis in her hand.

He closed his eyes and moved against her, and groaned as she slid her finger to the top of his penis and stroked it with a fingernail. Then, holding his penis tightly she rose on her haunches, lifted her skirt with her left hand and forced herself onto him. Gordon held her tightly, pressing her whole body down onto him, harder with every thrust.

"Deeper, deeper," she groaned writhing against him, and as he pushed ever harder into her his sap rose until all control was hopelessly lost. He felt her vagina tighten and as he exploded into her he could feel her squeezing, tighter, tighter until he yelled out in exquisite agony.

As they reached the climax together her whole body quivered. They held each other in a feverish embrace, her long nails digging into his naked back. As they relaxed and the fever of passion ebbed she kissed him gently on the lips. She spoke softly, whispering to him, "Gordon, I could love you. No one ever made love to me the way you do."

He kissed her turned-up nose, said nothing, and wished he could stay this way forever.

Gordon rose early next morning, leaving Jean still sleeping. After making love he had carried her to his bed and they had drifted into sleep. But while she had slept like a baby, he had slept fitfully, waking often, his mind disturbed, preoccupied with worries about the day ahead.

He arrived at the gallery early. Margaret was just about to open up and was surprised to see him.

"Well," she exclaimed, "I thought you weren't due back for another four days."

He explained that there had been a change of plan.

"Well, you should have rung me," she scolded.

"I know – I'm sorry."

"Any news of your wife?" she asked.

"No, nothing."

"Don't worry too much," she said touching his hand. "I'm sure she'll turn up. Anyway, I'm always here if you need anything – you know that."

"Yes, I know that, and thank you." He withdrew his hand, and

Margaret looked fidgety and uneasy.

"Well," she said at length, "this won't do. Would you like a coffee?"

That would be nice, thank you," he said, and went into his office. Everything seemed normal, nothing disrupted, all the familiar things in their place. It was an ordered office and his world revolved around it. 'If only,' he thought. 'If only.'

Chapter 59

Inverness Police Department

O'Donnel had finally left the power station at two in the morning; it was now 9.30 a.m., and as he sat in his office he pondered on the previous night. It had crossed his mind to ask Lucy back for a drink, but he had decided that the time wasn't appropriate and he had too much on his mind. He had also wondered what the mayor had said to Claire, or what she had said to him. The mayor hadn't looked too pleased when he left.

He'd tried to sleep, but sleep wouldn't come. His mind was too active. Too many things demanding attention: Tom's killer, Sheila's torso, the alligator, the drugs cartel, all swam in his mind, tossing about in a whirlpool.

His secretary found him at his desk deep in thought, and told him he looked awful. "I'll make you some coffee," she said. "That'll clear the head."

He glanced up at her, thankful for an understanding face. "Any messages?" he asked.

"Several," she replied. "Mark took them, all except these two." She laid the two memo notes on the desk in front of him. "For your eyes only," she added. "I know – coffee."

The first note was from Officer Partridge. It read: '7.00 a.m. at gator hole. Still no sighting. Can we come in now?'. The second was from the hospital: 'Mr Critchley died in the early hours of this morning at 3.30 a.m. His life support machine malfunctioned'.

O'Donnel brought his fist down heavily on the desk. "Damn! Damn! Damn!" he cried as his secretary came in with the coffee. "Barbara, get Mark to look into this, will you," he said handing her the note. "Support machines don't simply malfunction."

"What shall I do about the boys at the gator hole?" she asked.

"Bring them in," he told her. "By the way, how's Nokes?"

"The hospital said he's making steady progress – he should pull through."

"Thank God for small mercies," he said.

"Have you spoken to Mr Richardson about his wife, yet?" she wanted to know.

"Later," he said.

"Well, you'll have to tell him sooner or later. No use putting off the evil day for too long."

He scowled at her. "Out, Barbara," he told her, "I've got some telephone calls to make."

Chapter 60

Everglade Canal, Inverness

At around 10.00 a.m. the small boat edged its way under the bridge and into the old disused canal. The alligator had picked up the vibrations from the propeller as soon as the boat had left Alligator Island. It was hungry and its jaw still ached. And now as the craft approached it moved slowly from its hiding place beneath the eroded foundations.

The two men in the boat were unaware they were being watched as they passed beneath the bridge. One of them dropped the throttle and they looked about them.

"Why the hell the mayor wants this canal cleared I'll never know," said the older man. He was wearing green overalls with Inverness City Authorities embroidered on the breast pocket. "No one every uses this now," he said, scratching the back of his head. "Not since the old prison on Whale Island closed down."

"How long ago was that?" the younger man asked.

"Oh, some twenty years or so, maybe longer."

"He says he wants this finished by nightfall," the younger man said sourly, "so let's get to it – there looks like a lot to do for twenty bucks."

The weed cutter, fixed to the bow, whirred into action, the meshing teeth cutting and clearing a trough through the reed beds, the debris floating on the surface.

As the boat worked its way methodically forward, the old alligator slid unobserved into the water. Using the floating debris for cover, it headed towards the boat. It was a dozen feet away when a large bass appeared. The movement of the fish triggered instant action and the alligator went for it, catching it neatly in it jaws. In doing so its tail broke the surface sending a flurry of ripples towards the boat. Both men turned, alert to the disturbance, but they could see nothing. "Must have been a good ten-pounder to make a wave like that," the older man said.

"Or a gator," said the other. "Whatever it was, it's moved on."

The alligator lay still on the bottom of the channel. Above him the boat chugged slowly on. It would wait its chance.

"We'll go right through to the river," said the older man, "and then drag the reeds on board on the way back."

Chapter 61

A Hotel, Orlando

At 10.30 a.m. in a small dingy back street hotel room in Orlando, four men were huddled around a small metal table. They had arrived at different times and were all dressed casually – open-necked shirts and jeans. The idea was to make them look inconspicuous. The deception was not totality successful. Senator Page was wearing glasses and an ill-fitting blond wig. Hunaz Potra had shaved off his moustache. The room in which they sat was oppressively hot, and the mayor, in particular, was suffering from lack of air; his face was puffy and red.

The senator, who appeared to be unaffected by the heat, and had appointed himself chairman of the meeting, spoke first: "Thank you for coming, gentleman. We all know what this is about, so let's get straight down to business."

Hunaz Potra interrupted him before he had a chance to continue. "I think we should kill Richardson now," he said coldly. "I do not like being double-crossed. No one ever does this to me."

"What good is that!" said the mayor. "He's deposited a letter, apparently, with his solicitor, to be opened if anything happens to him. It's got our names on it."

"I don't believe it," Potra growled. "Anyway, I don't care. I still think we should kill him."

The senator took a deep breath. "I understand how you feel, Hunaz, but we can't do as you say. We must pay the money and recover the cocaine. After that you can deal with him in whatever way you please."

Potra's face relaxed a little. He was not one to show outward emotion, but his teeth ground inside his head.

Macceffy, who had an expression of perpetual dread on his face, asked nervously, "Why does he want to meet us? What is the point?"

"The point is," explained the senator, "that with all of us in the one place he'll feel protected, by virtue of the fact that we are all involved."

"I will not go," Macceffy stammered. "I'm not as involved as you are. I haven't killed anyone."

Potra reached over the table and with two fingers struck Macceffy in the chest. The force of the blow nailed him back into his chair, where he appeared to wilt with terror.

"Have you got the money?" the mayor enquired of Senator Page.

"I have mine," replied the senator patting his pocket. "You owe me two hundred thousand each."

"I don't have the money," stammered Macceffy, glancing furtively at the three men.

"Don't worry, Mr Macceffy," the senator said, "I'll sort something out." There was a malevolent tone in his voice that did not go unnoticed by Macceffy, whose hands began to shake.

"For God's sake give him a drink," someone said.

Potra picked up a glass, filled it with whisky and slammed it in front of a frightened Macceffy, who disposed of it in one gulp.

"When you've finished playing," Senator Page said with irritation, "we'll discuss where we're going to meet Richardson." He cast a glance at the mayor. "Abe, you know the area. Any ideas?"

The mayor stood to his feet and said, "I've given this some thought over the past twenty-four hours, and I think there's only one possible place – Whale Island."

"Where the hell's that?" Potra asked.

"It's an old prison on the Withlacoochee river," the mayor explained. "It's an island – no bridge, and it's at the junction of the canal that leads into Little Lake Henderson. There's only one way onto it without being seen, and that's by boat or," he added, "by helicopter."

"Anyone living there?" the senator asked

"No one," replied the mayor. "I checked it out yesterday. I've also had my men staked out along the river to make sure no one goes near." He said this with a certain amount of pride. He'd taken the initiative for once.

"That sounds good," Potra said, "but how will Richardson get there?"

"I'll arrange for a boat to pick him up at the Withlacoochee Bridge crossing. He'll be blindfolded. He won't have a clue as to where he is. He won't even know what state he's in."

"Impressive," the senator said, "but how do we get there?"

"By chopper," the mayor explained, "and then we take a power

242

boat back to Little Lake Henderson. The canal's overgrown, but I have men clearing a way through at this very moment."

Macceffy then spoke up: "But Mr Richardson will know that the location is close to Inverness, he'll only be travelling for about twenty minutes."

"No. He'll be blindfolded, as I said, and he'll be travelling for two and a half hours; we have a little detour planned."

"Well done, Abe," said the senator. "If Hunaz agrees, and of course Mr Macceffy here, we'll adopt the plan."

Potra nodded and so, reluctantly, did Macceffy.

"Okay. We'll meet tomorrow at the old landing off Alligator Island at 10.00 a.m. The mayor will organise the chopper."

The four men shook hands and the meeting broke up.

As Potra turned to leave, the senator beckoned him over and whispered to him, "Macceffy worries me. I think he should be taken care of."

Potra nodded slowly. "I'll see to it," he said, almost with relish.

Macceffy died that afternoon. His car was forced off the road by a truck at the Orlando turnpike. It had rolled down the steep embankment and exploded. The local police logged it as just another unfortunate accident on a notoriously dangerous bend. More caution signs were needed, they concluded.

Chapter 62

The Gallery, Inverness

Gordon drummed his fingers along the polished walnut of his desk. He found concentrating difficult. Waiting for phone calls that wouldn't come was like watching a kettle boil – it took forever. Even the appearance of a potential customer failed to spark any interest. Besides, Margaret was better with customers than he was. She would deal with the situation with her usual efficiency.

After the customer had left, Sheriff O'Donnel arrived. From the open door of his office he could just see the sheriff. He was talking to Margaret but he couldn't hear what they were saying. Margaret glanced his way. She looked upset.

Then the sheriff came towards the office. He didn't knock but went straight in, greeting Gordon with a nod, and lowered himself into a chair opposite the desk. He looked somewhat ill at ease, and couldn't stop fiddling with his hat. After a long silence, he said, "You know of my involvement in all of this?"

Gordon nodded. He didn't very much care about the sheriff's involvement. He cared only about the telephone call.

Another long silence ensued, then O'Donnel glanced across at Gordon and caught his eye. "You've got to be patient," he said slowly. "They'll ring."

Gordon shifted nervously in his seat and said nothing. He wondered what was in the black plastic bag the sheriff was carrying.

O'Donnel read his thoughts. "I have something in this bag," he said. "Something I want you to look at. It may cause you distress, but I'm asking you to examine it – it needs to be properly identified."

With that he placed it on the desk. Gordon picked it up and reached inside. He felt a soft, silky material and when he withdrew it he recognised it immediately as the remains of his wife's blouse. Half the sleeve was missing and there was a jagged tear down the right-hand side. His heart was thumping and his mouth felt dry; a kind of weakness seemed to take over his body. His hands began to shake and for some seconds he couldn't speak. When he eventually did he said, "It's my wife's. Where is she?"

The sheriff took a deep breath. "I'm afraid to have to tell you that she's almost certainly dead."

Gordon stared at him blankly. "Almost certainly?"

"If that blouse belongs to your wife, sir, and you seem to be convinced that is does, then I'd say with almost 100% certainty that she is."

"How did she die?" Gordon asked quietly, feeling a strange sense of calm decent upon him.

O'Donnel knew the question would come up, and he was prepared to answer it, but he didn't think the man in front of him would cope well with knowing. For that reason O'Donnel wanted to let him down gently. "I think, sir," he said, "that until we have more details it's best not to speculate."

"Speculate! What do you mean, speculate?" Gordon was furious. "Do you know how she died? Was she run over by a car? Was she murdered? Did she drown herself?"

"Mr Richardson."

"Damn it, Sheriff, tell me. Do you know how she died?"

"Yes, I think so."

"Well – tell me."

"You won't like it much, sir, but I'll tell you what I think happened."

"Thank you."

"I think she was killed by an alligator. We found what was left of a female body in an alligator's den over near the power station. The body was draped with the garment you're holding."

Gordon's face turned ashen white. He seemed to crumple. What stopped him from falling over was his elbows, which he planted firmly on the desk top as a prop. He then buried his face in his hands and rubbed his fingers into his scalp, backwards and forwards until they began to leave red wheals on his forehead. Eventually he lifted his face and his eyes were red with tears. He asked in a broken voice, "Sheriff, can what's left be identified as my wife?"

"I'm afraid not," replied the sheriff. "There's only the remains of the blouse and part of a rib cage. There can be no positive identification, until we do a DNA test."

"So, she'll be listed as a missing person?"

"Yes, sir," replied O'Donnel. "There's nothing more we can do. You see, we can't find any . . ." He hesitated. "We can't find any teeth, or other items. There's only part of a female rib cage. I'm very sorry."

Gordon looked down at the tattered piece of silk in his hand. "She may still be alive, then?" he conjectured.

"Mr Richardson, it's possible, just possible, but I fear highly unlikely." O'Donnel had seen this in people before. They grasped at straws, unable to accept the unthinkable. 'I suppose,' he thought, 'it's another way of nature numbing the pain.' "I'll fetch your assistant," he said. "She can stay with you a while."

"No," said Gordon. "Thank you, but I'd rather be alone. If you'll just close the door as you leave. I'll be okay." As the sheriff got up from his chair, Gordon held up the silk remnant, "Can I keep this?" he asked.

The sheriff nodded. He put the garment carefully back in the bag, but as he did so a small pearl button dropped onto the desk. Gordon snatched it up and clenched it tightly in his fist.

The sheriff left him sitting there, fist clenched, eyes glazed, staring into nothing. It was the shock before the horror set in, O'Donnel thought. Some men coped, some didn't. He wondered in which category Gordon Richardson belonged.

Chapter 63

FBI Headquarters, Tampa Bay

Commissioner Brown was exhausted. He'd been working through the night, briefing his officers on the day's operations, and it was now 10.30 a.m. The department had been working on this case for five years, years of hard slog with very little to show for it. Gordon Richardson's innocent involvement had been the chance they'd been waiting for, but, if they were to capitalise on their good fortune, the operation must swing into action like clockwork. Everything was ready. He had three choppers from Tampa on standby, two fast launches and six unmarked Mustangs at his disposal.

As yet he did not know where the meeting would be, though he had an idea. Wherever it was, he felt he could cover it. He had to. The department had spent ten million dollars so far. There would be no more funds forthcoming if he fucked this one up.

He took his mobile phone from his pocket and phoned Jean Manley. "Jean, it's me," he said with a sense of urgency. "Look, everything is ready our end. I decided it would be too risky to tap Richardson's phone. Go down to the tracking department. They'll give you a black cowboy belt with a big silver buckle. There's a tracking device in it. Make sure your boyfriend wears it. We've only got one hit at this, you understand." He pressed the 'end' button and walked briskly down the corridor to the main desk. Leaning over towards the sergeant he said, "I'm in the cells for two hours' kip – you hear me? Two hours, then you wake me – then, and not before."

The sergeant was a black girl from the Bronx, buxom and tough, with a smile that split her face into a white toothy grin. She was smiling now and showing a ripe set of molars. "Sure, boss. You want company?"

The commissioner fixed her with a hard stare that betrayed a rare flash of humour. "One of these days, Sergeant, I'll take you up on these offers you keep making, but today I must sleep – two hours – don't forget."

Chapter 64

The Gallery, Inverness

It was exactly 11.00 a.m. when the telephone rang in Gordon Richardson's office. He hadn't moved since the sheriff had left and was still clenching the button from Sheila's blouse in his fist. He was startled by the ringing – it brought him back to reality."

He placed the button on the desk in front of him and picked up the phone.

"Mr Richardson?"

"Yes. Who is that?"

"Hunaz Potra. Do you have the merchandise?"

Gordon's heart began to beat fast. The events of the morning had driven everything else from his mind, and now it all came back to him with a rush. "Yes," he said, attempting to gather his thoughts. "Yes, I do. But more importantly, do you have the money?"

"We have the money," said Potra. "Now listen carefully. These are your instructions. Don't write anything down, just listen." Gordon heard a rustling of paper, and then Potra resumed: "At 11.00 a.m. tomorrow be at the Withlacoochee Bridge – with the goods. You will be collected from there by motor launch. You will be blindfolded. When we reach the rendezvous the blindfold will be removed, but not until then."

Gordon felt the now familiar sensation of hairs stiffening on the back of his neck.

"And do you have the letter that you gave to your solicitor?"

"I do not," Gordon said. "He has instructions to take it to the police if I fail to call him by 7.00 p.m."

"So, when do we get the letter?"

"You don't," Gordon replied. "He burns it when he knows I'm safe."

"Burns it!" Potra reacted with scorn. "You don't seriously expect us to believe that, do you?"

"It's your decision," Gordon replied with equal sarcasm, and at that point the phone went dead. He replaced the receiver, not quite sure in whose court the ball now rested.

As he was pondering this dilemma, Margaret popped her head around the door. "That woman's here to see you," she said with a whisper of disdain. "She say's it's urgent. What do I tell her?"

"You mean Jean Manley?"

Margaret nodded.

"You'd better show her in," he said.

Jean seemed to be genuinely pleased to see him. "How are you?" she said with a cautious smile.

"I guess okay," he replied. "Still alive at least."

She sat down opposite him, this being the only seat available, and said, "I've just spoken to the sheriff. He told me about your wife. I'm sorry, truly I am." She sounded clearly upset.

"Thanks," he said.

"Look, about last night. It really meant something to me. It wasn't duty. It just happened." She took a deep breath. "I needed you – very much. You do believe me, Gordon? Please say you do."

"It's not important, Jean," he said quietly. "Not now."

Jean sighed and closed her eyes, and for a few moments she sat there in meditation. When she eventually came round she simply said, "You're right," and reached down for her briefcase which stood beside the chair. She placed it on the desk and snapped it open. From inside she took a cowboy belt, surmounted by a huge garish buckle, and then closed the case. Looking him straight in the eye and with all semblance of familiarity now gone, she instructed him to put it on and to wear it at all times.

His reaction was rather what she had expected. "I can't wear that!" he exclaimed. "It's ridiculous."

"You can put it on, and you will," she said with a firmness that surprised him. "This belt may well save your life."

"What do you mean by that?"

Jean explained. "There's a transmitter in the buckle. It's the only way we can track you." She thought for a moment and then said, "Have you had the telephone call?"

"Yes, I have," he replied. "They want me to be at Withlacoochee Bridge at 9.00 a.m."

"That's all?"

"That's all, except that they say they are going to blindfold me and lead me to God-knows-where." The whole thing, it rather struck him, was becoming a farce.

But Jean Manley didn't appear to be amused. He felt he detected a shadow of concern in those deep eyes, but he might have been wrong.

"I reiterate," she said, "that the belt will be our only contact with you. You must keep it on at all times."

"What else have you got in there?" he asked, nodding toward the briefcase.

She hesitated for a moment, then slid her fingers to the locks and snapped it open again. "Cocaine. The real stuff. The packets we took from the picture frame. It's all here. It has to be because they'll check it out."

"But . . ."

"Don't worry, they won't have it in their hands for long." She looked at him long and earnestly and then she said, her voice softening, "Gordon, be careful. Keep that belt on and don't take any unnecessary risks."

He nodded. "I'll keep it in mind," he said.

Chapter 65

Everglade Canal, Inverness

On the canal, the two men had cleared much of the weed and were making their way back towards the bridge, throwing out grappling nets as they went along, collecting floating debris and stacking it on the boat.

The alligator, sensing their approach, slid silently into the murky water and submerged. Above it, the boat was silhouetted against the light, with the dark forms of the two men, leaning out raking in weed, standing out sharp against the sky.

The old man leaned right out to reach for a floating mass of reed, and the alligator accelerated upwards. It came out of the water like a rocket and took the man just above the waist, dragging him from the boat, spinning its body beneath the water like a top, dividing the top of the man's body from its lower half. There was the hiss of air escaping from the man's lungs, and the water boiled, blood mixing with vegetation into a thick scarlet broth.

The younger man, who had been working the other side of the boat, heard the sound of rushing water, looked about him, and saw that his companion was missing. He had heard the splash and had seen the disturbance on the surface of the water, and had assumed Jake had fallen overboard.

For a moment he hesitated, staring down into the murky water, and then he stripped off his coat and dived. The water was too dark for him to see beneath the surface, so he felt about him with his hands, but he made no contact with a body. He swam frantically to the rear, thinking that perhaps the older man had been sucked under by the wash from the propeller, but apart from the underside of the boat all he made contact with was water.

The alligator had been returning to its den with its prey when it heard the second splash. Instinctively it dropped the shattered body and turned back towards the boat. The man was feeling along the hull with both hands and was just about to rise for air when the alligator struck. It came up from below, with a force that sent the second man spiralling several feet into the air and, as he came down, the alligator's jaws closed, snapping and crushing the young body as it fell back into the water.

Its jaws moved swiftly, carving great chunks of flesh and bone from the torso. An arm became dislodged and slipped unseen into the current.

It was during that short period of twilight before day turned to night when Mark Wall found the empty boat drifting by the edge of the lake, the engine still running, and no one on board. There were no signs of damage or collision. Everything appeared normal, except that the boat was full of chewed-up reeds.

The deputy was at a loss to understand what had happened. He telephoned the sheriff who had his own suspicions, but for the moment kept them to himself.

He told Mark to check with the council, but he reported back that as far as they were aware the boat was still at its moorings. They rang back ten minutes later to say that the boat had gone, perhaps stolen. No, none of their operatives was on the boat as far as they knew. The whole thing was a mystery.

For his part, O'Donnel was uneasy. There had been too many unusual happenings, too many unexplained deaths. Why would anyone steal a boat, fill it with chopped-up reeds, and then leave it with the engine running? Nothing made sense, unless . . .

He picked up the phone and rang the commissioner.

The commissioner's voice came over sharp and businesslike. "Kevin. Problems?" It was as if every telephone call Commissioner Brown ever received automatically carried problems.

O'Donnel paused before answering. "Well, maybe," he said trying formulate his answer into a credible answer. "We've found an abandoned launch on Lake Henderson. No one on board, but the engine still running."

"Any sign of foul play?"

"No, nothing. No blood stains, nothing. I'm going to investigate further."

"Kevin. Put it on ice." The commissioner's voice was firm.

Yet this was something that needed investigating fully, and quickly. "But, Commissioner . . ."

"Leave it, Kevin, at least for a few days. I don't want anything to fuck up tomorrow. Understand?"

"I guess so," said the sheriff.

"Okay," the commissioner continued. "We know the time and place of the rendezvous with Richardson, but we don't know where they'll take him. Providing he does what he's told and wears the belt we'll be able to track him. If he's failed to put it on, then we're lost."

"What can I do?" O'Donnel asked.

"Only one thing. Call all off your officers away from Lake Henderson; we don't want some do-good cop getting involved."

"Okay," said O'Donnel. "I'll organise a false alarm on the Inverness Bank at about 10.00 – that should keep them all busy for a few hours at least."

"Good," said the commissioner. Then he added, "Kevin, you know that without your undercover work I don't think we could have cracked this. I owe you. It'll be good to have you back in the office when this is over."

"Let's get it over first," said O'Donnel, and thought that perhaps the old man was counting his chickens a mite too soon. And getting back into the office in Miami? He wasn't so sure about that. He'd begun to get used to it here – liked it even. He looked out of the window. The old town was silent, sleeping, unaware of the danger lurking so close to the surface. Tomorrow? Tomorrow everything could change.

Chapter 66

Mitcham Creek, Inverness

It was early in the evening when Gordon Richardson arrived home. All day he had been busy at the gallery, checking accounts and tax returns, a job he loathed at the best of times, and today had not been the best of times. He'd been unable to concentrate. The gallery had been quiet, so quiet in fact that he had sent Margaret home early. At first she had refused to leave him on his own, but he insisted, so she left, not in the best humour.

As he opened the front door and stepped inside the porch, he thought he heard a sound. He hesitated. Yes, he could hear voices. For a moment he froze, fear pricking his skin. He crept along the corridor, trying not to make a sound. The door to the lounge was ajar. The television was on. It was the CNN News.

"Hello," he called nervously, and was startled when a woman's blonde head appeared round the edge of the settee.

"Hello," Jean said, "you look surprised to see me."

"I thought you were lying low."

She smiled. "I was, but my boss had other ideas."

"What?"

"He told me to come to see you – in fact he insisted on it."

"Senator Page?"

"He said I had to keep you company – make sure you didn't go out anywhere tonight."

"But how does he know . . ."

"That we're lovers? He doesn't. But he knows you fancy me. He saw us talking at the gallery. He doesn't miss much."

"Are you sure he doesn't know anything else – your involvement with the FBI, for one thing?"

"I'm sure he doesn't," Jean said. "He thinks I'm a dumb blonde – and a good lay."

Gordon felt his stomach churn. "I don't understand you," he

said angrily. "You with that bastard! Why do you do it? Why do you let him?"

"Forget it, Gordon. It means nothing – just part of the job."

"So was I – if you remember."

"You know that's not true," she said with irritation. "Let's enjoy what we have."

She reached out for him, but he pulled away. He wasn't in the mood; there was too much on his mind, and he couldn't help thinking that she was still playing with him. He'd have to be on his guard.

Jean cooked rib-eye steaks for dinner, which they washed down with vintage wine. They talked, though she did most of it. She talked of her childhood and growing up and about her father whom she adored, but with whom she had an uneasy relationship, and then she talked about the gallery and asked him about the future, though not once did she mention his wife or the present situation, but he was inattentive.

At about eleven she said she was going to bed. At the bedroom door she hesitated. "You know where I am if you need me," she said enticingly.

In spite of the wine and the convivial evening, he declined the invitation, though his desire for this woman was as strong as ever, and the food and wine had lulled him into a sense of mild recklessness. His thoughts were not for her, but for his wife. He closed his eyes and fell into a fitful sleep on the sofa.

Chapter 67

Lake Henderson, Inverness

By 9.00 a.m. Commissioner Brown's men were positioned at various points around Lake Henderson. He had three boats within 100 feet of the bridge, with two agents in each. Two helicopters, painted in the colours of the local pest control company, had been equipped with spraying arms which could be ditched at a moment's notice. They were due to begin spraying soon after 9.45 a.m.

Gordon woke with a start. Jean was leaning over him with a tray of coffee and toast. His body felt stiff; he was not accustomed to sleeping on settees.

"What time is it?" he asked, rubbing his eyes.

"Quarter after nine. Don't panic, you've got plenty of time. Enjoy your breakfast. I'll see you this evening."

"You going?"

"Sure," she said. "I have to get back to the office – the senator's expecting me."

"But you know he won't be there," Gordon said.

"I know that, but I don't want to cause any suspicion. Everything has to appear as normal. Just make sure you're there on time." She picked up the heavy belt from the arm of the settee where it was draped and handed it to him. "Don't forget this," she said. "It's our lifeline."

He took the belt from her, slipped his own belt off and threaded the thick leather through the loops and snapped the clasp of the silver buckle shut. He tried to carry out this operation as nonchalantly as possible so that she wouldn't see that his hands were shaking, but she was good at picking up on things like this.

"Are you okay?"

"Of course," he said, squaring his shoulders.

"Well, good luck then," she said and closed the door quietly behind her.

He was alone now and he was scared. He picked up a coffee cup but his hands were trembling so much that he spilt coffee over the tray. "Damn! Damn!" he cried out. He always liked to be in control, but this thing was playing havoc with his emotions. He shut his eyes tight and counted to ten. "Pull yourself together. Pull yourself together. Everything's going to be okay," he said to himself over and over again.

His eyes fell on the briefcase and on the single handcuff lying beside it. He took a very deep breath, picked up the case and snapped on the handcuff. The key he put inside his shoe. He was ready to go.

At 10.45 precisely he parked his car at Withlacoochee Bridge and slowly walked to the end of the pier. It was a beautiful October morning with mist still hovering above the surface of the lake. The sky was already a deep blue and the sun was playing tricks through the cedars.

A hundred yards from the shore, three fishing boats lay at anchor. He wondered which one of them he would be boarding, blindfolded and helpless. He sat down nervously on the edge of the landing and placed the briefcase next to him, grasping the handle so tight with his left hand that his nails dug into his palm. He had never felt so afraid in his life, and he fought to control his fear, because he knew that in dangerous situations fear became the enemy. He needed to think clearly, rationally. He glanced at his watch. It was 10.55. Any time now.

Overhead he heard the thud, thud of helicopters. They were descending over the lake and he could see they were spraying. He remembered later thinking this was strange as they usually sprayed at night. He turned his gaze back to the lake and to the three boats. There was no movement aboard and he wondered, with a brief lifting of the spirits, if the whole thing had been called off, but he was unwilling to risk deceiving himself. He glanced at his watch, and felt the buckle on his belt. It was cold to the touch, yet it gave him some comfort.

Suddenly from across the lake, in a direction almost opposite the three boats, came the deep throaty roar of a power boat. It was thundering across the water at top speed and it was heading directly towards him. It ran in close to the fishing boats, skewed past them and pulled alongside.

In the boat were two men, both of whom had the swarthy appearance of Hispanics. Both wore blue jeans, plain white shirts and sunglasses. One of the men had a grey beard and long grey hair tied in a ponytail. By complete contrast, the other, much younger, was clean shaven which included his head. Their appearance alone was little cause for comfort.

One of them shouted from the boat, "Mr Richardson?"

Gordon nodded.

"Come and join us. We're taking you on a little cruise."

Gordon got up awkwardly. His legs felt weak and on their own recoiled from the action moving forward.

The voice called again, this time more urgently, to which his mind, body and soul eventually responded.

The younger man held out his hand to help him climb aboard, and then went to take the briefcase. Gordon wrenched it away from him. "This stays with me," he said firmly. The man simply shrugged his shoulders as if it were no matter.

He'd hardly placed his feet upon the deck when the engine roared and the boat reared up like a stallion with a spur beneath its tail, and set an onward course across the lake. The violent movement threw him off balance and he fell sprawling onto the deck. He lay there for a few seconds, winded and anxiously clutching the briefcase to his chest. The two men glanced at him and smiled.

Halfway across the lake the older man throttled down and the boat slowed. The younger man told him that he would now be blindfolded and not to resist. A silk scarf was produced and placed across his eyes and pulled tight with a knot at the back of his head. The man tugged at it to check that it would not slip. The blindfold was too tight, it bit into the corners of his eyes and the knot hurt his neck, but he dared not complain. The engine roared once again and the boat accelerated away. Gordon staggered, but this time kept his balance by holding onto the boat's rail.

The sun on his back of his neck meant that they were heading west; he could feel its warmth and roughly gauge the direction of the boat, but that idea was quickly extinguished as blackness suddenly descended as a large black hood was placed over his head.

The boat motored on, sometimes turning left, sometimes right. He lost all sense of time and place. He was frightened; his world was blackness, and black thoughts churned inside his mind. Then the engine sound changed, it bounced off something solid like a wall, as if the boat was passing beneath a bridge or entering a tunnel. The echo pressed down upon him and accelerated his fear.

From the helicopter above the lake, Commissioner Brown had been watching the antics of the power boat for some time. He marvelled at the intricate manoeuvres deemed to be necessary to confuse a man's sense of direction, especially when he was already wearing a hood over his head *and* a blindfold.

He turned to the pilot to ask a question and when he looked back the launch, to his utter astonishment, had disappeared. "Where . . .?"

The pilot shrugged. "It was there a minute ago," he said, looking baffled. "Maybe it's the light on the water throwing up reflections." The pilot tried to get its bearing on the map. "This is about where it's disappeared. There, that's the route it must have taken, into the old canal."

"Right, so we've got him," the commissioner said.

The pilot looked sceptical. "But that canal's been closed for years – since they closed Whale Island."

"What's Whale Island?" the commissioner asked.

"The old penitentiary," the pilot told him. "That's where they're heading."

The commissioner got on the phone. "Ken, keep tracking. We think they're heading for Whale Island in the middle of Withlacoochee river. They must have cleared the old canal."

Chapter 68

Whale Island, Inverness

After a long wait, Gordon felt the boat accelerate once more and move into open water. The roar of the engine confirmed they were now on full throttle. Then, without warning, the boat lurched and slowed. It turned, the engine was cut and he felt a dull thud as it stopped up against a pier or some such solid object.

He heard two men jump off onto a wooden landing and the sound of ropes being manhandled as they secured the boat. One of them then jumped back on deck and came towards him. Instinctively he backed away, expecting any minute to feel a blow. Instead a pair of rough hands grasped his shoulders, spun him round, removed the hood and, to his intense relief, the scarf around his eyes. As it came off he was met by a blinding sun and threw up his hands to shield his eyes from the glare. A hand pushed him forward and a rough voice ordered him onto the wooden plank laid from boat to shore.

The man pointed towards a brick building on the dock facing them some thirty feet away. "See that door over there," he said. "That's where you go."

Gordon hesitated, but the man shoved him forward so that he almost lost his footing and just managed to get a foothold on the plank and stumbled across.

As his eyes became accustomed to the light he looked about him. He was standing on a concrete wharf, pitted and weed strewn through long neglect. It ran to the left and right of him for a hundred feet. Facing him was an immense red brick building, its high walls pockmarked by small, dark windows in which most of the glass was broken, leaving only rusting bars behind them. Directly in front of him was a pair of huge iron gates.

He drew a deep breath. He could smell the evil, feel the despair. It pervaded the air like some malignant vapour. He wanted to turn and run, but there was nowhere to which he could flee. He felt for the heavy belt buckle beneath his jacket; it was his contact with the world outside, and once again it gave him strength. He straightened his shoulders, gripped the briefcase more firmly and walked slowly up to the gates.

To his surprise they opened easily and he passed into a wide passage beneath the building which led into an enclosed quadrangle hidden from the sun. He blinked a few times as he was plunged into half light. There appeared to be nobody there. He looked around him but all he saw were dank brick walls which encircled him, bore down upon him with a grim oppressive intensity. It was an old prison.

'Why am I here? Have they brought me here simply to kill me? Am I to die here among the ghosts of tortured convicts?' Nightmares hovered in his mind. Panic began to well up inside him and when he heard the sound of an approaching helicopter, his heart leapt and he rushed back towards the open gates, but hardly had he reached them, when a figure stepped in front of him with a sawn-off shotgun, barring his way.

"Turn round. Face the wall. Try to move outside and I'll kill you."

Gordon backed into the yard, back into the space between the four walls. He heard a chopper land, then depart. It hovered above for a few seconds like an eagle above its prey, and then it turned about and faded away, the sound of its rotor blade becoming fainter by the second.

He stood there in silence, like a mouse waiting for a cat to strike. Then, suddenly behind him came footsteps. He turned to see against the light of the gateway the silhouettes of three figures. They were coming towards him. He couldn't see their faces as they were shielded by the light. They danced in the light, vaporous forms shimmering like phantoms without real form, but as they came closer the forms melted into substance. The three men were dressed in suits and all wore dark glasses.

One of them spoke and he recognised the voice with a mixture of relief and foreboding as that of the mayor. He narrowed his eyes to make out more clearly the rotund personage of the man speaking to him.

"Not the best of circumstances," the mayor said. "You've been a naughty boy, Mr Richardson – put us to a lot of trouble."

Gordon said nothing. Then one of the men stepped forward and he felt the cold muzzle of a gun against the side of his head. He closed his eyes – he knew he was going to die. He heard a click as the hammer was drawn back, and he waited, sweat beading his forehead, for the bullet to smash into his brain. "I want to kill you."

"Hunaz!"

The voice was unmistakable, the effect immediate. The man with the gun stepped back and then leaned forward and spat in his face. Gordon slowly pulled a handkerchief from his pocket and wiped away the phlegm. He had been so near to death that this latter humiliation was so disgusting that it strengthened not his fear but his resolve. He was outraged.

At this point the senator stepped forward and ordered him to place the briefcase on the floor.

Gordon hesitated. "The money," he demanded.

The senator reached out a hand to the man standing at his left shoulder and flicked his fingers. In response the man handed him a brown leather briefcase. The senator then turned to Gordon and said, "I have the money, now let's see the goods."

Gordon bent down slowly, slipped of his shoe, took the key from inside, and unlocked the handcuff. He then placed the briefcase flat on the ground and flicked open the clasps. The lid of the briefcase snapped open revealing neatly packed rows of plastic bags, each containing cocaine.

The Cuban stepped forward, still holding his gun, and picked up one of the bags and, holding it up to his mouth, bit off a corner. He tasted the contents with the tip of his tongue and then nodded approvingly. Then he knelt down, snapped the briefcase shut, tucked it under his arm and stepped back.

"Now the money," Gordon demanded once again.

The senator stepped forward and rammed the briefcase into his chest. "It's all in there," he said. "You'd better count it."

The two men held one another in a cold stare.

The senator reached inside his coat pocket. Gordon was convinced he was reaching for a gun and his muscles tensed, but instead of a gun he withdrew a mobile phone. "Okay, Sam, bring her in – we're ready to leave."

Within seconds the sound of helicopter blades filled the air, and within minutes it was hovering above the courtyard.

"I thought we were taking the launch back," shouted the mayor above the noise.

"We were," the senator shouted back, "but I changed the arrangements. I felt this would be quicker."

Suddenly, over his left shoulder, Gordon caught a movement from Hunaz Potra. He looked to his side just in time to see the little man level the gun at his chest. As Potra squeezed the trigger, Gordon dived for the ground, but he was too late, the bullet smashed into his shoulder with a sickening thud, splitting the collarbone. The force of the blow sent him sprawling, but instinctively he rolled and kept on rolling.

There was some fallen masonry which offered some cover. He managed to get to his feet and, in a half crouch, he staggered towards it. Potra shot wildly but the bullets went wide. Still he kept on coming. Gordon reached the masonry and crouched against it, but it was meagre cover. Potra closed in. He had a smile on his face as he raised the gun and aimed for Gordon's head, but as he did so a second helicopter blocked out the light above.

The Cuban glanced up as a burst of machine-gun fire rippled around his feet and the FBI chopper passed overhead.

The pilot of the chopper on the ground hauled back on his joystick and with full throttle rose vertically above the quadrangle, fading to the right to avoid the oncoming machines, but his angle of flight was too acute and his rotor blade struck the top of a chimney, scattering loose bricks and rubble into the courtyard.

Potra dashed across the open space towards the protection of the archway as the helicopter exploded. Like a demented Catherine wheel it rotated in the sky, shedding fire and metal as it went, until it plunged into the water in a plume of steam as burning metal hit the surface.

Gordon heard the explosion but didn't know what had caused it. He rolled over onto his back, the numbness in his shoulder beginning to turn to pain, and what pain. Red-hot knives sliced through his shoulder so that he clamped his teeth together to keep from screaming. Above him the sky was still blue. Vaguely he could hear the sound of helicopters, but it was a distant sound beyond his comprehension, almost as if in a dream, but then the sky changed and standing above him was Hunaz Potra with the gun still there, levelled at his head.

And then, from the far gateway, came a cry and Potra spun round. The mayor was yelling to him over the noise of the chopper engines. "The boat! Get to the boat. It's our only chance!"

Yet still the Cuban hesitated. He hesitated as the sky above once more filled with the thud, thud of helicopter blades, and then he turned and ran. All three were running, through the archway, the gateway, beyond the building toward the boat. The two men on board had the engine running and one was already struggling to release the rope from its mooring. Any second they would be gone, leaving the three fleeing men stranded.

The senator stopped, raised his gun and fired. The man on the rope dropped and rolled away and the three men came on. The older man leapt to the rope with an axe in his hand and swung it above his head, but by this time the Cuban was upon him, and sent a bullet slamming into his head at point blank range. The man fell across the rope and, with one great heave, Potra hefted him over the side and into the water.

Engines running, the boat was straining at the rope like a frantic dog on a lead. The senator made a lunge for the boat and landed heavily on the deck. Potra drew a knife from his belt and hacked at the restraining rope. In a second it had split and the boat leapt into space, sending Potra crashing to the deck. The force of the impact might have disabled a weaker man, but Hunaz Potra took the fall in a roll and came back on his feet. Mayor Thompson was still trailing. Because of his weight he couldn't run as fast as the other two, and he reached the boat seconds after Potra had cut the rope. Senator Page was at the controls, struggling to calm the bucking vessel. He managed to back the boat toward the quay again and yelled at the mayor to jump, but the mayor stood frozen to the spot, shaking his head.

Potra screamed at him, "Jump, you bastard, jump!" but the mayor refused to move.

The Cuban threw a glance towards the senator who instantly returned it with a quick nod of his head.

Potra fired. The bullet hit Mayor Thompson in the chest, sending him spinning backwards. The senator rammed the throttle full on, the boat lurched forward, its bow rising clear of the water, but two FBI choppers had spotted the boat and were now in pursuit behind a hail of bullets which spattered the water in their wake.

The Cuban's face was distorted with rage. He returned their fire, but to little effect. The senator was fully aware that it was only a matter of time before the helicopter's fire caught up with them, but to make it more difficult for them he threw the boat into such contortions that his companion held on to the rail as if his life depended on it.

As they sped upriver, swerving and dipping, he caught sight of the old canal on his far left. He raced towards it and, at full speed, torpedoed through the reeds and into safety. The two men crouched to avoid the overhanging branches as they sped through the sluggish water. The two helicopters veered off.

Senator Page looked across at the small Cuban and they exchanged smiles. "We've lost them," Potra said.

"Two more minutes and we'll be on the lake," the senator said.

"We should be okay if we can get to the airport ahead of them."

The old alligator had heard the noise of the boat, and it slipped into the canal and awaited its approach. It lay near the surface, its great armoured bulk half submerged like a waterlogged tree trunk, waiting. The boat came on, running directly into its path. Thirty feet -- twenty – ten – and then the alligator struck, turning on its side, and as it did so the bow struck its soft belly, slicing along it like a knife through a pumpkin.

The senator reeled beneath the impact and the steering wheel jarred violently to the right, snapping both his wrists and throwing him backwards. Then the boat rose into the air like a missile spiralling out of control. The two men stared ahead in frozen terror, unable to move. The boat hit the bridge abutment at full speed, shattering the hull into a thousand fragments. Seconds later it exploded as the fuel tanks felt the impact.

Senator Page died on impact, but the Cuban had instinctively dived over the front rail as the boat struck. The explosion catapulted his body twenty feet into the air, and when he opened his eyes he was lying on his back, half submerged, hidden by thick reeds. Slowly and painfully he turned onto his stomach and began to crawl through the thick black mud away from the blazing wreck of the boat. With each movement he felt pain, but he did not cry out, pain had been a part of his life for so long that he had become hardened to it. He inched his way forward, bit by bit, to a new beginning.

The old alligator floated down through the water, its soft underbelly gaping red with blood, its huge deformed jaws open wide as if waiting to strike, the current drawing its huge body down towards the bridge foundations.

Commissioner Brown saw the explosion from his launch far out on the lake. There was nothing he could do. By the time his men reached the scene there was little but broken pieces of charred and smouldering wood. Flames flickered on the surface like small altar candles.

The commissioner spotted a brown alligator shoe bobbing on the surface. He leant over with a landing net and drew the shoe into the boat.

Chapter 69

Inverness, Police Department

Kevin O'Donnel was sitting in his office when the telephone rang. It was Commissioner Brown. He was unusually cheerful. "Hi, Kevin," he said, "I've just seen the papers."

O'Donnel glanced down at his own copy of the *St Petersburg Times*. The headlines read: 'Three Celebrities Killed in Freak Boating Accident'.

"Well done," the commissioner said. "No suspicions – no fucking nosy reporters."

"No," replied the sheriff. "I told them that the town was grieving for the loss of two of its worthy citizens, Senator Page and Mayor Thompson. They didn't take it further – put it down to a tragic accident – left it at that."

"Good. By the way, Mrs Larimer talked. Looks like we'll get them all now."

"She talked?" queried O'Donnel. "Why would she do that?" And then he knew why. "You did a deal. You've given her immunity."

The commissioner didn't answer.

"You bastard! That bitch deserves to rot."

"Calm down, my friend. We've got some big fish – it was worth it. We had to deal."

O'Donnel slammed the phone down in a fit of anger. Why did the FBI always have to compromise with these bastards, he wondered. But he knew to get at the big fish you have to compromise with the little fish. It made him mad but he understood the logic of it.

At that moment the office door opened and in walked Lucy Foster. She had a smile on her face, and immediately his anger died.

The telephone rang again but he let it ring.

"Aren't you going to answer that?" she said.

"It's not important."

"Please. It's not going to stop."

O'Donnel picked it up. It was Commissioner Brown again and he was hopping mad. "Kevin, don't you ever slam the phone down on me again."

"Accident," O'Donnel said. "Phone slipped out of my hand."

"Okay. We'll leave it this time. Now, we want you back at headquarters next week. I trust that's okay?"

O'Donnel glanced at Lucy. "No, Commissioner," he said, "that's not okay. I'm staying on here as sheriff. I'm getting married."

"Married! Are you mad!"

"Maybe," said O'Donnel smiling, "especially as I haven't told the bride yet."

With a squeal of delight, Lucy threw herself into his arms and hugged him tight. For the second time that day O'Donnel slammed down the telephone on Commissioner Brown.

Chapter 70

St Petersburg Hospital

Slowly Gordon opened his eyes. His shoulder throbbed with a dull ache, though the rest of his body felt numb. He looked around him. He could see he was in hospital. By his bed sat a police officer.

"How are you feeling?" asked the cop.

Gordon didn't answer that. He didn't really know how he was feeling. If anything he felt drunk. What's more he couldn't focus properly. "Where am I?" he asked.

"St Petersburg Hospital. You've been unconscious for six days. The doctors weren't sure you'd pull through."

Gordon began to close his tired eyes. Just as the door opened slowly, he raised his weary eyelids to find his three children stood by the door with Sheriff O'Donnel. When they saw his eyes opening, the children all rushed to his bedside. The two girls kissed him gently on the cheek and Neil held his hand.

"Thank God you are okay," said Faye.

Gordon spoke softly. "Have you heard about Mum?"

All three nodded. They could not speak as tears welled in their eyes, and even Neil's eyes were full of sadness.

"I'm sorry," said Gordon.

"How did I get here? I remember the pain, but then nothing. I must have blacked out."

"We brought you here on the chopper," the sheriff told him, "and you've been flat on your back ever since."

Gordon was trying to think back. "What about . . ." He hesitated, trying to clear his mind. "Have you arrested them?"

"No," replied the sheriff, "we didn't arrest them. They were all killed."

Gordon stared at him. "Killed? All?"

O'Donnel explained: "The mayor was shot by our Cuban friend on the quay, and both he and Senator Page were killed when their boat hit a bridge. It exploded. They both died instantly."

Gordon closed his eyes and relaxed into his pillow. A warm feeling of relief washed over him. He shouldn't feel glad when people got killed, he thought, but this time he did.

268

Chapter 71

Inverness, Florida – Newquay, Cornwall

Lake Apopka shimmered in the early morning sun. Slices of light filtered through the trees by the shore. The lake was like glass, the surrounding world at peace with itself.

Gordon stood in the garden watching the sun climb. Across the water he could see the power station, silent and sinister, a monument, not so much to failed technology as to the greed of men. To the east the old white house on Alligator Island glittered in the sunlight. It had been four months since he had lain broken and confused in that hospital bed – four months of mending and contemplating. But if his body was healed his mind remained unsettled. He suffered from frequent depression. Periods of self-doubt, and a feeling of guilt lay heavily upon him. Sheila was dead, gone forever, and much of her pain had been his doing, he could not escape that.

He felt in his inside pocket for his passport. Taking his passport from his inside coat pocket, he looked at the photograph. "Thank goodness I can keep my own identity now that they are all dead –" he said aloud to himself, "an old name, but a new life ahead."

He heard a car pull up in the drive and the sound of a horn. A man was waving to him. It was Kevin O'Donnel. "You ready, Gordon?" he called. "We need to get you to the airport by one o'clock."

"Just give me a minute," he called back. "I'll be right with you." He looked out across the lake once more and tears clouded his eyes. "Sorry, Sheila," he said out loud. "I hope you've found your peace." He picked up his suitcase and walked slowly towards the sheriff's car. His shoulder still ached, but he was alive.

"Is that all the luggage you have?" the sheriff asked as he threw his case onto the back seat.

"No, the rest is being sent on later with the paintings."

The sheriff said, "Didn't work out, your move to Florida, did it?"

"An understatement," Gordon replied.

O'Donnel dropped the car into gear and the tyres crunched in the gravel. Gordon didn't look back

Half a mile along the highway the sheriff slowed the car; they were passing Rastos's cottage. He was sitting there, his good leg firm against the floor, his other trouser leg hanging loose like a deflated balloon. The sheriff beeped his horn and he waved. Then from the bushes near the house came a barking dog. It ran straight to Rastos and leapt into his lap. He hugged it and kissed it and ruffled its floppy ears.

"He'll be okay," the sheriff said. "Lucy gave him that dog – thought it would help him."

Once on the interstate, O'Donnel put his foot down. If they didn't get a move on they'd miss the flight.

"By the way," Gordon asked, "did you ever find that alligator?"

The sheriff grimaced and shook his head. "No, but we're still looking."

It was late in the afternoon when Virgin Airways Flight 747 touched down at Gatwick. Gordon tried to see through the misted-up window. Outside the sky was grey, rain coming down like a shower of copper needles. 'Quintessentially English,' he thought. He was going to miss the Florida sunshine.

The woman next to him rested her head on his shoulder. "Are you okay now, darling?" Jean said.

He squeezed her hand. "No, but I guess I'm alive, which is more than you can say for some of those I've left behind."

She cuddled into him. "Look, we'll be in Cornwall this time tomorrow. A new life, new start. Just the two of us."

It was mid-afternoon when the silver Jaguar pulled up outside Ocean Manor, a palatial Victorian rectory overlooking Fistral Bay, Newquay.

"Reminds me of Curdridge House," he said. "My God, was it only twelve months since I left there? It feels like a lifetime."

A stab of pain shot through his shoulder as he got out of the car. That pain would never leave him, he knew that. It was there to remind him that life was precious.

"Come on," said Jean, taking his arm, "let's try the bedrooms before your children arrive."

Chapter 72

Colombian Rain Forest

The Land Rover lurched along the muddy track. Rain was still falling, as it had fallen for the past five days, heavily without respite. Towering above and pressing in from all sides, the forest hung limp, its trees weighed down with water.

Straining his eyes, the driver peered between the wiper blades. He could just make out the villa, high up on the plateau, startling white against the dark backdrop of mountain foliage. "Thank God," he said to himself, "at least I can rest. Calcus will be glad to see me."

Suddenly, as if from nowhere, the air reverberated with the thud, thud, thud of helicopter blades. Instinctively he pulled the Land Rover off the track into the camouflaging foliage by the side of the road. Four helicopter gunships passed overhead just above the tree line. They were heading for the white house.

He wound down the window to get a clearer view, and as he did so the first helicopter released its missile. This was followed by the second, third and fourth, one after the other. To his horror, all eight rockets struck the house, sending a dark-blue smokescreen into the air, splintered with glowing red embers, cascading through the trees.

Just as quickly as they had appeared the helicopters were gone, fading away over the tops of the trees, the thud, thud of their blades becoming ever fainter.

Once more, except for the swish, swish of the wiper blades, the forest was silent.

Hunaz Potra was shaking with rage. He rammed the lever into first gear and eased the car out of the cover of the trees onto the open track and headed towards the house.

As he drove through the huge iron gates, the extent of the damage became quickly apparent. It was carnage. No person had survived. Women and children lay on the charred lawn, torn and twisted into grotesque shapes. One or two of the bodies were still twitching. Through the blackened windows he could still see flames, and smoke hung over the house like a shroud.

He got out of the car. His legs felt unsteady and he staggered slightly. Slowly he walked over to the veranda.

Calcus Anando was still sitting there at his table, his eyes fixed on a distant point. The Cuban touched his shoulder and the man fell forward, eyes still open, the back of his head blown away.

With tears in his eyes, Hunaz Potra bent over his friend's body, pulled it towards him and held it tight in his arms. He looked upwards to the heavens and vowed on all that was holy in this world to avenge the death of Calcus Anando.

"The Englishman," he whispered through tight lips, "Richardson. He will pay for this."